PRAISE FOR LUIS SENARENS

"We too had a Jules Verne, a man whose industry in turning out reams of copy was as remarkable, as was his ingenuity in evolving the strange machines, prototypes of so much of the present, out of his imagination..."

— *"Amazing Stories"* magazine, June 1928

"Luis P. Senarens, creator of the fabulous Frank Reade, a robot genius of fiction... thrilled boy readers in the nineties."

—*The New York Times*, December 28, 1939

"In his tales are passages of striking beauty and imaginative power that rival Jules Verne at his best."

—*"The American"* magazine, April 1921

"Mr. Senarens, a true genius, the same as Jules Verne, had one of the most fertile imaginations."

—*"Science and Invention"* magazine, October 1920

THE COLLECTED EXTRAORDINARY ADVENTURES OF FRANK READE JUNIOR

VOLUME 1

LUIS SENARENS

This 2020 edition is a revised and updated re-publication of the stories first published in 1892 in the *Boys Of New York* dime novel serials.

Although some of the most objectionable language has been edited to better suit contemporary sensibilities, as much as the original wording as possible has been retained for the sake of historical accuracy.

This revised and updated version is Copyright © 2020 Ornamental Publishing LLC. All rights reserved.

ISBN: 978-1-945325-20-5

Style editors: Rhea Reed (Book 1), Brett Chrisner (Books 1, 2, and 3)

Published by Ornamental Publishing LLC

Contents

BOOK 1 9

Frank Reade, Jr. And His New Steam Man;
or, The Young Inventor's Trip To The Far West

BOOK 2 115

Frank Reade, Jr. With His New Steam Man In No Man's Land;
or, On A Mysterious Trail

BOOK 3 219

Frank Reade, Jr. with His New Steam Man In Central America

LUIS PHILIP SENARENS
APRIL 24, 1865 - DECEMBER 26, 1939

"I was born in Brooklyn, N. Y., April 24th, 1865, of Cuban father and American mother." So begins Luis Senarens' short 1942 autobiography in "*Dime Novel Round-Up*" magazine, an early fan 'zine dedicated to the old "Penny Dreadful" adventure stories which had been extremely popular with kids during the latter half of the 19th Century.

By then, Luis Senarens was the elder statesman of dime novels, enjoying a celebrity not unlike Walt Disney in the 1960's or Stan Lee in the 2010's. As the brightest star of the "story paper" authors of the 1880's and '90s, millions of children had grown up with his breathtaking detective stories, his astonishing super-inventors, and his grand adventure tales of every imaginable sort.

But before he was an entertainment legend, he had been a hopeful twelve-year-old kid mailing story submissions to New York publishers. Incredibly, his improbable gamble actually worked! Young Luis became a successful writer, selling numerous adventure stories, comedy sketches, and miscellaneous articles to a variety of periodicals. Since all of the arrangements were handled by mail, none of the magazines had any idea their enthusiastic correspondent was, in fact, just a teenage boy.

Luis was around fifteen when publisher Frank Tousey asked him to take over writing a neglected Jules-Verne-style adventure series. In Senarens' hands, Frank Reade Junior, his youthful virtuoso of steam technology, would become his greatest and most famous character. Inspired by the science and technology of his day, Luis sent Frank on incredible voyages in machines that defied belief, navigating land, air, sea, and even space itself. Every week, Frank would find himself in exotic lands, exploring unknown places beyond the map, discovering peoples and cities that lit children's imaginations on fire.

Frank's globe-trotting was generally motivated by letters from around the world pleading for rescue from some peril or by scientists requesting the use of his wonder machines for research and discovery. The modern reader will quickly notice that in his travels, Frank tended to help himself to whatever treasure the locals possessed, frequently over the bodies of scores of dead natives who did nothing wrong except try to stop him from plundering their valuables.

This disregard for the rights and dignity of foreign peoples is paradoxically in tension with the sense of social justice that Luis Senarens gave Frank Reade Junior. Frank's closest companions and indispensable sidekicks were Pomp and Barney, a Southern black man and an Irish immigrant, the most marginalized Americans of his day. They accompanied him on every adventure, and were portrayed as unfailingly resourceful, reliable, capable, intelligent, and admirable in their bravery and tenacity. In the America of the 1880's, these two sidekicks were quite possibly the most positive black and Irish heroes that children grew up with; perhaps the only ones.

We encounter a striking example of this sense of justice in Book 27, where a group of ex-Confederate ruffians is exchanging heated words with Pomp, and Frank Reade Jr. steps in to defend him. The goons ask Frank if he can really call himself a white man, since he's defending a black man. Frank responds:

"Yes; I think I am, and man enough to say that a negro is a man as well as any other human being. This black man here is my faithful friend, who carried me on his shoulders when I was a child. I am his friend now, and his quarrel is my quarrel."

It is in this strained balance that Luis Senarens' writing lived. The tension between the Cuban and the American, between the America that had just fought a bloody civil war to abolish slavery and the America of Manifest Destiny which was slaughtering Indians and Pacific peoples to expand its vision of civilization.

As a Hispanic writer creating stories for the mostly white American reading public, Luis Senarens walked that fine line that minorities must tread to balance their duality as insiders yet outsiders. In the end, Luis Senarens succeeded in his balancing act, rising to become Editor In Chief, then writing novels, plays, and even screenplays for that new-fangled invention, the moving pictures.

It is in the spirit of exploring this tense balance between the Cuban and the American that we present Luis Senarens' signature creation: Frank Reade Junior.

— Gil Ruiz, Editor

Frank Reade, Jr.

And His New Steam Man

OR

THE YOUNG INVENTOR'S TRIP TO THE FAR WEST

BY LUIS SENARENS

Author of "Frank Reade, Jr.'s Electric Cyclone"; or "Thrilling Adventure in No Man's Land,"
etc.

CHAPTER I.
A GREAT WRONG.

Frank Reade Sr. was noted the world over as a wonderful and distinguished inventor of marvelous machines in the line of steam and electricity. But he had grown old and unable to knock about the world, as he had been wont once to do.

So it happened that his son, Frank Reade, Jr. a handsome and talented young man, succeeded his father as a great inventor, even excelling him in variety and complexity of invention. The son speedily outstripped his sire.

The great machine shops in Readestown were enlarged by young Frank, and new flying machines, electric wonders, and so forth, were brought into being.

But the elder Frank would maintain that, inasmuch as electricity at the time was an undeveloped factor, his invention of the Steam Man was really the most wonderful of all.

"It cannot be improved upon," he declared, positively. "Not if steam is used as a motive power."

Frank Jr. laughed quietly, and patted his father on the back.

"Dad," he said, with an affectionate, though bantering air, "what would you think if I should produce a most remarkable improvement upon your Steam Man?"

"You can't do it!" declared the senior Reade."

Frank, Jr. said no more, but smiled in a significant manner. One day later, the doors of the secret draughting-room of design were tightly locked and young Frank came forth only to his meals.

For three months this matter of closed doors continued. In the machine shop department, where the parts of machinery were secretly put together, the ring of hammers might have been heard, and a big sign was upon the door:

No admittance!

Thus matters were when one evening Frank left his arduous duties to spend a few hours with his wife and little boy.

But just as he was passing out of the yard, a black man, short in stature and of genial features, rushed excitedly up to him.

"Oh, Boss Jun'r," cried the sable servitor, "Jes' wait one moment!"

"Well, Pomp," said Frank, pleasantly, "what can I do for you?"

This man, who was a faithful servant of the Reades, and had accompanied both on their tours in foreign lands, ducked his head, with a grin, and replied:

"Yo' fadder wants you, Li'l Boss, jes' as quick as eber you kain come!"

"My father," exclaimed Frank, quickly. "What is it?"

"I don' know nuffin' 'bout it 'tall, Li'l Boss. He jes' say fo' me to tell yuh he want to see yuh."

"Where is he?"

"In his library, suh."

"All right, Pomp. Tell him I will come at once."

The employee darted away. Frank saw that the doors to the secret rooms were locked. This was a wise precaution, for hosts of cranks and demented inventors were always hovering about the place and would quickly have stolen the designs if they could have got at them.

Not ten minutes later Frank entered the library where his father was.

The elder Reade was pacing up and down in great excitement.

"Well, my son, you have come at last!" he cried. "I have much wanted to see you."

"I am at your service, father," replied Frank. "What is it?"

"I want you to tell me what kind of a machine you have been getting up."

"Come now, that's not fair," said Frank Jr. with twinkling eyes.

"Well, if it's any kind of a machine that can travel over the prairies tell me so," cried the elder Reade, excitedly.

Frank, Jr., was at a loss to exactly understand what his father was driving at. However, he replied:

"Well, I may safely say that it is. Now explain yourself."

"I will," replied the senior Reade. "I have a matter of great importance to give you, Frank, my boy. If your invention is as good as my steam man even, and does not improve upon it, it will yet perform the work which I want it to do."

A light broke across Frank, Jr.'s face.

"Ah!" he cried. "I see what you are driving at. You have an undertaking for me and my new machine."

Frank, Sr. looked steadily at Frank, Jr. and replied:

"You have hit the nail upon the head."

"What is it?"

"First, I must tell you a story."

"Well?"

"It would take me some time to go into the details, so I will not attempt to do that but give you a simple statement of facts; in short, the outline of the story."

"All right. Let us have it."

The senior Reade cleared his throat and continued:

"Many years ago when I was traveling in Australia I was set upon by bushmen and would have been killed but for the sudden arrival upon the scene of a countryman of mine, a man of about my own age and as plucky as a lion.

"His name was Jim Travers, and I had known him in New York as the son of a wealthy family. He was of a roving temperament, however, and this is what had brought him to Australia.

"Well, Travers saved my life. He beat off my assailants, and nursing my wounds brought me back to life."

"I have felt ever since that I owed him a debt which could not be fully repaid. At that time I could make no return for the service.

"Jim and I drifted through the gold fields together. Then I lost track of him, and until the other day I have not seen or heard from him.

"But I now find that it is in my power to give him assistance, in fact to partly pay the debt I owe him. This brings us to the matter in hand.

Six months ago it seems that Jim, who is now a man of great wealth, still a bachelor and for a few years past living at a fashionable hotel in New York, went to his club. When he returned in the evening he found a note worded like this:"

Mr. Reade laid a note upon the table, Frank read it:

"Dear Travers:—I would like to see you to—night upon a very important matter. Will you meet me in twenty minutes at the café on your corner. I must see you, so be sure and come.

"A Friend."

"Of course Jim wondered at the note, but he did not know of an enemy in the world, so he felt perfectly safe in keeping the appointment. He started for the cafe.

"The night was dark and misty, Jim walked along and had got near the cafe when somebody stepped out of a dark hallway and grasped his arm.

"'Come in here,' a sharp voice said, "we can talk better here than in the cafe."

"Before Jim could make any resistance he was pulled into a dark hallway. Two men had hold of him and something wet was dashed across his face and over his hands, then he felt some liquid poured over his clothes and some object thrust into his pocket.

"Then the door opened again and he was flung out into the street. Jim was unharmed, but amazed at such treatment. He had not been hurt and was at a loss to understand what it all meant.

"The incident had taken but a few moments in its course. At first a thought of foul play had flashed across Jim. Then it occurred to him to look at his hands which were wet with some substance.

"He gave a great cry of horror as he did so. There was blood upon them.

"In fact his hands and face and clothes were almost soaked in red blood. For an instant he was horrified.

"What mystery was this! But he quickly changed his opinion and actually laughed.

"It occurred to him as a practical joke upon the part of his club friends. Satisfied of this he resolved to get even with them.

"He tried to open the door, through which he had been pulled. It was locked and would not yield.

"Then he decided to go back to his room and wash off the blood. But he had not gone ten steps before he was met in the glare of the lamplight by one of the club men.

"'Thunder! What's the matter with you, Travers?' asked his friend..

"'Oh, nothing, only a little practical joke the boys have been playing on me,' replied Jim with a grin. Two or three others come along and Jim explains in like manner. Then he goes to his apartments.

"When he arrives there he is amazed to find the door open and a fearful scene within. The furniture, the light carpet and the walls in places are smeared with blood. Jim now got angry.

"'This is carrying a joke a little too far!' he cried, testily. 'This spoiling fine furniture is too much.'

"But he went to washing the blood from his hands. This was a hard job and took time. Suddenly half a dozen officers came into the room and seized him.

"'What do you want?' cried poor Jim in surprise.

"'We want you,' they replied.

"'What for?'

"'For murder.'

"Instead of being horrified, Jim was mad, madder than a March hare. He just got up and swore at the officers.

"'I don't like this sort of thing,' he declared. 'It's carrying a joke too far.'

"The officers only laughed and slipped manacles upon his wrists. Then they led him away to prison. Not until brought into court did poor Jim know that he'd been made the victim of a hellish scheme.

"Murder had really been committed in that house into which he had been dragged, and where he was smeared with blood. A man unknown was there found literally carved to pieces with a knife.

"Blood had been found upon Jim in his room. A trail led from the house to his room, A knife was found in his coat pocket. The evidence was all against him and his trial had just come off and he had just been sentenced to death by hanging with only three months of grace."

Frank Reade, Jr. listened to this thrilling tale with sensations which the pen cannot depict. It was so horrible, so strange, so ghastly that he could hardly believe it true.

He arose and walked once across the floor.

CHAPTER II.
THE NEW STEAM MAN.

Then the young inventor paused before his father, and in a deeply impressed manner said:

"Then an innocent man stands convicted of murder?"

"Yes."

"In that case it is the duty of every philanthropic man to try and save the innocent."

"It is."

"We must do it."

"I am glad to hear you say that."

"But the question now arises as to how we shall be able to do it. Is there no clue to the real assassins?"

"No definite clue."

"That is very strange. Of course there must have been a motive. That motive would seem to be to get Travers out of the way."

"Yes."

"And he has no enemies?"

"None that he knew of."

"Ah, but what would any one gain by putting him out of the way—"

Frank Reade, Jr. paused. He gazed steadily at his father. Much passed between them in that glance.

"His fortune is a large one," put in the senior Reade, "the right to inherit would furnish the best motive. There is but one heir, and he is a nephew, Artemus Cliff, who is a stockman, somewhere in the Far West. It could not be him."

"Could not?" Frank Reade, Jr. sat down and dropped into a brown study. After a time he aroused.

"I am interested in this case," he declared. "And my Steam Man is at the disposal of justice at any time. But you spoke of the prairies. Is there a clue in the West?"

"The only clue possible to obtain at present," declared Mr. Reade, Sr. "You see, detectives tracked two suspicious men to Kansas. There they lost track of them. Everybody believes that they were the assassins."

"Well, I believe it," cried Frank Reade, Jr. with impulse. "I can see but one logical explanation of this matter. Either Artemus Cliff has employed two ruffians to do this awful deed for the sake of Travers' money, or—the case is one not possible to solve with ease." Frank Reade Sr. did not display surprise at this statement of his son.

"Now you have the whole thing in a nutshell, my boy," he said. "Of course, you can do as you please, but if you wish to take any kind of a journey with your new invention, here is a chance, and a noble object in view. That object should be to track down the murderers, and clear Jim Travers. It may be that the nephew, Artemus Cliff, is the really guilty one, but in any case, I believe that it is in the West you will find the solution of the mystery."

"That is my belief," agreed Frank Reade, Jr. "but now that this matter is settled, let me show you the plans of my Steam Man."

Frank Reade, Jr. drew a roll of papers from his pocket and spread them upon the table.

Upon them were the blue print plans and drawings of the mechanism of the Steam Man.

Frank Reade, Senior examined them carefully and critically. From one piece to another he went and after some time drew a deep breath saying:

"Well, young blood is the best after all. I must say, Frank, that I am beat. There is no doubt but that you have improved upon my Steam Man. I congratulate you."

"Thank you," said Frank Reade, Jr. with gratification.

"But I am anxious to see this marvel at work."

"You shall," replied the young inventor. "Tomorrow the Steam Man will go out of the shop upon his trial trip."

A few minutes later Frank Reade, Jr. was on the way to his own house.

He was in a particularly happy frame of mind. He had achieved great results in his new invention, and here, as by design, was a chance afforded him to use the Steam Man to a philanthropic and heroic purpose.

The idea of traveling through the wilds of the West was a thrilling one.

Frank could already picture the effect of the Steam Man upon the wild savages of the plains and the outlaws of Western Kansas and Colorado.

Also the level floor—like prairie of that region would afford excellent traveling for the new invention.

Frank Reade, Jr. was a lover of adventure.

It was an inborn love. The prospect before him fired his very soul. It was just what he desired.

That evening he unfolded all his plans to his wife.

Of course Mrs. Reade was averse to her husband undertaking such a dangerous trip. But after a time she overcame her scruples and reconciled herself to it.

The next morning at an early hour, Frank was at the engine house of the steel works. The wide doors were thrown open and a wonderful sight revealed.

There stood the Steam Man.

Frank Reade, Sr. and a great number of friends were present. Pomp, the negro, was also there, as well as a strange—looking little Irishman with a genuine Hibernian mug and twinkling eyes, which bespoke a nature brimming over with fun. This was Barney O'Shea.

Barney and Pomp had long been faithful servants of the Reades. In all of their travels with their inventions they had accompanied them. Of these two characters we will say no more, but permit the reader to become acquainted with them in the course of the story.

The senior Reade examined the mechanism of the new Steam Man with deepest interest.

"Upon my word, Frank," he cried, "you have beaten me out and out. I can hardly believe my eyes."

Frank Reade, Jr. laughed good humoredly.

Then he went about showing a party of friends the mechanism of the new Steam Man.

The Man himself was a structure of iron plates joined in sections with rivets, hinges or bars as the needs required.

In face and form the machine was a good imitation of a man done in steel.

In no wise did he look ponderous or unwieldly, though his stature was fully nine feet.

The man stood erect holding the shafts of a wagon at his hips.

The wagon itself was light but roomy with four wheels and a top covering of fine steel net work. This was impervious to a bullet while anyone inside could see quite well all about them.

There were loop—holes in this netting to put the rifle barrels through in case of a fight.

A part of the wagon was used as a coal bunker. Other small compartments held a limited amount of stores, ammunitions and weapons.

Upon the fender in front was a brake to regulate the wagon on a steep grade, and a slit in the net work here allowed of the passage of the reins, two long lines connecting with the throttle and whistle valves. A word as to the mechanism of the man.

Here was really the fine work of the invention.

Steam was the motive power.

The hollow legs and arms of the man made the reservoir or boilers. In the broad chest was the furnace. Fully two hundred pounds of coal could here be placed, keeping up a fire sufficient to generate steam for a long time.

The steam chest was upon the man's back, and here were a number of valves. The tall hat worn by the man formed the smoke stack.

The driving rods, in sections, extended down the man's legs, and could be set in motion so skillfully that a tremendous stride was attained, and a speed far beyond belief.

This was the new steam man. The improvements were many and manifest.

All the mechanism was more nicely balanced, the parts more strongly joined, and the steel of finer quality. Greater speed was the certainty.

Fire was burning in the furnace, steam was hissing from the retort, and smoke was pouring from the funnel hat of the man.

Frank Reade, Jr. suddenly sprung in the wagon.

He closed the screen door behind him. Pomp was engaged in some work in the coal bunker.

Frank took up the reins and pulled them. The throttle was opened and also the whistle valve.

Three sharp shrieks the new Steam Man gave and then he was away on the trial trip.

Out of the yard he went and out upon the highway.

Everybody rushed to the gates and a great cheer went up. Down the highway went the Steam Man at a terrific gait.

His strides were long and powerful. So rapidly were they made that a tremendous amount of surface was covered.

It was a good smooth road.

Just ahead was a man riding a horse. Near him was a bicycler who was noted as a fast rider.

Both had heard that the Steam Man would make his trial run that morning.

Bets had been made by both that they could beat the Man.

Frank guessed the truth at once.

"Hi dar, Boss Jun'r," cried Pomp, with a chuckle and a shake of his greying head. "Dem two chaps got a pile ob gall. Jes' you show dem dat dey ain' in it. Won't you?"

Pomp had more than one reason for beating the horse and bicycle. He had made a small bet of his own on the result.

It was evident that the parties ahead were ready for the fun.

Frank Reade, Jr. smiled grimly, and opened the throttle a little wider.

The next moment the Steam Man, the bicycle rider and the trotter were all flying neck and neck down the road.

Heavens! what a race that was!

Down the road they flew like a whirlwind. The dust flew up behind them in a cloud.

But the Steam Man just trotted by his competitors with seemingly no exertion at all. Frank turned with a laugh to see how easily they were distanced.

After a good trial, the new Steam Man returned to the foundry yard. As Frank stepped down out of the wagon, his father came up and grasped his hand in an ecstasy of delight.

"Bravo, my son!" he cried. "You have eclipsed my invention. I wish you luck, and I know that you will succeed in clearing Jim Travers."

"I shall take only Barney and Pomp with me," said Frank Reade, Jr. "There will not be room in the wagon for more."

"Well, they will be useful companions," said the Senior Reade.

"My son; may God be with you in your enterprise."

Frank Reade, Jr. at once proceeded to make preparations for his western trip. He visited Travers in prison and talked with him.

"To tell the truth, I am distrustful of my nephew, Artemus Cliff, he is an avaricious villain, and a number of times has tried to swindle me out of money. I know that he has led the life of an outlaw out there on the border."

"But if he aspired to gain your wealth, why did he not attempt your life in some direct manner?" asked Frank.

"I presume be may have feared detection," replied Travers. "If I am hung for the murder of this unknown man, the mystery will be sealed forever. The real murderer will never be known."

"I believe you are right," agreed Frank Reade, Jr. "Well, I will find this Artemus Cliff, and do the best I can towards clearing up the mystery and setting you right."

"Thank you!" said Travers with emotion. "I feel that you will succeed."

CHAPTER III.
ON THE PLAINS.

The scene of our story now undergoes a great change.

We will transfer the reader from Readestown to the plains of the Far West. Fully five hundred miles from civilization, and right in the heart of the region of the hostile Sioux.

Frank Reade, Jr. had transported the Steam Man as far as possible by rail.

From thence he had journeyed the rest of the ways overland.

Nothing of thrilling sort had as yet marked their journey. But they were upon the verge of the most exciting adventures, as the reader will hereafter agree, possible to be experienced by man.

With the broad expanse of rolling plain upon every hand, one morning in June the Steam Man might have been seen making its way along at a moderate gait.

Frank Reade, Jr. with Barney and Pomp were in the wagon.

Frank held the reins and his keen gaze swept the prairie in every direction.

As far as the eye could reach there remained the same broad expanse. There was little to break the monotony.

Barney and Pomp had taken advantage of a lull in their duties to play a social game of poker in the rear of the wagon.

These two unique characters, although the warmest of friends, were nevertheless always engaged in badgering each other, or the perpetration of practical jokes.

"Bejabers, I'll go yez ten better on that, ye buffalo," cried Barney, throwing down a handful of chips. "I'll take me worrud it's a big bluff yez are playin'. Yez can't fool me."

"Yo'll jes' find out dis ole chile neber plays a bluff game," retorted Pomp with a chuckle. "Jes' you look out fo' yo'sef, I'ish."

"Begorra, I ain't afraid av yez an' I'll go ye the tin," cried Barney. There was a broad grin upon Pomp's face. He quietly picked up ten chips and then put in ten more.

"Hold on, I'ish, I'll go yuh ten better."

"Call yez, be hivens!" cried Barney, chucking in ten more.

Then he threw down his hand.

"Can yez bate that?" he cried, triumphantly. "Give us the pot, eejit. Yez are no good."

But Pomp put one dark hand over the pile of chips.

"Jes' wai' one minni', I'ish."

"Whurro! Yez can't bate it!" cried Barney, confidently.

He had thrown a good hand containing four kings and two aces. But Pomp quietly laid down four aces!

The picture was one well worthy of an artist. For a moment the two card players gazed at the six aces in amazement. It was a very curious anomaly that there should be six aces in one pack of cards. Then Barney sprang up furiously.

"Begorra, it's a big cheat ye are!" he cried, angrily. "Whoivver saw the loikes av that? By me sowl, the hull poile is moine!"

"Don' you pu' yo' hands on dem chips, I'ish!" cried Pomp, angrily. "P'raps you kain tell me wharfore you got dem two aces, maybe you kain?"

"Bejabers, they war in the pack, but yez Kin tell me perhaps where yez got those four aces yez put down there?"

"I tell yuh, I'ish, dey was in de pack."

"Bejabers it's the fust pack av cards I ever saw with six aces in it," retorted Barney.

"Now don' you gib me any mo' ob yo' sass, I'ish!" blustered Pomp. "I'll jes' make you sory if you does."

"Bejabers yez ain't the size!"

"Look out fo' yo'self, I'ish!"

"Whurroo!"

Over went the table leaf, down went the chips in the bottom of the wagon, and the two angry poker players closed in a lively wrestle.

For a moment Barney had the best of it, then Pomp tripped the Celt up and both fell in a heap in the bottom of the wagon.

They chanced to fall against the wire screen door in the rear of the wagon.

It was unlocked and gave way beneath the pressure, and the two practical jokers went through it and out upon the hard floor of the prairie.

They were rolled about in a cloud of dust, and had they not been of something more than ordinary composition they would have suffered from broken bones.

But as it was both picked themselves up unhurt.

The Steam Man bad gone on fully one hundred yards before Frank Reade, Jr. perceived that his companions were missing, and at once closed the throttle and brought the Man to a halt.

"Serves the rascals right," muttered Frank, as he saw them pick themselves up from the dust. "They are always skylarking, and no good comes of it."

Frank had stopped the Steam Man. He waited for the two jokers to pick themselves up and return to the wagon.

But at that moment a thrilling thing occurred.

Barney and Pomp had fallen near a clump of timber.

From this with wild yells a band of mounted Sioux Indians now dashed.

They were a war party—pointed and bedecked with feathers, and in the full paraphernalia of war.

The peril which threatened the two jokers was one not to be despised.

It was quite evident that the savages meant to cut off their rejoining the Steam Man. In that case their fate would be sealed.

But Barney was quick—witted, and saw the situation at a glance.

With a wild howl he broke into a mad run for the Steam Man. It was a question of life or death and he ran as he had never ran before.

Pomp was not so lucky. While Barney was distancing his pursuers, and actually succeeded in reaching the wagon, Pomp suddenly found himself cut off.

Indian ponies were circling about him, the red riders whooping and yelling like veritable demons.

The poor servant was beside himself with terror and perplexity.

"Golly sakes alibe!" he yelled, with his hair literally standing on end. "Whatebber is I gwin to do? I's a gone man fo' suah."

It certainly looked that way. The natives circled nearer and half a dozen of them dismounted and rushed upon Pomp.

Now Frank Reade, Jr.'s employee was unarmed.

He had not even a pistol or a knife. Of course he was at their mercy. In less time than it takes to tell it, the savages had closed in about the terrified man, and he was quickly thrown upon his back and bound.

Then he was laid across the back of a pony and tied on securely. Then a lariat was attached to the pony's bridle, and the natives with their prisoner in their midst dashed away.

Barney had reached the Steam Man and climbed into the wagon. Frank Reade, Jr. had seen the whole affair, and for a moment was too astounded to act.

Then as Barney came tumbling into the wagon, Frank turned the Man around and sent him flying toward the red riders.

This move was quickly made, and the Steam Man ran forward rapidly. But quick as it had been, the savages had yet succeeded in making Pomp a prisoner and getting away with him.

"Bejabers, they've got the eejit bound to a horse," cried Barney, wildly. "Wud yez luk at the loikes, Mister Frank. We must catch the omadhouns and give them a lessin of the right sort."

"I hope we may," replied Frank, with great anxiety, "but I fear the red fiends will get to cover before we can overtake them."

"Whurroo! It's mesilf as will spoil the loike av some av thim," cried Barney, as he picked up his rifle.

The natives were racing like mad across the prairie.

They had caught sight of the Steam Man, which was to them some fiend incarnate, some evil spirit which would seek their certain destruction.

Terror of the wildest sort made them whip their ponies to the utmost.

It was a mad race.

But the Steam Man was gaining.

He took tremendous strides. Frank pulled the whistle valve, and the shrieks sent up on the air were of a terrifying kind.

The red aggressors had all gazed with wonder upon the white man's iron horse that followed its steel track across their prairies.

But this latest appearance, the Steam Man, was too much for their nerves.

They could not bear it, and fled.

The Steam Man would certainly have overtaken them.

But, not visible until one had turned the timber line and made a rise in the prairie was a distant range of hills.

Toward this the natives were going. If they reached them, they would certainly succeed in eluding their pursuer.

And the chances seemed good.

Frank saw, with a peculiar chill, that they were really liable to reach the point aimed at.

He sent the Man on at full speed.

Barney placed himself at a loophole, and commenced firing as rapidly as he could at the fleeing foe.

The result was that many of them fell, and the others redoubled their exertions to make an escape.

On went the chase toward the distant range of hills.

Nearer and nearer drew the ponies to the objective point.

With sinking heart Frank saw that the Indians were likely to reach them before the Steam Man could overtake them.

Of course this would mean safety for the red riders, for the Steam Man could not hope to follow the ponies over the rough surfaces there encountered.

"Heavens, we are not going to save Pomp!" cried Frank, with a thrill of despair in his voice. "What shall we do, Barney? Is it not awful?"

Barney was busily engaged in placing fresh cartridges in his Winchester.

"Begorra, it's save the cabbage I will if I sacrifice me own loife!" cried the big—hearted Celt. "It's me own fault, for sure, that he iver fell troo the door and got picked up by the red min."

Frank put on all the steam he dared, and the Man took tremendous strides forward.

"We will make a mighty effort," he gritted, as he piled on the steam.

"Bejabers, here goes for wan av the spalpeens!" cried Barney.

Then the Irishman's rifle cracked.

One of the natives tumbled from his pony's back.

Barney continued to load and fire as fast as he could. But the opportunity was not long granted him.

Suddenly the cavalcade of red men dashed into the mouth of the pass.

They were out of sight in a twinkling. The Steam Man was obliged to come to a halt.

There were huge boulders and piles of stones to block the passage. Barney and Frank Reade, Jr. exchanged glances of despair.

"That is the end of Pomp," declared the young inventor, with a chill. "I have no doubt that is a part of Black Buffalo's band, and he never spares a life."

CHAPTER IV.
THE COWBOYS.

Frank had spoken truthfully. The band of aggressive natives was really a part of the tribe of which Black Buffalo was the chief.

Throughout all the Kansas border this blood thirsty fiend was known and feared.

He had ravaged more wagon trains, burned more settlements, and committed more massacres than any other Sioux chief in the Far West.

His name was a synonym of terror among the settlers, from Dakota to the boundary line of Texas.

By many he was claimed to be a white man or renegade. Others averred that he was a recreant Pawnee chief.

However this was, certainly no red warrior was better known and feared than Black Buffalo.

And it was into his hands that Pomp had fallen.

Small wonder then that Frank Reade, Jr. was much alarmed, and even inclined to believe his faithful servitor's life lost.

The merciless Black Buffalo would not be likely to spare Pomp's life. The savages had captured him alive simply to drag him into the hills and torture him to death.

Barney began to bemoan the situation in violent terms.

"Och hone, the poor soul," he cried, "he was a Buffalo Soldier with a good heart jist that same. Be jabers av' we cud only get near enough to the red omadhouns I'd loike to shoot ivery mother's son av thim."

"Well, I don't see why the red fiends haven't the best of us," declared Frank.

"It luks that same, Mister Frank," wailed Barney.

"I don't see how we can ever get through that pass. The Steam Man might go there, but the wagon won't."

This was true enough.

The Steam Man on the level prairie was invincible, but on rough ground like this wholly useless.

Frank and Barney were beside themselves with solicitude and perplexity.

Frank even thought of going forth on foot to try and overtake the redskins. But of course the folly of such a course was quickly apparent to him.

Barney even attempted to carry out literally this plan.

He went so far as to open the door in the wire screen and leap down to the ground.

But Frank cried sternly:

"Barney, come back at once. You can gain nothing by such a course."

"Shure, Mr. Frank," cried the Irishman, "if yez will only let me go—"

"Come back," was Frank's terse command, which was reluctantly obeyed by the Celt.

Frank took a careful look at the hills.

He chanced to see a smooth pathway up the height, and which seemed to follow the course of the canyon or pass.

Up this the Steam Man cautiously advanced. As they continued to ascend higher a good broad view of the prairie was obtained.

And suddenly reaching an elevation from which a southward view could be obtained, Frank gave a sharp cry, and taking a glass from a locker, sprang to a loop—hole in the netting.

He scanned a number of objects upon the prairie far beyond.

At that distance they looked like a herd of buffaloes.

But with the glass Frank saw that they were mounted men and white men at that.

They looked like a roving band of cowboys. In any event they were white men and it was quite enough for the young inventor to know this.

"We can depend upon them to help rescue Pomp!" cried Frank, exuberantly. "Luck is yet with us, Barney."

"Be jabers I hope so," cried the excited Celt. "If they be white men and have a heart they'll shurely do it."

Frank instantly turned the wagon about and sent the Steam Man rapidly down to the prairie.

He blew shrill blasts upon the whistle to attract the attention of the white men.

In this he was successful.

As the Steam Man reached the prairie floor, the cavalcade of cow boys came dashing up.

They did not seem surprised at sight of the Steam Man somewhat singularly and drew up fifty yards distant while one of their number rode forward.

He was evidently the leader, and was a tall, dark, evil—looking fellow. Frank Reade, Jr. was not favorably impressed with his appearance.

As the young inventor noted that the whole gang had a forbidding appearance and with a chill Frank realized that he could hardly expect any assistance from such a cut—throat looking band.

The tall, dark leader doffed his sombrero as he rode forward and made a low bow.

"Buenos señores!" he said with a Spanish accent. "I wish you a fair day. Do you travel far with your Iron Man?"

"I am glad to meet you," replied Frank, eagerly. "We come from the East and we are here upon an important mission."

The stranger smiled and bowed again with a peculiar affectation of politeness.

"I am pleased to hear it. Are you not the gentleman called Frank Reade, Jr.?"

Frank gave a start of surprise.

"I am," he replied, quickly, "then you have heard of me."

"I have, Señor Reade," replied the cowboy chief, with another exaggerated bow and smile.

"Perhaps you know of my mission here?"

"I do," was the reply.

Frank was more amazed than words can express. What mystery was this?

How had this fellow, who bore the stamp of a Spaniard, learned of his mission to the Far West? The young inventor was staggered for a moment.

"Your mission here," replied the cowboy chief, politely, "is to hunt down two men who you believe are guilty of a murder which they skillfully foisted upon a certain man by the name of Jim Travers."

"You are right!" cried Frank. "But how in the name of wonder did you know that?"

"I prefer not to say. It is enough that I know it."

"It is strange that you should have learned it," said Frank, "but I will ask no more questions just now in the face of a terrible exigency."

"Ah!"

"I want to ask your help."

"My help?"

"Yes."

"Pardon, señor, but I cannot see in what manner I can serve you."

"You must assist me. One of my men—a black man—has fallen into the hands of the Indians. They have made him prisoner and have just escaped with him into these hills. I ask your assistance in effecting his rescue."

A peculiar smile played about the cowboy's lips.

"Is he not the one you call Pomp?" he asked.

"Yes."

"And that man with you in your cage there is called Barney?"

"Yes."

"Ah, I see—Barney and Pomp. Well, señor Reade, pray accept my compliments and the wish that you may see civilization again alive, which I do not believe will be the case. Ha—ha—ha! You have blundered into a death—trap!"

Something like a correct comprehension of affairs now began to dawn upon Frank.

"What do you mean?" he gasped in surprise. "Who are you?"

"Well, since you ask me, I will tell you," replied the cowboy chief with a laugh. "I am no Spaniard, as you might have thought. I am as good an American as you, and you will have good cause to remember my name in the near future, provided you escape from this trap. I am the man you are so eagerly looking for—I am Artemus Cliff."

"Heavens!" gasped Frank Reade, Jr. "the man I am looking for!"

"The same," replied Cliff, mockingly. "You have undertaken quite a daring deed, my fine inventor, but you will find that you have bitten off a very much larger slice than you can masticate."

"We will see," began Frank.

"You see these men?" continued Cliff. "They are my followers, tried and true. What is it to you whether my uncle, Jim Travis, should hang for murder? You can never prove him innocent—at least, never will, for you will never go from here alive."

"Scoundrel!" cried Frank. "You are the real murderer!"

"Ha, ha, ha! Prove it if you can!" laughed the cowboy chief, derisively.

"I will prove it, if I have to drag the confession from your lips!" cried Frank, resolutely.

"Pshaw! Talk is cheap. Attention, men! Grab the throttle rein of the Steam Man and you can destroy him! Forward! Charge!"

Frank Reade, Jr. heard the command and knew well the danger. He was at a loss to account for Cliff's knowledge of him and his invention.

The young inventor was not aware of the fact that for weeks previous to the starting forth of the Steam Man spies had been busy in Readestown.

But such was the truth.

Artemus Cliff had covered his tracks well. He knew that Frank Reade, the young inventor's father, was a friend of Travers and would see him through, if possible.

Therefore, he had provided well for giving Frank Reade, Jr. and the new Steam Man a hot reception on the plains.

With hoarse cries the cowboys descended upon the Steam Man. They urged their horses forward at a full gallop.

Frank Reade, Jr. knew well that it was possible for them to greatly injure his invention, so he made quick action to defeat their plans.

He shouted to Barney:

"Give it to them, Barney. Shoot every man you can."

Then Frank opened the throttle and let the Steam Man out for all he was worth.

It was an easy matter to outstrip the horses, and the Steam Man kept ahead, while the cowboys came thundering on in the rear.

Then Frank slackened speed so as to keep up a uniform distance between the Man and the horses.

While Barney poured in shot after shot into the midst of the gang of pursuers.

The cowboys began to drop from their saddles one by one. It was a destructive and telling fire.

And they strained every nerve in vain in an effort to reach the Steam Man. Frank kept the Man just far enough ahead to ensure safety and enable Barney to pick off the cowboys with ease.

It took Cliff some time to tumble to this little game.

When he did, and realized that he was simply decimating numbers without gaining ground, he called a halt.

The cowboys were now near the banks of a wide river which was really the Platte, Frank Reade, Jr. saw his advantage and brought the Steam Man to a stop.

Then he seized a rifle and joined Barney.

CHAPTER V.
POMP'S RESCUE.

But it was hardly likely that the cowboys would stand their ground long under such a fire.

As fast as they could Frank and Barney worked the repeaters.

The result was that quite a number of the foe lay dead upon the prairie.

But Artemus Cliff knew the fatality of remaining there. Being unable to catch the Man, he knew that their only hope was now in retreat.

All of the cowboys fired at the Steam Man. The bullets rattled harmlessly against the steel cage.

Frank at once sprang to the reins and the brake and started the Steam Man in pursuit. It was quite a turning of tables.

The pursuers were now the pursued.

So it continued until suddenly, by the orders of Cliff, the cowboys turned their horses into the river and forded it.

Once on the other side they were soon beyond the reach of the rifle balls. The Steam Man of course could not follow.

The encounter with the cowboys was at an end.

They did not return to the attack, somewhat singularly, but kept on until the rolling plains hid them from view.

Cliff's direful threat against the Steam Man and its inventor, had not been carried out. But Frank did not, by any means, delude himself with the belief that the villain would relinquish the attempt so easily.

"Well, Barney," he cried, cheerily, when satisfied that the scrimmage was over. "We came out of that scrape a little the best of it. It has all turned out as I expected. That Cliff is the real murderer."

"Begorra, it luks that way, Mister Frank," agreed Barney.

"So it does. We must plan to capture the villain, and wring a confession from him."

"Bejabers that's true. If I only bad an opportunity I'd pretty quick wring his loon neck for him."

"But that does not settle the question of Pomp's fate," declared Frank. "He must be saved."

"Shure, Mister Frank."

"But how can we do it?"

This was yet a conundrum.

Frank and the faithful Irishman stood looking at each other. It was a long time before either spoke.

Finally Frank said:

"There's only one way, Barney."

"An' what's that?"

"We've got to get into those hills in some way. I don't like to leave the Steam Man, but to save Pomp I'd—"

The young inventor ceased speaking. A strange medley of sounds came from the direction of the pass.

There were wild yells and pistol shots, and then, out upon the prairie, the two astonished travelers saw a motley crew of horses and Indians emerge.

The natives were fighting furiously. Frank knew enough of the Indians of that region to know what it all meant.

A band of Sioux and a band of Pawnees, the deadliest of enemies, were engaged in a terrific battle.

Frank took in the scene at a glance.

He at once understood all.

The band which had captured Pomp was undoubtedly the one engaged in this conflict. They had very likely met the Pawnees in the upper part of the pass.

When the Pawnees and Sioux met a fight always followed. Generally the latter came off victorious.

As it seemed now, however, the Pawnees had the best of it.

They were worsting the Sioux in good fashion. Frank and Barney watched the scene a moment until suddenly a sharp cry burst from Barney.

"Begorra, Mister Frank, if there ain't the eejit," he cried, wildly.

Barney was right. Frank glanced in the direction indicated and saw a thrilling act.

In the midst of the Sioux was Pomp bound to the back of a mustang.

Suddenly in the midst of the melee the horse was seen to bolt from the rest and dash out upon the prairie.

Of course, Pomp had no control over the beast, having his hands tied behind him.

The mustang took his own course and ran like the wind.

The Sioux did not dare to any of them attempt pursuit. The foe in their front claimed their attention.

"Bejabers, the horse is runnin' away wid Pomp," cried Barney. "What will we do, Mister Frank?"

"Catch him if we can," cried Frank, seizing the throttle rein.

He opened the throttle and let the Steam Man go ahead; with long strides the machine began to gain upon the mustang.

Pomp was vainly endeavoring to free his hands.

If he could have done so, and could have got hold of the reins once, he could easily have stopped the horse.

But this he was unable to do.

As a result, the animal carried him along swiftly, and along the base of the hills.

Suddenly the mustang swerved and darted into a narrow pass.

Barney, at the loop—holes of the wagon with rifle in hand, had been sorely tempted to fire at the runaway.

But the fear of hitting Pomp had restrained him.

Now, however, the horse was out of range. But Frank headed the Steam Man for the pass.

Fortunately, it was unobstructed by boulders, and had a good level floor. The Steam Man was enabled to forge along with safety.

But the mustang and his black rider had gone from sight. However, the pursuers kept on.

Suddenly they came out upon a broad plateau with steep descent upon all other sides. This extended among the Hills for a distance of several miles.

A great cry of horror now went up from Frank and Barney.

The mustang was seen racing along the edge of a mighty chasm. In a few seconds he would be almost sure to take an impossible leap over a deep gorge.

If he should go to the bottom of that gorge it would be the end of Pomp and the mustang.

This was seen at a glance and with the most intense of horror Barney cried:

"Shall I fire, Mister Frank? It's the only thing as will save the old soldier."

"You will have to do that," replied Frank, sharply. "Look out for your aim, Barney. God help Pomp!"

Barney pulled the trigger.

Crack!

The bullet sped true to its mark. It struck the mustang in the side.

The animal faltered, threw up its head, stumbled, and then pitched forward in a heap.

Pomp lay beneath the horse. It did not require but a few moments for the Steam Man to reach him, however.

In a twinkling Barney sprang out of the wagon and cut Pomp's bonds.

Pomp was not in the least injured. He lay with one leg under the mustang, but was easily extricated.

The joy of Frank's employee at his rescue cannot be expressed in words.

He embraced Barney effusively.

"Shure I thought yez kilt intoirely, eejit," cried the big—hearted Irishman. "It's moighty glad I am to see yez aloive."

"You kain jest bet dis chile be glad to get out ob dem red debbils' hands," cried Pomp, exuberantly.

And then he dashed aboard the Steam Man and grasped Frank's hand.

"Oh, Boss Frank, I's dretful glad to see you!" cried Pomp, excitedly.

"I am glad to have you back, Pomp," cried Frank. "And to know that you are unharmed in any way. But it was a close shave for you,"

"'Deed it was dat, Li'l Boss. But dis old sojer is powerful hard to kill, an' specs dat's why I lib. But I's got lots to tell you, Boss Jun'r."

"You have?" exclaimed Frank.

"'Deed I has. P'raps you kin find it valuable fo' yuh. I'll jes' tell yuh dat when we went up troo dat pass we jes' come out pretty quick in a valley. Dat valley was a scrumptious one, an' dar was a trail leadin' down inter it. But afore the Injuns could ride down inter it along come six white men on hossback an' a right pert young lady on a hoss, too.

"Sakes alibe I nebber seen so pretty a gal in all mah life. Well, dese here men, dey seemed like dey was 'quainted wid der Injuns. Dey jes' talked as free like wid old Black Buffalo, an' I jes' opened my ears an' listened.

"Dey said dat de gal was a prisoner an' dey was takin' her from a cave in de hills to Ranch V. Dey mentioned de name ob Artemus Cliff. Den dey rode on, suh, an' mah sakes, jus' den up from the valley dere came a hull gang ob Injuns and pitched into us. Ob cose you know all de res'."

Frank Reade, Jr. listened with the deepest amazement to this exciting story.

"A young girl!" he gasped. "Of course those men were Cliff's, but where on earth were they going?"

"Dey done said it was to Ranch V. suh."

"Ranch V!" repeated Frank. "That is not very definite. But it must be the headquarters of Cliff and his gang. You didn't hear them say just where that ranch was located, Pomp?"

"No suh, but I jes' took note ob de direckshun dey was goin' an it was to de souf—wes'."

"Well," said the young inventor as he turned the Steam Man about, "I cannot imagine who the young girl is or how she fell into the hands of Cliff's gang. But it is certain that she is in their power and we must save her."

"Bejabers that's roight, Mister Frank," cried Barney, gallantly, "the O'Sheas from Brian 'Boru down war always known as men av honor an' defenders av female virtue."

The Steam Man started on the return across the plateau.

It was Frank Reade, Jr.'s, intention to reach the prairie once more and strike out to the southwest, in the hopes of locating the Ranch V.

The Steam Man ran swiftly to the mouth of the pass which led down to the prairie.

Barney had filled the furnace with fresh coal, and the indicator showed that there was plenty of water in the boiler.

Frank was about to enter the pass when suddenly Pomp sprang up with a wild cry.

Pomp sprang to Frank's side and tried to grab the throttle rein. Frank was astounded.

"Hold on there, Pomp. What are you trying to do?" he cried.

"Hi dar, Li'l Boss. Stop de Man, or fo' de Lawd we all be done fo', suah as preachin'!"

"What?" gasped Frank.

"If you don' believe it, jes' look up yonder?"

Pomp pointed one finger upward to the canyon wall above the pass. The sight which rewarded the startled gaze of the young inventor caused him to reverse the throttle and bring the Steam Man to a halt.

Two cowboys were crouching behind an enormous boulder which they had intended to roll down upon the Steam Man.

CHAPTER VI.
THE FIGHT IN THE PASS.

A more narrow escape could hardly be imagined.

The precipitation of the huge boulder upon the Steam Man would have destroyed the invention and the lives of those on board.

Just in time Pomp had seen the danger. Another moment and it would have been too late.

"Hi yi, don' you see now, Jun'r Bossman?" cried Pomp, wildly.

"I see," replied Frank, in thrilled tones. "My God that is a narrow shave. We would have been crushed to atoms in another moment as I live."

"Whurroo! Give the spalpeens a good bit av cold lead!" shouted Barney, rushing to one of the loopholes with his rifle.

"That's right!" cried Frank, doing the same.

"Golly, you kin bet we will do dat!" chimed in Pomp.

The two cowboys, seeing that their game was exposed, sprang up with wild shouts of dismay.

As they did so they were exposed to shots from below. The three rifles spoke sharply in chorus.

The two would—be destroyers tumbled in a heap. Their fall was followed by a wild chorus of yells from the thickets and boulder piles above.

A volley of bullets came from there and rattled harmlessly against the steel netting, showing that the cowboys were there located in great force.

How they had chanced to be there at that critical moment our adventurers could only guess.

But Frank mentally concluded that at best they were but a division of Cliff's gang, and they had happened upon the spot by chance.

Seeing the Steam Man they had seized what seemed to them a fine opportunity to destroy it.

How far short they came of it we have already seen.

A red—hot contest now began between the cowboys and those in the steel wagon.

Of course our three friends had a vast advantage inasmuch as they were protected from the shots of their foes.

Of course the outlaws far outnumbered them, but it was not at all a difficult matter to pick them off occasionally with a rifle bullet.

Volley after volley the cowboys fired at the Steam Man.

When at length it became patent to them that their shots were futile, they made the air ring with yells of baffled rage.

Then they ceased firing and silence ensued. Every cowboy had disappeared seemingly from the canyon wall.

But this did not deceive Frank Reade, Jr.

He knew that this was only a game of the foe and that it would yet be unsafe to try the pass.

"Bejabers, ain't there some other way av gettin' out av this place?" cried Barney, giving the plateau a sweeping glance.

But the chain of hills surrounding it did not lend color to such a possibility.

"It don't look like it," said Frank, dubiously.

"I jes' fink dat is de only way out ob dis place," said Pomp.

"We are in a kind of trap," declared Frank Reade, Jr. "We were not sharp or we would have avoided this scrape."

As it was, however, the best they could do was to watch for an opportunity to run the gauntlet through the pass.

But they had not long to wait for new and thrilling developments. Suddenly Pomp gave a startled cry.

"For massy sakes, Li'l Boss, jes' you look out yonder. Whatebber is dey up to now?"

Over the edge of the plateau there was visible a line of men advancing rapidly toward the Steam Man.

They were deploying right and left as if to surround him. This was certainly their purpose.

"They're troiyin' to surround us!" cried Barney.

Frank watched the maneuver with deep interest.

He smiled grimly.

This was certainly the purpose of the foe. But the young inventor saw in the move a betterment of his own chances.

"They will not gain what they hope to," he said, resolutely.

Then he saw that a line of armed men had deployed across the mouth of the Pass to prevent the Steam Man from escaping in that direction.

In Frank's judgment there were fully two hundred cowboys in the party. This was tremendous odds, but the young inventor did not fear the results.

With a wild cheer the cowboys began to close their line in about the Steam Man.

Frank Reade, Jr. opened the whistle valve and let out several defiant shrieks. Then he started the Steam Man in a straight line for the pass.

Pomp and Barney with their repeaters began to fire upon the line of men there.

The repeaters did deadly work.

It was a constant fusillade, and the cowboys dropped like sheep. The error of their plan could now be seen.

In dividing their forces to make the surrounding line, they had weakened themselves. Frank had seen this.

If they had been merely content with holding the pass, it would have been extremely doubtful if the Steam Man could so easily have escaped.

Just as fast as they could work the sixteen—shot Winchesters, Barney and Pomp mowed down the opposing line of cowboys.

The line was thin, and it would have required a very solid corps to have withstood that scathing fire.

Down went the Steam Man toward the pass with fearful speed.

Heaps of the dead and wounded cowboys lay upon the ground. As the Steam Man reached the pass, a number of the cowboys tried to grasp the throttle reins and stop the machine.

But the ponderous body of the Man knocked them aside like flies and the wheels of the heavy wagon crushed them into death or insensibility.

The Steam Man literally forged his way through the Pass like a rocket.

Barney and Pomp cheered wildly and fired parting shots at the discomfited foe.

In a few moments the Steam Man ran out upon the prairie.

Frank did not waste time but set his course at once to the Southwest.

He was anxious to locate Ranch V. This he believed was his first and most important duty.

He was satisfied that nothing was to be gained by remaining in the hills.

He was confident that Cliff had gone to the Ranch V wherever it was. More than all else, he was powerfully interested in the mysterious young lady as described by Pomp.

He was determined to know who she was, and what Cliff held her in captivity for.

THE FIGHT IN THE PASS.

The day was rapidly drawing to a close.

After a short while the hills faded out of sight, and the rolling prairie was visible upon every hand.

Then, as the Steam Man took his long strides across the even plain, Frank suddenly caught sight of a beaten path or trail.

It was plainly a trail much used and bore a trifle east of south. Frank brought the Man to a stop.

"I would like to know where that trail goes to!" he declared. "I am not sure but it is the route to Ranch V."

"Golly, Boss Frank!" cried Pomp, craning his neck and looking to the southward a little ways. "What is dat jes' ober dat roll in de perairy? Ain' dat some berry sumspicious objec'?"

Frank gazed in the direction indicated and saw a tall, black—looking timber seeming to rise out of the roll in the prairie. But he knew that it was beyond.

Frank let the Steam Man go along for a quarter of a mile, and topping the rise a startling sight was revealed.

There, scattered over several acres of land were the blackened ruins and charred timbers of some buildings.

It was easy to see what these buildings had constituted.

A large ranch with stockade, extensive cattle pens and yards, had once stood upon this spot. Frank allowed the Steam Man to pass through the ruins.

Thrilling sights were accorded our adventurers.

There were heaps of ashes, the bones of animals, and several charred skeletons of human beings.

There was every evidence that a fight had occurred at the place, and that the ranch had been burned by either Indians or rival cowboys.

As chance had it the sign which, painted in broad letters, had once hung over the yard gate, had not been destroyed, and lay upon the ground near.

Our explorers were enabled to read it plainly.

"Rodman Ranch."

Burney and Pomp descended from the wagon, and spent some time in exploring the ruins.

"I jes' fink de Injuns burned up dis place," averred Pomp.

"Begorra, it's the divil's own job they med avit," declared Barney.

But Frank said, with conviction:

"Just as likely it was the work of Cliff and his gang. They are outlaws at best, and if Rodman Ranch was a respectable place, they would be sure to wish it destroyed."

Barney and Pomp re—entered the wagon now, and once more the quest for Ranch V was begun.

But night came on, and they had obtained no clue.

A good place was found to camp, and it was decided to wait until morning before pursuing the journey further.

Accordingly everything was made comfortable with this end in view.

No camp fire was made, for this was not deemed necessary.

At night they always slept in the wagon, and Barney and Pomp served turns in watching.

The fires in the furnace were banked, and the Steam Man was given a rest just the same as the others.

One place was always as good as another in camping out thus, save that it was necessary to be near a body of water, so that the boilers could be filled with ease the next morning.

The Steam Man was thus cared for, the fires banked, and everything made shipshape when, after Barney had been on watch not more than two hours, the first of a series of thrilling incidents occurred

The night was as dark as Erebus, not a star twinkled in the ether for heavy black clouds overhung all.

Suddenly Barney saw a light glimmering far out on the prairie.

It increased to quite a respectable size and continued to blaze for a long time.

The Celt watched it for a long while. Then is curiosity got the better of him.

"Bejabers, that's strange," he muttered. "I'll make sure there's something wrong about that now."

Barney, acting upon impulse, leaned over and grasped Frank's shoulder. The young inventor awoke with a start.

CHAPTER VII.
THE VIGILANTS.

"W-what's the matter?" gasped Frank, sleepily arousing himself.

"Whist now, Mister Frank! There's a strange loight out yonder on the prairy, an' I thought I'd jist call yewr attintion to the same, sor."

"A light?" muttered Frank, now fully awake.

He got upon his feet, and rubbing his eyes, stared at the distant blaze.

"That is odd," he muttered. "It will do to investigate that."

"Sure, it may be a camp fire," ventured Barney.

"If so, then we must find out who the campers are," declared Frank.

It was but an instant's work to arouse Pomp.

Then the fires in the furnace were started, a line of hose was run to a creek near, and the boiler was filled.

In an incredible short space of time steam was got up, and the Steam Man moved ahead.

Frank held the throttle reins and directed the Steam Man's course toward the distant camp—fire.

For such it was, as became evident as they drew near.

At first no movement was made by the camping party, and Frank fancied that they had nobody on guard.

But as the Steam Man with clanking tread came within one hundred yards of the camp, a wild shout went up and a gun was discharged at the Steam Man.

Frank was now able to see the circle of the camp as revealed by the firelight.

Men had been rolled in blankets upon the ground to the number of a score.

But these were now upon, their feet. Just beyond it could be seen that mustangs were corralled.

Frank Reade, Jr. had no way of knowing whether the campers were friends or foes.

Be had fancied them a part of Clift's cowboys. Still there was a possibility they were not.

At any rate he could not treat them as foes until he learned positively that they were such.

So he brought the Steam Man to a stop just fifty yards from the camp.

The scene in the camp now was a ludicrous one.

The men were filled with mingled fear, amazement and stupefaction at the sight of the Steam Man.

The fiery eyes and nostrils and mammoth proportions of the Man in the darkness made him look like a monster from the infernal regions.

The startled cries of the campers came to the amused hearing of those in the wagon.

"Great Jericho! What d'yer call that thing?"

"It's the devil hisself!"

"He's after us!"

"That last drink at the cross trails was too much for us boys. We've got 'em bad."

"I reckon we'd better fix up a prayer. The old gentleman has come to git us."

Barney and Pomp exploded with laughter. It was very funny.

But as soon as the pandemonium had for a moment subsided, Frank Reade, Jr. hastened to shout:

"We're human beings the same as you. Have no fear. Who are you?"

The words had an astounding effect upon the campers. After a moment of stupefied silence the answer came back.

"Who the dickens are you?"

"I am Frank Reade, Jr., and this is my new invention, the Steam Man," replied Frank. "You have nothing to fear."

The campers now saw the three men in the wagon as Barney turned on the light of the calcium and illuminated the vicinity.

At once their fear lied and a comprehension of all dawned upon them. "A steam man, by thunder, and built all of iron!"

"Wail, that beats all!"

"What'll come next?"

"That beats the iron hoss all holler!"

The campers now came thronging about the wagon. As the number was limited, Frank did not feel particularly uneasy, though he held the throttle ready and Barney and Pomp had their repeaters at hand.

But the fears of our three adventurers were quickly allayed.

One of the men, a tall, powerful framed man, came forward, and said:

"Wall cap'n, we're glad to meet you an' yer Steam Man. My name is Sim Harmon, an' I'm captain of this band, who are all Vigilants from Poker Gulch. We're out on the trail of a gang of ruffians."

"Vigilants!" cried Frank Reade, Jr. with joy. "Then you are not members of the Artemus Cliff gang?"

"Artemus Cliff!" cried Harmon. "He is the chap we want. If we can lay hands on him we'll stretch his neck, you bet. D'yer know whar we kin find him?"

"I am on his trail myself."

"The deuce ye are?"

"It's the truth."

"What for?"

Frank opened the door of the wagon, and descending shook hands with the Vigilant captain.

He told him explicitly of the mysterious murder of which Jim Travers had been adjudged guilty, but which it was believed was the work of Cliff.

Harmon listened with interest.

"So that's another game of the cuss!" he cried. "Wall, that's a bad one, but I reckon we've a wuss count agin' him, stranger."

"Indeed!" exclaimed Frank.

"Did ye come across the ruins of a ranch out hyar on the peraiy some miles?"

"I did."

"Wall, that was onct Rodman Ranch, an' Ralph Rodman was one of the best men in this part of the West But that ornery cuss Cliff fell in love with pretty Bessie Rodman, his darter, an' when Ralph denied him the right to come a— courtin' her, the scoundrel jest brought down a gang of hoodlums an' burned down the ranch, toted off the gal, an' killed all the rest about the place."

"Horrible!" exclaimed Frank. "But you have not told me of Rodman. What became of him?"

"Wall, that illustrates the villainy of the cuss. Just previous to burnin' the ranch, two men, Sid Bowen an' Jem Ducey, hired by Cliff, enticed Ralph to New York by bringin' him a bogus message from a brother, who was represented as bein' in great distress. That's the last seen of Rodman. What they did with him we don't know. But I've heard that Bowen an' Ducey have returned, an' Rodman didn't come with 'em. It's my belief he's been done away with, an' it's all a game of Cliff's to get the gal Bessie into his possession."

A great cry broke from the lips of Frank Reade, Jr.

This story of Harmon's he had listened to eagerly, and, as it was unfolded, bit by bit, a clear, concise comprehension of all now came to him.

He saw the hideous details, the cold, scheming construction of a deep and awful plot, involving murder and abduction and terrible wrong.

"Great heavens!" he gasped, wiping cold perspiration from his brow. "Your story throws a great light upon the matter which I have in hand, Mr. Harmon."

"The deuce you say!" gasped the captain of the Vigilantes.

"It is the truth," cried Frank. "I think I can tell you the true fate of Ralph Rodman, and you will agree that Cliff is the projector of one of the most awful double plots of crime that human being could be capable of.

The Vigilantes all gathered around the young inventor, agog with interest.

"Ye don't mean it?" gasped Harmon, with amazement. "Ye're huntin' Cliff then the same as we are?"

"Yes."

"What fer?"

"To force a confession or explanation from him of a mysterious murder of which his own uncle, James Travers, of New York, has been adjuged guilty and who is now in prison awaiting his sentence of hanging about a year from now.

"Oh, this villain is a deep one. But I have told you of that mysterious murder and, as Heaven is my judge, I believe the victim of that murder which was purposely thrown upon Travers was Rodman. You see Cliff's object in throwing the murder upon Travers was to see him hang and thus inherit his vast wealth."

For a moment after this statement silence reigned.

Appalled with the magnitude of the villain's plot all remained silent. But the mystery was cleared up at last.

All understood now exactly the deep game of Artemus Cliff.

But one sentiment reigned supreme in the breasts of all. Artemus Cliff should be brought to justice.

It was easy enough to see how the wretch in planning to win Bessie Rodman had enticed Rodman to the East and there murdered him. Then to Hill two birds with one stone he had caused the awful crime by clever circumstantial evidence to be thrown upon his wealthy uncle, James Travers.

Of course, with Travers' death, he would inherit the millions left by him.

Ralph Rodman was dead. The ranch was a heap of ashes.

For these crimes Artemus Cliff was responsible. But Bessie Rodman was yet in his power. Travers was near the gallows.

These two people must be saved.

Frank Reade, Jr. saw the mission, as did Harmon.

Instinctively they clasped hands.

"I reckon we both know what to do," declared the Vigilant captain tersely. "P'r'aps we kin work together. I'll help you all I kin."

"And I will help you," replied Frank. "We will bring Cliff to justice if the Steam Man can help us to do it."

"He will hang if I kin get my hands onto him."

"But we must make no mistake. He is strongly backed up. You have only twenty—five men with you."

"But they air all men," replied Harmon, pluckily.

"I will not question that," replied Frank, "but the weight of numbers would defeat you. Cliff has several hundred men in his command."

"We're not afraid of 'em. Yet ye're right enuff. It's well fer us to go easy."

"It is well to be careful," said Frank. "I think that you had better keep along with us for a time."

"All right!"

"I think there is no doubt but that the young girl whom Pomp saw in the hills was Bessie Rodman."

"Of course it was her."

"They were taking her to Ranch V. Do you know where it is?"

"Yas," replied Harmon, quickly, "that's on Stone River, an' it's a pesky big place too. Thar's a big stockade around it an' armed men are allus a—watchin' for fear an outsider will git in. So that's the place, eh? Wall, it will be hard to git Bessie out of Ranch V."

"She shall be got out or I will give my life in the attempt!" cried a tall, handsome young plainsman with flashing eyes.

He looked much in earnest. Frank gazed at him critically. A little later he was introduced to him as Walter Barrows, a rising young stockman, and the lover of pretty Bessie Rodman.

CHAPTER VIII.
ON TO RANCH V.

PLANS were quickly made.

It was decided to work upon strategical grounds, as their force was so much lighter than Cliff's.

"You see, if we can strike Ranch V at a time when Cliff and the majority of his men are in the hills we can capture the place," declared Frank, shrewdly.

"That's bizness," agreed Harmon, "but ye're the boss. I kin see that ye've got a better head piece nor I have, Mister Reade."

"We will not admit that," said Frank, modestly, "but rathe let us work together, Mr. Harmon."

"All right, cap'n. I'm with ye."

Further plans were elaborated, then as only a few hours yet intervened until dawn, it was decided to snatch a few brief hours of sleep.

With the early dawn all were astir. The Vigilants saddled their mustangs and all was soon ready for the start.

The Steam Man was an object of great wonder to the plainsmen.

"By Jinks!" exclaimed one of them, "the sight of that weird—lookin' critter oughter scare the life out of any number of Injuns."

"I think the Steam Man will aid us much in accomplishing our ends," said Frank, modestly."

The start was made just after daybreak. The Vigilants rode alongside the Steam Man on their mustangs.

Of course Frank was compelled to go more slowly on this account.

But the Vigilantes knew the way to Ranch V, and this was, after all, the most important thing of all.

Frank considered it a great piece of luck in having fallen in with the Vigilantes.

He now understood exactly how matters stood all around.

It was near noon when a halt was called in a small basin near a lake of water.

Here camp was briefly made, and also at the same time an important discovery came to hand.

A broad trail made by a cavalcade of men and horses was discovered.

It pointed to the north.

Harmon examined it carefully and finally, with great exuberance, cried:

"It's good luck, friends. That thar trail I believe was made by the cowboys an' it leads to the hills. It's over three days old, an' they haven't come back this way. I should think that the most of their men must be up there, in which case Ranch V will he almost deserted. Come on, boys, let's capture the hull place."

With a cheer the Vigilants sprang to saddle.

Soon they were once more galloping over the prairie.

Not two hours later, or in the middle of the afternoon, Harmon drew his horse alongside the Steam Man and pointing to the south cried:

"Look yonder, Mr. Reade. Do ye see them lines of high ground? Wall, jest this side is the Ranch V."

A cheer went up from all.

"Begorra, it's Ranch Ours it'll be, if iver we get there," declared Barney.

"Golly, won't dis be a big 'sprise party fo' dat vilyun Cliff," cried Pomp.

Frank Reade, Jr. held the Steam Man at a steady stride, and very soon the ranch came in sight.

It was truly a most extensive establishment.

The stockade and buildings covered acres of ground. A great herd of cattle were feeding on the open plains.

The main ranch itself was surrounded by a high stockade, which would resist most any ordinary attack with small arms.

As the Vigilants and the Steam Man came swiftly rushing down upon the place, a great commotion was seen to take place.

Men rushed out into the yards, horsemen went scurrying about, and down came the stockade gate.

But Harmon and his men rode boldly down to the gate, and began to assail it with axes.

While Frank Reade, Jr. kept the Steam Man on an elevation near, from which he, with Barney and Pomp, covered the work of invasion by a hot fire with their Winchesters.

The cowboys could not get upon the stockade to fire at the assailants for this reason.

Harmon's men therefore worked with perfect immunity.

No more favorable time for an attack could have been chosen.

There were but few of the cowboys in the ranch, and these were picked off by the fire from the Steam Man as fast as they appeared on the stockade.

With lusty cries the Vigilants chopped through the timbers of the gate.

In a remarkably brief time a hole was cut through and the gate raised.

The Steam Man rushed into the yard, and in less than ten minutes every cowboy in the place was a prisoner, and Ranch V was captured.

Walter Barrows, the brave young stockman, was the first to enter the main ranch.

The instinct of a lover took him to the chamber in which Bessie Rodman was kept a prisoner.

He burst in the door and clasped the young girl in his arms.

That was a joyous meeting.

When they appeared in the yard the Vigilants cheered wildly. It was a brilliant victory.

Ranch V was captured.

The stronghold of the outlaw Cliff, the den of villainy and vice, was captured. It did not require much time for them to reach a decision as to what to do.

"Every building must be laid low!" cried Harmon. "Put the torch to every accursed timber."

The cry was taken up and spread from lip to lip.

In haste torches were procured. Harmon himself lit the first, and was about to apply it to a building.

But he did not do so.

A thrilling incident stopped him. A loud cry went up.

"The cowboys! They are coming! To arms everybody! There comes Cliff at their head!"

Every eye was turned to the plain beyond the stockade.

There was no disputing the truth. Cliff and his gang returning from the hills had come just in time.

It would be folly now to burn the ranch.

Harmon seeing the desperate exigency dropped the torch, and cried: "To the stockade! It's for life or death, boys. Fight to the last!"

But the command was not necessary. Already the brave Vigilants were at their posts.

Cliff with his small army of followers came on at a swinging gallop. He could see that the ranch was in the possession of a foe.

This inflamed his wrath, and, with loud curses and yells, he rode down in the van of his followers.

Frank Reade, Jr. had taken in the situation at a glance.

He knew that it would be flatly impossible for the score, of Vigilants to hold those three hundred desperadoes long at bay.

It would mean the eventual massacre of every Vigilant. This Frank wished to avoid.

The young inventor had induced Bessie Rodman to seek refuge in the wagon. Otherwise, she would certainly fall into the hands of the foe again.

Frank started the Steam Man ahead, and went down to the stockade. He made the vigilantes a hasty address.

"Nothing will be gained by holding this place," he declared, with force. "You cannot do it. The odds are too great."

"But we cannot surrender," cried Harmon, "and how can we retreat?"

"Easily enough," replied Frank, "there is a rear gate. Open it and cut out upon the prairie."

"But they may overtake us?"

"It is your only hope. You'll have to work lively, for they are trying to surround the stockade. I'll cover your retreat easy enough."

Harmon saw that Frank was right.

He did not pause to argue the point further. With quick commands he caused his men to fall back.

The stockade gate in the rear was opened just in time, and the Vigilants rushed out upon the prairie.

They set out at a mad gallop for the distant hills.

The cowboys with mad cries followed. But they met with quite a serious obstacle in their pursuit.

The Steam Man kept exasperatingly between them and the Vigilants.

From the rear loopholes of the wagon Barney and Pomp kept up a steady fire with the Winchesters.

Nearly every shot emptied a saddle, and despite their superior numbers, the cowboys soon found it better and safer to keep well out of range.

The pursuit lasted for ten miles. Then the horses of both parties became fatigued and they were compelled to halt.

But Harmon's men, by dint of careful work, got their horses into the fastnesses of the hills. Here they felt more secure.

The Steam Man had well covered the retreat of the Vigilants. But darkness was now coming on and a serious question presented itself to Frank Reade, Jr.

To remain where they were for the night would be to incur the risk of a midnight attack from the cowboys.

This might result seriously.

At least Frank was disposed to evade it.

He consulted with Harmon, and the result was an arrangement which it was believed would be better for all.

In the fastnesses of the hills Harmon felt sanguine of holding his own against the cowboys.

Therefore it was decided that the Steam Man should leave the vicinity and go far enough away over the prairie to make sure of safety for the night.

Accordingly Frank left the vicinity and sent the Man striding over the plain in the dusk of evening.

There was no visible indication that the cowboys intended to pursue.

They had apparently gone into camp not five miles distant.

Frank kept on with the Steam Man until twenty miles had been covered.

Then he came to a halt.

It seemed as if they must feel safe here. Accordingly, arrangements were made for passing the night.

A comfortable seat was arranged for Bessie Rodman and, much exhausted by the fatigue of her experiences she quickly fell asleep.

But tears had wet her cheeks and trembled on her eyelashes. Frank had told her of her father's death.

"Oh I fear it is more than I can bear, she declared, in agony of spirit. "My dear, dear father. Oh, if I were a man, how I would avenge him!"

"There are plenty to do that," replied Frank, cheeringly. "The villain shall surely pay for his evil deeds."

"I hope it may come to pass," she said, sincerely.

Then she dropped off to sleep. But even as she slept, deadly peril hung over her young and beautiful head.

CHAPTER IX.
POMP'S MISTAKE.

Frank Reade, Jr. felt comparatively safe as he rolled himself up in a blanket and went to sleep. He did not believe that the villain, Cliff, would be able to molest them that night.

It was Barney's first watch.

The Hibernian, until midnight, kept a good lookout in the cage. Then he called Pomp to succeed him.

The former soldier kept a good lookout until the early morning hours.

The darkness was most intense.

At about this time Pomp experienced a deadly faintness at the pit of the stomach and a great longing for water.

His thirst became most consuming, and it seemed as if he must, at any cost, gratify it.

But he found, upon looking in the tank, that it was empty.

There was not a gill of cold water in the wagon. Pomp grew sober with this dampening reflection.

"I jes' fink if I had a bit of watah I would be a'right," he muttered; "but how ebber am I gwin to get it, dat's what I'd like to know."

Pomp went to the steel screen and tried to penetrate the darkness.

He knew that not ten yards distant were the waters of a small creek. He could hear them rippling now.

It was directly at variance with his orders to open the cage door. Yet it seemed to Pomp as if he must do so.

The risk did not seem great.

There seemed little likelihood of the proximity of a foe.

Pomp felt certain that he could reach the creek, get his drink, and get back safely to the wagon.

He was sorely tempted. The desire was most powerful.

"Golly!" he muttered, with a wry face. "What am I gwin to do? I don' beliebe dar's any danger ob going out dar, but if the Li'l Boss knew it he'd fix me putty quick. Sakes alibe! But what am I gwin to do? I am a'mos' dyin' fo' a drink ob watah."

Pomp thought of awakening Barney and enlisting his aid.

But he reflected that the Celt would he certain to disagree with his scheme.

There was no other way but to assume the responsibility himself. Pomp drew a deep breath.

Then he fell to listening.

All was silent as the grave.

"Sho!" he muttered. "Dar ain' no danger at all. I'll jest hab dat watah as suah as I'm born."

He quickly slid back the bolt in the door and opened it.

Then he stepped out of the wagon. In another moment he glided down to the water's edge.

Pomp flung himself flat and began to drink of the creek water.

But he had not taken one drink when he became aware of an appalling sensation. He turned his head and glanced back at the Steam Man.

The lantern banging in the cage showed the open door and all as plain as day. But, great heavens! What did he see?

Dark forms were swarming about the machine. One was already in the wagon.

Pomp saw this much, and then his attention was claimed by another matter. He suddenly felt a heavy body descend upon him and talon fingers clutched his throat.

In that flash of time Pomp had turned partly over.

He was just in time to see the flash of a knife blade. He made a convulsive upward blow, and grasped the wrist of his unknown assailant.

By the merest chance the death blow had been averted.

But it was a close call.

Then with a herculean effort Pomp rolled over the edge of the bank, and the next moment, with a powerful swing, he had brought himself and assailant into the water of the creek.

The sudden bath caused Pomp's adversary to relax his grip.

Pomp had no further motive for continuing the struggle, and striking out swam for the opposite bank.

He clambered out of the water, and crawled into a thicket.

There he lay shivering, and witnessed a thrilling scene upon the other bank of the creek.

The occupants of the wagon had all been aroused, and were every one prisoners, in the power of Cliff and his cowboys.

The outlaw had managed to cover the twenty miles, skillfully following the trail by means of a dark lantern.

He had been hovering with his minions about the Steam Man, just as Pomp committed the indiscretion of leaving the door open.

Of course it was an easy matter for the cowboys to board the wagon and make prisoners of all on hoard.

The glee of Cliff was beyond expression.

He danced and clapped his hands with fiendish joy. He pinched Bessie's arms until she screamed with agony, and with brutal laughter roared:

"Oh, I'll make ye all dance. Ye thought ye'd git away from me, did ye, gal? I'll show ye that ye can't get away from Artemus Cliff. Ha, ha, ha! What a good joke."

He laughed uproariously.

"All mine," he continued. "And this Steam Man, this wonderful invention, is just what I want. I can travel around in great style. Oh, Mr. Frank Reade, Jr., I'll dance on your grave yet."

"Monster!" cried Frank, writhing in his bonds. "You'll never succeed. A righteous God will never permit it."

The villain gave his men carte blanche to make camp and indulge in a carousal.

They did so until daybreak, and then Cliff stated that it was his purpose to go back to Ranch V.

It did not take him long to understand the mechanism of the Steam Man.

He quickly found out how to use the throttle reins. He was aided by the fact that he had once been a locomotive engineer.

With the early morning light the start for Ranch V was made.

And Pomp, wet and shivering and horrified, crouched in the thicket upon the bank of the creek, saw the Steam Man and his friends, all in the power of the foe, take departure.

When they had gone Pomp came out of his hiding place.

"Golly!" he muttered, with distended eyeballs, "I jes' fink dis ol' fool hab done de berry awfulest t'ing eber known. Dar's only one way fo' Pomp to sabe his honor, an' dat be to fix some way to rescue Mistuh Frank an' all ob de odders, an' I'll do it if I can."

Pomp was very much in earnest.

He was a brave and generous fellow, and willing at any time to sacrifice his life for the Reades.

In some manner be must certainly vindicate himself. He crossed the creek again and stood upon the spot where the Steam Man had been.

Of course the machine was out of sight by this time, but nevertheless, Pomp took the trail and proceeded to follow it.

For some hours he trudged on over the prairie. All the while he was revolving in his mind some plan for the relief of his friends.

He was bound to admit that it was a puzzle. Yet he did not lose hope.

The hills were every moment becoming plainer. Already Pomp had covered five of the twenty miles.

Pomp was a good walker, and no distance was too great for his trained muscles.

The sun was beginning to run high in the heavens, and a brisk breeze blew across the prairie.

Pomp kept on steadily.

The trail kept on toward the hills, and the sagacious employee reflected that Cliff was likely going to join the main body of his men.

"I jes' fink I can see what dat rascal be up to," muttered Pomp. "He be jus' too sharp to let de game slip him once he gits his clutches onto it. He be jus' goin' to take de Steam Man to his Ranch V, and dar's whar dis chile must go an' try to work some leetle plan to rescue Frank Reade, Jr. an' de odders. Dat be a fac'."

With this logical conclusion Pomp trudged on.

He was now on the last five miles of his journey to the hills. The sun was long past the noon hour when Pomp, by dint of rapid walking, had made the hills.

There was no sign visible of the Steam Man or of the cowboys.

But Pomp saw that the trail continued around the base of the hills. This puzzled him a moment.

He paused and scratched his head in deep thought.

"Dat be a drefful queer thing," he muttered. "Dat ain' de way to go to Ranch V, if I's right in mah conjeckshun."

Then he paused, and a light of comprehension broke across his face. A distant sound had come to his hearing. It was the faint rattle of fire—arms far up in the hills.

"Golly!" he exclaimed. "I see de trick ob dat berry sharp fox, Artemus Cliff. He gwin to gib de Vigilants a good lickin' afore he goes to Ranch V. Dat jus' my bes' way for to jine Mistuh Harmon an' his men, an' help dem trash the cowboys."

Pomp's mind was made up.

He would join the Vigilants and do his best to give the cowboys a good drubbing. He at once struck into the hills.

But alas for Pomp!

Luck seemed against him for the time being. He had not more than fairly entered a narrow pass when an appalling incident occurred.

The air was suddenly broken by wild yells, and in an instant he was surrounded by half a hundred painted savages, who burst from niches and crevices in the rocks about.

They pounced upon him, and before Pomp had even time to think of resistance he was a prisoner.

The natives swarmed about him like bees. Words cannot express Pomp's dismay at this turn.

His eyes bulged, and his knees shook as with the ague.

"Fo' de good Lor' dis be dretful!" he groaned. "I'se done fo' dis time, an' dar ain' nobody to rescue Boss Frank!"

It was truly a dubious outlook. The Indians were of Black Buffalo's gang of Sioux, and they seemed much elated at getting the prisoner once more into their clutches.

They chattered and gesticulated like a flock of magpies, and some of them approached Pomp with their tomahawks as though they would fain make an end of him then and there.

But the others held them back and an excited wrangle followed.

All this while Pomp was writhing in his bonds. In vain he tried to break them.

For some while the natives wrangled. Then a compromise was made and Pomp was picked up bodily, and carried through the pass and into a small glade among some trees.

Here he was tied to a tree and a great heap of branches was piled at his feet.

With a chill of horror, the old soldier saw that the savages meant to take his life in a horrible manner.

He was to suffer death in the flames. Pomp felt sick and faint. But ever, in that moment he thought not of himself, brave fellow, but of Frank Reade, Jr. and the others.

"Golly sakes, whoebber gwin to sabe Li'l Boss now?" he groaned.

CHAPTER X.
IN THE ENEMY'S POWER.

Artemus Cliff shouted in evil glee and triumph as he manipulated the Steam Man and let him out for a swift run across the prairie.

He amused himself by racing with his followers who were on horseback.

"By jingo!" he roared, "this is more fun than I ever had before. Why this beats the steam—cars all to smash. And it's all mine. Why I can travel like a prince now. Ha—ha—ha! I'm the luckiest man on earth."

He turned and fixed a glowering gaze upon Bessie Rodman.

"And ye're mine too," he cried, "the lily of the prairie. The happy life companion of Artemus Cliff. When I get my hands onto Uncle Jim Travers' millions, we'll travel the world over, my daisy."

Bessie did not appear to heed his words, though her face increased a trifle in its pallor.

"Monster!" cried Frank Reade, Jr. with intensity. "You will never succeed. Heaven will not permit it."

"Heaven don't have much to do with me," cried the villain, with a lurid oath. "The devil has been a good friend of mine, and I ain't afraid of his place either."

"Begorra, they wudn't have ye even there," cried Barney. "Yez are too wicked for avin that place."

"Oh, ho, Irish, you've got your tongue, eh?" cried Cliff, with a vicious laugh.

"So ye think I'm too bad, eh?"

"By me sowl, thar cudn't be a place too bad for yez!"

"I'll have a nice little hades fixed fer yer right on this earth an' I'll give ye a fair taste of it in advance, too," said the villain, vengefully.

"Arrah, yez can't scare me at all," he retorted. "Yer threats are jist the same as a puppy dog's hark."

"You'll find that I'm the kind of a dog that bites," averred the villain.

"It's not me that cares fer yer bites."

"We'll see about that. Don't blow your horn too soon."

"Begorra, that's good advice fer yersilf, ye blatherskite! Av I on'y had me two hands to use now I'd haste the rascality out av yez or I'd make a good job fer the undhertaker."

"Talk is cheap," sneered the villain. "Ye'd better save yer wind."

"It's yersilf as nades it most," said Barney, bound to have the last word.

Cliff evidently found Barney's tongue equal to his own, for he abandoned the conversation in a sullen fashion.

Bessie Rodman made no attempt at speech.

She sat silently in one corner of the wagon.

Frank Reade, Jr. also remained silent.

The twenty miles were quickly covered by the Steam Man. It was yet far from the noon hour when they arrived at the camp of the previous night.

The cowboys in full force were there, and as Cliff appeared with the Steam Man, they made the welkin ring with yells of delight and satisfaction.

All crowded around to examine the steam wonder and inspect its mechanism.

The prisoners looked out upon a sea of faces. They were not kindly regarded by the cowboys.

"Take 'em out and shoot 'em, Cliff!" cried a voice in the crowd. "Give 'em twenty paces and a grave seven feet deep."

But Cliff refused to do this.

"Leave it to me!" he cried. "I've got a better plan."

"What is it?" was the cry.

"I want ye all to be ready in half an hour to go into the hills an' corner Harmon an' his gang. There must not one of the Vigilants go out of here alive."

"Hurrah!" yelled the cowboys.

"We can give them the worst thrashin' they ever had."

"In course we can."

"In regard to these prisoners, the gal is going to be my wife. The others I'm going to have some fun with down to the ranch. We'll have a rabbit chase with 'em, or something of the kind."

"Good!" yelled the mob, carried away with the plan.

Thus the fate of the prisoners was decided by their captors. But the question of attack upon the Vigilants was now the one in order.

Preparations were at once made for cornering Harmon and his heroic little band.

Several parties of cowboys were dispatched to head off any possible attempt at escape from the hills.

Harmon's men were certainly hemmed in on all sides, and it was a most dubious outlook for them.

The exultation of the cowboys was beyond expression.

"We've got 'em dead sure!" cried Cliff, triumphantly. "Not a one of 'em can possibly escape."

The cowboys now began to close the line in about their prey.

A pass was found through which the Steam Man was taken, and to a point within easy range of the position held by the Vigilants.

Harmon had chosen an elevated position on a kind of small table land or plateau.

Here behind boulders he had concentrated his forces. The position was not a bad one to defend.

To charge upon it the cowboys would have to ascend a height of fifty feet or more in the face of a strong fire.

But this sacrifice of men Cliff did not intend to make, at least not at once.

There were other points of vantage about, which the cowboys quickly took possession of.

From these, a desultory fire was kept up with the Vigilants with some loss upon both sides.

But Harmon's men could not very well withstand any loss whatever. This the cowboys could stand better.

The Steam Man, however, could advance to very close proximity with the Vigilants, and those on board were safe from any shots of retaliation.

This made it bad for Harmon for he had no way of checking this most destructive fire.

It was a most galling thing for Frank Reade, Jr. to remain idle and see his invention used in such a manner.

He groaned aloud with horror and dismay. Barney did the same.

"Oh, if I could only free myself," declared the young inventor.

"Begorra, I wish I cud do that same," muttered Barney.

Cliff and the three cowboys with him in the cage were doing their best to shoot every Vigilant who exposed himself.

They were thus so deeply engrossed that they paid no special heed to the prisoners for the time.

Barney, quick—witted Irishman, noted this fact.

At a favorable moment he leaned over and whispered to Frank:

"Bejabers, Mister Frank, I think I know av a way to turn the tables on them blasted omadhouns."

"The deuce!" gasped Frank. "What is it, Barney?"

"Whisht now an' work quiet, me gossoon!" whispered Barney. "I'll lay down ferninst the side here an' yez kin turn yer wrists toward me mouth. Me teeth are no good av I don't cut them in two before so very long."

Frank experienced a thrill.

"Can you do it, Barney?"

"Av course I kin."

"But if they see us."

"They'll niver do that. Be aisy now, me gossoon, an' roight on the shelf there there's a knoife an' yez kin cut my bonds at the same toime. Thin we kin take care av the four av thim. I'll take two mesilf."

"And I'm good for the other two or I'll die!" muttered Frank. "All right, Barney, do your best."

"I will that."

But at this moment Bessie Rodman leaned forward, and in a soft whisper said:

"Wait! There is a quicker way."

Frank and Barney were astonished.

"What?" exclaimed the young inventor.

By way of reply Bessie drew both hands from behind her.

They were free. There were livid lines upon the fair wrists, where the cruel throngs had cut in.

But the shapely hands were so small that Bessie had been enabled to slip them through the bonds and free them.

Up to this moment neither Frank nor Barney had looked upon the young girl as more than the ordinary weak woman.

That is to say, they had not given her credit for the amount of nerve she possessed.

But they were given ample evidence of it now.

Quick as a flash, and with commendable resolution, she reached over and seized the knife upon the shelf.

It was but a moment's work for her to cut Frank's bonds. As they snapped, the young inventor took the knife and quickly cut Barney's.

Their captors were at the loop—holes firing, and had not seen this move.

Nothing could have worked better.

Frank picked up a club, and Barney an iron bar. Nobody can handle a weapon of the sort better than an Irishman.

"Whurroo! Bad cess to yez fer a pack av omodhouns," cried Barney, dealing one of the cowboys a crashing blow on the head.

Before one could think, the iron bar came down upon the head of another. Both sank senseless to the floor of the wagon.

Frank Reade, Jr. had knocked Cliff senseless. Only one of the foe was left, and he was quickly knocked out.

In a twinkling, as it were, the tables were turned.

Barney and Frank Reade, Jr. were now masters of the Steam Man once more. The irrepressible Irishman pulled the whistle valve and sent up a shriek of defiance and triumph.

Then Frank Reade, Jr. swung open the wagon door.

"Throw them out!" he cried; "all but Cliff."

Barney obeyed the command. The three cowboys were quickly dumped out upon the ground.

But Cliff was allowed to remain. The villain lay insensible in the bottom of the wagon.

Frank was about to bind him, when an imminent peril claiming his immediate attention prevented him.

The cowboys were aware of the turning of the tables in the wagon.

With mad yells they were rushing forward in a body to surround the Steam Man. Unless immediate action was made they would succeed.

Frank knew well the danger of this move.

It would be an easy matter for the cowboys to ruin the invention by a single blow. There was but one way, and that was to beat a retreat.

Barney seized his repeater and began firing into the crowd of cowboys. Frank opened the throttle and sent the Steam Man up the incline toward the stronghold of the Vigilants.

Of course, the latter had seen and understood all.

They embraced the opportunity to pour a flank fire into the ranks of the cowboys. It was a moment of thrilling sort, but the Steam Man seemed to have the best of it when a thrilling incident happened.

CHAPTER XI.
WITH THE VIGILANTS.

In another moment the Steam Man would have been in the ranks of the Vigilants.

It would have been a great point scored, for Cliff would then be a prisoner and the way to save Jim Travers from the gallows would have been paved.

But it was not to be.

The villain had come to in the meanwhile, but cunning rascal that he was, had laid inanimate in the bottom of the wagon.

He had seen all that was going on, and when he saw that the Steam Man was certain to escape, he knew that only desperate action upon his part would save him now.

Accordingly, while Franz and Barney were occupied at their posts, he made a sudden lightning leap for the door in the cage.

Unfortunately, Barney had not fastened it.

A little scream of warning came from Bessie, but it was too late. The villain flung open the door and sprung out.

He tumbled heels over head down the decline.

This was partly done on purpose to avoid any bullets sent after him. But none struck him, and he was the next moment in the ranks of his men.

Frank turned just in time to see the daring escape.

The young inventor's disappointment was so great that he came near leaving the wagon to pursue the villain.

"Begorra, av the divil ain't got clane away entoirely!" cried Barney in dismay."

"I'm sorry," returned Frank. "But take the precaution now, Barney, to bolt that door."

Barney complied with alacrity.

Then he was obliged to return to his post, for the enemy were thick in the rear. But the next moment the Steam Man topped the rise.

A volley from the Vigilants drove the cowboys back for the time. Then Frank Reade, Jr. brought the machine to a halt upon the plateau.

The Vigilants were wild with delight, and crowded about the Steam Man. Frank Reade, Jr. opened the door and descended among them.

In an instant Harmon was by his side and had gripped his hand.

"God bless ye, Mr. Reade!" cried the whole—souled plainsman. "It's like takin' the paw of one brought back from the dead. Dog—dast it, but I'd given ye up entirely when I see that your Steam Man was in the hands of that coyote. It's all like a kind of miracle."

"I think we may congratulate ourselves," said Frank, "but do you know that we are in a tight box?"

"Nobody knows it better," declared Harmon.

"I doubt if we pull out of it."

"What Kin we do?"

"Is there no avenue open for retreat?" asked Frank.

"Not a one."

"Then we can only stay here and fight to the last. Of course, I might be able to elude them with the Steam Man, but I'd never try that while any of your band are left."

"P'raps it would be the best way," said Harmon, generously. "At least you could save the gal. It don't matter so much about us. We're only rough men, and not a one of us afeared to die."

"You are heroes!" cried Frank, with fervor, "and if I should desert you, I would forswear any honor as a man. No, the Steam Man will stay here and fight for you until the last, depend on it."

"In course we need your help," replied Harmon. "Mebbe we'll whip the skunks yet."

"We'll try it."

"Begorra, that we will," cried Barney. "Whurroo! Av' I only had a good whack at that baste av' a Cliff now I'd spoil his beauty foriver."

Walter Barrows and Bessie had been holding a joyful conference. But now the order went up:

"Every man to his post. The enemy are coming."

There were no delinquents. Not one in that heroic little band hung back.

It was true that the foe were coming again to the attack.

With Cliff leading them they were charging furiously up the hill. But the Vigilants stood firm and gave them a raking volley.

For a moment they wavered. Then once more they came on.

Cliff's voice could be heard as he rallied them.

"Curse ye, go on up thar and kill the hull crew of 'em!" he yelled. "Don't let one of them escape alive! Kill 'em, every one, and don't give any quarter!"

"We'll see about that," muttered Frank Reade, Jr. "It may not be so easy to do all that, Mr. Cliff."

Frank and Barney, from their position aboard the Steam Man, could pour a terrible fire into the ranks of the foe.

It was a terrible battle!

The cowboys were mowed down like grain before the sickle; yet they did not waver, but came on faster.

Every moment they drew nearer the top of the rise. If they surrounded it the sequel would be brief.

Overpowering muscles would quickly tell the story, and the little band of Vigilants would be wiped out of existence.

It was, without doubt, Cliff's purpose to give no quarter. A wholesale massacre would be the result.

The Vigilants were now fighting for their lives. As well die facing the foe as with back turned. Every man was resolute in this.

But the tremendous body of men swept over the rise and gained the plateau. In a twinkling the Vigilants were surrounded, and it seemed as if no power would intervene to save them from sure and total extinction.

Frank Reade, Jr. took in the situation at a glance, and cried despairingly:

"Barney, we are lost! Our end has come, and we are as good as dead men already!"

Poor Pomp saw no way out of the awful situation in which he was placed.

Death in its most awful form was upon him.

A worse fate could not be imagined.

The natives piled the brushwood about him, and danced with demoniac yells about the pile.

If Pomp could have turned pale, he would have been whiter than chalk at that moment.

But for all this, his fears were even now more for his friends than for himself.

"Golly Massy!" he chattered, shivering like one with the ague. "Whatebber will be de end ob all dis. Here I's gwin to be burned to death, and Li'l Frank in de clutches ob dat rascal Cliff, an' nobody to rescue him. Oh, good Lor' it be dretful."

It was indeed a dreadful thing.

But Pomp was certainly powerless. Higher the brushwood was heaped, and then one of the savages advanced with a torch.

In a moment he had applied it to the pile.

The dry wood burned like tinder. In an instant, great flames sprang up.

But they were at the edge of the pile. However, Pomp felt their heat and they would soon reach him.

The poor man was nearly insane with a frenzy of desperation.

The red men now began a fiendish dance about the pile. They leaped and ran and swung their tomahawks and made hideous faces at their victim.

But fate had not ordained that this was to be Pomp's end.

Even while death seemed certain, rescue was close at hand.

Suddenly there smote upon the air the ring of horses' hoofs, and a quick sharp order, followed by the crash of carbines.

Indians fell in heaps before that volley. A panic resulted and the next moment through the smoke Pomp saw the gleam of uniforms, and knew that a body of United States cavalry had happened upon the spot just in the nick of time.

Pomp was beside himself with the realization.

He tried to break his bonds, and cried:

"Sabe me, sojers—sabe Pomp! I's suah to barn to death ef youse don' sabe me!"

But the call was not necessary.

Through the smoke sprang two dismounted soldiers. In a twinkling the burning brush was kicked aside, and Pomp's bonds were cut.

Then the old soldier was face to face with a tall, handsome young officer.

The Indians had been dispersed and the fight was over.

"I am Col. Clark, of the United States Seventh Cavalry," said the young officer. "Who are you?"

"I am Pomp!" was the black man's prompt reply.

The officer smiled.

"Well, who do you belong with?"

"I belongs with Mistuh Frank Reade, Jr.," replied Pomp, with emphasis. "I's a free born negro, but I goes wherebber Boss Frank goes jes' de same."

"Oh, I see," replied the officer; "well, where is your man just now?"

"Golly, for goodness!" cried Pomp, excitedly. "He be in a heap ob trubble, an' you kain help him out of it."

With this Pomp told Clark all about the Steam Man and their mission in the West.

The young colonel listened with deep interest, and then when apprised of the fact that the Steam Man and its passengers were in the hands of Cliff, he cried, excitedly:

"By Jupiter! That man Cliff is just the chap I am after. Word was brought to the fort some time ago of a den of thieves up here with a rendezvous called Ranch V. Do you know of it?"

"Golly sakes, Colonel Clark," cried Pomp, excitedly, "you kin jest bet I does! Jes' you find de cowboys and rescue Mistuh Frank and he done show you where de Ranch V are."

"It shall be done if we are able," said Colonel Clark.

He turned to his men who were scattered about the vicinity, having been engaged in driving the Indians out of the valley.

But the bugle quickly recalled them.

A spare horse was brought forward for Pomp and then the cavalrymen in solid body rode out of the valley.

As they struck the prairie below, the distant sounds of firing came to their ears.

It was the din of the conflict between the Vigilants and the cowboys. Aided by the sounds, Colonel Clark was able to gallop straight to the scene.

Through a pass in the hills they reached the plateau. They burst upon the cowboys in the rear just at the critical moment when it seemed as if Harmon's heroic little band was doomed.

It required but a glance for Clark to take in the situation.

Whirling his sabre aloft he spurred his horse forward with the thrilling command:

"Forward! Charge!"

CHAPTER XII.

THE FORTUNES OF WAR.

Just at that moment, when utter destruction threatened the brave little band of Vigilants, the U.S. soldiers came upon the scene. Nothing could have been more opportune.

It was the saving of the day. The emotions of all at sight of the glittering uniforms may be imagined.

A great shout of triumph went up. A yell of dismay came from the cowboys.

Then followed the rattling of steel and the flash of sabre blades. Before that charge what force could stand?

Backward the followers of Artemus Cliff were forced.

In vain the villain tried to rally them. They would not respond. The odds were too great, and they broke and fled in wild confusion. The next moment Pomp dashed up the incline and dropped from his horse almost at Frank Reade, Jr.'s feet.

"Bless de Lor', Li'l Boss," he cried ecstatically. "Youse alibe an' well, an' dis ole chile hab brought you a rescue aftah all. P'raps you forgib me fo' leabin' de Steam Man when I hadn't ought?"

"You are forgiven, Pomp!" cried Frank, lightly. "I might have done the same thing myself. I am glad no harm came to you. I had given you up."

"'Deed no, Boss Frank!" cried the delighted servant. "I is too bad to die. Hi dar, I'ish, I is glad to see you!"

"Well, if it ain't the cabbage!" cried Barney, with a wild rash at Pomp. "Whurroo, it's glad I am to see yez once more alive an' well! Bejabers that's so!"

The two friends embraced warmly. Then Colonel Clark rode up and saluted all.

"It seems that you've been having a bit of a squall here," he declared, "but at any rate you've vanquished the enemy."

"With your timely assistance," replied Frank. "But I believe we are not strangers, colonel."

"Frank Reade, Jr. the inventor!" cried Clark, springing from the saddle and seizing Frank's hand. "Well, now, I'm glad to see you. But come to think of it, your man mentioned the name of Frank Reade, but I never dreamed that it was you."

"It is nobody else," replied Frank with a laugh. "And I well remember you."

"And I do you," replied Clark. "I was once one of an army commission to visit you and make you an offer for one of your inventions on a gun."

"You are right."

"You would not sell it."

"No," replied Frank. "I do not care to sell any of my inventions. They are for my own use. I will always, however, put them at the disposal of the weak and oppressed."

"Truly a noble sentiment," agreed the colonel, "but I am anxious to capture this man Cliff. Hello! what have you there? A giant in iron? One of your new inventions is it? Well, that beats all."

With this Clark proceeded to make an inspection of the Steam Man. A great crowd of the newcomers were doing the same.

It was an object of great wonderment. Frank showed its working to the entertainment of all.

But Cliff's men had not been so easily beaten as the natives.

They had dispersed into the passes and were somewhat scattered, but here they made a stand and resisted stubbornly.

It was necessary to dislodge them as quickly as possible.

At any moment they might avail themselves of the fortunes of war and turn victory into defeat.

So Clark quickly called his men together.

Only a brief rest was all that he would accord them.

The bugle sounded "boots and saddles," and every man was quickly mounted.

A plan was quickly outlined between Frank Reade, Jr. and Col. Clark.

This was that the cavalry should pursue and thoroughly rout the cowboys, even going down to Ranch V to effect its destruction.

The Vigilants were to return home, and the cavalry would see to the punishment of Artemus Cliff.

But the Steam Man was to remain at a point below until the return of the cavalry.

If possible, Cliff was to be captured alive and a confession wrung from his lips.

This plan had been agreed upon.

The Vigilants were not wholly satisfied, yet did not demur.

Clark and his command dashed away into the hills.

The Vigilants and the Steam Man started for the open prairie.

This division of forces very soon proved to be an unwise and unfortunate thing.

The fortunes of war are proverbial for changes.

Strongly intrenched in the hills, Cliff's gang gave the soldiers a disastrous battle.

In vain the plucky young colonel tried to dislodge them.

They fought like tigers, and having the advantage of location, actually decimated the cavalry one half in number.

Until nightfall, Col. Clark kept persistently waging the battle. Then he began to think of retreat.

But, to his horror, he found that this was by no means as easy a matter as he had fancied.

The foe had actually closed in upon him, and nearly every avenue of retreat was closed.

He was literally surrounded by the foe.

"My soul!" he muttered, in deep surprise; "this is not very good generalship on my part."

What was to be done?

It was plainly impossible to dislodge the foe.

The little band of cavalrymen were now hardly adequate to cope with the foe in their front.

It really seemed as if Cliff had received reinforcements. The number of his band had in some mysterious manner been increased.

Darkness was coming on rapidly.

Something must be done, and at once. Col. Clark racked his brain for an expedient.

Certainly they must extricate themselves from this position, and without delay. Men were falling every moment about them, and the enemy's line, like a cordon of death, was every moment drawing tighter about them.

Cold sweat broke out upon the intrepid colonel's brow.

"My God!" he muttered. "What is to be done?"

It was a terrible question. They were literally in a trap of death.

Cliff was aware of this, and his men made the air hideous with their yells. Closer they crowded the line.

In this extremity Clark regretted having separated himself from the Vigilants and the Steam Man.

But this error had been made, and it was too late to correct it.

But the brave colonel was not long without an expedient.

He called out one of his pluckiest privates, and said:

"Jason, do you want to undertake a ticklish job?"

"I'm ready, sir," replied the private, with a salute.

"You know we are in a tight box?"

"Yes, sir."

"We must have reinforcements or the enemy will surely get the best of us."

"It looks that way, sir."

"Now, I want you to try to get through the enemy's line. Look for the Vigilants and the Steam Man and tell them to come to our aid. Then ride to the fort as fast as you can for a fresh squad. Tell the officer in charge to send two hundred mounted men."

"Very well, sir."

"Do you think you can do this?"

"I will do it or I will not come back."

Clark knew that Jason meant just what he said.

A few moments later the courier for relief slipped carefully into the shadows and was gone.

A prayer trembled on Clark's lips.

"I don't care for myself," he muttered, "but I cannot bear to see my brave boys slaughtered like sheep."

Darkness now thickly settled down. Of course no fighting could be done until the break of day.

But the cavalrymen were not in a position to guarantee them much rest.

Few of them dared to sleep, and then it was upon their arms.

As the night hours dragged by, Clark paced the ground upon the outskirts of the camp and listened for some sign of the return of Jason.

He knew that it was not possible for the faithful courier to return from the fort under two days.

But if the cavalry division was reinforced by the Vigilants and the Steam Man they might be able to keep the foe at bay until the fresh squad should arrive.

Thus the plucky young colonel clung to hope.

Time passed. It seemed an age to Clark before a silent shadowy form slipped out of the gloom and into the camp.

As it drew nearer he recognized the courier Jason.

"Well, my man!" he said, sharply. "You are back."

Jason saluted quickly.

"Where are the reinforcements?"

"I did not find them."

"But did I not tell you to find them?" began the colonel, angrily

"Easy, colonel," said Jason, respectfully. "I think I have done a better thing, sir."

"What do you mean?"

"It's a good ways to the fort. You might be cut to pieces before I could return. I have found an avenue by which I think we can escape."

Clark's manner changed instantly.

"You don't mean it?" he exclaimed, excitedly. "What is it?" Jason drew nearer and lowered his voice in a mysterious manner. "Just over that pile of boulders," he whispered, "I found a narrow passage through the mountain side. It is almost a cavern, for the top is so closely overhung with bushes. It's a close squeeze for the horses, but I think we can all get through and out upon the prairie before daybreak."

Col. Clark was intensely excited.

"Good for you, Jason!" he cried, in a joyful manner. "Arouse the camp, but do it quietly. Put every man in his saddle within ten minutes. You have solved our salvation, and you shall be promoted."

Jason hurried away to do the bidding of the colonel.

In a brief space of time the camp was aroused.

The weary soldiers, worn out with fighting, were only too glad to learn of the possibility of an escape.

At once preparations were made to steal a march upon the enemy. The passage described by Jason was found. It was necessary to first pry aside a huge boulder before passage could be made.

Into the passage the little band went, and one by one filed out into the valley beyond.

So skillfully was the move executed that the foe never dreamed of it. Daybreak came, and Cliff was furious to find that his intended victims had given him the slip during the night.

The cavalrymen had reached the prairie in safety, and galloped away from the hills.

Clark knew that his only and best move now was to return to the fort for reinforcements.

He could not hope to do anything with the foe with such a mere handful of men.

Accordingly, just as the sun appeared above the horizon, the little cavalcade, with its shattered ranks, galloped away across the plain. No effort was made to search for the Vigilants.

Clark knew that even with their aid it would not be feasible to give battle to the cowboys.

Clearly it was necessary to have two hundred more men. The colonel set his lips vengefully.

"I will teach that desperado a lesson," he muttered. "He shall be swept out of existence together with his rascally crew, and before another week."

On over the prairie they galloped toward the fort.

And as they rode, thrilling adventures were the lot of Frank Reade, Jr. and his friends on board the Steam Man.

Let us, therefore, for a time, deviate here and follow their fortunes.

CHAPTER XIII.
THE ABDUCTION.

Chief Harmon of the Vigilants was not wholly content to abandon the trail of the cowboys, just here.

He indulged in quite an argument with Frank Reade, Jr.

His remarks were not without logic.

"Why, only look at the sense of the thing," he declared. "It is by no means possible that the soldiers are going to have an easy time with Cliff and his men. They may turn the tables on them yet. I tell you it was a premature thing for that colonel to do, to set us adrift so quickly."

"Yet he ought to know his own strength," said Frank.

"I don't believe he does."

"I cannot but feel that he is doing the right thing."

"I don't feel that way."

"Well, in case of defeat the stigma will not fall upon you."

"Ah, but that is not the idea. We must not let Cliff defeat them. If he does, he will defeat us."

"What do you propose?"

"I am not going back home yet. We will make a camp down here on Willow

Creek. When we learn for a fact that Cliff has been done up, then we will go home. Until then we are on duty."

Frank saw that Harmon was right. He extended his hand and said:

"I agree with you."

"I knew ye would," replied the Vigilant leader. We can do this upon our own responsibility. You are to wait for Clark at a point below here, I believe?"

"Yes."

"Very good. That point is on Willow Creek. We will accompany you there."

It was nightfall before Willow Creek was reached.

In a convenient spot camp was made. The darkness became most intense in the vicinity.

Camp-fires were made and guards posted.

The fires in the furnace of the Steam Man were banked, and the occupants descended and mixed with the Vigilants.

The men gathered around the fires, and told stories and cracked jokes.

Walter Barrows, the young Vigilant who was so deeply in love with Bessie Rodman, had waited upon her at the wagon step, and together they took a lover—like walk down the bank of the creek.

Nobody saw them go, and it is doubtful if any one would have sought to restrain them.

But they were committing unwittingly an act of great risk and folly. For unknown to any in the camp a coterie of dusky natives lurked in the tall prairie grass about.

Barney and Pomp were entertaining the camp with some of their munchausen stories.

The plainsmen roared with laughter until their sides ached.

Both were comical mokes and were continually playing roots upon each other. Barney had just worked a gag upon Pomp when suddenly the distant crack of a pistol was heard.

Instantly every man in the camp was upon his feet.

The most intense of excitement reigned. All was confusion.

Then one of the guards came rushing in.

"There's a hull lot of Apaches down yonder," he cried, "the grass is full of 'em and I reckon they've surrounded the camp."

"Steady all!" thundered Harmon, the Vigilant leader. "Who fired that pistol shot?"

"I don't know," replied the guard.

"Is anybody outside the line?"

"Yes."

"Who?"

"Walter Barrows and the young lady passed me not an hour ago. They went on down the creek."

"My soul!" gasped Harmon, with white face, "that was Barrows' pistol without doubt. He an' the gal have certainly fallen into the grip of the Injuns. We must make lively work to save 'em."

Frank Reade, Jr. had listened to this report with a sensation of horror.

Barney and Pomp had at once desisted in their fun—making, and Barney proceeded to open the Steam Man's furnace.

The crack of rifles now sounded all around the camp.

The Indians, without doubt, were drawing their line closer, and meant, if possible, to exterminate the little band of Vigilants.

But a line of defense was then thrown out, and the skulking raiders were held at bay.

But a desultory and very unsatisfactory species of warfare was kept up in the darkness.

It was impossible to tell how to move or where.

The enemy fired from all directions and practically at random.

Many of the Vigilants were wounded, and Captain Harmon was angry.

"Confound an Injun!" he muttered, in disgust. "They have sich a sneakin' way of fighting. They allus attack one after dark, an' hain't got the pluck to come out in the open an' fight."

Everybody was bound to acknowledge the logic of this.

But the natives kept up the same mode of attack until Frank Reade, Jr. made a diversion.

Barney had succeeded in getting up steam once more in the Steam Man. and now Frank Reade, Jr. approached Harmon.

"Give me five men," he declared, "and I will whip the foe for you."

"Five men!" gasped Harmon. "Why, they're ten to one out there."

"I don't care if they are."

"But—"

"Will you give me the men?"

"Oh. yes, but—"

"There's no time for questions, Captain Harmon. Leave it all to me."

"Alright, Mr. Reade."

By Harmon's orders five of the Vigilants joined Frank Reade.

He led them aboard the steam wagon. Then he closed the door and seized the reins which connected with the throttle.

The Steam Man gave a shriek loud enough to perforate the ear drums of any one in the vicinity.

Then it dashed out upon the prairie.

The effect may be imagined.

The monster with fiery eyes and all flame and smoke, with clanking thunderous tread plunging into the midst of the foe, was an apparition well to be feared.

Right into the midst of the aggressive natives the Steam Man ran.

While the armed men in the screened wagon poured destructive volleys into the midst of the red foe.

Pen cannot adequately describe the situation.

For a moment the Apaches held their ground. Then, with wild, baffled yells they fled before the conqueror.

In less than twenty minutes the vicinity had been practically cleared of hostiles.

They retreated to a point below where their ponies were corralled. Mounting, they dashed away to the westward. The Steam Man pursued until finding a creek, they escaped for good.

Then the Steam Man returned to camp.

But although the foe had been repulsed, matters were still bad enough.

Walter Barrows and Bessie Rodman were missing.

That they were captives was a forlorn hope. That they had been murdered was a dreadful fear.

Delay was almost fatal in this case. Without loss of time a good trailer was put upon the trail of the lovers.

Daylight was breaking in the east, and this enabled him to easily follow the trail.

Along the banks of the creek it ran for nearly a fifth of a mile.

Then the trailer paused.

Here without doubt was the spot where Barrows bad been attacked by the Apaches.

There were footprints and marks of a struggle. A rifle, with broken stock, was picked up.

"It is Barrows' gun," said one of the Vigilants.

Blood was found upon the ground, but no trace of the bodies.

"They have been taken away as captives," declared Harmon, positively. "There is no doubt of that."

"Or thrown into the creek," suggested one of the Vigilants. Investigation for a moment gave the pursuers a thrill of horror. There were footprints down to the water's edge, and the mark of some heavy body dragged thitherr.

In the shallow water, protected by reeds, was a body.

For a moment all expected to recognize Barrows. But all drew a breath of relief. It was not him.

The body was that of one of the Apaches. Doubtless it was one shot by Barrows, and his body had been thrown into this place to escape the notice of the white pursuers.

"That's an Injun trick," declared Harmon, positively. "I'm mighty well satisfied that the captives are alive."

"I hope you are right," said one man.

"Ditto!" said another.

"Then let us take the trail," cried Frank Reade, Jr. "If possible, we must rescue them."

The question was settled at once. All sprung to saddle, and the trail, which was quite plain, was followed.

Across the prairies went the Steam Man, with the Vigilants behind. Of course, their horses could not compete with the Man on a level stretch, but Frank did not try to run away from them.

The Indians bore away to a southwesterly course, and soon a range of hills became visible above the horizon.

Harmon made them out as the Black Bear range.

"If they get into those hills with the captives," he declared, "we'll have mighty hard work diggin' 'em out."

"Why?" asked one of his men.

"Bekase, there's more holes and out of the way dens there than you could shake a stick at."

Barney and Pomp crouched down in the wagon and kept their rifles in readiness for business.

Frank Reade, Jr. watched the plain ahead with eager eye, but though the trail was plain there was yet no signs of overtaking the red foe.

As they drew nearer the hills it became almost a certainty that the natives had sought refuge there.

A long stretch of plain intervened to the hills.

This was easily to he inspected with a glass, and Frank did so. There was no sign whatever of the Indians.

All hope was thus given up of overtaking the redskins before reaching the hills.

It seemed a certainty that they had reached their caves, and the only alternative left was to scour them thoroughly.

But when quite near an entrance between high hills, suddenly the pursuers topped a rise in the prairie and were rewarded with a startling sight.

Just below, in a depression, was the band of braves, seemingly engaged in making camp.

A small creek ran through this depression.

As is well known, Indians always encamp upon the banks of a stream. Yet it was a surprise to the pursuers that they should venture to camp in this open spot.

At sight of their foes the astonished redskins were thrown into a tumult.

Instantly a mad retreat was begun for the mountains.

A wild cheer pealed from the lips of the Vigilants.

Harman settled himself in his saddle and shouted:

"Forward, all! Charge!"

With a yell the Vigilants put spurs to their horses and made for the Indian encampment.

Frank Reade, Jr. started the Steam Man on a circuit to head off the natives.

But as he did so Pomp clutched his arm.

"Hi dar, Boss Frank!" cried Pomp. "Does you see dat little party ober der making fo' de hills?"

Frank did see them.

"Yes," he replied.

"Well, dat be Missy Bessie an' her lover jes' as suah as yu' am bo'n, Boss Jun'r, an' dar be half a dozen Injuns jes' holding onto de bridles ob der hosses. I makes it out, suh, dat dey fink dey kin reach de hills afo' de Steam Man, suh."

"By Jupiter, you're right, Pomp!" cried Frank, with inspiration. "But we'll try and spoil that little game."

"Dat's right, Li'l Boss!" cried Pomp. "I jes' fink de Man kin obertake dem hosses suah enuff."

Frank seized the reins and pulled open the throttle.

As the Steam Man went forward with his mighty stride Frank opened the whistle valve and let out a mighty shriek of such loudness that the echoes were repeated a hundred—fold in the recesses of the hills.

CHAPTER XIV.
IN HOT PURSUIT.

The party of raiders with the two captives in their midst, evidently intended to reach the hills, if possible, before being overtaken by the Steam Man.

At first Frank had fancied it easy to cut them off.

But there were several depressions in the prairie which the Man had to circuit, and the distance was greater than Frank had really dreamed of.

Like a runaway locomotive the Steam Man raced over the plain.

The Vigilants were having a running fight with the Indians.

But Frank Reade, Jr. was doomed to disappointment.

He failed to cut off the band of abductors, and they vanished from sight in a deep pass.

It was too rocky a trail for the Steam Man to follow. Thus far the villains had the best of it.

"Golly sakes, Boss!" cried Pomp, "dey done git away wif dem prisoners fo' suah."

"It looks like it," agreed Frank, in a baffled tone, "but there ought to be some way to cut them off."

"Begorra, there's only won way," declared Barney.

"What is that?"

"Let the eejit stay with the Man, an' you an' I will go after the divils a—foot," said the Celt.

For a moment Frank entertained no hopes of the success of such a plan.

Then he glanced back to the prairie where the Vigilants and the Indians were having their battle.

It was nip and tuck between them, but Frank saw that the Vigilants were fast getting the best of it.

Not more than half a dozen of the raiders had the captives in charge. To be sure, the odds were three to one, yet Frank believed that with the plucky Barney's help, they could defeat them.

To think with Frank Reade, Jr. was to act. He did not waste time, but seizing a rifle, cried:

"Your idea is a good one, Barney. We will act upon it. Pomp, keep a sharp eye out for danger until we return."

"A'right Boss Frank," replied the faithful servant.

Barney, delighted that Frank had seen fit to adopt his plan, was quickly ready and they left the wagon.

The Indians, to be sure, had the start of them, but the pass was rocky and it was hardly likely that they would succeed in getting a great lead.

Swiftly the two rescuers pressed forward.

They climbed over piles of boulders, crept through narrow defiles, and climbed high steeps.

It seemed that progress must be slow for the ponies of the Indians, and they should be overtaken before long.

Suddenly Barney paused with a sharp cry.

He seized Frank by the arm and pulled him back into the cover of an angle in the mountain wall.

He was none too soon.

The crack of rifles smote upon the air and the shower of bullets came down into the pass.

"Bejabers, I saw the spalpeens just in the nick av time!" declared Barney, peering around the edge of the cliff wall. "Av I hadn't we'd have been dead gossoons as sure as me name is Barney."

"You're right there!" cried Frank, slipping extra cartridges into his rifle; "that was a close call."

"Indade it was."

"I had no idea we were so near the rascals."

" Bejabers, I didn't mesilf till I see the top—knot av wan of thim over that ridge yender."

"They are ready for us, then."

"Bejabers, and we're ready too. If I iver get a bead on any wan av them there'll be a job for the coroner, bad cess to thim."

"Where are they? I can't see their position very well."

"Aisy, Mister Frank," said Barney, "they're hiding up yonder jist ferninst that big scrub av an oak on the edge of the cliff."

Frank looked in that direction. Suddenly Barney gave a sharp cry.

"Whurro!" he yelled.

Quick us a flash his rifle went to his shoulder.

Crack!

A yell of agony rang through the gorge. Then down over the cliff tumbled an Indian almost at the Celt's feet.

The bullet had pierced his skull and his final account was settled.

"Good shot, Barney!" cried Frank, that only leaves five for us to tackle."

Then quick as a flash the young inventor threw his rifle to his shoulder.

Crack!

Another yell, a death cry went up on the air of the defile.

"Bejabers, that's only four av the divils left," chuckled Barney. It's only two to wan, Mister Frank."

"You're right, Barney!" cried Frank, with enthusiasm, "but the odds are yet too great."

The outlook now was certainly encouraging for the rescue of the prisoners.

But the two rescuers knew better than to essay an open attack.

The Indian method of warfare was in this case far the best. They remained strictly under cover.

All was quiet on the bluff above.

But it was not by any means likely that the foe were inactive.

The great danger now was that they would continue to slip away deeper into the hills and reach some inaccessible hiding place.

Our rescuers waited as long as seemed consistent with safety.

Then Frank said:

"I think we'd better make a break, Barney."

"All roight, sor," replied the Celt. "Do yez think it safe?"

"We must use caution. It may be possible that they are trying to draw us from our hiding place."

"So I thought, sor."

"Again, they may be far into the hills by this time. We will gain nothing by staying here.

"All roight, sor."

Barney began to scan the side of the cliff. A path was not visible anywhere. Yet the Celt did not believe it impossible to climb to the top.

If this could be done they might then succeed in getting upon level ground with the foe and escape the risk of their bullets.

Frank divined Barney's purpose and said:

"I think we can climb it, Barney."

"Bejabers we'll try."

Barney had just got his hands and feet into niches in the cliff when a startling sound came up the pass.

"Hark!"

"What is it?"

The tramp of ponies' feet could be heard and the distant baffled yells of native raiders were wafted up on the breeze.

"The Indians are coming up the pass," cried Frank, with dismay. "Barney, there's not an instant to lose."

"Begorra, ye're roight," cried the Celt, beginning to make his way up the cliff.

It was a smart climb up the steep wall, but it was safely made at length.

They were now on level ground with the four captors. But a careful reconnoitering of the vicinity showed that they had left.

In the lull in the conflict they had slipped away into the hills.

But Barney took the trail and they went forward again in pursuit. The sounds of the foe coming up the pass in their rear, however, every moment became plainer.

But fortunately, just at a point where the trail diverged deeper into the hills, the foe must have turned in another direction for very soon the sounds died out.

"We have nothing to fear from them," cried Frank, with a breath of relief. "They have gone in another direction."

Very soon the hills began to merge into a deep valley. Through this there ran a swift stream.

As Frank and Barney entered the valley Barney shouted:

"By me sowl, there be the spalpeens now."

"Where?" asked Frank.

"Jist down there ferninst that grove of trees, Mister Frank."

"Sure enough."

The four savages and their captives were plainly seen on the banks of the creek.

They were just in the act of embarking in a canoe.

Frank saw that he must act quick if he would prevent this.

So he said, sharply:

"Go to the right, Barney, I will go to the left, and we must head them off."

"All right, sor."

Away went Barney on the mad run. The savages had already got the canoe into the water.

They saw him coming and a yell was the signal. The captives were hustled into the light craft and it was pushed out from the shore.

Down into the current it went. There was no time to lose.

Frank Reade, Jr. came to a stop and raised his rifle. It was a desperate chance but he took it.

A quick aim, a bead skillfully drawn on one of the paddlers and—

Crack!

A wild Indian yell went up and the prow of the canoe swung around.

Over into the water went the doomed savage. The shot had been a good one.

But the canoe was at the moment at the head of some swift rapids. The next moment it was racing down them, and turning a bend in the stream vanished from view.

Frank had not time to draw another bead before it was out of sight, and when it reached the lower level and came into view again it was out of range.

Barney came along now and shouted:

"Bejabers, yez did well, Mister Frank. That was a beautiful shot. There's only three av the red divils left."

This was true, but the three Indians seemed likely to elude their pursuers after all.

The canoe was racing down the stream, and fast nearing a defile in the hills.

If it should enter this, there was little doubt but that the fugitives would make their escape.

Frank and Barney, saw this in the same moment.

"Begorra, Mister Frank, we must cut the divils off!" cried the Celt.

"Forward, then!" cried Frank. "Is there not a short cut?"

Both looked for this. In the same instant they espied it.

The creek took a long turn and by cutting directly across a meadow the two pursuers saw that they would be likely to cut off the raiders.

Accordingly, they started forward on the run.

The Indian captors saw their move at once, and an angry yell went up from them.

One of them rose in the canoe and took quick aim and fired.

The bullet whistled close to Barney's ear. The Celt stopped and cocked his rifle.

"Bejabers, I'll spoil that fellow!" he cried. "Have at yez, ye blatherskite!"

Barney's rifle spoke.

But the motion of the canoe very likely destroyed the aim, for the bullet did not take effect.

At this point the canoe took a swift course, and in the twinkling of an eye seemed to have overcome the skilled hand at the paddles.

In a flash it went over and the entire party were dumped into the waters of the creek.

A great cry went up from Frank Reade, Jr.

"My God! They will be drowned!"

Forward the brave young inventor rushed. He thought of poor Barrows with his hands tied.

Thrown into the waters of the creek, it did not seem as if any power on earth could save him.

But two of the natives had seized the prisoners. The canoe had overturned in close proximity to the shore.

The third raider gave assistance, and as the water did not chance to be deep, all got ashore.

"Now we have them!" cried Frank, confidently.

But his statement was premature.

Even as it seemed that the rescue was certain, an incident occurred to prevent.

From behind a small hillock appeared Red Bear's gang of Apaches, full half a hundred strong.

CHAPTER XV.
THE VIGILANTS TO THE RESCUE.

The appearance of the savages was most inopportune.

Mounted on their fleet ponies, with wild yells they swept down upon the party.

The three Indian captors yelled with delight.

Frank and Barney of course came to a halt. Of course it was folly to tempt fate.

To attempt to stand against that gang was folly.

"By Jupiter!" gasped the young inventor. "It's all up with us, Barney! We are badly beaten!"

"Tare an"ounds!" grumbled the angry Celt."That beats all me woife's relations! Whativer shall we do now, Mister Frank?"

"Beat a retreat," declared the young inventor. "Come on, Barney!"

"It's mesilf as hates to retreat," said Barney, stubbornly. "Oh, if we only had the Steam Man an' the eejit here now we'd moighty soon turn the thing about."

The two rescuers now turned about and hastily beat a retreat across the valley.

But they had not gone far when the Indians began to ford the creek for the purpose of giving pursuit.

Barney saw the move and called Frank's attention to it.

"By me sowl, Mister Frank!" cried the Irishman, excitedly, "we've got to make quick toime, or they'll have our scalps."

"You are right, Barney."

But at that moment Frank Reade, Jr. lifted his gaze, and a mighty cry escaped his lips.

Directly in front of them, a body of armed men swept into the valley.

They were the Vigilants, and at their head rode Harmon. At sight of Frank and Barney they urged their horses on faster with a loud cheer.

This was answered by the two fugitives, with a will.

The savages, seeing the Vigilants, now changed their tactics. They turned their horses about and rode swiftly on the back trail.

Frank could hardly wait for Harmon and his men to come up.

Enthusiastic greetings were exchanged, and also experiences.

The Vigilants had driven the Apaches before them into the hills.

But upon entering the fastnesses, with which they were not familiar, the Indians had given them the slip.

In the search, they had come upon the scene at an opportune moment.

There seemed no better thing to do than to give pursuit to the red men at once.

Accordingly, a couple of spare horses were provided for Frank and Barney, and they rode forward on the charge.

The delay had been brief, but it had enabled the raiders to cross the creek and start for the defile beyond.

Down thundered the Vigilants in hot pursuit.

The creek was quickly forded and the pursuers seemed to be gaining at every bound.

But of a sudden the Indians executed a peculiar and inexplicable maneuver.

Suddenly and without warning they split in two sections, one going to the right and the other to the left.

In one division was the girl captive, Bessie Rodman, and in the other Walter Barrows.

The party who had the girl in charge started for the defile.

The other made directly across the valley. In a flash of time the purpose of the savages was made apparent.

The Vigilants could not go both ways without splitting up.

As they were much less in number than the Apaches the result of this would be to greatly weaken them, if not actually place them at the mercy of the red foe.

On the other hand, it was a problem as to which direction to pursue or which party to follow.

Harmon drew a slight rein upon his horse and wavered a moment. The Vigilants naturally were inclined to go to the rescue of their comrade, but Frank Reade, Jr., comprehending the folly of this, cried:

"The girl first. We can rescue the man later."

"Yes!" cried Harmon, in a voice of thunder; "that is our duty! The girl first, boys; then we will try and save Barrows."

The Vigilants cheered, and away thundered the troop toward the defile.

A few moments later they reached it and entered it.

High walls of black, forbidding rock arose on either side to a mighty height. The bed of the defile was rough and strewn with boulders.

It was harder for the horses of the Vigilants to pick their way through here than the fleet—footed ponies of the savages.

Accordingly, the Indians, gained quite a lead. But after a quarter of a mile of the defile had been traversed the Vigilants were brought to a halt in an unceremonious manner.

The defile seemed suddenly to take an upward trend here, and high piles of boulders made a barrier of some height.

Suddenly from behind this barrier there came the flash of rifle muzzles, and a volley of bullets came rattling down through the defile.

Two of the Vigilants were wounded, and Harmon instantly called a halt.

Cover was quickly sought behind rocks and corners near.

It was evident that the Indians had here made a stand. The Vigilant leader was puzzled.

But suddenly Frank Reade, Jr. gave a sharp cry:

"Listen!"

His acute ear had caught the sound of horses' hoofs coming up the defile in their rear.

"By thunder!" ejaculated Harmon, with sudden terrible comprehension, "we are trapped!"

The men gazed blankly at each other.

Nothing was more apparent. The Apaches under the shrewd Red Bear had certainly very cleverly outgeneraled them.

Led into the defile by one division of the Apaches, the other had proceeded to block up the outlet, and thus literally the Vigilants were in a trap.

There was not the advantage in facing a foe in this manner that there was in having him wholly in the front.

To be attacked both front and rear would demoralize even the largest and bravest of armies. Harmon was completely taken aback.

"Wall, I swan!" he exclaimed, with earnestness, "I never believed an Injun could beat me in any such way as that. But we are in fur it, boys, and no mistake. We've got to fight hard."

The red raiders in front were keeping up a raking fire.

Those in the rear had now drawn near enough to also open fire. The fun had begun.

But the brave band of white men had no thought of fear or of retreat.

They at once, by Harmon's direction, sought safe places of cover and proceeded to return the fire.

Every time an Indian's top—knot showed above the fringe of rocks, it was made a target of.

Thus, the battle was kept up for over an hour.

Then an idea occurred to the inventive mind of Frank Reade, Jr.

He had carefully examined the face of the pass. In doing so he had discovered what looked like a feasible foot path over the cliff. At once he called Harmon aside and explained a plan to him.

"I think we can defeat the savages easily in this manner," he declared. "Give me five men and I will guarantee a surprise for them."

"Mr. Reade, take what force you need," declared the Vigilant leader. "I have full confidence in your ability to do as you say. May you succeed."

Frank at once selected five men from the troop.

Then with Barney he led the way cautiously up the path. Fortunately, it was overhung with foliage to a large extent, so that they were hidden from the view of those in their rear.

In a few moments a position near the brow of the cliff had been reached. Then Frank's surmise was verified.

The little party could look down upon the heads of the natives. It was an easy matter to pour a volley amongst them with most demoralizing effect.

Frank sent one of the men back down the cliff, to give Harmon the cue when to make a charge.

Then at a favorable moment Frank gave the order to fire.

Six repeating rifles were turned upon the raiders, and as fast as they could be worked, they were engaged in firing a volley down upon the heads of the exposed Indians.

The effect was startling.

The native brave is never the one to stand in open field and fight. At once a panic seized them.

It was the moment for the charge, and Harmon's men rushed forward.

Up over the rocks they went. In a twinkling the braves were driven from their entrenchments and utterly routed, and completely dispersed.

Frank Reade, Jr. and Barney saw their opportunity, and rushed upon two of the red foe who had Bessie Rodman in charge.

In a moment the girl captive was free once more and among friends. The two guards fled for their lives.

All this had happened in a twinkling of an eye, comparatively speaking. But the fight was not over.

The force in the rear were coming to the attack.

But Harmon's men were now in a position to command the defile. A quick, sharp conflict ensued, and the Apaches were driven back with great slaughter.

The Vigilants had thus far the best of it.

The enemy had been routed, and Bessie Rodman rescued.

Only one other thing now remained to be accomplished, and this was the rescue of Walter Barrows.

But even as the question was being discussed a loud cry arose, and the next moment a listless, blood—stained young man came dashing down over the cliff and fell half fainting in the midst of the Vigilants.

It was Barrows.

In the midst of the fight the plucky young plainsman had succeeded in breaking his bonds, and after a desperate fight with two of his captors, had made his escape.

Everybody extended congratulations to the young couple, and then plans for the future were discussed.

It was not certain that the Indians would not return to the attack. But a report was brought in by a number of scouts sent out that the Apaches had withdrawn from the field entirely.

It was therefore decided to go back to Willow Creek.

It was not known whetherr Col. Clark had been victorious with the cowboys or not.

Until this question was settled Harmon had no idea of returning home.

"Until Cliff and his gang have been wiped out of existence," be declared, "I shall not give up the chase."

Frank and Barney were anxious to return at once to the Steam Man and Pomp.

They were, by no means, assured that Pomp was safe or that he might not have got into trouble.

Accordingly, the start was at once made for the prairie.

Down one of the defiles the Vigilants rode. Coming out into the little valley they crossed this and entered the pass.

But they had not proceeded a hundred yards into the pass when one of the advance scouts came rushing back and gave a thrilling report.

"The cowboys are coming up the pass!" he cried. "Thar's a host of 'em, and Art Cliff is at the head of 'em."

"The cowboys!" gasped Harmon.

The greatest excitement ensued.

"My soul!" exclaimed Frank Reade, Jr. in dismay. "Clark has been defeated!"

"Bad luck to the omadhouns!"

"But what of Pomp?" exclaimed Frank with alarm. "Barney, we ought at once to ascertain where he is."

"To be shure, Mister Frank," agreed the Celt, "but how in the name av all the saints are yez goin' to do it? Bejabers, these cowboys have got us cornered."

In a very few moments a large sized battle was in progress in the pass.

CHAPTER XVI.
POMP MAKES ACTION.

Now let us return to Pomp and the Steam Man, whom in the detail of the thrilling adventures just chronicled we have neglected.

The former soldier entertained nothing like fear at being left alone on board the Steam Man.

Indeed, he rathe enjoyed the responsibility thus put upon him.

He could occasionally hear rifle shots from the hills, which assured him that Frank and Barney were making it hot for the raiders.

"Golly!" he muttered. "I jes' reckon dem Injuns git de worstest ob dat fight. Hi dar, if dey amn't comin' dis yer way. I spec's I better move."

This was true.

The Indians had been driven before the Vigilants, and starting for the hills were coming straight toward the Steam Man.

It was evident that they meant to enter the hills at this point.

Pomp knew that it would be folly to remain where he was with the Steam Man.

They might ruin the machine as he could not hope alone to hold them at bay.

So he opened the throttle and started away with the Man.

He kept on until satisfied that he had reached a safe point.

Meanwhile the Indians reached the pass and entered it.

The Vigilants, however, did not seem in a hurry to pursue. They remained on the battle ground for some while looking after their dead and wounded.

When they did start for the pass Pomp had returned and was there stationed.

As they came up Pomp put his head out of the screen door and shouted:

"Good fo' you, Mistuh Harmon. Jes you gib dem Injuns a good lickin' fo' luck. I reckon you kin do it."

"I reckon we can, Pomp," replied Harmon. "At least we'll try it."

"If you sees Mistuh Frank, jes' tell him fo' me, dat his carriage be wailin' fo' him. Will you?"

Harmon replied that he would and rode away laughing immoderately.

The Vigilants all vanished up the pass. It seemed ages after they had gone, when Pomp received another great surprise.

Suddenly, hearing the clatter of hoofs he turned his head, and scrutinized the prairie.

A thrilling sight met his gaze.

There, coming over a swell in the plain was a body of horsemen.

It required but a glance for Pomp to recognize them.

They were the cowboys with Artemus Cliff at their head. They were riding directly down upon the Steam Man.

They were just coming from the scene of their victory over Clark. Pomp's eyes stuck out like agates and he sprung to his feet.

"Glory fo' goodness!" he gasped. "Dat's Cliff and his debbils. I jes' reckon I get out dere way."

In an instant he opened the throttle and let the Steam Man race out upon the prairie.

The cowboys gave a wild yell, and attempted pursuit.

But they could not keep anywhere near the Man, and finally abandoned it. With baffled yells they returned and disappeared in the pass.

"Golly, dat's a berry bad fing for Boss Frank an' de oders," muttered Pomp. "Dey will neber be anticipating de comin' ob dem rapscallions, an' dat will make t'ings berry bad, indeed."

Pomp at once began to wax anxious as to the fate of his friends.

He began to feel as if it was very much his duty to enter the hills and render what assistance he could.

But what was to be done with the Steam Man?

Pomp reflected that he might take it with him if he could only find some way of doing so.

To attempt to traverse the rocky Pass was out of the question.

The old soldier was in a quandary.

Soon he heard the sounds of firing. The battle was on, and at no great distance, either.

Pomp could hardly contain himself. Hs walked up and down in the cage like a prisoner in his cell.

"Ob co'se, I has Boss Frank's ordahs to stay here," he muttered, "but it be evident dat Li'l Bos needs all de help dat he can get. What ebber I kin do, I jes' don' know what."

He sat down and began sober reflection.

He was a shrewd fellow, and as a result he was not long in formulating a plan.

He sprang up finally.

"By golly, I'll jes' do dat fing!" he cried, finally. "It de bes' fing I kin do."

He opened the throttle and started the Steam Man along the base of the hills. With keen eye he studied the possibility of entering them.

By the pass it was impossible. But he imagined that it would not be difficult to find another means.

Nor was he disappointed.

At a certain point the hillside was shorn of trees and boulders. It made a smooth surface even over the brow of the height.

As the Steam Man was provided with power to climb any height of this sort, Pomp at once set his course up the height.

Up went the Steam Man with prodigious strides.

Nearer the top he drew. Pomp had no means of knowing whether it would be possible to go further or not.

But his best hopes were realized upon reaching the summit.

Down a gentle incline the Steam Man went, and through a scattered grove of trees, and came out into a valley deep in the hills.

The sound of firing was now quite plain.

Indeed, as Pomp guided the Man down into the valley, he saw the powder smoke of the conflict in the pass, just a short way up the valley

"By golly!" muttered Pomp, joyfully, "I reckon dat I get dar jes' in de bes' time. Won't Li'l Boss be glad to see me!"

Bat at that moment a startling thing occurred.

The Man was traveling slowly, when just as the bottom of the incline was readied, two powerful braves sprung out of the grass and seized the throttle rein.

Pomp was so taken by surprise that for a moment he could not act.

The pulling of the rein closed the throttle, and the Man came to a halt.

Pomp could not use the rein to open it again, and had there been more of the red foe, the Steam Man would have been at their mercy.

But there were only two of them, and while one held the rein the other essayed to hack his way into the wagon with his tomahawk.

Pomp acted with the rapidity of thought.

"G'way from dar you red imp!" he yelled, picking up a revolver. "If you don't I'll jes' bore a hole in you."

But the red man did not desist, and Pomp, springing to a loop—hole fired at him.

The bullet went true to its aim, and the Indian fell dead.

The other native, seeing the fate of his companion, let out a baffled yell, and relaxing his grip on the valve rein fled precipitately.

Pomp did not take the pains to fire at him, but coolly picked up the valve rein, opened the throttle and the Steam Man went on.

Straight for the scene of the conflict at the mouth of the Pass Pomp went.

When he came upon the scene he found a thrilling and sanguine conflict in progress.

At sight of the Steam Man a cheer went up from the Vigilants.

In a moment Frank and Barney were aboard and shaking hands with Pomp. The situation was quickly explained.

"I thought mos' likely you would want de Steam Man, Boss Jun'r," said the faithful servant. "So I jes' fetched him ober to you."

"You have done well, Pomp," said Frank, joyfully. "Of course, this insures our safety. With the Steam Man we would easily escape the cowboys. But it will never do to leave these brave Vigilants to their mercy."

"Ob co'se not, Li'l Boss," cried Pomp, seizing his rifle. "Jes' you let dis chile draw a bead on dem rapscallions. I'll show dem dat Pomp kin use a rifle."

The Steam Man was placed in the van of the line of battle. Protected as they were by the impervious screen, those on board could fire with advantage at the cowboys.

The battle was a hot one, but every moment the cowboys slowly gained ground.

What was worse, the ammunition of the Vigilants seemed to be giving out.

With plenty of ammunition, it was possible that the Vigilants could have held them at bay for a long while.

But, of course, when the ammunition should give out, the battle would be ended.

White—faced, but determined, the brave plainsmen stood their ground.

Not a man of them thought of retreat. All were prepared to give up their lives like heroes.

There seemed no way of getting out of their present desperate situation.

To retreat was about equal to an impossibility, for it would be out upon the open plain where they would be shot down like sheep.

The situation was an awful one.

"Durn it, I don't keer for myself," said bluff Harmon the Vigilant leader, "but some of the boys have families dependent on 'em. Ah, that dog of a Cliff has sins to answer fer."

"You are right," agreed Frank Reade, Jr. "But there must be some way of getting out of this scrape."

"How?"

"Ah, that is a sticker. There is no hope of reinforcements near?"

"None whatever."

"The Steam Man could be sent for them in quick time, if such a thing were possible."

"But it is not. The nearest place is Ranch V, and that is Cliff's own den. We know that."

"Certainly."

"The fort is too far off. There is just one forlorn hope."

"Ah!"

"The cavalry."

"But they may have been all wiped out."

"Very true. Well, we must die then like men. But, Mr. Reade, there is no reason why you should not take the girl in your Steam Man and make your escape."

Frank placed a hand upon the Vigilant captain's shoulder.

"Yes!" he said, briefly. "I could do that."

"Then do it. We will hold the foe at bay until—"

"Stop!"

Harmon looked his surprise.

"You do not know me," said Frank Reade, Jr. determinedly, "do you think I would desert you in this hour of need?"

"But—"

"Never! If you die, so do we. Until the last, the Steam Man will stand his ground."

With tears of emotion in his eyes Harmon gripped Frank's hand. "God bless you!" was all he could say.

At this moment one of the Vigilants came up excitedly.

"We are just firing the last cartridges," he declared. "What shall we do? Is it a retreat, Harmon?"

"Retreat!" cried the Vigilant leader, clubbing his rifle. "Never! Come on one and all. The crisis has come. Now let us show them how brave men can die."

The cowboys with their wild cheers were forcing the crippled Vigilants back.

But even in the moment of their victory a strange sound came from the rear and a mighty cry went up from the throats of the Vigilants.

"Hurrah! We are saved! Rescue has come at last."

CHAPTER XVII.

ONCE MORE— IN THE ENEMY'S POWER.

It had been Col. Clark's firm intention to return to the fort for reinforcements.

It was a long ways, but he did not reckon this. He thought only of securing a sufficient body of men to cope successfully with the cowboys.

So on they rode, the little remnant of the squad for the far distant fort.

But after a night had been spent in camp, just as the bugle called "boots and saddles," one of the guard sighted a body of horsemen just coming over a swell in the prairie.

The alarm was given and Clark rode out to investigate.

One glance was enough and a cry of joy escaped his lips.

"Hurrah!" he cried. "We are in luck. It is Romaine's company of one hundred men. Forward all!"

With cheers the little band rode out to meet the reinforcements.

The command had been sent out under Captain Romaine to search for Clark and his men.

The two officers shook hands and explanations were made.

"You have come just in the nick of time, Romaine," declared Clark. "We can now return and whip the cowboys."

"We are with you, colonel!" declared the captain with a salute. "The boys are itching for some hot work."

"Well, I will promise it to them," laughed Clark, as he took command.

At once the cavalry set out at full gallop for the hills.

It seemed like a strange fate that guided them almost to the very scene of the conflict.

The firing was heard long before the pass was reached, and Clark hurried his men forward.

He at once threw them into the pass in the rear of Cliff's gang.

It was an opportue moment, too.

Just as the last cartridge of the Vigilants was used the cavalry struck the rear of the cowboy gang.

Instantly a panic seized Cliff's men. They made a brief stand, and then were driven up a side defile into the hills.

Here they made a stubborn stand.

The cavalry literally cleared the pass, and riding through came into the midst of the Vigilants.

The scene which followed baffles description.

In a moment Clark and big Harmon were shaking hands with the deepest emotion.

"Ye came jest in the nick of time, Clark," declared the Vigilant chief. "In ten minutes more we might have all been dead men."

"Then we are in luck." cried the colonel, "for which I am very glad. Ah, Mr. Reade, I am glad to see you."

"The same," replied Frank, as he gripped hands with the colonel. Then Clark rode away up the defile to see what was going on there.

He found the fiercest kind of a battle in progress. The cowboys had intrenched themselves once more and were making a bold stand.

The cavalry outnumbered them, but they were in a very advantageous position.

The best efforts of Clark's men would not suffice to dislodge them. For a long while the sanguine battle went on.

In vain Clark tried to eject them from their position. His bravest efforts met with failure.

The intrepid colonel knew that if he could get the foe into the open he could hope to whip them.

But as it was it looked certainly as if his plucky little band would be badly decimated in the accomplishment of the desired end.

In this quandary Frank Reade, Jr. appeared upon the spot.

The young inventor had borrowed a horse of one of the Vigilants and rode up to see how the fight was going on.

"Well, colonel," he said, greeting Clark, "how are you making out?"

"Not as well as I could desire," replied the colonel in a dejected manner.

"What is the matter?"

"Why, I can't drive the rascals."

"Why not?"

"They have a position up there in the hills which is unassailable."

"I disagree with you," said Frank, quietly. "I am not a military engineer, but I am a land surveyor and I tell you their position oh that hill is not of the best."

Clark was staggered.

"Why, it is the best position about here," he declared.

"No, said Frank, gravely. "Yonder is a much better position." He pointed to a hill to the right, and which the one upon which the cowboys were seemed to overlook.

"What—try to command the foe from that hill?" cried Clark, scornfully. "We would only expose ourselves, and they would sweep us from it like chaff before the wind."

"No, they wouldn't."

"Now, Mr. Reade, what is the use for you to talk that way? The hill upon which they are is higher than this one."

"It may be higher in the number of feet," replied Frank, "but not in advantage of position."

"How do you make that out?"

"It is easy enough to see. The top of this hill is smooth, is it not?"

"Yes."

"The top of theirs is craggy and they cannot climb up to it. Their position is far from the top. A position on the top of yonder hill will easily look down into their camp."

Clark was surprised, but he saw the logic of Frank's remark.

"By Jove!" he cried. "Perhaps you are right."

"I think you will find that I am."

"But I would have taken my oath that they had the highest position around here."

"Well, that would seem to be really so, for the hill itself is higher. Yet it is but an optical delusion."

Clark extended his hand to Frank.

"Mr. Reade," he cried warmly. "You are right. I acknowledge my mistake. Perhaps your opportune suggestion may enable us to whip the foe."

"If it is of any value, I am highly pleased!" said Frank, modestly.

"I feel that it is, and I shall at once proceed to take the hill."

Clark at once proceeded to do this. By his command his men moved up the back side of the hill.

This protected them from the bullets of the cowboys.

Arrived at the top of the smooth hill, it was found that Frank Reade, Jr. was right.

They were enabled to look right down upon the cowboys in their position.

"Hurrah!" cried Clark, jubilantly, "that means victory."

A volley was given the astonished cowboys. They returned with ill effect.

The tables were exactly turned upon them, and they were not slow to see the point.

A red—hot fire was kept up for some little time, but the cowboys no longer held the advantage.

Indeed, it began to look muchly as if they were to be driven from their position.

Suddenly all firing ceased.

The cowboy gang were not in sight, nor did they fire another shot.

Clark feared a stratagem or some fatal decoy, and dared not at once order a charge.

But finally he became convinced that the cowboys had evacuated their position and had made a retreat.

Flushed with victory Clark ordered his men to charge.

Up the slope they went with fixed bayonets. But when they cleared the top of the intrenchments, hastily thrown up by the cowboys, it was found that they had gone.

They had departed quite unceremoniously and completely.

Not an article of any kind was left behind.

Indeed, it also became a mystery as to the course taken by them. Not a sign of a trail could be found.

It baffled the cavalrymen.

"By Jupiter!" exclaimed Clark, in disgust, "how are you going to fight such a shadowy foe. If they would only come out like men and fight it out it would be all right. But they don't dare do it."

"You would whip them," said Frank Reade, Jr. with a laugh. "That is why they are playing hide and seek."

"I suppose so, but it makes it pretty hard for me. I suppose the best course now is to send out scouts and scour the hills."

"Exactly."

"All right. I will do it."

"I hope you will succeed."

"Thank you. I will do it or die."

"That is a good resolution."

"Well, I mean it, every word of it."

With this Clark ordered his men to horse, and the quest at once began.

Frank did not believe that he could be of further service just now, so he decided to return to the Steam Man.

Mounting his horse, he rode down through the defile. In a few moments he reached the spot where the remnant of the brave Vigilant band were.

There was the Steam Man intact, but Frank saw at a glance that something was wrong about the camp.

Everybody appeared to be deeply excited. Young Barrows was seen wringing his hands and rushing about madly.

Frank sent his horse forward rapidly.

Barney saw him coming and ran out to meet him.

"Och hone, Mister Frank!" he cried.

"Well!" exclaimed Frank, reining up his horse, "what is the matter!"

"Sure, somethin' terrible has happened since ye went away."

"Well, what is it?"

"Shure, sor, the young lady, Bessie, has gone, sor, an' divil awan av us kin foind her anywhere."

"Bessie Rodman gone?" gasped Frank. "Can that be possible?"

"Shure, sor, it is, an' faix they all do believe that the divils av cowboys, by the orders av Artemus Cliff, have got her agin."

"Great heavens!" cried Frank, with horror, "how on earth could they have done that? Is there not enough of you here to prevent?"

"Shure, sor, that is true enough," cried Barney. "But it's the girrul's fault hersilf, as ivery wan believes."

"Her fault!" cried Frank, in surprise. "How could that be?"

CHAPTER XVIII.
THE LOVERS QUEST.

"I'll tell ye how it was, Mister Reade," cried bluff Harmon, the Vigilant, as he came up. "Ye see the gal took big chances. Thar's a spring in that bit av bushes there an' she went over to git a drink of water. Nobody has seen her since."

"Have you made a good search?" asked Frank, sharply.

"An all fired good one."

"But how do you know that Cliff's gang have got her?"

"Because we know that it could not be Injuns, for the ground was marked with prints of the cowboys' shoes.

Frank received this information with sinking heart.

He knew that it must be too true that Bessie Rodman had again fallen into the hands of Cliff.

It was a dismaying reflection.

To effect her rescue would prove no easy task.

Just how to go to work to do it was a problem to Frank.

But he was not long in deciding upon a plan of action.

Meanwhile young Barrows, desperate over the thought that his girl love was once more in Cliff's power, had made a daring move.

Alone he rode away into the hills.

He was determined to rescue Bessie or sacrifice his life in the attempt.

Barrows was a youth of rare pluck and great determination.

In this quest he was aided by his blind love for Bessie Rodman. For her he would gladly give up his life.

Striking into the hills he sought to follow the trail of the abductors.

But it was soon lost in the flinty ground, and his best efforts to recover it were in vain.

However, he kept on with feverish resolution. It was now a blind quest, but this did not deter him in the least.

Soon Barrows had penetrated deep into the hills.

He heard the distant sounds of firing and knew that the soldiers and Cliff's men were yet having it out.

"God give me strength to rescue Bessie Rodman!" he prayed, as he rode on.

It had occurred to Barrows that the young girl might have been taken to Ranch V by her captors.

He had half made up his mind to proceed thither when a thrilling thing occurred.

Suddenly the sharp crack of a rifle smote upon the air.

Barrows reeled in the saddle and his horse gave a plunge.

A line of red blood trickled down over his face. The bullet had grazed his cheek bone.

It was a narrow escape.

The fraction of an inch in another direction, and the bullet might have penetrated his brain.

Young Barrows had faced danger and death times enough to know quite well what to do.

He instantly dropped from his horse and spoke a word of command to the animal.

The faithful and well—trained steed wheeled and galloped away into the cover of timber near.

Barrows himself sank down behind a pile of rocks.

All this was done in the twinkling of an eye.

The trained westerner whose life is in danger knows well the value of quick action.

It was this which saved the life of Barrows, for half a dozen bullets came whistling down the mountain side the next moment.

He had run unconsciously upon his foes. He experienced a thrill as it occurred to him that this was most likely the party who had Bessie Rodman in their charge.

"Heaven help me now!" he muttered, fervently. "I must save her or die!"

From his position he could safely scrutinize the mountain side.

He saw that far up on its side there was a rude cabin made of bark and logs.

From this the storm of bullets had come.

Nothing could be seen of those within the cabin.

But Barrows believed that not only was the foe within, but also Bessie Rodman.

He was somewhat at a loss now to know just what move to make.

To advance openly to the attack would have been an act of folly.

He would certainly have met his death in a summary fashion.

So while pondering on the subject he continued to watch the cabin windows.

He held his rifle in readiness for instant use.

Suddenly a face appeared for an instant at one of the windows.

It was quickly withdrawn, and Barrows had not time to fire. He recognized it, however, as the face of one of the outlaws.

The young plainsman's nerves were steel, and he watched his chance again with nervous anxiety.

Suddenly the opportunity came. Once more the face appeared.

Barrows raised his rifle quick as thought.

Crack!

A wild cry went up, the sound of a falling body was heard, and then the tramping of feet and bitter curses.

Barrows knew that his shot had taken effect.

Then he changed his position. But not a sound or a sign of life came from the mysterious cabin.

"If they are in the cabin they are keeping mighty dark," he muttered. "They surely must be there, for I have not seen them come out as yet."

A great length of time had elapsed.

Certainly an hour and a half of waiting had passed, and Barrows felt that he must do something and at once.

"I shall die of worriment if I stay here," he muttered. "Perhaps—"

He paused. A thrilling thought had struck him.

It was more than likely that he had been waiting all this while for nothing.

It would have been not by any means a difficult matter for the foe to have slipped out by a rear exit, and by this time be far from the spot.

But how was he to determine this fact?

It could only be done by approaching the hut boldly and searching it.

To do this was to incur the risk of a bullet from the outlaws.

This might be only a clever trick of theirs to draw him from his covert.

All these thoughts passed kaleidoscope like through Barrow's brain.

He was satisfied that the foe could be but a half dozen in number.

If he could have kept up a desultory battle with them in his present position he believed that he could have picked off a number of them, and thus reducing their numbers eventually bring the fight to a focus with a fair chance of winning.

But the outlook now was by no means so prepossessing.

It was more than likely that he would have great difficulty in cutting off the abductors before they should join the main body of the cowboys.

In this case it would be more difficult to rescue Bessie Rodman.

Barrows now realized his folly in starting out single handed to pursue the abductors.

If he had now several of his companions with him the hut could have been surrounded and there would have been little trouble in making the rescue.

But time was speeding and something had got to be done at once.

Barrows proceeded to act.

He began to cautiously climb up the mountainside keeping in the cover of rocks and trees.

He was very careful not to expose himself to a shot and in this way had soon reached a point from which he believed he could see the rear end of the cabin.

There it stood lonely and silent.

Was it really deserted or were the foe yet within its walls?

To all appearances it was deserted.

Barrows hesitated a moment and then took the desperate chance.

He emerged boldly from the woods and approached the cabin.

On he went until within ten yards of the door. Yet there was no sign of life.

The next moment he reached the door.

It yielded to his touch and he entered. The place was deserted.

There were evidences that the foe had been there.

Also Barrows made a thrilling discovery. In the soft dirt of the floor he discovered the footprints of Bessie Rodman.

At least it was safe to presume that they were hers, for there was no likelihood that the region for many miles held another of her gentle sex.

Feverishly Barrows examined the trail and followed it out through a rear door of the cabin.

It led into a narrow gulch and up the mountain.

It was quickly lost in the gravelly soil, but Barrows kept on up the mountain.

He now censured himself for not having acted with greater dispatch.

He believed that had he changed his position earlier he would have become aware sooner of the change of base of the abductors.

This was undoubtedly true, but on the other hand there had been the great risk of exposure to a bullet.

On the whole the lover felt that he had reason to be grateful for his success in so promptly striking the trail of the foe.

He kept on up the mountain with increasing hopes.

If he could once more overtake the abductors under more favorable circumstances he believed that he could effect the rescue of Bessie Rodman.

He still kept on up the mountain.

Then he suddenly halted at a point from which he had a good view of the country about.

He looked down upon a level plain below some distance which was fringed with trees.

In the verge of this timber line Barrows saw a number of moving figures.

He was satisfied that they were the party of abductors and he even fancied he could see the form of Bessie Rodman.

With deadly resolution Barrows started in pursuit.

Down the mountain he went and soon reached the level of the plain.

The party was now out of sight but Barrows believed that he could overtake them.

So he set out at a rapid pace along the verge of the timber. Exciting experiences were in store for him.

CHAPTER XIX
FRANK'S NARROW ESCAPE

Frank Reade, Jr. had decided to go at once in quest of the abductors of Bessie Rodman.

He called Pomp and Barney aboard the Steam Man, and the start was made.

Of course they were not aware that Barrows had started out upon the same mission.

It was decided to proceed up the Death Gulch, for Frank fancied that the abductors had likely struck out over the mountain range.

The gulch could be traversed by the Steam Man easily, and Frank deemed it safer to travel that way.

Up the gulch the Steam Man went.

For some distance all went well, and no incident worthy of note occurred.

But finally a branch of the canyon was reached, and here a halt was called.

This extended to the southward.

Frank knew that the outlaws could not have crossed this without a wide detour.

The ground was high above the walls of the canyon, and the young inventor decided upon a different move.

The Steam Man proceeded up this canyon for some ways.

Then Frank called a halt.

"We will stop here," he said.

"Shure, Mister Frank," cried Barney, "What iver do yez want to do that fer? It's a clear course ahead."

"I am well aware of that, Barney," replied Frank, "but I am not sure that we are following the right course."

"Indade, sor."

"I mean to climb to the top of the canyon wall here and take a look off at the country."

"Shure enough, sor!"

"Golly, Boss Frank, ain' youse gwin to let dis chile go wif you?"

"Begorra, not a bit av it!" cried Barney. "Shure, yez may stay wid the Steam Man, ye cabbage."

"You g'long, I'ish! I reckon Boss Jun'r take me dis time."

Frank smiled and said:

"Yes, it is no more than fair, Pomp, for you to go this time. You will remain with the Man, Barney."

Barney did not demur, for he knew that it would be of no use. But he had been with Frank on excursions many times, and perhaps felt that it was no more than fair that Pomp should have this chance.

No time was lost.

Armed with rifles and revolvers, the two explorers left the Steam Man.

A good path up the canyon wall was selected, and after an arduous climb they finally reached the summit.

From here a mighty view of the country about was obtained.

As far as the eye could reach to the eastward was the level expanse of plain. In the other direction mountain peaks rose above them to a great altitude.

Frank had a powerful glass, and with this proceeded to scrutinize the country below.

But he could see nothing of the cowboys, nor was he able to tell in what direction Clark's men had gone.

He descried at once what he believed to be smoke ascending from behind distant trees, and fancied that this might be from the guns of the military and the cowboys.

But of this he was not sufficiently positive to venture to go thither.

"Well, Pomp!" he said dubiously, as he closed the glass. "I don't see that we can locate the abductors of Bessie Rodman from here. I declare I am befogged."

"Golly, Li'l Boss," cried Pomp, with dilated eyeballs, "what eber you fink we bettah do now?"

"I declare I don't know."

"I's reckon dat de cowboys hab gone back to dat ranch ob dere's wid dat lily gal."

Frank gave a start.

It had not before occurred to him that the abductors might have taken their captive to Ranch V.

Indeed, so strongly did he become impressed with the possibility that he was half inclined to start at once for the ranch.

But sober second thought impelled him first to think of searching the hills.

If she could not be found in them then it would be time enough to think of paying Ranch V a visit.

An incident happened at the moment also that for a time prevented any move of the sort.

Pomp had begun to scale a small peak near.

"P'ra'ps I kin get a bettah look from up here, Boss!" cried Pomp. "Jes' de same, I tries it fo' you."

"All right, Pomp," replied Frank. "Tell me if you see anything of importance and I will come up."

"A'right, suh."

Pomp went up the peak.

He reached the top and began to look over the country, when suddenly he beheld a thrilling scene below.

Frank had gone to the edge of the canyon to look over and see what the Steam Man was about.

As he leaned over the edge of the deep gorge he did not see a giant form suddenly glide from a crevice in the cliff behind him.

It was, in reality, an enormous black bear.

The brute had caught sight of Frank, and being in an ugly mood, started for him.

The bear advanced so quickly and noiselessly that Frank was all unaware of his presence until the brute was upon him.

Then a terrific blow from the bear's paw sent him reeling over the edge of the cliff.

Over the edge went the young inventor, and a yell of horror and pain went up from Pomp's lips.

"Golly sakes, Li'l Boss, hab you fallen down to yo' death?" cried the affrighted servant, as he came tumbling down the peak like a madman.

Frank had certainly gone over the edge.

The bear stood upon the verge of the precipice growling savagely. Pomp was in a frenzy of fear and horror. He could not see what was to prevent his beloved employer from going down to his death.

He would have rushed to the spot where Frank had stood but the bear was there.

At this moment the stillness of the gorge was broken by the shrill whistle of the Steam Man.

This was enough for Pomp.

In a moment he raised his rifle and fired at the bear.

Ordinarily, he would have been compelled to fire many times, but as chance had it, this single shot proved fatal.

It struck the bear full in the eye and went crashing through his brain.

The big brute went over the edge of the precipice and crashed down into the gorge.

Pomp heard plainly the crash of the bear's body as it struck the bottom of the pass.

Then he rushed to the edge and looked over.

He saw the bottom of the gorge plainly enough. There lay the inanimate form of the bear.

The Steam Man stood not twenty yards distant from this spot, and Pomp saw Barney far below, yelling and waving his hands.

Pomp answered, and then caught sight of something which thrilled him.

Clinging to a jutting bit of rock in the canyon wall he saw Frank Reade, Jr. hanging between heaven and earth.

The astonished soldier fell upon his stomach and leaned far over the edge of the gorge.

"Golly, Boss Frank!" he cried, excitedly, "I done fought you was a—goner fo' suah. Hab you got a strong hold dar?"

"Pomp!" cried Frank, in sharp tones, "I am nearly exhausted. I fear I shall lose my hold here soon."

"Fo' Hebben's sake," cried the affrighted servant, "don' you say dat, Li'l Boss. If you fell down to de cornah ob dat gorge you would be killed fo' suah. You jes' wait an' dis chile will help you."

"You'll have to hurry, Pomp!" cried Frank, in an exhausted manner.

"Yu' kin jes' bet I will."

"Whurroo, there buffalo!" cried Barney from below. "Wud yez be after letting down a rope to Mister Frank. Quick, now, or yez won't have the toime."

Pomp acted quickly.

He carried constantly a lariat at his waist.

This he lowered over the edge and down to the point where Frank was hanging suspended between earth and sky.

Pomp had acted with great dispatch, but even as the rope went over the edge, a warning cry went up from Barney below.

"My God! I am falling!" cried Frank, with horror.

His hands were slipping over the edge of the jutting bit of rock to which he clung.

The next moment they released their grip entirely and down he went.

But, as good fortune had it, just below him was a stump growing out of the cliff.

Against this he fell and his clothing caught upon a jagged root.

It held him firmly, and there he hung safe and secure.

A cry of joy went up from Pomp and Barney.

"Jes' you hang right on, Li'l Boss!" cried Pomp, earnestly. "Don' you gib way at all, an' dis chile he pull you up a'right."

"All right, Pomp," cried Frank, regaining the coolness so habitual to him. "I think I am safe here."

"Praise de Lor' fo' dat!" cried the elated servant. "Jes' hol' right on."

Down went the lariat.

In a moment more it settled over Frank's shoulders.

As Pomp drew on it, Frank made it secure under his arms.

Then he began to draw up on the rope. It required some exertion of strength, but in a few moments Frank cleared the edge.

But at this moment a loud shout came up from the gorge below.

It was Barney's voice raised in a note of alarm.

"My soul!" cried Frank, excitedly. "What can have happened?"

Both rushed to the edge of the canyon and looked over.

CHAPTER XX

THE FLOOD—CORNERING THE FOE

It was a thrilling sight which met their gaze.

They saw Barney leaping up and down and gesticulating wildly.

"What is the matter?" cried Frank.

But before the words had fairly left his lips he saw what was the trouble.

Along the bottom of the gorge a thin stream of water was flowing.

Every moment it was increasing.

"Bejabers, Mister Frank, is there much more water comin'?" cried Barney. "Shure if so, I'm thinkin' we'd better be after getting out of here."

"Right?" cried the young inventor, excitedly, "but where can it come from?"

He ran to an eminence nearby and from which a good view of the upper canyon could be had.

And there Frank beheld a thrilling sight.

At the upper end of the canyon was a large lake made by an accumulation of logs and debris across the source of the canyon.

Here half a score of men with axes and iron bars were engaged in breaking the dam so as to let the whole lake down into the gorge.

It would mean a flood of awful sort if they succeeded.

It would surely sweep the canyon clear, and the position of Barney was a most perilous one.

Frank saw this with horror.

He knew at once that the workmen were of the cowboy gang.

Already the dam could be seen to be giving way.

In a very few moments the flood must come. No time must be lost.

Into the canyon the water would plunge and engulf everything in its path.

Frank waited no longer.

He sprung to the edge of the canyon and shouted to Barney:

"Go, for your life, Barney. Run for the plain. We will take care of ourselves."

"All right, sor!"

Barney sprung into the cage and away went the Steam Man with a shriek down the canyon.

The next moment a terrible roar came from the headwaters of the gorge, and then Frank and Pomp saw the mighty flood coming. Like a race horse it surged down through the canyon.

It was now a mad race between the Steam Man and the flood.

It was a long way to the plain below, and Frank groaned with horror as he realized the uncertainty of the Steam Man's reaching it.

There were places where the Steam Man must go slowly, and this would mean overtaking by the flood.

But Barney, with his shrewd Irish wit, had realized this.

He knew that it would be impossible for him to reach the plain before the flood.

So he decided upon a wise move.

He reached the junction of this canyon with the other.

There was not a moment to spare.

Looking back, he could see the water coming in mountainous billows.

The Steam Man had to be checked a trifle in order to turn into the other canyon.

But Barney made the turn all safely, and the Steam Man shot up the canyon far enough to avoid the back current of the flood.

"Bejabers, I'm in luck this toime!" cried the Celt, jubilantly, as he opened the whistle valve.

The note of safety was heard by Frank and Pomp with a sensation of great relief and joy.

They understood at once the move made by Barney.

"That was a capital thought of Barney's," cried Frank. "It is lucky that he did not keep on the plains. He would have been overtaken."

"I jes' reckon dat am a fac'!" cried Pomp. "Well, I fink we'd bettah get back to de Steam Man as quick as eber we can."

"You are right, Pomp," declared Frank. "Our position here will be hardly a safe one now."

"Yo' right, suh."

The flood in the canyon was now rapidly subsiding.

The great lake had quickly emptied itself into the canyon.

In a short while the bed of the canyon was once more dry.

Barney then ran the Steam Man back into the main canyon, and Frank and Pomp hailed him.

"You did well, Barney!" cried the young inventor, joyfully. "You made the best possible move."

"Begorra, I knew well enough that I had to git out of the way of the waters, sor," replied Barney. "But shure, are yez comin' down soon?"

"We are comin' right down," replied Frank.

Down the canyon wall they scrambled and safely reached the gorge.

Then they greeted Barney with joy and clambered aboard.

"Shure, Whativer will yez do now, Mister Frank?" cried Barney. eagerly.

"I shall follow the canyon up and try to dislodge the outlaws," replied Frank.

"Very good, sir!" Cried Barney with readiness. "We'll go ahead thin?"

"Yes."

Barney took the reins and the Steam Man went on up the gorge.

In a short while they had reached the dam which had held back the lake.

Here a course was found directly out upon a vast plain.

Frank was about to direct the Man's course thither when an incident occurred to for a moment delay them.

A loud and harsh voice came from the cliff above.

"Hello, down there!"

The speaker could not be seen. The Steam Man came to a halt.

"Well?" cried Frank.

"Ye're Frank Reade, Jr., eh?"

"That is my name."

"Wall, I'm Artemus Cliff. I give ye fair warnin' to surrender. Ye're in a death trap."

"Thank you for informing us," retorted Frank, "but I don't believe I'll surrender yet."

"Ye won't then?"

"No."

"Then take the consequences."

"I can do that."

A savage curse come down upon the air. Then the crack of rifles was heard and bullets pattered against the steel netting.

Of course no harm was done, and Frank only smiled grimly.

He sent the Steam Man up the gorge, and in a few moments came out upon the plain, which was deep among the hills and hemmed in with a line of timber.

The cowboys continued to pour volley after volley into the Steam Man.

Frank waited until he had reached a favorable position.

Then he stopped the Steam Man, and picking up his rifle, said: "Come, boys!

let's give them as good as they send."

Of course Pomp and Barney were ready and eager.

A destructive fire was sent into the covert of the cowboys.

In a few moments it grew so hot that they could not remain there, and had to get out.

With baffled yells they retreated deeper into the hills.

"Whurroo!" yelled Barney jubilantly. "Shure it's aisy enough to whip such omadhouns as they be!"

"Golly! don' you be too suah, I'ish," remonstrated Pomp.

"What do yez know about it, eejit?"

"Suah, I know jes' as much as you does, I'ish."

"G'long! Yez are a big stuff."

"I ain' so big a wan as you be."

"Say that agin, an' I'll break the face av yez."

"Huh! You kain' do it."

The two rogues would have had a friendly set—to then and there, but Frank interposed.

"None of that," he cried, sternly; "there is serious work before us."

This was a quietus upon the two rascals, and they ceased their skylarking.

The cowboys had been driven back, but now a thrilling sound came from the distant hills.

It was the heavy volleying of many rifles. There could be but one explanation.

Evidently the cavalry had come into conflict with the cowboys.

A good—sized battle was in progress. An impulse seized Frank.

He realized that he ought to join that conflict. There was no doubt but that the Steam Man could do much to aid the cavalry.

So he started the Man across the plain, looking for an opening into the hills in the direction of the firing.

This, however, seemed not easy to find.

But as the Man was skirting the line of timber, a thrilling scene was suddenly brought to view.

In a small clearing in the verge of the timber two men were striving to down one. It was a terrific and deadly struggle which was in progress.

The single fighter was holding his own well.

Nearby, with arms tied behind her, was a young girl.

It was Bessie Rodman.

"My God!" cried Frank. "Quick, for your life, boys! We must put an end to that struggle. Don't you see it is young Barrows, and he is fighting to rescue the girl."

"Golly, dat a fac'!" cried Pomp, excitedly. "Jes gib me a chance at dem rapscallions."

Up to the spot the Steam Man swiftly ran.

A cry of wildest joy and hope welled up from Bessie Rodman's lips.

Young Barrows also saw that rescue was at hand and made extra exertions to overcome his foes.

The cowboys, however, seeing that succor had come tried to break away.

As Barrows was too exhausted to restrain them, they succeeded and dashed away at full speed.

Reaching their ponies, they mounted and were out of sight in a twinkling.

The next moment Barrows had clasped Bessie in his arms, first cutting her bonds.

"Thank Heaven!" he cried. "We are united once more, and this time let us hope never to part."

Those aboard the Steam Man pretended to be busy during the affecting meeting.

But soon the lovers came to the cage and a general welcome followed.

An explanation of all followed, and then plans for the future were quickly decided upon.

CHAPTER XXI
WHICH IS THE END

The sound of firing now came from the hills quite plainly.

It was evident that Clark's men were having a hard battle.

Barrows detailed his experiences as we have recorded in a previous chapter.

Then it was decided at once, if possible, to join the cavalry.

"If I can place Miss Rodman in your charge, Mr. Reade," said young Barrows, gallantly, "I will gladly join the soldiers and aid in the repulse of the foe."

"You may do that," replied Frank, readily. "In fact, I think it safer for the lady to remain in the wagon hereafter."

"You are very kind."

"It is nothing."

Accordingly, Bessie was given a seat in the wagon. Then Barrows mounted one of the ponies left by the cowboys.

"I will see you later," he said, lifting his hat to Bessie.

Then he rode away to join the cavalry in their battle.

The Steam Man, of course, could not hope to follow so quickly. The fleet pony could go through narrow paths, and of course Barrows reached the scene of action long before the others.

But Frank Reade sent the Steam Man along at a good pace.

After some search a pass was found, and the Man made its way carefully through, and suddenly came out upon the field of action.

The cowboys were strongly intrenched in the hills, and seemed disposed to make a final stand.

Col. Clark's men were making desperate attempts to drive them from their position.

As the Steam Man came dashing up to the spot a great cheer went up from the soldiers.

Frank answered it by pulling the whistle valve of the Man and sending up a sharp note.

The Man could not hope to reach the position of the outlaws, for the ground was too uneven.

But a position was taken up from where the battle could be easily watched.

Then Col. Clark came up to the wagon.

Warm greetings followed, and Frank said:

"Is there anything I could do to help you, colonel?"

"I think not," replied the gallant officer. "I believe we shall drive them out very soon now."

"I hope so."

"If I am not mistaken the day of Cliff and his gang are numbered."

"That is joyful news."

"Yes."

"I hope you will succeed."

"Thank you."

The colonel rode away and the voyagers watched the contest with interest.

One watching the beautiful face of Bessie Rodman could have seen that she was inwardly praying for her lover's safety.

But fortune was with the troops, though they had experienced a hard battle. The position of the outlaws was a very strong one and almost unassailable. High walls of rock were there for them to use as a breastwork.

It was not easy to dislodge them except at great loss of life.

But Clark was not a man to be defeated.

He urged his men on and slowly but surely drove the foe before him. Frank Reade, Jr., now with Barney and Pomp and Bessie Rodman on board, took the Steam Man out on to the prairie.

For over an hour a kind of desultory conflict was kept up in the hills.

Then Col. Clark suddenly came dashing up to the wagon.

"We have got them dislodged," he cried. "And I think they have struck out for Ranch V. Now if you will show us the way, Mr. Reade, we will try and exterminate this poisonous gang."

"With pleasure!" cried Frank.

He started the Steam Man at once for Ranch V.

Across the prairie the machine ran rapidly, and the cavalry galloped in the rear.

It was in the latter part of the day that all came out upon a rise overlooking the stockade of Ranch V.

But the cowboys had got there in advance and had made ready for an attack.

Col. Clark was a man of immediate resources.

Without hesitation or a moment's delay he threw his men forward on the charge. At almost the first attack the gate was carried and the soldiers entered the yard.

But step by step Artemus Cliff contested the way.

His men by divisions surrendered half a dozen or more at a time. Being thus made prisoners, they were sent to the rear. In this manner the numbers of the cowboy gang were decimated.

Suddenly a thrilling cry went up.

"Fire! Fire!"

The stockade and ranch proper had been fired, and great columns of flame now arose.

The scene was fast becoming a thrilling one. Darkness was coming on, and the rattle of firearms the dark shadows of night partially dispelled by the flames, gave a weird aspect to everything.

Slow but sure was the conquest of Cliff and his gang.

Now he was driven to his last resort, the corner of the stockade nearest the river. Scarce a score of his followers now remained.

It was utterly no use for him to resist longer. The villain saw it but yet kept on lighting doggedly.

"Surrender, or die!" cried the lieutenant who led the squad. "It is your only chance."

The remaining cowboys threw up their hands. But Cliff pitched forward in a heap upon the ground, struck by a pistol ball.

There he was found later under a heap of dead men. He was removed to the camp near and his wounds examined.

Ranch V was a thing of the past.

Not a stick was left standing, and of the cowboy gang fully a hundred had rendered up their final account.

Possibly twenty of the cavalrymen had been killed.

It had been quite a severe battle, but Frank Reade, Jr. and his companions could not help but feel overjoyed at the result.

Barney and Pomp had an old—time set—to over the victory, this time Pomp coming off victorious.

The night was passed quietly. Early the next morning a surgeon came to the Steam Man and called for Frank.

He announced that Cliff was dying and wanted to make a confession but would make it to nobody else.

Frank hurried to the dying couch of the villain. Cliff's filmy gaze was fixed upon him eagerly, and he said, huskily:

"Reade, I'm done for. I made a good fight but I've lost. The game's up. I might as well make a clean breast of it. Uncle Jim is innocent of Rodman's death. Sid Bowen and Jim Ducey, my trusted pals, killed Rodman and worked the whole game. That's all. I reckon I can die better now."

"You have done a good deed, Artemus Cliff," said Frank, kindly. "And may God forgive you your sins."

But the villain did not answer. Already his eyes were set. The Master had called him. He had cheated the gallows after all.

A grave was dug on the prairie and Frank saw that he was properly buried.

The confession was put in writing and duly witnessed. The mission of the new Steam Man to the far west was ended.

* * * * * * * *

The spirits of all were bright and cheerful, now that the end had come.

The extermination of the Cliff gang was certainly a blessing to that part of the State, and no one regretted the villain's demise. Preparations were now made for the return home.

Of course, Col. Clark and his command would return to the fort, but Frank now thought of Bessie Rodman.

"By Jupiter!" he muttered, "something must be done for her. Poor girl! she is without a friend in the world now."

Barney and Pomp winked at each other, and Barney cried:

"Bejabers, Mister Frank, have yez lost yer powers av penetration?"

"I reckon you way off, Boss Jun'r," rejoined Pomp.

"What are you fellows driving at?" asked Frank, in surprise.

"Why, dat gal, she got one ob de bes' friends in de worl'. Jes' you cas' yo' eye ober dar an' see dat spruce young feller what be walkin' wid her."

Frank did "cast his eye" in the direction indicated, and saw Bessie and young Walter Barrows approaching.

There was a particularly happy light upon the faces of both.

"Pshaw!" muttered Frank. "That young fellow can't marry her yet. She's got to have a home in the meanwhile. Miss Rodman, one moment, please."

The lovers paused, and Frank said brusquely:

"I can understand your position, Bessie, very well, and I know that you need a home. I can only offer to take you to Readestown with me, and my wife will do all in her power—"

"One moment, sir," said Barrows, with burning face. "You are very kind, but let me first explain. I am this lady's natural protector for life."

"What?" gasped Frank.

"Yes, she is my wife."

Pomp and Barney collapsed at the expression upon Frank's face.

"Your wife?" gasped the young inventor. "When were you married?"

"Just now, and the ceremony was performed by the chaplain of the regiment."

Frank thrust forth his right hand, and gave Barrows a grip which made him wince.

"You must pardon my conduct," he cried, "but it was such a surprise. I wish you both worlds of happiness."

Some hours later the new Steam Man was on its way homeward. A week later it was in Omaha, Nebraska, and not long thereafter was at home in Readestown.

The young inventor was received at home with an ovation, and his father, the distinguished Reade Senior, was overjoyed to learn that the evidence had been procured to clear Travers.

As for the latter he came from prison like one coming into a new life and from that time on regarded Frank Reade, Jr. as his greatest earthly benefactor.

The new Steam Man and his wonderful western trip was the talk of the country.

People came from near and far to see the invention and it was not long before the young inventor suddenly found himself involved in another daring project.

The new Steam Man was destined to make another trip, and become involved in adventures even more thrilling than these just recorded, and a full and detailed account of the second trip may be found in

NO. 2 OF THE FRANK READE LIBRARY,

ENTITLED

FRANK READE, JR. WITH HIS NEW STEAM MAN IN NO MAN'S LAND;

OR,

ON A MYSTERIOUS TRAIL,

BY LUIS SENARENS.

EDITOR'S HISTORICAL NOTE:

Between 1850 and 1890, the Oklahoma panhandle was known as "No Man's Land." At the time, it didn't belong to any of the surrounding states, so neither Texas, Colorado, Kansas, New Mexico, nor Oklahoma had jurisdiction. It was, legally, nobody's land. The Oklahoma Organic Act of 1890 gave the land to Oklahoma. Today, the area is known as Beaver County, Oklahoma.

Frank Reade, Jr.

With His New Steam Man In No Man's Land.

OR,

ON A MYSTERIOUS TRAIL

BY LUIS SENARENS

CHAPTER I.
A CASE OF MYSTERY.

One evening a man stepped into a cab at the Lake Shore depot in the city of Chicago and said tersely to the driver:

"Take me to the Palmer House."

"All right, sor," replied cabby, banging the door shut and mounting his box.

The cab rattled away over the pavings and the traveler, lounging back among the cushions, idly watched the passersby upon the great thoroughfares.

After a time, his gaze shifted and he took in the fixings of the interior of the cab. As he did so he gave a sharp cry of surprise.

Upon the opposite cushion and unnoticed by him when he entered the cab was a small satchel.

He reached over and took it in his hand. It was a ladies' shopping bag, and for a moment the finder thought of stopping the cab and asking the driver whose property it was with a view to restoring it to its lawful owner.

But a circumstance restrained him.

Upon the bag with something like a thrill of horror he saw that there was blood.

Moreover, it was fresh and liquid as if recently deposited there.

"Upon my word!" exclaimed the traveler, "here is a pretty how d'ye do. Can it be that I have stumbled upon the clue to a tragedy?"

For a few moments it was a question of no easy sort to the traveler as to whether he should open the bag or not.

Curiosity was powerful. A less courageous individual would have at once turned the bag over to the police authorities.

But the traveler hesitated only a moment.

Then he pressed the clasp and the satchel flew open. Miscellaneous articles were revealed, small articles of a ladies' toilet, a letter among all the rest.

Again, the traveler's curiosity gained the upper hand. He unfolded the sheet of plain white note-paper and read:

"Dear Miss — A matter of great importance to you I have in keeping. It concerns your future happiness and your life. Come to No. 823 L — street this afternoon at three. Do not fail or sorrow and misfortune are yours.

Madame White.

'Egyptian Mind Reader.'"

For some moments after reading this epistle the traveler was silent.

A strange light shone in his eyes.

"By Jupiter, this is strange!" he muttered. "What does it mean? Here is a matter for the police. I will send it to headquarters at once."

At this moment the carriage stopped before the entrance to the palatial hotel.

"Palmer House!" said the cabby, as he opened the door.

The traveler, with the satchel in hand, stepped out. Almost instantly two detectives had him by the collar.

"You are our prisoner," said one of the detectives, sharply. "You will make no resistance on peril of your life."

"Your prisoner?" exclaimed the traveler in surprise; "haven't you made a mistake?"

"No bluffing," said the detective, harshly. "It will do you no good. Put these on."

He held up manacles.

"One moment," said the traveler, coolly. "Upon what charge do you arrest me?"

"The charge of murder!"

"Murder!"

"Yes. We are onto you, Bill Dane. You cannot get out of it. You were seen to enter this cab with a young woman at No. 823 L — street. It is known that you have abducted her, previous to which you foully murdered her father in a room at 823. What you have done with the girl we know not, but you had better confess all and throw yourself upon the mercy of the law."

A tall young man, handsome, but pale as death now rushed up to the spot.

"You have caught the scoundrel!" he cried, breathlessly. "It is not Haynes, though."

"No, it is his tool, Bill Dane," replied one of the detectives.

"Wretch!" cried the young man, excitedly. "Tell us where Alice Wentworth is at this moment, or as sure as my name is Jack Arnold, I will make trouble for you."

The traveler all this while had been silent. He now said, calmly: "Gentlemen, listen to reason. If there has been any wrong doing, I am in sympathy with you, but I earnestly assure you that I am not the man you are after."

"That is a likely story," sneered the detective.

At this moment the young man who had given the name of Jack Arnold snatched the satchel from the traveler's hand.

"Ah!" he cried, wildly; "this proves that he is telling an atrocious falsehood. Here is Alice's satchel. My God! See, it is covered with blood!"

This seemed to settle the case beyond all peradventure. The cabman was also arrested, and a start was made for headquarters.

"Gentlemen," protested the traveler, "you are wasting valuable time. I am not the man you are looking for. The cabby will tell you that he just picked me up at the Lake Shore depot."

"That's true, sor," affirmed the cabby.

But the detectives would not be convinced. They were fully satisfied that they had caught the right man.

So straight to headquarters they went. Here at the sergeant's desk the prisoners were searched and questioned.

"I protest against this arrest!" said the traveler, firmly. "I tell you have got the wrong man."

"What is your name?" asked the sergeant.

"Frank Reade, Jr."

"What is your occupation?"

"I am an inventor."

At this declaration everybody in the room gave a start. All eyes were fixed upon the handsome young man, well dressed and distinguished, who dared to assert that he was identical with one of the most noted men in the world.

"Frank Reade, Jr.!" exclaimed the sergeant, looking at the prisoner as one would regard an insane patient. "What proof can you offer of your identity?"

"Here is my card, also a free pass over the railroad, signed by the president of the road, and made in my name. I ask you to send a messenger for these men, who will come here at once and identify me."

And with this the distinguished inventor of many wonderful machines wrote down with a pencil the names of half a dozen of Chicago's millionaires.

The sergeant and the detectives, as well as Jack Arnold, were completely taken aback.

The cabby grinned with pleasure.

"The gent's all right, sor," he said to the sergeant; "the young man an' young woman I sent off on an Omaha train six hours ago, sor."

"You scoundrel!" hissed one of the detectives. "Why didn't you bring them here?"

"Shure, sor. I didn't know thim from any wan else. They jest ped me me fare an' that was all I cud axe 'em."

"What condition was the young lady in when they boarded the train?"

"Shure, sor, if I hadn't seen that she was too respectable for it I should have thought she was drunk, sor."

"Drugged!" gasped Jack Arnold, sinking overcome into a chair. "Oh, my God! Alice is lost to me. She is wholly hopelessly in the power of that fiend."

Frank Reade, Jr., addressed the sergeant.

"Are you satisfied with my credentials?" be asked, tersely.

"Mr. Reade," said the sergeant, politely, "we are pained to have given you this trouble. I have no doubt of your identity, but you will pardon me if I ask the privilege of sending a detective with you to the Palmer House. You are known there?"

"I am," replied Frank Reade, Jr. "I will quickly satisfy you."

"Then the prisoners are discharged."

The bloody satchel was retained by the police. But Frank Reade, Jr., and the cabby, with one detective, returned to the street.

A short while later the world-famous inventor was in his apartments. A lunch was brought him, which he enjoyed.

But he could not banish the incidents of the day from his mind. Evidently some great wrong had been enacted, the real substance of which he had been only partially informed of.

Therefore, he was not displeased when a servant came in with a card: "Jack Arnold."

"Show the gentleman up," said Frank, quickly.

A few moments later the tall, handsome young man whom he had seen at the police station entered the room.

"You will pardon my effrontery in venturing to call upon you, sir," said Arnold, in a voice which showed that the speaker was the victim of deep emotion, "but—I felt that I must come to you. Something which I could not resist impelled me to do so."

"Have a seat," said Frank, pleasantly. "In what way can I serve you?"

"I am the victim of a fearful heart blow," said Arnold. "God knows that I have suffered more in the last twelve hours than ordinary man could stand."

"You have my sympathy," said Frank. "Pray name the cause."

"I will tell you the whole story," said Arnold, in a broken voice. "Upon the best part of M— street the home of Hiram Wentworth, one of the wealthiest men, was situated until within one short year. There he dwelt with his daughter Alice, a very beautiful society girl, and a favorite in the best circles of this city. All went well and happy with the Wentworths until a year ago.

"Then Harold Haynes, a dissipated and worthless young rogue of this city, ventured to propose to Alice. She rejected him and became engaged to me.

"Haynes at once went in a systematic manner to ruin Wentworth, and me as well. He managed through hired agents to get the old man into a financial deal which ruined him. Every dollar of his property was swept away in one unfortunate speculation in wheat.

"This he believed would humble the Wentworths and bring them to his terms. He once more had the audacity to propose for Alice's hand, offering to make Mr. Wentworth a rich man again, as he had a large fortune of his own.

"To his anger and surprise, he was again refused and had a heated encounter with Mr. Wentworth. Baffled in his plans, the villain at once resolved upon desperate measures."

"An infamous affair," said Frank.

"So, indeed, it was; but let me tell you all. The villain has associated himself with a brotherhood of crime, a clique of robbers and thieves, road agents and cut-throats, with headquarters in No Man's Land, where they fancy themselves free from justice.

"This morning two messages were sent out from 823 L— street, one to Hiram Wentworth and one to Alice. The latter note was sent an hour later. The note which you saw in the satchel was the decoy which drew Alice to her doom.

"Hiram Wentworth, decoyed into the house at 823, was foully murdered. His body is now awaiting an inquest. Alice arrived at 823 an hour later; was at once given a stupefying drug, under the peculiar influence of which she is wholly subject to the will of her captors, though possessed of most of her normal faculties. Bill Dane, an accomplice, and Harold Haynes, without any doubt, are on their way at this moment to Lonely Ranch, in No Man's Land."

CHAPTER II.

THE CONTRACT MADE.

Frank Reade, Jr., listened to this thrilling recital of villainy and crime with the deepest interest.

"Horrible!" he exclaimed. "That Haynes is without an equal as a villain."

"So say I," agreed Arnold, earnestly. "He is a fiend incarnate."

"His purpose—"

"Is to force Alice to marry him. In his brutal way he is deeply in love with her. Only think of what a fate for her."

"It is terrible," said Frank, all the sympathetic part of his nature aroused.

Arnold's face was very pale and set. "It is a horrible, monstrous wrong and awful crime," he said, in a rigid voice. "And, if it takes me a lifetime, I will surely hunt down and punish that wretch. He shall be made to pay life for life."

Frank was silent for a moment. Then be said:

"You are well justified, Mr. Arnold."

"But that is not all," said the young avenger, stopping suddenly in his walk to and fro. "I cannot but feel that it was the workings of a merciful Providence that brought us together in such a strange manner. Since learning your identity, Mr. Reade. I have dared to hope and to even come here and ask if you would lend me co-operation and help in my mission?"

Arnold regarded Frank earnestly and almost pleadingly. The famous inventor was silent a moment.

"Indeed," he said, finally, "I hardly know how to answer you. In what manner can I render you aid?"

"Oh, sir, if you will grant my prayer. I have heard of your wonderful Steam Man and the marvelous feats you have accomplished with your great invention. Dare I ask you to help me now?"

Frank Reade, Jr., sprung up and went to the window. Suddenly he tarried, after what seemed an inward struggle, and said:

"I feel tempted to accede to your request."

"Thank God!" cried Arnold, fervently. "I knew you would do it. Your heart is too full of noble motives and—"

"Sh!" said Frank, putting up his hands, "none of that. Mind, I do not promise. But if you will accompany me to Readestown I will examine the new

Steam Man, and should I deem the thing possible, I will certainly go with you to No Man's Land to rescue, if possible, Alice Wentworth and punish the murderer Haynes."

"God bless you!" cried Arnold, fervently.

We will not dwell upon the events of the next few hours. The late express that night took the two men on their way to Readestown.

This was a charming little town named after and founded by Frank Reade, the father of Frank Reade, Jr., who was an inventor before him.

Here the Reades lived in wealth, and here were their extensive shops devoted exclusively to the construction of their wonderful inventions.

Arrived at Readestown, Frank took Arnold at once to the shops.

As they reached the yard gate a commotion was heard.

Two men, one a negro, and the other a genuine type of the fun-loving Irishman, were engaged in a friendly wrestle.

"Hi, you good fer nutin' I'ishman!" shouted the black man. "Youse ain' able to put me on ma back. Youse kin bet life on dat."

"Bejabers, it's not the hit av a black man like yez as kin lay out Barney O'Shea. Whurroo! have at yez!"

The negro went down, but twisted under the Celt and was up again.

Then freeing himself, the black man lowered his head and rushed at the Irishman. The latter, struck full in the stomach, went down as if kicked by a mule.

This was the state of affairs just as Frank Reade, Jr., reached the gate.

"Barney and Pomp!" he said, with a frown, "none of that. Be off about your duties. Is the Steam Man in good trim?'

In an instant both men were bowing before the inventor.

Faithful servitors were Barney and Pomp, and they had accompanied Frank Reade, Jr., on many a journey about the world.

They were the warmest of friends yet given deeply to hectoring each other. In this respect they were evenly mated.

"All right, sor!" cried Barney, scraping and bowing, "the Steam Man, sor, is in foine shape an' ready for another trip, sor."

"Dat's right, Boss Jun'r," cried Pomp, earnestly. "Dat's de fus' time dis fo' days dat I'ishman have told de trooth."

"Take that back, Pomp, or I'll break the jaw aff yez."

"G'long, you no count I'ish!"

"Hold on!" cried Frank, authoritatively. "None of those pet names just now. Come, Mr. Arnold, and I will show you with pleasure the new Steam Man."

Frank led Arnold into a large, high roofed chamber. Here the young Chicagoan beheld a wonderful sight.

Before him, tall and of giant frame, was the image of a man, made of steel plates and holding up the shafts of a wagon, also made of metal plates.

Frank proceeded at once to describe to Arnold the workings of his wonderful invention, the new Steam Man.

"Wonderful!" exclaimed Arnold, with deepest interest; "but how does it work? Steam is the motive power, eh?"

"Yes," replied Frank. "If you will look at the man's chest you will see a capacious furnace. The steam chest is upon his back. The water is carried in the legs and lower body of the man."

Arnold received all these explanations with increased wonderment. "It is almost beyond belief," he said.

"These driving rods down the legs give them the treading motion and stride necessary," continued Frank. "The smoke-pipe you can see is the tall hat worn by the man. The gauge and indicator are upon his back, over the steam chest. The whistle is in his mouth. The throttle and whistle are both controlled by these strong reins which extend into the wagon. Now you understand pretty well the mechanism of the man?"

"I do," replied Arnold. "It is wonderful."

"Then let us look at the wagon. This is made of steel and the square section of network erected over it is of finest steel and capable of flattening a bullet.

"In this network are loopholes for firing, and in front is the aperture for the throttle reins. A door in the rear lets us into the wagon."

"Grand!" cried Arnold, enthusiastically. "Why, you could defy a small army with such a vehicle as this."

"Yes," replied Frank, "the wagon I have provided with four wheels. There is a brake upon the dasher.

"The wagon is capable of carrying the necessary coal for fuel, and also upon either side are bunks for sleeping, which being reversed make comfortable seats in the day time. Spaces are provided for provisions, weapons and ammunition. Now you have seen and understand the mechanism of the new Steam Man."

Arnold would have spent hours in examining the wonderful invention of which he had heard so much.

He was of a mechanical turn of mind himself and matters of the kind deeply interested him.

But Frank led the way into a private office.

"Mr. Arnold," he said, briefly, "I have never been known to refuse to give aid to the oppressed or the wronged. I have decided to undertake the rescue of Alice Wentworth and the punishment of the villain, Harold Haynes."

"Heaven will reward you."

"I shall start for No Man's Land in three days from now."

"Good! Can I not accompany you?"

Frank shook his head.

"Only my two trusted men, Barney and Pomp, are to go with me," he declared.

Arnold said nothing. But there was a peculiar gleam in his eyes.

He did not attempt to urge the desire he felt to accompany the Steam Man. He felt that it was much gained already in having enlisted the services of Frank Reade, Jr., and his wonderful invention the "new Steam Man."

As it happened a reporter was waiting outside and got the news. Instantly every telegraph wire in the country was flashing the report from one place to another that Frank Reade, Jr., and the new Steam Man would go to No Man's Land in pursuit of the villain Haynes.

At once floods of letters commendatory or denunciatory of his action began to pour in upon Frank.

But these the young inventor threw all into the waste basket.

Not in years had an event created more excitement. The sympathetic feeling for Alice Wentworth was powerful.

It was conceded that if Frank Reade, Jr. invaded a region where the life of a United States marshal was not safe, and actually succeeded in rescuing the young girl, he could be credited with having performed a mighty deed.

As for Frank himself, be paid little attention to the world's opinion or outside talk.

He went at once about preparing the Steam Man for the trip.

Some little repairing was in order, some welding, a few new bolts, and miscellaneous matters which were speedily adjusted.

Then, upon the third day, all was announced in readiness for the start.

Barney and Pomp were delighted with the idea of going upon the trip and had prepared themselves accordingly.

So it happened that at noon of the third day the Steam Man was in sections placed aboard a special train for a certain point in Texas, from which it was deemed best to strike into No Man's Land.

The Man was stowed away safely in sections, so arranged that when the destination was reached, he could be easily and quickly put together again.

Barney and Pomp occupied the same car with the Man.

Frank had a special coach, and several of his intimate friends accompanied him to the spot where he should leave the railroad.

The flying special was soon on its way to Texas.

When it rolled out of Readestown all of the people turned out in a vast body to see the famous inventor off.

They cheered lustily, and amid the hearty good will and well wishes of thousands of friends Frank Reade, Jr. started upon one of the most thrilling trips of his career.

Adventures of a most wonderful sort lay before him. Before he should again see Readestown he must experience much that was thrilling and strange.

Indeed, this premonition was upon Frank, and he had taken good care in fitting up the Steam Man, to provide plenty of ammunition and stores.

The special train was not many days in covering the hundreds of miles of track to the point of destination.

It was a small flag station, upon a branch line, and right in the midst of the vast plains of Texas.

Here the car containing the Steam Man was side tracked.

Skilled workmen bad been brought along and these now proceeded to put the Man together.

No time was lost. In a very short space, the machine was in working trim.

Pomp had a fire started in the furnace, and Barney had everything in the wagon ship-shape and in order.

"A'right, Li'l Boss!" cried Pomp, finally. "We'se ready to start."

Frank shook hands with the friends who had accompanied him.

Then he sprang into the wagon, opened the throttle, and the Steam Man sped out upon the plain with long strides.

CHAPTER III.

ON THE PLAINS.

The journey was begun. The Steam Man plunged at once into the unexplored wilds of the mighty West.

Few habitations were about the railroad station.

These rapidly disappeared from view. Ahead naught was visible but the mighty range, deserted and wild.

In a short while naught but the everlasting floor of the prairie could be seen about.

For hours the Steam Man kept on with long strides.

The plains soon began to grow more undulating, and quickly the effect was visible in the Man's speed.

But they yet forged ahead at a lively rate.

"Bejabers, there's too much of all the same in this country for to suit me, at all, at all," declared Barney.

"I reckon you right, I'ish," agreed Pomp, readily.

"Upon me sowl. I'd like to see a mountain wanst in a while, if it was only for the sake av me eyes."

"Dat is a fac'," agreed Pomp, readily, "but I jes' think we'll see enuff of dem when we reach No Man's Land."

"I think you are right, Pomp." cried Frank, with a laugh. "It will not be quite so easy traveling there."

"Fo' a certain fac', Boss Frank."

Frank chanced to glance prairieward at that moment. He gave a mighty start as he did so.

"Great heavens! What is that?"

Of course, Barney and Pomp gazed in the same direction. A long black line seemed to be moving along the horizon.

"It's a band of Injuns, Boss!" cried Pomp.

"Bejabers, if that is so, we had better look out for our scalps," shivered Barney.

But Frank's trained gaze taught him better than to draw this conclusion.

"They don't look like Indians," he declared. "And I don't believe they are such. Get me my glass, Pomp."

"A'right, sah."

Pomp drew a heavy field glass from a locker in the wagon. Frank went to a loophole and began to study the distant line. In a moment he shut the glass with a click and cried:

"No, that is not a line of Indians. It looks like buffaloes. If so, we had better take care to keep out of their path. If the herd descends upon us, they will likely wreck the Steam Man."

"Golly!" cried Pomp. "Whatebber shall we do, Boss Frank?"

"Wait a moment," said Frank, coolly. "Let me take another look."

Frank again adjusted the glass and took a look at the distant moving line. This time he was able to see more clearly. He quickly exclaimed:

"They are not buffaloes! They are a mighty drove of steers, and they have broken away from the round-up and are running amuck! The danger is just as great, however. We must look out for them!"

"Golly sakes!" cried Pomp, with chattering teeth. "Dis chile knows jes' what dem steers are. I jes' fink dey tear de Steam Man all to pieces!"

"If the whole body of them descend upon us we are doomed!" cried Frank. "We must act quickly."

Frank changed the course of the Steam Man a trifle. He bore more to the eastward so as to give the herd a chance to pass on the flank. In this way a collision was avoided.

On came the thundering herd.

Few who have never seen the fearful run of a mighty drove of a thousand wild steers can realize the irresistible force, the mad impetuosity of it. Nothing can stay their course save the ingenious skill and daring of the cowboy.

On they will go to their certain doom over the brink of some precipice or into the current of some wide stream.

A perfect sea of long horns they came thundering down in irresistible progress across the plain.

It was well for the Steam Man that it was not in the path of that fearful avalanche of beef.

Now the excited cowboys, half a score in number, could be seen riding along the flank upon their fleet ponies and madly trying to head off the herd and save them from destruction.

The voyagers on board the Steam Man watched the scene with breathless interest.

"Golly!" cried Pomp, with bulging eyes. "Dat is quite a hoss race, ain' it!"

"Begorra, it luks loike it, Pomp," agreed Barney. "May the Vargin Mary save 'em if they come to a precipice."

"They will split soon," said Frank, confidentially. "Ah—look out!"

The words were not out of his mouth when a maddened steer charged directly from the herd at the Steam Man.

Quick as thought Pomp picked up his rifle and fired at it. At the distance of twenty-five yards the steer dropped dead.

"Good shot. Pomp," cried Frank.

But one of the cowboys pulled up his pony angrily and halted not fifty feet distant.

He whipped out a revolver and shouted angrily:

"Hold off. stranger! What did ye do that for?"

Two other cowboys also halted, and all regarded the Steam Man with great wonderment.

"What kind of a fire-engine do ye call that, stranger?"

"'Tain't an engine, it's an iron man!" cried another one of the cowboys. "Don't you see it goes by steam?"

"By Jericho! that beats the railroad all out. I say, strangers, come out and shake paws!"

The cowboys surrounded the Steam Man, and sat upon their ponies like Centaurs and still viewing the Man with wonderment.

"By Gosh! that's better than ridin' pony back, ain't it?"

"What'll come next?"

"They'll have a steam hoss or an iron cayuse yet."

"Gentlemen!" said Frank Reade, Jr., from the loophole, "I extend you greeting. I'm sorry that I was compelled to shoot that steer. But the animal would evidently have damaged my invention if I bad not shot him."

"Yer right, stranger," cried the first cowboy, who had been examining the dead steer. "'Tain't none of my funeral anyway. That steer don't belong to this herd. It's a stray, an' bears the mark of the Lonely Ranch up in No Man's Land."

Frank gave a mighty start.

"The Lonely Ranch?" he cried.

"That's what I sed, mister."

"What do you know of the Lonely Ranch?"

"Wail, I allow to know a bit. I reckon I was cowboy on that ranch wanst."

Frank was instantly interested.

"Ah!" he cried. "What kind of a place is it, friend?"

"Eh? Do ye really want to know?"

"Yes."

The cowboy, a rough-bearded fellow, shifted the tobacco in his mouth, and replied:

"It's a pesky lonely place."

"Indeed?"

"I reckon as how honest men bad better not put up thar, leastwise them as has money. D'ye see?"

Frank nodded eagerly.

"I understand," he said. "Who is ranchero?"

"I reckon his name is Harold Haynes. He's a smooth cuss, but I've heerd tell that he an' Black Mask, the road agent, are one an' the same."

"Not an honest man, then?"

"Wail, I should say not, stranger."

"How far is it from here to the Lonely Ranch?"

"Ye don't think of going thar?"

"I might."

"Wail, ya'll have a long course to travel. It's nigh onto five hundred miles. I 'low ye'll git thar, though, with that ere long-legged Iron man of your'n."

"Five hundred miles!" exclaimed Frank. "What sort of a country?"

"Mostly open and clear."

"Not mountainous, then?"

"Not to git thar—no!"

"I thank you for this information."

"Ye're welcome."

The cowboys reined their horses nearer to the Steam Man and began to examine it curiously.

Mischievously, Pomp pulled the whistle valve. The result was comical.

The Man let out an ear-splitting shriek. The horses of the cowboys were quite unaccustomed to such a noise.

They leaped and bolted sideways, making desperate plunges toward the open plain.

It was a sheer miracle that they did not unseat their riders. The cowboys, however, did not attempt to control them, but dashed- away after the herd of steers.

Soon they were all out of sight beyond the horizon line.

The Steam Man went on toward No Man's Land at increased speed. It was quite a discouraging reflection that Lonely Ranch, the den where Frank believed that the villain Haynes held Alice Wentworth a prisoner, was five hundred miles distant.

And yet, upon the smooth prairie the Steam Man could easily run one hundred and fifty miles a day.

At that rate four days would bring them to their destination. Frank set the Steam Man at work at full speed.

The Man flew over the smooth ground with most tremendous strides.

Mile after mile sped by, and at length, at nightfall they camped upon the banks of a small creek.

It was necessary to cross this, but the water not being deep, a favorable place was found to ford.

In this manner the stream was crossed. Upon the opposite bank camp was made.

Pomp cooked a steaming supper, venison steak being served, Barney returning from a hunt with a fine antelope.

But the Irishman brought back a startling report.

"Bejabers, Mister Frank," declared the Celt, "I jist come across some Injun soigns."

"Indian signs!" exclaimed Frank, with a start. "What were they?"

Barney was no novice in the trade of plainsman. He had spent seasons before upon the prairies of the wild West.

He knew well enough what Indian signs were and could follow a trail with almost the skill of an old scout.

In pursuing the wounded antelope he had come across a trail. It was made by the feet of ponies and it was a large trail.

As nearly as Barney could reckon there were fully two hundred riders in the cavalcade.

The Indian shoes of raw-hide left an imprint in the soil which was tell-tale.

That they were Comanches and a hostile party there was no doubt in the Irishman's mind.

Of course, this war party might be many miles distant long before this. But the discovery was important, as it revealed the fact that savage foes were in the vicinity, and it would be necessary to look after things very carefully.

Accordingly, camp was made with all caution.

CHAPTER IV.
BATTLE WITH COMANCHES.

It was decided that Barney should stand guard the first half of the night and Pomp the latter part. The fires were banked in the furnace, yet in such a manner that a little blowing would revive them quickly.

Then Frank Reade, Jr., threw himself down upon a bunk and went fast asleep.

Barney and Pomp, however, sat up until midnight playing cards. This disposed of Barney's watch completely, but Pomp did not demur.

He had been victorious in the game and this he had cared more for than naught else.

"De nex' time you wants to play cards, I'ish," he declared, with a grin, "jes' you calls on dis' gemman an' you kin be accommodated at any time."

"Ye are a robber an' a chate," exploded Barney. "Av it wosn't for waking up Mister Frank I'd show yez a bit av moi fist for yer villuny, that I would."

"Huh! You is no count, I'ish," jeered Pomp. "I ain'' fraid of any such as you."

"Bejabers, ye wud be if I ever got a whack at yez wanst."

Pomp had a retort framed upon his lips when an incident checked him.

He chanced to glance through the netting into the gloom beyond the circle of light from the Steam Man's furnace.

There he beheld a sight which gave him a tremendous start.

Plainly visible in the shadows was the outline of an Indian's form. From his breech-clout to his top-knot of feathers the Indian was plainly visible.

Pomp gave a start and a crawling sensation of terror crept over him.

For a moment be could not speak, but remained staring blankly at the gloom, unable to move hand or foot.

The savage had vanished, evidently aware that be had been seen. Barney regarded his chum with amazement.

"Wat ever is the matter wid ye?" be exploded. "Yez look like a crazy man."

"Hush, don' you say a wo'd, I'ish," whispered Pomp, hoarsely. "Jes you wake up the Boss at once."

"Begorra, an' what wud I be doin' that for?"

"Because dere are a lot of Injuns all around us."

"Injuns!" gasped Barney; "Wat are yez larkin' about, man?"

"It a fac'. I jes' seen one of dem over yonder in de shadows."

"Mother presairve us! Air yez in earnest, gossoon?"

"Co'se I am."

Barney strained his gaze to penetrate the gloom. He saw nothing of the savages, but Pomp had awakened Frank.

The young inventor was upon his feet instantly, wide awake.

"Indians!" he exclaimed. "Are you sure of It, Pomp?"

"I's dead suttin, sur, Boss Jun'r," asserted Pomp, earnestly. The words were scarcely out of his mouth when they were substantiated in a thrilling manner.

The air was suddenly broken with a wild chorus of yells, and from the deep grass about shadowy forms were seen to spring up.

There was no doubt but that a large body of Comanche surrounded the Steam Man, and were coming to the attack.

The air was now made hideous with their fierce yells and whoops. Instant action was necessary.

Frank gave his orders quickly, and they were instantly obeyed. Barney opened the furnace drafts, and began to blow the fire and to get up steam.

Pomp seized a rifle, and with Frank went to a loophole.

It was easy enough to single out the foes in the gloom.

The Comanche were armed with rifles, and fired at the wagon, the bullets flattening against the steel cage.

But this did no harm to the occupants. On the other hand, every shot fired by Frank and Pomp took effect. With their repeating rifles they could shoot them down with terrible rapidity and precision.

The Comanche were not long recognizing this fact.

These Indians were at heart a coward. They never sought a battle on open ground, but by nature sought the cover of ambush and the resorts of strategy.

So it was not long before the Comanches fell back into the deep grass and sought to hide themselves from the aim of their white foes.

It became now more difficult for Frank and Pomp to draw a bead upon the redskins.

But Barney by this time had got up steam and Frank sprang to the throttle reins.

In a moment the Steam Man sprang forward and plunged into the deep prairie grass and into the very midst of the red foe.

In an instant the wagon was surrounded by a legion of the redskins. Yelling and brandishing their rifles, they attempted to stay the progress of the Steam Man.

Several threw themselves before the Man and tried to hold him back. But the powerful feet of the Man struck them and trampled them down like pigmies.

Those who came in contact with the heated part of the Man were burned severely and retreated in dismay.

A number tried to seize the wheels of the wagon and stay its progress.

But they might as well have tried to turn the wind in its course.

For their pains they were hurled from their feet and crushed under the Iron wheels.

"Whurroo!" yelled Barney, from his post at one of the loop-holes.

"Give it to ther omadhouns. Bejabers, we kin lick them to a stand still!"

As for those natives who were mounted, their ponies could not be brought within rifle shot of the Man.

One blast of the whistle would set them all plunging and tearing away across the plain at max speed.

The conflict resulted in a hollow victory for the Steam Man.

Straight through the foe's ranks he strode, and sped out upon the plain with the rapidity of a railroad tram.

In the darkness Frank was obliged to go much at random.

But the floor of the prairie was smooth for fifty miles about, so that he experienced no trouble.

A number of the savages attempted pursuit, but the killing fire from the wagon cage drove them back.

The Steam Man outstripped them, and in a short while not an Indian was to be seen or heard.

"Hurrah!" cheered Barney and Pomp. "Dat's de way to do it! Bejabers, the Comanches ain't in it."

All felt exultant at the result of the conflict. It was certainly gratifying.

The Steam Man kept on for miles.

At length, Frank concluded to call a halt again. He did so, and once more they went into camp.

This time they were not disturbed.

They rested securely until dawn. Frank was the first astir, and mounting the top of the cage, took a good survey of the country about with his glass.

He saw. as far as the eye could reach, only level plain.

For a hundred miles to the northward it extended like the calm surface of the sea.

This was encouraging, for the Steam Man would thus find few obstacles to bar his progress.

Barney and Pomp were soon aroused, and preparations were made for another start.

Soon the Man was under way again. For twenty miles not an incident of any kind occurred to break the monotony of the ride.

Then suddenly Barney who was at the dasher cried:

"On me word, Mister Frank, watever wud ye call that over yownder? Iv it ain't a foire, then I'm very much mistaken the same!"

Frank at once gazed in the direction indicated. Sure enough, a long black line extended along the horizon line and rising in a black cloud toward the zenith.

Half circling the prairie horizon, the line seemed to be closing in upon the rear of the Steam Man.

"A prairie fire!" gasped Frank.

This was doubtless the truth.

A glance at the dry, crisp grass long parched in the sun, showed well enough the reason for this.

The fire was a most tremendous one, and seemed to embrace a front of a hundred miles or more.

In fact, the whole vast plain seemed likely to be swept by the dread scourge.

A great shadow now began to obscure the sun. Far up into the zenith bung the mighty smoke clouds.

To be overtaken by that terrific storm of fire meant death.

None knew this better than Frank Reade, Jr. Fortunately he bad had experience with prairie fires before.

With practiced eye he scanned the horizon and weighed carefully the possibility of dodging the path of the fire to the right or left.

But he quickly saw that this was quite impossible.

It extended much too far in both directions to be eluded in such a manner.

There seemed but one way, and this was to run straight ahead and trust to fortune in outstripping the fire and reaching cover.

So the Steam Man was put to full speed. Like a race horse, the Man fled across the plain.

But fast as the Steam Man went, the fire seemed to gain.

There is no actual record of the speed of a prairie fire.

It is to be presumed that this must depend much upon the wind. But under a gale it has been known to outstrip the fastest horse.

The situation was fast becoming critical. Frank with his glass was studying the distant line of fire.

It was sweeping, with frightful rapidity, every moment nearer them. There was no doubt of this.

In vain Frank scanned the horizon ahead for some sign of cover.

Now with his glass he saw a large body of horsemen riding madly to the westward, seeking to outflank the fire.

That they were the Comanches there was little doubt.

In the van of the fire also could be seen a perfect host of wild animals.

There were antelopes, buffaloes, panthers, prairie dogs and all species of the animal life of the plains.

The creatures, terrified beyond measure, were racing for life even as our friends aboard the Steam Man were.

The situation was now fast becoming a desperate one.

It seemed as if they were certain to be overtaken by the flames. In view of this fact, Frank Reade, Jr., at once decided to act in a different manner.

There seemed to him only one desperate chance left for their lives, and this he accepted.

CHAPTER V.
ESCAPING THE FIRE.

With his mind thus made up Frank acted quickly.

With a word of command to Barney he sprang to the door of the cage.

"Stop the Man, Barney!" he ordered.

The Celt was astonished.

"Wat's that, Mister Frank?" he asked.

"Stop the Man I say."

For the first time in his life the Irishman failed to obey implicitly and without questioning his employer's command.

"On me sowl, Mister Frank, yez don't mean that, do ye?"

"Of course I do."

"But—shure the foire is coming after us the minnit, sor!"

"Will you obey me?"

"Yis, sor."

Barney shut the throttle and applied the brake. The Steam Man came to a quick stop.

In a moment Frank was out of the cage.

Pulling a handful of the dry grass he touched It with a match.

Instantly the flame leaped up. Running a dozen yards along through the grass Frank quickly fired it.

There was but little wind, the heavy clouds of smoke behind precluding this.

Yet the opposition fire blazed and ran leaping over the prairie.

In a few moments it had burned over several hundred yards of the prairie floor.

Gathering volume, it swept on, a new fire in the van of the other. The Steam Man now leisurely jogged along in the rear and over the burned ground.

Frank's scheme was a common one, and if used in good time always works well.

Of course, the fire behind must burn up to the edge of this newly burned district, and it could go no further.

If sufficient ground could be burned over in that space of time, so that those on board the Steam Man might escape suffocation from any vacuum created by the two fires, they would be surely saved.

This was the one chance, and Frank had accepted it.

As good fortune had it, it worked most admirably. The new line of fire gathered force every moment, and swept on like a thunderbolt.

The distant Comanche saw their opportunity, and dashed for the newly burned district.

The wild animals even, by instinct, seemed to understood this, and they also came flocking in upon the burned ground.

The fire in the rear burned to the edge of the burned district, and there quickly spent itself.

The fire in advance went roaring and whirling across the prairie, carrying destruction and desolation before it.

The Steam Man followed in its path for miles.

Then suddenly the smoke clouds were seen to lift, and the flame vanished as if by magic.

The green, undulating plain, unscathed by the fire blast, was seen beyond us far as the horizon line.

Then an explanation of the matter was quickly accorded the travelers.

A river, wide but shallow, ran to the westward here across the prairie, and this had barred the further progress of the disturbing element.

The fire had been smothered in the waters of the river.

A prairie fire is swift and terrible in its course, but as quickly out. The material, being light, is reduced to ashes so rapidly that the end quickly comes.

Therefore, when the Steam Man was brought to a halt upon the river bank, only a few smoking embers attested to the former existence of the mighty conflagration.

The rolling waters of the river now lay before the travelers.

It looked like a serious obstacle, for a bridge was out of the question.

"Bejabers, it's stuck intolerably we are!" cried Barney.

"Jes' looks dat a'way," averred Pomp.

"We must find a ford," declared Frank Reade, Jr.

But this seemed easier said than done. The river was exceeding broad and swift in current.

Frank got out of the wagon and went down to the water's edge.

At once he saw a welcome truth and proceeded to test it.

He waded out into the river and kept on until he reached the middle.

In no place was the water above his knees. It was a shallow though swift flowing stream, and its bed was hard and pebbly.

The bugaboo was disposed of in a summary manner. It would be an easy matter for the Steam Man to ford the stream at this point.

"Come on, Barney," shouted Frank; "it's all safe."

Then the famous inventor made for the opposite shore.

He reached it, and turned to see the Steam Man wading the stream. Fortunately, the water did not reach the furnace Ares, and the Man crossed safely.

Once upon the other bank, Barney and Pomp wiped the exposed parts of the machinery and oiled them again.

"Whurroo!" cried Barney, cutting an Irish jig. "We never get left. Is it on to the Lonely Ranch we'll be after going now, Mister Frank?"

"Yes." cried Frank, as he sprang aboard. "If we have good sailing, we'll be there in four days."

"I jes' hopes we will," said Pom, joyfully. "I jes' like to have a shot at dem rapscallions of outlaws, dat's jes' what I'd like to do."

"You will get the chance. Pomp, without a doubt!" cried Frank Reade, Jr. "Come, all aboard."

The Steam Man's whistle blew, and once more the ponderous iron feet were speeding across the plain.

Fifty miles more were covered before the middle of the afternoon. Then the travelers came to a line of timber which seemed to stretch away as far as the eye could reach.

The Man here came to a halt. Frank was undecided what to do. The timber line seemed to be an obstacle in their path much more formidable than the river had been.

It was easy to ford the river, but the tangled undergrowth of the timber seemed quite impenetrable.

Their course lay directly through the timber. To attempt to make a circuit was seeming folly.

But Frank was not long in making up his mind.

"Look here, Pomp," he said, sharply, "I want you to stay with the Man. Keep a sharp lookout for danger."

"Fo' de Lor' sakes! Whar is you gwin, Boss Jun'r?"

"I am going to see how deep this timber belt is. Come, Barney, I want you to go with me."

"All roight, sor," cried the Celt with alacrity, as he sprung for his rifle. "I'm jest the man for that."

Barney followed Frank out of the cage.

They stood in the verge of the timber.

Frank quickly selected a place of entrance. Both were provided with sharp axes to cut their way through the undergrowth where it was too thick to allow of the passage of their bodies.

For the first fifty feet the undergrowth was dense.

Then it seemed to disappear and they came upon perfectly smooth ground under the trees, and where the Steam Man could have run with ease.

"Good enough!" exclaimed Frank, with joy, "the most we will need to do is to cut our way through this thin fringe of undergrowth. Then I believe the Man can pick his way along all right."

Yet Frank had not solved the most important question of all.

This was the width or depth of the timber belt.

Accordingly, he led the way deeper into the timber.

But the situation remained unchanged for the first half hour's tramp. Frank reckoned that they bad traveled fully a mile and a half into the timber.

And yet there was no signs of its coming to an end.

Suddenly they came upon what seemed to be a well-defined roadway or broad path leading deeper into the timber.

The ground certainly bore the imprint of horses' hoofs, and Frank examined the trail with surprise.

"By Jupiter!" he exclaimed, with surprise, "this is a curious thing. It looks to me very much as If this was an Indian trail, and that it was much used."

"Bejabers, that's so!"

"I have it," cried Frank. "This is a path made by the savages for the purpose of going through the belt."

It seemed a fortunate discovery, for there would seem to be nothing to hinder the Steam Man from passing through the timber by means of the same trail.

Frank was deeply gratified by the discovery, and said:

"We will return at once for the Man. Come on, Barney."

"Are ye shure, Mister Frank, that this trail leads through the timber, sor!"

"Where else should it lead?"

"Shure, sor, I dunno, but —"

At that moment a thrilling sound smote upon the hearing of both. It was the distant muffled beat of horses' hoofs.

The next moment and before they could even spring to cover into view in the trail came a body of horsemen.

It needed but a glance to reveal their character and to apprise the two explorers of their most deadly danger.

The horsemen were half a hundred in number and were hostile Comanches.

They rode their nimble ponies as though a part of them, and gaily bedecked with war-paint and feathers their appearance was certainly hideous enough.

At sight of the two white men the Comanches let out a chorus of yells.

For a moment they had reined in their ponies, then incited by the commands of a tall, brawny chief who rode in advance, they came forward at a more rapid gait.

Frank quickly threw his rifle to his shoulder and pulled the trigger. The tall chief reeled in the saddle, threw up his hands and fell from his pony's back.

CHAPTER VI.
IN THE TIMBER.

WITH the fall of their chief the Indians seemed maddened. With savage yells they bore down upon the white men.

"Mather preserve us!" cried Barney. "We're in a devil av a fix, Mister Frank. Whativer will we do?"

"Steady!" cried Frank, in a commanding voice. "Keep with me, Barney."

He stepped back among the trees and Barney did the same.

Then both opened fire upon the savages, working the repeaters as fast as they could.

As a result, a perfect storm of bullets rained upon the red foe. Despite the fact that there were but two of the white men, the storm of bullets from the repeaters bad a salutary effect upon the Comanches.

They had no means of knowing the exact number of the white foe. The rapid fire of the repeaters deceived them into a fear that many times the number of whites were concealed.

Already half a dozen dead savages lay upon the trail. They wavered and then halted, and with wild and baffled yells broke for cover.

By nothing less than sheer will, force and clear grit, Frank and Barney had checked the advance of the foe.

But the danger was now more imminent than ever.

The savages had no intention of giving up the contest.

On the contrary, they were now in a better position to cope with their foes.

In the cover of the trees they would steal up on the white men and inaugurate that delight of the savage, the bush fight.

The young inventor knew that the time had come for a change of tactics.

He was by no means egotistical enough to believe it possible for him to beat the savages at their own game.

It was now better to adopt a discretionary move and make a safe and easy retreat.

There was great danger that the foe might close in upon their rear.

In such a case the outlook would be bad. It would be, by no means, uncertain that they might lose their scalps.

So Frank made a motion to Barney.

"Fall back!" he whispered. "We must get back to the Steam Man."

Cautiously and silently the two explorers made their way hack through the forest upon the back trail.

As luck would have it they did not encounter a savage on the way. In a short while they were in the deep fringe of undergrowth. Through this they quickly made their way.

They came out at a spot not ten yards from the place where they had left the Steam Man.

But now an astounding surprise was accorded them. Frank rubbed his eyes and Barney looked dumbfounded.

There certainly was the spot where they bad left the Steam Man. But the machine itself was gone.

No sign of Pomp or the Steam Man was visible.

As far as the eye could reach over the plains or along the timber line the man was not to be seen.

For a moment Barney and Frank were too amazed to speak. Then Frank managed to recover himself sufficiently to say:

"Upon my soul! What does this mean, Barney?'

"Tare an''ounds!" gasped the Celt. "I'm out av it, Mister Frank. Divil a bit do I understand it."

Frank knew well that Pomp would not disobey orders and leave the spot unless compelled by some strenuous influence to do so.

"Something has happened to Pomp," he declared. "Do you think it could be that he has been attacked by the Indians, Barney?'

"Divil a bit do I understand it, Mister Frank," he declared, earnestly. "Shure, he has gone, an' that is all I can make out of it."

Frank advanced to the spot where the Steam Man had been and began to examine the ground.

There were the marks of the Steam Man's ponderous feet and the wheel tracks.

Also intermingled with them were the prints of ponies' hoofs. In a heap of prairie grass near the dead body of a Comanche Indian was found. He had a bullet hole in his skull. At once Frank comprehended all.

"Pomp was attacked by the Indians!" be cried, with conviction. "He made a good fight, and then was obliged to relent. The Indians have probably pursued him. Here is the trail leading to the westward."

"Shure, it's roight yez are!" cried Barney, readily. "He wud niver stay an' be captured by the red divils. It's a big head he has."

"That is right, Barney!" cried Frank. "We can only hope that he escaped."

The two men looked at each other in a nonplussed fashion. It was truly not easy to decide upon a move.

At any moment the Comanches who were upon their trail might appear. The situation was a dubious one.

"Upon my word!" muttered Frank. "We run our noses into a nice little trap here. It seems to me that this region Is alive with hostile Indians. I wish I had tried to enter No Man's Land from the north. But it was so hilly there that I fancied these level plains would make the easiest traveling."

"Shure that wud be so, Mister Frank, iv it warn't fer the Injuns," said Barney.

"Yes."

"Bejabers, I 'ave a plan."

Frank turned quickly.

"What is it?'

"Bejabers, I tink iv we climbed a tree hereabouts mebbe we cud see the Steam Man an' wherivver he is."

"Not a bad idea, Barney," agreed Frank. "But we had better be expeditious or those Indians upon our trail will be in upon us."

Barney selected a tall cottonwood and went up into it like a monkey. When he had reached the highest point, he took a good survey of the country.

As a result, he presently shouted:

"Shure, sor, I kin see the smoke av the Steam Man away out to the westward, sor. I reckon it's comin' this way, sor."

"Good!" cried Frank, jubilantly. "Pomp has probably outwitted the savages and is coming buck after as. Come down as quickly as you can, Barney, and we'll go to meet him. If we can once get aboard the Steam Man we shall be all safe."

Barney slid down out of the tree.

Then together they started along the verge of the timber belt.

In a few moments the smoke from the Steam Mini's pipe was seen.

It was evident that Pomp was returning. Soon the Man came into view not more than two miles distant.

To attract Pomp's attention. Barney fired his rifle into the air.

The answer came buck quickly in the shape of a whistle from the Man. It was plain that Pomp had seen them.

Thus far nothing had been seen of the Comanches since leaving the trail in the timber.

Our two adventurers had begun to congratulate themselves upon having given the red foe the slip, when an unlooked-for calamity occurred.

Suddenly from the timber belt a score of painted warriors leaped.

With wild yells they were quickly upon our adventurers, and in a twinkling, they were surrounded.

Frank shot down two of the redskins and Barney one. Then they were disarmed and thrown heavily to the ground.

Stout thongs bound their wrists. The very worst of misfortunes had befallen them.

The purpose of taking the foes alive was to be plainly seen. The redskins intended to torture them at the stake.

"My soul! it is all up with us, Barney!" Frank groaned.

"Bejabers, it luks loike it, Mister Frank!" replied Barney, "bad luck to ther spalpeen. Iv the Steam Man was only here now."

But the Steam Man was not on hand. Even if it bad been it was hardly likely that Pomp could have coped single handed with that murderous crew.

But the savages did not wait for the man to come up. Their first move was to hurry their prisoners away into the forest.

When Pomp came up a few moments later not au Indian was in sight.

He had experienced some thrilling adventures since being left alone in charge of the Steam Man.

After Frank and Barney had gone, Pomp had made himself comfortable in the wagon cage.

He opened a box of choice cigars and gave himself up to a consoling smoke.

All the while he was muttering away in disgust at his ill-fortune.

"Now, Li'l Boss no business to take dat no 'count I'ishman wif him," he muttered. "He ain' no use whatebber. I jes' fink Boss Jun'r is beginnin' to show favoringtism' an' I's jes' gwin to kick on it, you bet."

But the mild fumes of the cigar soothed Pomp's ruffled temper.

After all it was not by any means unenjoyable to sit there in the cage enjoying the cigar.

He became somewhat reconciled, and was wrapped in reverie when a thrilling incident aroused him.

A strange pounding noise came to his ears and he sprang up. A startling sight met his gaze.

There over the prairie, a large body of savages were riding down full tilt upon the Steam Man.

Pomp was so amazed that for a moment he could not act.

CHAPTER VII.
JACK ARNOLD APPEARS.

But Pomp quickly recovered himself and made action.

"Massy sakes!" he cried, rolling his eyes comically, "dis a bad fix an' no mistake. Whatebber am I gwin to do now I'd jes' like to know."

One thing he was sure of. It would never do to let the savages surround the Steam Man.

He knew well, that against such an overpowering force he could do nothing single-handed.

Therefore, he quickly decided to beat a retreat in as graceful a manner as possible.

So he sprang to the dasher, unloosed the brake, and opened the throttle.

The Steam Man leaped forward, and in a few moments was flying across the prairie at a tremendous gait.

The savages came yelling in pursuit, but they might as well have tried to overtake an ignis fatuus.

Now that the race bad begun, Pomp threw himself into the spirit of it.

"Ki dar!" he yelled, in glee. "Mebbe you fink you catch dis chile, but you kin jes' bet dat you don' do it."

Then he caught up his rifle and began firing at his pursuers with deadly effect.

Pomp felt sure that the Comanches were a part of the band who had attacked them the day before, for they did not manifest any surprise at sight of the Steam Man, and, in fact, seemed familiar with its appearance.

The ponies of the savages were urged to their utmost.

But they could not outrace the Steam Man. Pomp run them a hot race for six miles at full speed.

Then the Indian ponies began to give out. One by one they dropped back.

At the end of ten miles Pomp had left them all out of sight. He was exceedingly jubilant.

"Golly!" he exclaimed, with dancing eyes, "when dey fink dey can catch dis chile, dey jes' bettah try it. Dat's all I's got to say fo' m'sef."

Pomp brought the Steam Man to a halt now. He knew that Frank and Barney were still in the timber, and that if they returned in the meanwhile they would be much alarmed at his absence.

So he concluded that the sooner he returned to the starting point the better.

But this did not seem easy.

On the return trail there was much danger that he might run across the savages again.

Yet it was imperatively necessary that he should return. He hit upon an idea finally which be believed would work safely. This was to make a wide detour and thus avoid meeting the savages.

His mind was quickly made up, and he set the Steam Man to going at full speed upon the return.

As fortune had it, his ruse worked well. In no case did he meet with a foe, and presently came in sight of the timber line.

"I spec's dey's returned afo' dis an' is lookin' fo' me," muttered Pomp, "but I reckon if dey waits dey'll see me soon enuff."

Just at that moment he saw two men in the edge of the timber.

At once he recognized them.

They were Barney and Frank.

Pomp was overjoyed at the sight and sent up a whistle from the Steam Man.

"I'll be jus' glad fo' Boss Frank to come abo'd agin," he muttered joyfully. "I ain' a bit scrumptious about bein' lef' alone on bo'd dis 'ere masheen."

But even as he saw his two friends in the edge of the timber, a thrilling sight rewarded Pomp's gaze.

He saw the savages spring out of the forest and overpower the two white men.

Pomp saw this, and was beside himself with horror and the knowledge of his inability to give them help.

He opened the throttle to its widest and sent the Steam Man along.

It was of no use.

When he reached the spot the two prisoners had gone, and there was no visible way of effecting a rescue.

Pomp was nearly frantic, and tried to affect an entrance into the limber with the Steam Man.

He even thought of abandoning the man and going to the rescue of his friends single-handed.

But sober second thought showed him the futility of this, and he changed his mind at once.

"Mah sakes alive!" the distraught man cried, wringing his hands forcibly. "I mus' fin' some way or other to rescue Mistuh Frank an' dat I'ishman from dem Injuns. I mus' do it some way."

But just how to do it was certainly a conundrum to poor Pomp.

At length, in sheer desperation, he started along the line of timber looking for an opening by which he might enter. And as he did so he witnessed a startling sight.

Suddenly over a swell in the plain there came into view a white horse, upon which was a man - a white man certainly, as Pomp told himself — and riding at mad speed.

Just behind and close upon him were full a dozen Comanche Indians.

Their fleet ponies were gaining upon the heavier horse.

Once the white fugitive turned and fired back at his pursuers.

But the shot did not seem to take effect. With wild yells, the savages swept down upon their victim.

Pomp witnessed the race with tingling veins. He quickly sprung to the Steam Man's lever.

"Fo' goodness sake." he cried, breathlessly, "I must jes' rescue dat man, fo' if dem Injuns overtakes him I done fink dey habe his scalp fo' shuh."

He started the Steam Man ahead at full speed.

He was well within range of the savages, and with his rifle Pomp sprung to one of the port-holes.

He quickly drew aim and fired.

He was an excellent shot, and the bullet took effect plainly. One of the savages threw up his arms with a wild shriek and fell to the ground.

Again Pomp fired.

Another of the savages fell. The others now swerved in their course to get out of the range of the Steam Man.

But the white fugitive turned his horse toward the man.

Only four of the savages were left.

Again Pomp worked the repeater and another savage fell. This turned the tide of battle.

The other three, with maddened yells, cut for the cover of the timber.

The pursuit was abandoned, and through Pomp's prompt intervention the white fugitive was saved.

But before be reached the Steam Man his horse stumbled and fell.

Exhaustion had overtaken the beast and a blood vessel was ruptured. A few convulsive throbs and the noble animal was dead.

The rider picked himself up very luckily unhurt and approached the Steam Man.

He lifted his hat and shouted:

"Hullo. Pomp! Where is Mr. Reade?"

He was a tall handsome young man and at sight of him Pomp gave a gasp of surprise.

"Fo' de Lor' sakes if it ain' Mistuh Jack Arnold he cried.

"It's nobody else," replied Arnold, with a laugh. "A little surprised to see me, are you, Pomp?"

"Of co'se," replied Pomp. "De last time I seed you was in Readestown."

"That is right."

"But how comes you to be out here in dis here place?"

"Oh, I thought I might be of some help to you in the hunt for Alice."

"Bless yo heart, but how you dare to go aroun' among all dese Injuns alone an' on hossback?"

"Well, Mr. Reade wouldn't allow me to accompany him in the Steam Wagon, so I thought I'd come on my own hook."

"Well, I never did see de beat of dat," exploded Pomp, "but jes' you come right abo'd, Mistuh Arnold, I's done glad to see you."

But Jack hesitated.

"Where is Mr. Reade?" he asked.

"Oh, now, dat is de worst of all," replied Pomp, with agitation. Would you beliebe it, he an' de I'ishman am curried off by dem Injuns." "Heavens! You don't mean it!"

"Yes, I does."

"But—can nothing be done to save them?" asked Jack.

"Sometin' must be done, Mistuh Jack. Jes' you come right abo'd." Jack refused no longer.

He leaped into the cage and Pomp told him the story of their adventures. The young Chicagoan listened with interest.

"By Jove!" he exclaimed. "Something desperate has got to be done and that right away. What shall we do, Pomp?"

Pomp's eyes glistened.

"I's jus' got a plan," he said.

"What Is it?"

Pomp felt sure at that moment that he had hit the key-note.

"If you will jus' stay abo'd of de Steam Man I'll jus' go out an' rescue dem if I hab to break mah neck to do it."

Jack drew a long whistle.

"That won't do, Pomp," he declared.

"Why?"

"I don't know how to operate this machine. Supposing I was attacked by Indians before you got back?"

Pomp saw the point at once.

His cherished plan was exploded. He knew that it would not do to abandon the Steam Man.

Much crestfallen, he arose and started the Man along the edge of the timber belt.

"What are you going to do?" asked Arnold.

"I's jus' gwin to fin' some way to get into dem woods."

"Ah, that is not a bad idea."

Pomp kept the Man along at a sharp gait just in the verge of the timber.

Suddenly Arnold gave a sharp cry.

"A trail!" he cried.

Pomp applied the brake.

"Whar is dat?" he asked.

"Right here and it goes right into the timber," replied Jack.

"Massy sakes alibe!" cried Pomp, eagerly. "Is dat a fac'?"

"It is, and I'll bet my life it is the entrance used by the Indians!" declared Jack, with earnestness.

Pomp went to the cage door and sprung out. It required but a brief examination to satisfy him that Jack was not far from right.

"Golly, you hab jus' got de fac's in de case, Mistuh Jack!" he cried. Then without a moment's delay, Pomp started the Steam Man along the trail.

Into the timber the Man went at full speed.

The trail was good and broad and the Man kept along at a good pace. For several miles the trail was followed through the dense forest.

Thus far no signs of the savages had been seen.

Now, however, Jack Arnold suddenly sprung up with a warning cry.

"Look out, Pomp!" he shouted. "We are going right into a nest of them. Sheer off a bit."

CHAPTER VIII.
RESCUED BY THE STEAM MAN.

When Barney and Frank were led away into the timber by their captors their sensations were of a varied sort.

A cloud of depression hung over them both.

It did not seem as if they could possibly escape death. In the power of these merciless Comanches the outlook was by no means bright.

Yet neither betrayed outwardly any sign of fear or trembling.

The savages stoically marched in single file through the deep forest.

None of them made speech save the painted chief, who occasionally uttered a guttural command.

After a time, they came out into the trail discovered a short while before by Frank and Barney.

This was followed for a distance of three miles.

Then the woods broke away into a deep clearing, and a strange sight was revealed to the captives.

In the center of the clearing was a miniature lake of clear sparkling water.

About this were a score of Indian teepees. A number of braves were lounging about, squaws were at work skinning wild animals, and pappooses and dogs were gamboling beneath the tree arches.

It was an Indian village in the heart of the timber. It was to this then that the trail led.

"Bejabers, we've got to the end av our journey," muttered Barney, as they entered the clearing.

"You are right," replied Frank. "The question now is, what will they do with us?"

"On me worrud they can't any more than kill us intoirely," replied Barney.

"That is poor consolation."

"Shure and it is."

But the prisoners were not allowed further conversation.

They were now led into the center of the village. The excitement was intense.

All the Indian braves, squaws and pappooses thronged about them. After a while a council was held.

Then a war dance followed. The suspense of the prisoners was quickly relieved.

Suddenly they were led into the edge of the clearing.

Here a couple of stakes had been driven in the ground.

To these they were tightly bound. A heap of brush was piled about each. Then the savages danced about the victims, making the air ring with hideous yells.

After a time, this ceremony closed, and quiet reigned for a time. Both Frank and Barney had given themselves up for lost. There seemed no power at hand to save them.

Yet both were resolved to die game.

Suddenly a savage was seen advancing with a torch. It was plainly his purpose to set fire to the brush pile about the stakes.

But before be reached them a startling intervention occurred.

It was at this critical moment that Jack Arnold and Pomp and the Steam Man reached the end of the trail.

Jack saw the Indian village and the savages ahead and yelled a warning to Pomp.

But the plucky man did not heed it. He had seen another and more startling sight.

He saw the two captives at the stake and knew in that moment that their lives depended wholly upon him.

This was enough for the faithful employee.

He would rescue them or die in the attempt. In that flash of time he made up his mind what action to make and acted.

He dashed right down into the midst of the Comanches with the Steam Man. With a full head of steam on, the Man went crashing through the village.

Braves were knocked down, squaws and papooses fled for their lives, wigwams were demolished, and general havoc made. Round and round the clearing went the Steam Man, trampling any opposing braves under foot, and Pomp kept the ear-splitting whistle going all the while.

The terrific iron monster, plunging among them in such a fashion, thoroughly demoralized the Comanches.

They literally fled for their lives before the grim monster.

At a favorable moment Pomp pulled the Man to a halt opposite the prisoners at the stake.

Jack Arnold leaped out and cut their bonds. In another moment Barney and Frank were aboard the Man.

Pomp started on through the village for the prairie on the other side of the timber belt which was now in sight.

The Steam Man was soon far out on the level plain and safe from pursuit.

Then mutual congratulations were in order.

Frank and Barney were astonished at sight of Arnold, but were glad to see him, nevertheless.

"If you do not want me aboard," said Arnold, apologetically, "I will get off here anywhere."

"Not much!" cried Frank, heartily. "I can see that you are a man of sand, and I am glad to have you along."

"I think I can help you a little in the rescue of Alice Wentworth," said Jack.

"I have no doubt of it," replied Frank. "On the whole I am glad you came! We shall need you."

This restored a harmonious feeling, and matters went smoothly thenceforth.

It soon became evident that the Steam Man had passed through the outlaw country, and was coming to a different series of perils.

Henceforth the battles would be likely with outlaws instead of Indians.

The Man made fifty miles before dark. Frank calculated that they had but two hundred miles further to go before reaching Lonely Ranch.

"We will be in No Man's Land tomorrow night," he declared. "That will be none too soon to suit me," declared Jack Arnold, eagerly.

"Bejabers, it'll be none too soon for me either," put in Barney.

"Golly! I jes' like to set mah eyes on dat Lonely Ranch," cried Pomp, with a display of his ivories. "Dat vilyan, Harold Haynes, is my mark, an' don' you fo'git it."

The Steam Man kept on all that day, and camp was made at night on the banks of a small creek.

The next morning the Man was again on the trail.

And, as Frank had predicted, at night they were in No Man's Land. The Texan plains bad ended and now a wild mountainous country lay before them.

It was now necessary to find the Lonely Ranch. First it was

Necessary to come across someone who bad a knowledge of its whereabouts.

Suddenly Barney, who was at the dasher, cried:

"Bejabers, whativver wud yez call that! It luks loike a house." Frank picked up a glass and leveled it at the distant object.

It was at the foot of a hill, and as Frank studied it, he became satisfied that it was a building of some sort.

He conjectured that it was a small sheep ranch, and fancied he could see the flock upon the hillside.

However, the Steam Man's course was set for it.

In a short while the distant ranch became plainer to the view.

It was then seen that Frank's conjecture was correct.

Very soon the Steam Man drew quite near to the ranch. Then a man on horseback was seen to ride out to meet them.

He was a tall, gaunt Texan, and as he reined his pony up fifty yards from the Steam Man, shouted:

"Heigho! What kind of a railroad do ye call that? It's the first time I ever seen a bullgine goin' without rails to go on."

"Hello, stranger!" cried Frank. "Come nearer. I want to talk with you."

"Are ye friend or foe!"

"Friend of course."

"I'll have to take yer word for it. But I say, what kind of an invention is that anyhow! A man made out of iron!"

"That's what it is, a Steam Man."

"Wall, I'll be damned! I've heern tell of ther Iron Hoss, but I never heern of ther Steam Man afore."

"Oh, the world is full of new inventions."

"By gosh, it might be for all of me, fer I ain't bin off this ranch fer nigh onto two years."

"You don't say so!"

"Yos, I do."

"It must be a lonely life!"

"Wall, you bet."

The plainsman now rode nearer to the Steam Man. He took a keen scrutiny of it and then said:

"Wall, you're welcome to my ranch, friends. Won't ye stop an' have a bite o' whisky? My pard he's off on t'other side of the ranch just now. Ye're welcome!"

"Thank you just the same," declared Frank politely, "but I don't think we'll stay. We're in a bit of a hurry."

"For a fact, eh?" exclaimed the ranchero, riding nearer. "I say, pard, ye hain't got a bite of terbacker, have yer?"

Barney produced a plug and tossed it out to the ranchero.

"With me compliments!" he shouted. "May yez injoy it."

The stranger regarded Barney gratefully and took a huge bite.

"Ireland is the home of people of good heart," he said, warmly.

"Yez are right thar!," retorted Barney. "An' ye show yez good since in the appreciation av it."

Everybody laughed, and then, Frank who had an eye to business exclaimed:

"I want to ask a favor."

"It's already granted, stranger."

"Where is Lonely Ranch?"

The ranchero gave such a violent start that he seemed likely to fall from his saddle.

His gaze shifted, and he unconsciously expectorated his fresh quid of tobacco.

"Lonely Ranch?" he exclaimed in a peculiar voice. "Pardon me, stranger, but do ye mean the real Lonely Ranch of which Harold Haynes or Black Mask is the master?"

"That is it!" cried Frank, eagerly.

"Then I might as well say that I know well whar it is?"

"Ah!"

"Are ye goin' thar?"

"Yes."

"Friends of Haynes, eh?"

"Not much!" replied Frank. "We are after him with the authority of the law. Wait until we get a grip on him."

The ranchero slapped his hands together excitedly.

"By ther great bufflers!" he cried in his cracked voice, "that's what ye are here with that bullgine fer, eh? Well, I swan! I hope ter Mary Jane that ye'll do the cuss up brown. Thar ain't ther life of a ranchero on this range are safe nowadays with Haynes an' his hounds around. Kill him, I say!"

"That is what we intend to do," declared Frank, "but we must first find him."

"He ain't a hard man to find," declared the ranchero. "As sure as my name ar' Bill Simmons, I'll go an' direct ye jest how to go to Lonely Ranch."

Good for you!" cried Frank, gratefully. "We will repay you well."

"Don't want no pay," replied Simmons. "I'll be only too glad to see ye wipe him out."

"Then he is not a good neighbor?"

"Thunder! he's a robber, an' a murderer, too. Whenever he wants any of my sheep he jest sends a gang down here an' takes 'em without ther askin'. I know of several of our kind who have been found dead with a bullet in ther heart, an' Black Mask did it, as we well knew."

"Then he is a kind of despot in this region, a sort of terror?"

"Ye're right he is."

"Well," said Frank, quietly, "if you will show us where the ranch is, I will be much obliged to you."

"I'll do that, cap'n. Jest trot around hyar to t'other corner of the cabin."

"All right."

Frank started the Steam Man up and went as far as the corner of the ranch.

As he did so a cavalcade of horsemen was suddenly seen coming down the hillside. At sight of it Bill Simmons turned deadly pale and gasped:

"My God! there is the Black Mask himself. It is Harold Haynes and his dogs. What does he want here?"

The situation was a most thrilling one.

CHAPTER IX.
A MEETING WITH THE OUTLAWS.

As Simmons made this thrilling declaration, Jack Arnold sprang up.

The veins upon his forehead were like whip cords and his eyes like burning lights. He seized his rifle.

"Dog!" he exclaimed, tensely. "Our day of reckoning has come. It is your life or mine now."

He would have sprung out of the cage but Frank restrained him.

"Hold on, Arnold," he said, sharply. "Where are you going?"

"Outside!"

"But you must not."

"Let me go."

"No."

"Why not?"

"Because you will needlessly expose yourself. It is safer and better to remain here and keep cool and quiet. We are sure to win the game."

Arnold drew a deep breath. Frank's words calmed him and he sat down.

Haynes and a dozen rough-looking plainsmen came dashing np to the spot.

The villain's features were contorted with passion, and he cried in a hoarse voice:

"Surround that machine, men!"

The dozen outlaws did so, making a line about the Steam Man. Haynes rode forward a step.

"Eh, Bill Simmons!" he gritted, glaring at the ranchero. "What are you doing here, I'll ask?"

"This my ranch," replied Simmons, respectfully.

"And you entertain these invaders of our domains, eh? The Steam Man! I have heard that he was coining here to crush me. Well, Mr. Frank Reade, Jr., you'll have a large-sized contract on your hands to do it."

"Perhaps not so very large," replied Frank, coolly. "Time will decide that, sir."

"So that's what yer here for?"

"I am here to demand that you give up to me safe and sound a young girl whom you have in your power, whose name is Alice Wentworth."

The villain's lip curled.

"You demand it, eh!" he hissed, savagely. "Well, you are certainly blessed with assurance. Lookee, sirrah, you may not be aware that you have ran your head into a nice trap from which you will not escape alive."

"I am not aware of It," said Frank, coolly.

"Curse ye, then I'll make ye aware of it!" hissed the villain. "I'll not kill ye outright, but ye shall die by inches. Close in, men, and tip that machine over. Capture them alive if you can."

The outlaws with a yell rushed upon the Steam Man.

They came on foot, having dismounted from their horses. Their plan was to demolish the Man first if they could.

But they failed to take into consideration the fact that four very determined men were in the wagon cage.

"Steady!" cried Frank Reade, Jr. "Give them the repeaters, boys!" A volley was fired from the Steam Man. Three of the outlaws fell. "Let me draw a bead on the ring-leader," said Arnold, with set teeth.

He did so, and fired at Haynes the next moment.

The villain reeled in his saddle but recovered himself. The fact that he did not fall seemed evidence that he was not badly injured.

"That's queer!" cried Arnold. "I aimed for his heart and I am sure that I hit him."

Again the young Chicagoan fired at the villain.

But as before Haynes reeled slightly in the saddle and did not fall. The villain was urging his men on like a fiend.

But they were unable to reach the Steam Man on account of the raking fire poured into them from its defenders.

Suddenly Haynes turned in the saddle and shouted to his men. Then he blew a shrill whistle.

An answering blast came from the mountain side above.

Then into view galloped a squad of half a hundred armed men. These bore down directly upon the Steam Man. Frank Reade, Jr. at once sprang to the throttle.

He knew it would be of no use to stand ground against such an overpowering force.

The result would certainly be disastrous. Discretion in this case was certainly most commendable.

Therefore Frank opened the throttle and let the Steam Man run away from the spot.

The villain Haynes saw that his victims were likely to slip from his grasp.

This enraged him and he furiously rode forward to intercept the Man.

"Upon my soul, that brute has a charmed life!" cried Jack Arnold. "I have tried in vain to fetch him down, and I am sure that I hit him, but the bullets do not seem to have any effect."

This time Jack fired at the horse which Haynes rode.

The bullet took effect.

The animal plunged and fell, throwing the outlaw with great force to the ground.

He lay like one dead, while his followers all desisted in their pursuit of the

Steam Man and went to his assistance.

It was the opportunity for escape, and Frank let the Man run away at a very rapid gait.

Into a deep pass in the hills the Steam Man went.

After following this, at an upward coarse for some miles, they finally came out upon a sort of plateau or level plain in the heart of the hills.

Here a halt was called.

The question now on hand was as to the locality of the Lonely Ranch.

"I do not believe that it is far away," declared Frank, positively. "In fact, the meeting of Haynes and his raid I consider as good evidence that it is near at hand."

"I agree with you!" cried Jack.

"Bejabers, av me eyesight is any good, that luks a bit loike it over yender," said Barney.

The Celt pointed to a dark object upon the side of a distant mountain.

"Golly, dat is a fac', Boss Jun'r!" cried Pomp. "An' if dat ain' a lonely 'nough place, den dis chile hab miss his guess fo' suah."

Frank said nothing, but picked up the glass and began to study the distant object.

"There are certainly buildings," he declared, "and a high stockade upon the brow of a cliff. As I live, I believe it is the Lonely Ranch!"

"Of course it is!" cried Jack Arnold, excitedly. "We are in luck."

"Let us go ahead and investigate," said Frank. "Start the Man up, Pomp."

"A'right, sah!"

Pomp proceeded to obey orders. The Man went forward at a rapid gait.

Soon the distance was covered to the verge of the plateau. Here a halt was called upon the brow of a canyon cliff, extending as far as the eye could reach into the hills.

A quick consultation was held.

First of all, it seemed a good plan to reconnoiter the ranch, and see if many of the outlaws were about.

Frank had thought of doing this himself, but Arnold begged the privilege.

"Give me one of your men," he said. "I will take the Irishman."

"Very well," agreed Frank. "I need not adjure you to move with great care."

"Have no fears."

So it was decided that Arnold and Barney should go forth to reconnoiter.

They left the Man and disappeared in the thick forest upon the mountain side.

Frank and Pomp waited long and anxiously for their return. But an hour passed, two of them sped by and no sign of the two men.

"Golly! I jes' reckon dey is lost, Li'l Boss!" cried Pomp.

"I am beginning to get anxious," said the young inventor. "Something most have happened to them."

Yet nothing could be done but to wait patiently for their return.

The position of the Steam Man was not a very safe one all things considered.

Upon one side was the steep face of the cliff. Upon the other the impenetrable woods. The ground was rough and covered with stones.

Suddenly a sharp cry pealed from Pomp's lips.

"Golly sakes, Boss Jun'r," cried the excited man. "Jes' you hear dat! I fink de enemy am comin' fo' suah."

The loud beating of horses' hoofs was plainly heard, and suddenly into view swung a troop of armed men.

They were outlaws as Frank saw at a glance.

They saw the Steam Man at once and with loud yells bore down upon it.

It was a thrilling situation.

Frank was at a loss to know just what move to make. Retreat seemed impossible.

The Steam Man was started ahead but a pile of stones opposed its progress. It was impossible to turn either to the right or the left.

In the rear were the enemy. Truly it was a desperate predicament.

Yet pluckily, Pomp and Frank opened fire upon the foe. And their shots were not without effect.

The outlaws came to a halt and held themselves out of range.

But the respite was a temporary one.

At length the outlaws dismounted.

They then proceeded to creep up behind huge boulders and ledges and opened fire upon the Steam Man.

A sharp battle at once began.

Of course for a time Frank and Pomp had the best of it, for they were protected by the wire cage.

But after a time reinforcements came. Then a barrel of gunpowder was rolled from behind the rocks, and a voice cried:

"Surrender, or be blown to perdition!"

There was a fuse in the end of the barrel, and it was in a position to be rolled down toward the Steam Man.

Frank saw at a glance that it would be a very easy matter to blow the Man to pieces.

There seemed no other course but to surrender, in the face of this most appalling fact.

CHAPTER X.
IN THE ENEMY'S POWER.

The Steam Man was certainly in a trap. Frank and Pomp viewed the situation with the utmost of dismay.

There seemed no way but to surrender in an undignified and unqualified manner to their deadliest foes.

Frank's heart sank. He knew well enough what it meant to fall into the hands of Harold Haynes.

Death would be certain. An escape seemed impossible.

Yet, if the barrel of gunpowder was exploded beneath them, they would certainly be blown to pieces.

That the outlaws would do this there was no doubt.

It was a trying position.

Frank was for a moment at a loss just how to act.

He turned a white face to Pomp.

"My soul!" he gasped. "We are in for it, Pomp."

"Golly, dat is a solemn fac', Boss Jun'r," agreed the servant.

"It means death to surrender and death to refuse."

"But I jes' finks dat we stan's mo' o' a chance for escape if we s'renders, Li'l Boss."

"Perhaps you are right."

At this moment a sharp call came again from the outlaws.

"Last chance. Will ye surrender or not?"

Frank went to a loophole and made reply:

"What are your terms?"

"Unconditional."

"We will surrender If you'll allow as to retain our rifles and our personal liberty."

"That is cool. You will surrender if we will set ye free again. That don't go down, boss."

"What are your best terms?"

"I told ye once. Without conditions""

"That is not fair treatment."

"That is not our lookout. Will ye surrender or not?"

Frank saw that there was plainly no way out of the scrape.

The only way was to make a virtue of necessity. Perhaps rescue would come or there would be a chance to escape.

So he made reply:

"Very well, we will surrender."

With a cheer the outlaws sprang from their covert and rushed upon the Steam Man.

They gathered about the wonderful invention, and one of them entered the cage.

By like direction Frank was compelled to return with the Steam Man to the plateau.

Then a trail up the mountain side was taken, and a short while later the Steam Man came to a halt before the high stockade of the Lonely Ranch.

A huge gate swung open and the Man steamed into the yard.

Frank Reade, Jr., and his Steam Man were prisoners in the power of Harold Haynes.

It was a thrilling realization and most appalling to Frank himself. But the young inventor had figured in many positions of peril before. He was therefore cool and calm and upon the alert.

If possible, he would seize the first opportunity to escape.

Therefore Frank kept his own counsel, and maintained a good lookout for the desired opportunity.

The Steam Man was examined with great curiosity by the outlaws. Haynes himself was not present at the moment. But suddenly the big gate in the stockade opened and Frank saw him come riding in.

The villain's face lit up with fiendish joy at sight of the Steam Man.

It was a moment of triumph and evil satisfaction to him and words cannot express his state of mind.

He leaped from his horse and advanced toward the prisoners.

"Ha, ha, ha!" he laughed discordantly. "So soon, my fine bird. I told you to beware of the Lonely Ranch. You could not keep your bead out of the trap could you."

Frank smiled contemptuously and replied:

"Your victory is not one to boast of, villain. You cannot triumph always. The evil doer comes to his deserts sooner or later."

"Pshaw! don't yer preach to me."

"It would be a waste of breath."

"Yer right."

"The sun never shone upon a more unconscionable scoundrel."

"Ye're complimentary in yer remarks."

"It is my opportunity to speak the truth," said Frank. "If it is cutting so much the better."

The villain's face flushed.

"Take care!" he hissed. "I'll not stand everything."

"Bah! I defy you!"

"Thunder and blazes!" roared the villain, "I'll take that out of you if it takes a leg! Ho, men, take this chap down into the dark hole. Leave him there without food and drink for awhile."

Four or five of the outlaws sprang forward and laid hands upon Frank.

"This set Pomp into a fury. The faithful employee tried to break his bonds.

"Fo' de jan' sakes, kain' I do nuffin' to help you, Li'l Boss?" he cried, desperately. "I jes' mus' do somefin. Lemme go, you rapscallions, and I'll lick de whole ob youse alone. Don' you do no harm to Mistuh Frank, or you will pay well for it."

But poor Pomp was quite helpless.

He could not break his bonds and was obliged to see his dear master dragged away to the black hole spoken of by Haynes. This was beneath the main body of the Lonely Ranch.

A trap door was lifted in the door, and Frank was unceremoniously pitched down into the place.

He struck heavily upon the damp earth, having fallen a distance of fully a dozen feet.

For a moment he was stunned and unable to rise.

After a time, however, he was able to sit up.

All about him was pitchy darkness.

The ground beneath him was wet and slimy.

It was a noisome, bad-smelling place, and a chill, engendered by the transition from the warmer air above, crept over Frank.

He fell sick and faint.

But with an effort he overcame this feeling, and managed to get upon his feet.

Through some singular inspiration of mercy the captor had cut his bonds and he had the use of his hands.

This was certainly an advantage.

Frank was some time in composing his mind sufficiently to decide upon a plan of action.

Then be began first to out, if possible, the capacity and character of the place into which he had been thrown.

He felt his pockets for a small folding lantern which he carried.

It was an invention of his own, and capable of burning some hours. But before he could draw it out, the trap door above opened a crack, and a gleam of light shot down into the place.

A harsh voice said:

"Well, my fine inventor, how do you like it down there? What do ye think of Harold Haynes now? Don't want to meddle with him ag'in, do ye? Oh, I tell ye it's a piece of luck in yer coming out here. That Steam Man is jest the machine I've been waiting for a good while. I'll make things terrible for the stage line now, an' they'll fear Black Mask more than ever, be sure."

"Scoundrel!" gritted Frank. "Justice will overtake you yet."

"There is no justice in No Man's Land," jeered the villain. "Ha! Ha! Ha! You ran your head into a fine trap. But I will not disturb your quiet for long. You will no doubt enjoy life down there. Fine place, isn't it? After you have enjoyed it for three days, you will agree that it is a little better than Hades. Well, enjoy yourself, old friend. Good-bye."

The trap door went down with a bang. Frank drew a breath of relief when he realized that he was once more alone.

He waited with caution a reasonable length of time.

He knew well that if the outlaws knew that he possessed a pocket lantern they would make a move to take it away from him.

When he was satisfied that the coast was clear he drew the lantern from his pocket.

It was but a moment's work to adjust and light it. All about him at once became as plain as day.

He saw that he was in a square, cellar-like hole, dug deep in the ground.

The door was wet and slimy, as also were the walls.

Decaying vegetation was in the place, and the odor from it was most awful to bear.

The germs of deadly fever lurked in the air. Frank knew that a sojourn of any length of time in the place was as good as a death warrant.

He carefully examined every part of the walls and floor. The walls were of slabs of sandstone, carefully packed and laid.

The young inventor could see no way of escape from the terrible death hole, at least by easy means.

A chilling reflection came upon him.

"My soul!" he muttered. "I am certainly doomed. This is my awful end. What a horrible fate."

Despair naturally succeeded this conclusion. But Frank Reade, Jr., was a man of grit.

He made a mighty effort to overcome the sensation and succeeded. Then he set at work coolly and calmly to weigh the possibility of an escape.

His active brain was not to be baffled by a problem like this.

That inventive faculty which had made him world famous did not desert him now.

It was destined to extricate him from even a worse position than this. He soon hit upon an expedient.

When captured, both prisoners had been disarmed.

But Frank bad managed to retain a Florentine dagger, which he had secreted in his vest.

This he now removed. First, he began work upon the foundations of the cellar wall.

These were sandstone, a soft material, and easily worked with steel tools.

By sawing upon the sandstone, Frank succeeded in extracting several of the largest blocks.

These he placed in a tier against one side of the wall.

Soon this tier was so high that by mounting it be was able to reach the wood flooring of the ranch.

Now the most difficult part of the work began.

First Frank cut a small hole up through the flooring.

To his joy he found that it consisted of a single layer of boards. By listening at this opening be was enabled to tell when anybody was in the room above.

By degrees he began to cut through the boards. Soon he had the ends of two of them sawed through.

Daylight streamed down into the cellar. Frank reckoned that he had been in the place a day and a night.

He believed that with the coming of another night he might make a break for liberty.

He was weary and faint.

He had not slept or ate anything since being thrown into the hole. Now, exhausted nature succumbed.

He lay down upon the topmost slab of sandstone and slept soundly. When he awoke he felt assured that it was midnight and the time for action had come.

CHAPTER XI.
THE QUESTION OF RESCUE.

After leaving the Steam Man, Barney and Jack Arnold had struck out up the mountain side directly for the Lonely Ranch.

They were in the midst of thick forest of maples and beech and deciduous trees.

For some time they made their way through almost impenetrable undergrowth.

Then suddenly Arnold came to a halt.

"What is that?" he gasped.

A dismaying sound came to their ears.

It was the distant crack of rifles. But one conclusion could be formed.

"Bejabers, there's only wan thing it cud be," declared Barney. "They've attacked the Steam Man."

"Heavens!" exclaimed Arnold. "We ought to be on hand to help."

"Shure enough; but, me fried, it will lake an hour to get back to the Man."

"Of course."

"Shure the red divils or the outlaws, which iver they be, cud overcome thim afore thin."

"What will we do?"

The two men looked at each other in utter dismay.

It was certainly a serious question.

Duty would seem to demand that they go at once to the relief of their friends.

On the other hand, the Steam Man in the hands of Frank Reade, Jr., they reflected, ought to be safe enough.

But valuable time was passing.

The distant sounds of the firing became plainer.

It was evident that a hot fight was in progress. This reflection made Arnold's blood boil.

It at once decided him in the course to pursue.

"Enough!" he cried. "Let us go back and help them."

"I'm wid yez!" cried Barney.

"We would be shirking our duty not to do it."

"Shure, Mr. Arnold. If yez will lead the way. I'll folly on." Arnold lost no time in doing this. In a very short time they were flying down the mountain side.

It was found much easier going down than coming up.

To be sure the thick undergrowth bothered them some.

But they kept on rapidly.

Every moment the sounds of firing became plainer. The battle seemed to be a hot one.

Then suddenly the firing ceased.

"Bejabers, it's one way or the ither now," cried Barney, his face paling. "Do yez think they have kilt 'em entoirely?"

"Let us hope not," said Arnold, hopefully. "We will not have it so just yet at any rate."

On they plunged. It required some time to reach the edge of the timber.

The spot was now seen where the Steam Man bad been.

It was no longer there.

Both Barney and Arnold were given a shock. Certainly the Man was not there.

Either it had eluded the foe and taken up another position or Frank and Pomp had been killed or surrendered.

For a moment Barney and Arnold were unable to reach any conclusion.

Then the latter espied the dead bodies of the outlaws scattered about.

"By Jupiter!" be cried. "Frank made it expensive for them, didn't he."

"Bejabers, I'm glad of that," cried Barney. "Iv he 'ad salted a few more av 'em it would av bin a mercy."

The idea occurred to Jack to look for the trail of the Steam Man and ascertain if possible where it had gone.

Accordingly with Barney's help an examination of the ground was made.

This resulted in the finding of the wheel marks leading up the mountain side.

The trail told the whole story and the hearts of the two searchers sank.

"It's all up!" exclaimed Jack, dismally, "They were captured by the villains."

"Och, hone! that's a pity!" wailed Barney. "Iv the omadhouns do any harrum to Frank I'll niver rest till I 'ave 'ad revenge."

But Arnold was more hopeful.

"It may come out all right yet," be declared, "We must make up a plan to rescue them, Barney."

"If we kin."

"Can we not?"

"How wud ye do it?"

"I am not prepared to say yet. Some one of us might play the part of spy or something of the sort"

"Bejabers, that's so."

"At any rate we must rescue Alice Wentworth. That is my particular mission here."

"I'm wid ye!" cried Barney. "Jest tell me what to do."

But the words had barely left Barney's lips when a thrilling thing occurred.

Suddenly from a clump of trees a dozen man sprung forth.

They rushed toward Barney and Arnold, crying:

"There they are. Don't let 'em escape. They must not get away." In a flash Jack Arnold comprehended their great peril.

He knew that these were some of Haynes' gang.

To fall into their hands would be fatal. Prompt action was necessary.

"Quick, Barney!" he cried, leaping toward the timber. "For your life!"

But the Celt needed no urging.

They had already started for the trees and was quickly safe in their midst.

Arnold was close beside him.

It was for a time a lively race.

But the dense undergrowth favored the fugitives and soon they had reached a safe point.

Sounds of pursuit had died out in their rear and they felt safe.

Out of breath and much exhausted they came to a halt.

At the moment they were at the head of a mighty gorge choked with huge boulders and debris.

Just above, far up on the mountain wall, was the Lonely Ranch. The stockade leaned over the cliff at this point and looked like the battlements of some old time castle.

Jack and Barney were now at a complete loss as to what move it was best to make.

The locality was certainly a hot and dangerous one for them.

There was the momentary danger of falling into the clutches of the outlaws.

On the other hand, they could not think of leaving their friends in the power of Haynes and his fiends.

No, in some manner their rescue must be effected.

Barney was an astute schemer, and Arnold was possessed of a great power of execution.

It did not require them long to hit upon a plan.

"I tell you, Barney, we have got to work lively," declared Jack, positively. "Now that these chaps know of our presence hereabouts they will leave no stone unturned to find us."

"Bejabers, ye're roight," agreed Barney. "What iver can we do!"

"I have a plan."

"What is it!"

"The only way we can rescue Frank and the others is to effect an entrance to the stockade."

"Shure, that's plain enough."

"Of course it is."

"But howiver can we do it?"

"It looks to me as If under cover of darkness that we might crawl up to the foot of the stockade under the cliff and tunnel our way under. It looks like soft earth up there."

Barney was silent a moment.

His keen brain was carefully weighing the feasibility of the move. Suddenly he cried:

"By me sowl, I belave yez are correct, Mister Arnold. Shure we had ought to dig our way through there very quickly."

"So it would seem. Now we must wait for darkness."

"Thin we had better foind a safe hiding place somewhere afore it's that time."

"That's so."

There was little danger of their trail being followed. The flinty character of the ground hereabouts forbade that.

A little search in the gorge found a small cavern or aperture in the cliffs the face of which was covered with vines.

Here they found a safe hiding-place.

They remained quietly in this place till long after dark. Their position was not without its perils. As they crouched there silently the sounds of their pursuers could be plainly heard.

Indeed they became well assured that the gorge was full of the outlaws.

Several of them passed very near to the cave.

Had they lifted the vines they must have surely seen the inmates-of the cave, and the result would have been disastrous for Barney and Arnold.

But they did not do so.

Fortune was with the fugitives.

After a time the sounds of pursuit died out, and the two fugitives drew a breath of relief.

Hope once more began to dawn about them. The future looked brighter.

Their spirits rose and they welcomed the coming of darkness.

Soon the shadows of night settled thickly over all the wild land.

They waited until midnight before venturing to go forth from their covert.

All was now quiet in the gorge.

Lights above showed the locution of the stockade. This would guide them in their work.

Each had a stout, broad bladed hunting knife.

Primitive tools with winch to dig in the earth, but this did not deter them in their purpose.

Up the sleep ascent they crept side by side. It was not long before they bad reached the foot of the stockade.

Arnold had reckoned that the timbers were driven possibly four feet into the earth.

To tunnel under them it would necessitate making a beginning some distance below the banking.

This was done. With the hunting knives for picks and their hands for shovels the two rescuers worked valiantly.

They dug a circular opening into the hill several feet deep in a very short space of time.

They were making rapid progress, when a thrilling incident occurred. Suddenly Barney clutched Arnold's arm.

"Whist, now!" he whispered, shrilly. "Wud yez luk at that?"

Arnold did look, and saw a dark form emerge from the gloom and come straight toward them.

CHAPTER XII.
THROUGH THE TUNNEL.

Barney und Arnold were for a moment so startled that they could not act.

Then Arnold whispered:

"Into the tunnel, Barney—quick!"

There was just room enough for them both in the tunnel. Into it they quickly crawled.

They were out of sight in a twinkling.

The man, whoever he was, evidently had not seen them.

He passed along the foot of the stockade above and vanished from sight.

If he had seen them he showed no signs of it in manner or voice. He went straight on at the same rate.

But Barney and Arnold dared not risk exposing themselves for some time.

They were much alarmed, and in doubts as to the safety of remaining longer in the vicinity.

"He may have seen us," whispered Arnold, "and be working a strategy to capture us or spring a surprise upon us."

"Begorra, that's so."

"I hate to abandon the work, and yet if we would make sure of our safety we should leave this spot at once."

There was no doubt of this.

It was a doubtful problem to solve. Bui Barney finally said:

"Bejabers, we've got to take some risk, Mister Arnold. I say, let's take the chances an' stay here."

"Agreed!" cried Arnold. "We would be faint-hearted to be so easily scared away."

"Truth, an' that's so."

With this they went again to work with increased effort.

Every moment the tunnel grew deeper. Most excellent progress was made.

The dirt was easily worked, although large stones were encountered, but these were dislodged and rolled out.

Suddenly Barney's knife came in contact with something which gave forth a dead, hollow sound.

He knew at once that it was wood, and a cry of joy escaped him.

"Bejabers, we've reached the stockade!" he cried. "All we've got to do now, Mister Arnold, is to go under and upwards."

This was true.

A very little effort now would suffice to place them inside the stockade of the Lonely Ranch.

Arnold's calculation of the depth of the stockade posts were so accurate that they had hit the bottom of them.

It was an easy matter to clear away the dirt beneath them.

Their mutual pressure upon each other prevented their sliding down and the diggers felt safe in going under them.

It was now a matter of seven feet upward tunneling.

Barney began to assail it vigorously.

As fast as he brought the dirt down, Arnold carried it out of the tunnel.

Suddenly Barney's arm went up into the outer air and the final crust of turf caved in.

The Celt cautiously raised his bead above the level and looked about him.

The place chosen proved an admirable one.

As it happened, there was quite a distance between the tunnel and the main building of the ranch.

This was enshrouded in gloom.

But beyond, camp-fires could be seen, and a guard paced up and down by the stockade gate.

It was evident that everybody about the ranch had retired to rest.

It looked aa if the coast was clear, and Barney felt elated with the prospect of rescuing the prisoners.

He cautiously crept up through the tunnel, and stood upon the level ground.

He bent over, end in a whisper sent word down to Arnold.

"Whisht there, me hearty!" be called. "Come an up."

"Is it alright?"

"YA."

Arnold took no time in obeying Barney's advice.

He stood upon the ground a moment later beside the Celt.

The spot where they stood was deepest gloom. There seemed but very little danger of being seen.

For a moment they stood in the shadows, undecided what move to make.

Then Barney said:

"I tell yez Mister Arnold, I'd loike to git me bands on that guard at the gate. I'd moighty soon spoil his beauty."

"At present he is not troubling us," suggested Jack. "We would incur a great risk in attacking him."

"Begorra, that's true enough," agreed Barney, "but what wud yez do about it, Mister Arnold?"

"I think if we can liberate the prisoners, we can all make our escape as well through the tunnel."

"Bejabers, ye're right."

"First of all let as cautiously reconnoiter the vicinity. If we see the coast is clear we can work quickly enough."

"Iv yez will lead the way I'll folly on," declared the Celt, eagerly. "All right."

Arnold did lead the way.

Together they crept toward the ranch. As they neared the main building, however, they heard some strange sounds.

At first it was difficult to interpret them, but presently the murmur of voices raised high in song and laughter came to their ears.

Then turning the corner of the main building they saw light streaming from the door and windows of a small cabin not twenty yards distant.

Song and laughter and rough jest came floating out upon the air.

It was evident that some of the outlaws were holding carousal there.

"By me sowl, it's a merry owld ruction they're havin'," declared Barney, in a whisper.

"You are right!" replied Arnold.

"That's a bit av lack fer us, I take it, Mister Arnold."

"I believe it. Of course they are not on guard while drunk."

"To be shure."

Arnold now left Barney in the shadow of the main ranch and crept up cautiously to the cabin.

He was able to apply one eye to a crack in the shutters.

He saw the interior of the cabin quite plainly.

The outlaws, half a hundred in number, were seated at tables playing cards and drinking whisky.

Piles of money upon the tables showed that they were gambling.

But the leader, Harold Haynes, was not there.

Arnold carefully noted every particular of the ribald scene.

He counted the men and studied their faces. Satisfied that the most of them were intoxicated, he crept back to Barney's side.

"We have little to fear from them," he declared. "Unless a general alarm is given."

"Shure we must luk out for that."

"Of course."

But the words bad barely passed Arnold's lips when he was given a great start. He clutched Barney's arm.

"Back!" he whispered, "back! for your life!"

Back into the deep shadows the two men crouched. They were none too soon to escape a great danger.

Two men loomed up in the darkness. They were conversing in ordinary tones, and went directly toward the cabin.

They passed so near to the two rescuers that they might have touched them.

Yet the glare of the light was in their eyes, and Barney and Arnold escaped detection.

This was the best of luck. As soon as the peril had passed they did not fail to congratulate each other.

"By me sowl, we got out av that scrape lucky," said Barney.

"You are right."

"Iv those chaps had seen us, the game would 'ave been up."

"Surely. Now, Barney, let us make action. Hullo! there is the Steam Man."

This was a fact.

Not fifty yards distant stood the wonderful invention. But the fires in the furnace were out, and the man was not able to go.

At first the daring plan bad suggested itself to Barney of taking possession of the Man.

But sober second thought disposed of this.

The high stockade prevented an escape with the man. Overpowering numbers of the outlaws would prevent it also.

Again, it would not be possible to fire on the furnace without attracting attention.

So that plan was disposed of.

Barney, however, visited the machine and looked it over.

He saw that it was quite unharmed, and muttered:

"I wisht there was only some way we cud seize the darlint. But niver moind! Iv we resky Mister Frank he'll soon foind a way to do it."

With this firm belief Barney at once agreed with Arnold upon a plan of action.

They believed that the prisoners were confined in the main ranch.

Arnold saw a grated window and climbed up to it.

All beyond the grating was darkness, but he bad a pocket lantern, and he flashed its rays into the place.

He was given a thrilling shock of surprise as he did so.

The room which was opened up to his view then was about fifteen feet square.

It was rudely furnished, containing a cot bed, some chairs and a table.

Some skins were upon the floor for rags, and a few coarse prints upon the wall. A grated door was at one end.

It had the appearance of a prison chamber, as such it was.

But the prisoner was a fair young girl, slender and petite, with large lustrous eyes and wavy, golden hair.

She started up from a chair where she bad been sitting, with an exclamation of terror.

But a passionate, tender cry burst from Arnold's lips.

"Alice, my darling! Have no fear! It is your Jack!"

"My Jack!" welled from the girl's throat, as with a convulsive cry, she flew to the window. "Oh, God be praised! My prayers are answered. You have come to save me!"

"I have, and Heaven has directed me," replied the passionate lover.

What followed between them for the next few moments at the grated window was not for other eyes to see.

Barney was employed in keeping watch discreetly, and of course had little interest in that direction.

"But how am I to get out of this awful place?" asked Alice finally. "Oh, the danger is great. If Haynes should find you here he would kill you."

"Fear not, my love!" replied Arnold, warmly. "I shall take you away from here safely or sacrifice my life."

But at that moment a startling sound reached the ears of both.

There was a shuffling sound outside the cell door, the latch rattled, the click of a padlock was heard and the door opened.

A man crossed the threshold and stood in the room.

CHAPTER XIII.
POMP TO THE FRONT.

The very instant that he heard the latch raised, Jack Arnold gave a start.

"My soul! Some one is coming!" exclaimed Alice, in a thrilling whisper. "Save yourself! Go quick!"

Arnold needed no further bidding.

Quick as a flash, he closed the lantern and slid down from his perch.

He reached the ground before the door had opened. When it swung open, Alice Wentworth stood in the middle of the chamber.

It was dark as Erebus in the room, and the intruder could not be seen.

For a moment Alice stood like a statue, a fearful sense of terror upon her, then she said tensely:

"Who are you, and what do you want here?"

There was a shuffling sound and then there came a hushed voice:

"Sh, missy, I's come to sabe you. I's Pomp an' youse don't need to be afraid ob me. I's on'y a po' black man, dat's all, missy, fo' a fac'."

"But I don't know you," said Alice, distrustfully.

"No, missy, I s'pose how you don't, but I's with Boss Franke Reade, Jr., an' Mistuh Jack Arnold; you know him?"

"Yes," replied Alice.

"Well, we'se come in de Steam Man to sabe you an' carry you back home. But dat nasty Harold Haynes he done capture de Steam Man an' Boss Jun'r an' I. He jes' put me in dis nex' room an' I knowed youse was here cos' I heerd you talkin' wif de old Spanish woman wot bring us our suppers; you see?"

Alice was deeply thrilled.

"Are you telling me the truth?" she asked, with wildly beating heart.

"Fo' de good Lor', I's doing dat, missy," replied Pomp, for he it was.

Alice took a match from a shelf and ignited it.

By its flame she saw the face of the honest black employee before her and all doubt was settled.

"Heaven be praised!" she exclaimed, "this is too good to believe."

"But it is a fac', missy, an' if you jes' trust in dis chile I's gwine to try to git you out ob here purty quick."

"But how on earth did you escape from your cell?"

"Ki dar, jes' you lets dis chile alone fo' dat. Dere ain' no locks on dis do', missy, only a big wooden bar on de outside. I just had a small steel saw an' I done saw a hole in my do' an' lif' dat bar an' walk right out, den I come to yo' do' an' lif' de bar an' here I is."

It was a straightforward story. Certainly it was gratifying knowledge.

"But—where is the guard who usually sits out in the corridor?"

"Dunno, missy I spec' he's gwine away somewhar. He ain' dere now fo' suah."

The guard, fancying his prisoners all safe was at that moment enjoying himself in the cabin with the carousing party.

It had all worked admirably for Pomp, and be certainly had played in great luck.

Alice saw the point at once and was much overjoyed. It seemed for a moment too good to believe.

She clapped her hands joyfully.

"Oh, it looks as if we were going to escape!" she exclaimed. "Do you know, Mr. Arnold and Barney are just outside the window. They tunneled their way in here and are ready to help us out."

Pomp pave a cry of joy.

"You don' mean dat, missy!" he cried. "Dat is de bes' ob good luck."

Pomp rushed to the window and sent forth a thrilling whisper: "Bah! is dat you, I'ish? I's done glad to see you."

"Bejabers, ye can't see me yit, eejit!" retorted Barney, his Irish wit cropping out, in spite of peril.

"Dat's a fac', I'ish," returned Pomp, in the same spirit. "An' dat's why I's so berry glad."

"I'll par'lyze ye whin I get yez on level ground."

"Hah! Youse ain' able to do dat, I'ish."

But it was not the time and place for skylarking, and Jack hastily illuminated this to Barney.

The Celt cooled down at once, and said:

"That's roight, Mister Arnold. Shure I'm wid ye to the ind."

A short consultation followed.

The result was that Pomp went on an investigating tour to the main door of the ranch.

The result was that, to the joy of all, he was able to open it.

A few moments later Alice was in Arnold's arms, and Pomp and Barney were embracing each other.

All this had occurred in the deep shadows, and not one of the outlaw band had suspected anything wrong.

After the first greetings were over Arnold started to lead the way to the tunnel so as to leave the enclosure.

But he had not taken ten steps when he halted.

Barney and Pomp were still by the Ranch. A sudden startling recollection had come to Arnold.

"Heavens!" he exclaimed. "I had nigh forgotten. Where is Frank Reade, Jr.?"

But Pomp and Barney had been discussing this same question.

"I fink dat dey hab put Boss Jun'r in some out-ob-de-way place," said Pomp, with conviction. "It's suah dat he ain' in de same buildin' whur I was."

"Where can they have put him," said Arnold, anxiously.

Before an answer could be made, however, the sound of approaching footsteps was heard.

Then a tall, dark form loomed up through the gloom.

The little party shrank back into the gloom in doubt and suspense.

"Heavens!" gasped Arnold, "that is Harold Haynes. I know his step. We shall be discovered. Let us skip while we can."

Haynes, for he it was, reached the door of the ranch.

He lifted the latch and went in. It seemed hardly a moment before he came rushing out excitedly.

But the prisoners had reached the mouth of the tunnel and were making their way out through the same.

Haynes' yells und curses and commands filled the air.

The alarm was instant and most startling.

All of the outlaws came rushing from their quarters. Lanterns flashed and the clank of arms was heard.

Barney was the last to pass through the tunnel. All were now outside the stockade, but not in safety by any means.

Barney and Pomp felt a powerful inclination, which amounted to a mad desire to attempt the rescue of Frank Reade, Jr.

But this was clearly out of the question just now.

It was at present necessary to make good their own escape. Then later they could attempt a rescue.

After passing through the tunnel the little party of fugitives started down the gorge.

They knew well enough that there was no time to be lost.

Only the promptest of action would save them now. Down into the deepest of the woods they went.

They could hear a great clamor about the Lonely Ranch far above. But there were no immediate sounds of pursuit and they felt for the nonce safe.

Of course it was a surety that the villain Haynes would leave no stone unturned to find them.

The region about would be thoroughly scoured by armed men.

If escape were to be made sure it would seem necessary to secure some method of transportation other than walking.

If they were only possessed of horses now, they could speedily bid defiance to the foe.

But on foot, in a wild and peril infested region, so many miles from a friendly settlement, the situation was not by any means a salubrious one.

In this extremity an idea occurred to Arnold.

He suggested that they proceed to the cavern in which they had so safely sought refuge a few hours before.

It was an admirable hiding-place, and seemed to be just the needed spot. The move was agreed to.

It was not for to the cave, and reaching it, they entered and proceeded to make themselves comfortable.

The sounds of pursuit came to their ears plainly enough.

Even the flash of lanterns could be seen through the leafy screen which covered the mouth of the cave.

Once voices were heard very near, and a terrible fear seized the fugitive that the foe had discovered and were following their trail. But this proved an unfounded fear, and quiet once more reigned. Thus the night hours passed slowly away and dawn at length came.

All was quiet in the vicinity and it seemed certain that the outlaws bad given up the search.

Yet, for aught they knew the gorge might be filled with foes.

So Jack decided that it would be safer for all to remain quietly where they were for that day and possibly another night.

Then some scheme would be devised whereby horses might be procured and a start made for civilization.

This was Arnold's plan.

But Barney and Pomp shook their beads, saying determinedly:

"Bejabers, we'll niver leave this place until Mister Frank is rescued."

"You kin jes' bet on dat."

"Indeed, it is my inclination to do the same," said Arnold warmly. "But look at my position. We are without provisions and would starve here. Moreover, Miss Alice ought to be removed to a place of safety at once."

"Dat's a'right, Mistuh Arnold," declared Pomp. "You kin jes' take de lady away to a safe place jes' as quick as you please. Me an' I'ish we stay here."

This was the plan agreed upon.

In many respects it seemed the best course to pursue.

Certainly Alice would be in constant peril by remaining in the vicinity.

To the active rescuers she would be but an encumbrance. It seemed certainly best, therefore, to send her at once homeward as far as possible. In this Arnold was the best to figure as an escort.

Plans were at once made to that effect. By great good luck Barney and Pomp contributed materially to the success of the scheme.

They went out upon a scouting trip that night, and in the morning returned with four horses, saddled and bridled.

They had by luck discovered an enclosure above the ranch, into which the outlaws turned their horses to feed.

Saddles and bridles were found in an old lean-to on the verge of the enclosure.

The two daring fellows went boldly in, helped themselves, and came away without discovery.

It was a literal God-send to them.

With the horses, escape began to look certain. At the hour of sunrise Arnold and Alice mounted and started down the gorge.

Arnold's plan was to reach the plain, and avoiding the ranch, strike out for Texas.

By traveling cautiously he hoped to avoid the Comanches and reach the railroad.

They bade good-bye to Barney and Pomp.

"May you have success in your efforts to rescue Mr. Reade," said Arnold, warmly.

"Thanks to yez," replied Barney. "We wud niver show up in civilization agin widout Mister Frank."

"Dat's a fac'," chimed in Pomp.

The two travelers set out on a gallop and were soon out of sight down the gorge.

Barney and Pomp led their horses into the cavern and secured them.

There was work before the two faithful fellows, and it consisted in effecting the rescue of Frank Reade, Jr., and the recovery of the Steam Man.

The sun was just rising and Barney and Pomp were at a loss just what move to make, when suddenly a piercing whistle came from the mountain side above.

The two servitors of Frank Reade, Jr., looked up and were astounded to see the Steam Man coming out through the stockade gates.

CHAPTER XIV.
A PLUCKY ESCAPE.

WE left Frank Reade, Jr., in a critical position in the filthy, reeking cellar hole of the Lonely Ranch.

The famous inventor reckoned that be had been a day and a night in the vile place.

Midnight of the second night was at hand, and he believed that the time for action had come.

All depended upon the success of his efforts now.

It seemed to him that if he should fail now all hope would be lost.

He mounted the sandstone platform once more and listened.

Not a sound could be heard from the interior of the ranch.

All was quiet.

The coast seemed to be clear.

The ends of two of the floor boards bad been sawed through. A little more work would complete it.

So he began work with a zest.

It was necessary to proceed carefully. There were periods of listening and moments of anxious waiting.

But success was destined to be his through persistent effort

At length after patient work the other ends of the boards were cut and the aperture completed.

It was fully large enough for him to pass through and he did so.

He stood upright in a large square chamber. All was intense darkness.

Frank listened carefully to make sure that the room held no other occupant.

Then he had resort once more to the pocket-lantern which had done him such good service.

Turning its rays on gradually he was able to see the whole interior of the room.

To his joy it did not contain an occupant. This was encouraging.

There was a single window and Frank went to it.

It overlooked the gorge.

All was blackness outside.

A low, sobbing wind, was playing among the tree-tops below. All was quiet at the grave otherwise.

Escape by this window did not seem feasible.

Frank quickly abandoned the idea, and turned his attention to the door.

This, to his surprise, stood ajar.

The room itself had the appearance of a store-room.

There were heaps of old saddles and equipments thrown about.

There were rusty cavalry sabers and disused carbines. Upon the walls were hung moldering suits of buckskins and jeans.

Frank quickly took an inventory of the contents of the room.

He felt the possible need of a weapon, and selected one of the sabers.

This he gripped tightly in his hand, and crept toward the door.

He passed through the door, and was in a narrow corridor. Here he felt a draught of air.

This told him that the outer door must be open. He cautiously made his way along the corridor.

He had not gone far before he saw the open door of the ranch.

And upon the threshold sat the figure of a man.

His head was bowed upon his knees, and he seemed to be either buried in reverie, or deep in slumber.

Frank concluded that this was the guard placed to watch the door. The young inventor was cool and decided.

He crept cautiously nearer.

"There is just one thing that will save the guard's life," he repeated as be gripped the handle of his saber, "and that is the fact of his being asleep."

Nearer he crept to the guard.

It was the night previous that the other captives had escaped and Haynes had ordered guards stationed everywhere in the stockade.

But if this guard had not been so deep in the carousal of the night before he would have been on duty.

As it was, the deep snoring told Frank plainly enough that he was fast asleep.

The young Inventor therefore did not venture to attack him.

He crept cautiously and silently by him into the outer air.

Not thirty yards distant a small fire burned, and by its light Frank saw another guard pacing up and down.

Frank had escaped from the ranch but he was yet within the stockade.

This it did not seem so easy to escape from.

The young inventor cautiously made a half circuit of the campfire, keeping in the deep shadows.

In this way he brought himself in sight of the stockade gate.

Two heavy lanterns hung there on tall posts. An armed guard was standing statue-like by each post.

Escape by the stockade gate was out of the question.

Again, Frank turned about and took a new course. This time he came in sight of an object which caused his heart to leap.

It was the Steam Man.

The Man loomed up giant-like in the gloom.

The fires in the furnace were out -and there was no guard by the machine. Frank approached the cage.

He opened the door and entered.

It was then that the most during idea occurred to him.

Upon one side of the wagon near the dasher there was a secret locker.

He pressed a spring and opened the lid. It was a roomy space, and several openings in the side covered with a screen admitted plenty of air.

Frank reflected that Haynes would be sure to make use of the Steam Man on the morrow.

There was no doubt but what he could do it, for it was as simple a matter to engineer it as a steam engine.

The young inventor counted the costs upon all sides. Then he closed the lid of the locker

From another secret compartment which opened with a spring he took a couple of revolvers heavily loaded.

Then he stretched himself out in the wagon and proceeded to make himself easy.

Frank, however, kept upon the alert, so that he would not be surprised or discovered in his position.

The night hours passed rapidly and soon daylight began to appear in the east. With this the entire camp was astir.

The outlaws came from their quarters quickly in answer to a bugle call.

Frank saw them eat breakfast in one of the small cabins near. Then he was given a bit of a start.

Two of the outlaws now approached the Steam Man.

Frank saw the imminent danger of exposure and acted quickly.

He crept into the secret locker and closed the lid.

It was not a very comfortable position. but he yet maintained it.

He knew that in order to gain his liberty it would be necessary to take some risks.

The two outlaws approached the Steam Man and sprang aboard.

They were talking excitedly, and the voice of one Frank recognized as belonging to Harold Haynes.

"By Jupiter!" Haynes exclaimed, vehemently, "they must be over-taken and recaptured. The next time kill every one of them but the girl. Do ye understand, Bill Bunch?"

"I do, Harold!" replied the other, "but p'raps ye can show me how to work this blasted machine?"

"You've hired on the rail road?"

"I reckon so."

"Then ye'n ought to know all about it. Jest start a fire in the furnace. The gauge shows that there's water enough. Just like a regular locomotive, you know."

"Sure; quite convenient ain't it? Here's coal all aboard, too."

"It's a big thing an' beats steam railroads all to smash, for you can go anywhere you please with the Steam Man."

"By Jove, that's so! This will make you a good rigging to tackle stage coaches with."

"You bet! Now, I want you to be engineer, Bill Bunch."

"All right!"

"First, fire her up. Then you and I will take a run out around the country here and look for the escaped prisoners."

"That we will."

Bill Bunch went to work at once with a will.

In a very short time he had the furnace roaring and steam up. Frank, in the locker, had listened to and heard all.

He was given a wild thrill of joy to know that the other prisoners were safe.

"That was the shrewd work of Arnold and Barney!" he mattered. "No doubt they looked for me, but, of course, couldn't find me. Ah! it is the best of luck, and, if I can only once more get possession of the Steam Man, we will very quickly spoil all of Mr. Harold Haynes' plans."

But at this moment a loud cry went up.

The guard at the ranch had just discovered the escape of Frank Reade, Jr. The report reached Haynes and he was furious.

With a volley of oaths he leaped from the wagon and directed a thorough search of the enclosure.

"Find him if you can," he yelled. "He could not have got beyond the stockade fence."

The whole outlaw garrison was at once engaged in the quest.

But though they looked everywhere most assiduously not a trace of the escaped prisoner could be found.

Haynes was furious and the air was black with his oaths.

He threatened the guards with the direst of vengeance.

In the heat of his wrath he leaped aboard the Steam Man and yelled: "Open the gates! Let her go, Bill Bunch, and we will burn down the dogs or break our necks."

Bunch pulled the whistle valve and then the Steam Man glided through the gates and down the mountain side.

CHAPTER XV.

FRANK RECOVERS THE STEAM MAN.

It was at this moment that Barney and Pomp had been considering a plan of to how to learn the fate of Frank Reade, Jr.

The appearance of the Steam Man was a genuine surprise.

They looked at the Man as it fled down the mountain side with amazement.

"Golly!" cried Pomp, with dilated eyes. "What's dat fo' I'ish?"

"Why it's the Steam Man, lad. Can't ye see?" retorted the Celt.

"I kin see jes' as well as yo kain, I'ish," replied Pomp.

"What did yez ax me that for, then, I'd loike to know?"

"I axed you what dat Man was out dat-a-way fo'?"

"Whurroo! I reckon that Mister Haynes, the dimmygog av this country about here, is out for a ride. Bad cess to the baste, iv I could only draw a bead on him with me trusty rifle."

"Ki dar," cried Pomp, with sudden inspiration. "I's got it, I knows what it be out fo'."

"Well, what is it, eejit?"

"He be gwine to catch Mistuh Arnold an' dat gal."

Barney looked serious.

He fumbled the lock of his rifle and stood irresolute for a moment. "Do yez raly think that, lad?"

"Of course I does."

"Thin, by St. Patrick, it's mesilf as must go after the Steam Man at once. It will niver do to let Haynes overtake Arnold, for shore he'd kill him and git his clutches on the gal agin, the omadhoun."

"Dat's jes' de troof."

"Begorra, git out yer hoss, Pomp. We'll give 'em a hoss race on me worrud."

It was but a moment's work for the two faithful fellows to bring out the horses.

Then they mounted and rode down the gorge.

with whip and spur they urged their horses on.

They well knew the need of this.

Arnold was undoubtedly out on the prairie now.

The Steam Man would be sure to sight him on that broad expanse. It would be easy enough to run him down, and this would mean death to Arnold and a horrible fate, a return to captivity for Alice Wentworth.

Very quickly Pomp and Barney came out into the valley below. They were riding at a headlong pace.

Suddenly Barney turned his head.

He caught sight of something on the mountain side which made his teeth chatter.

It was a large body of the outlaws, mounted and armed, and coming down at full speed.

"Bejabers, wud yez luk at that, Pomp!" cried Barney.

Pomp did look.

Had it been possible, the black man would have turned pale. As it was, his teeth chattered.

"Fo' goodness sakes, I'ish, we'se in a bad place!" he cried. "If dem rapscallions should see us-"

"Whurroo! Luk out wid yez!"

A yell came from the mountain side.

The outlaws sent their horses on at a more rapid gait.

The truth was plain.

They had seen she two servitors of Frank Reade, Jr., and had set a course for them.

Barney and Pomp realized that they were in a bad position.

Yet they rode on until suddenly they came out of the hills and upon the vast tableland.

Here it was level ground, and there was no doubt but that it would be a question of equine speed and endurance.

Far out over the plain there was visible a couple of black specks. That these were Arnold and Alice Wentworth there was little doubt. The Steam Man was after them at full speed.

Barney and Pomp were literally between two fires.

In their zealous endeavor to go to the aid of Arnold they had run their heads into a trap which seemed likely to prove fatal to them.

Out over the plain they rode at breakneck speed.

It was a hard race, and for a time the result was doubtful.

Then Barney with white face looked back and cried:

"Go on wid yez, Pomp, me hoss is givin' out and the divils are gainin' on us."

"Golly, you don' say dat!" cried Pomp. "Well, I jest fink we kin die hard, kain' we, I'ish?"

"By me sowl, what will become av Mister Frank if harrum comes to us?"

This was characteristic of the free-hearted Irishman who was so deeply attached to his muster that he did not stop to think of himself. But now a strange thing happened.

The cage door of the Steam Man was seen to suddenly open and a man's form went tumbling out upon the plain.

He picked himself up unharmed, however, and as he did so Barney cried:

"Bejabers, what's the manin' av that, Pomp?"

"Ki, dar, kain' you see?" cried Pomp. "Dat be dat rapscallion, Mistuh Haynes. He hab falled out ob de waggin."

"Begorra, and what for, I'd loike to ask yez?"

"How you s'pose I knows about dat? But jest you look dar."

The Steam Man was seen to suddenly change its course.

It went at an angle to the right and now some queer events took place.

The outlaws in pursuit of Barney and Pomp had seen the fall of their leader from the wagon of the Steam Man.

Haynes, upon reaching a point some distance away, halted and beckoned furiously to them.

This resulted in their deviating in their pursuit of Barney and Pomp, who in their turn also went in the direction of the Steam Man. The Man suddenly switched about and came to a halt.

A man sprang to the cage door and stood revealed to Barney and Pomp.

To the two faithful fellows it was like a complete miracle. For a moment neither could believe his senses. Barney rose in his saddle and yelled in delirious joy:

"Tare an' 'ounds, iv it ain't Mister Frank himself, safe an' well! St. Peter be praised for that same!"

Pomp was completely overwhelmed.

"Fo' de lan' sake'!" he gasped, "Howebber did all dat happen? It be jes' one ob dem miraculous t'ings, dat's jes' what it be."

Frank Reade, Jr., it was, and no mistake.

The famous inventor had played his card well, and had won. Secreted in the locker he had waited until satisfied that the Steam Man was well out on the plain and that it was safe for him to act.

Then he made quick action.

Throwing open the locker he rose quick as a flash with a revolver in each hand to confront his foes.

"The devil!" gasped Haynes, falling over backwards in fright.

But Bunch reached for his pistol.

Frank did not want to take the life of either. But Haynes fired at him quick as a flash.

The ball pealed a bit of skin from Frank's cheek, it was a close call.

There was no hesitation now.

It was a plain question of life or death, and Frank pulled the trigger. His aim was deadly.

Bunch fell, shot through the heart. His body lay in the bottom of the wagon.

But the cowardly Haynes did not stay to face the music. He sprang to the cage door and leaped out upon the prairie.

Frank might have shot him then but he did not care to do it.

He sprang to the throttle rein and changed the Steam Man's course.

Then he took in the scene about.

He comprehended the situation at a glance and recognized the deadly peril of Barney and Pomp.

He was more overjoyed than words can express at the prospect of once more reclaiming his faithful servants.

He at once changed the Steam Man's course so as to hail them.

A few moments later Barney and Pomp dropped from their horses and rushed forward to embrace their dear employer.

"Och, hone, an' yez don't know how glad I am to see yez wanst more, Mister Frank," cried Barney, effusively.

"You jes' suah dat dis chile be glad too," cried Pomp.

"You are not more glad than I am," replied Frank, with emotion. "Heaven has sided with us, and we are snatched from a fearful death. We have the Steam Man once more in our possession and can bid defiance to the foe."

"Whurroo, we'll give it to the omadhouns," cried Barney. "It's thirstin' for a ruction wid 'em that I am."

"But Arnold," cried Frank. "What of him?"

Both Barney and Pomp turned and looked across the plain.

The forms of Arnold and Alice riding to the southward were not to be seen.

They had vanished from view, probably into the mesas beyond.

But the matter was explained to Frank who looked grave and at once said:

"We must go after them at once. This will never do. Arnold does not realize the mighty risk of falling into the hands of the Comanches."

"Bejabers, I belave yez." cried Barney. "Shure the Steam Man ought to overtake thim I think."

"It can." replied Frank. "Let us take the trail at once."

But at this moment the air was broken with the crack of firearms.

The outlaws fired volley after volley at the Steam Man.

But paper pellets would have done fully as much harm.

The leaden bullets smote harmlessly against the steel cage.

Barney and Pomp responded with telling effect.

Indeed so hot a fire did they pour into the outlaws' ranks that the enemy were fain to beat a retreat.

But they filled the air with maddened and defiant yells and whoops.

Frank paid no further attention to them, however.

He started the Steam Man away over the plain. For full ten miles the Man ran at railroad speed.

The horses of the outlaws were left far behind.

The Steam Man followed Arnold's trail with ease until the mesas were reached.

Here halt was called upon the banks of a willow fringed creek. And here a thrilling discovery was made.

Upon the tangled meadow grass lay the forms of two dead Comanches.

There were signs of a terrible struggle. The ground was tangled, the grass bloody and a wide horse trail led toward the hills to its right.

"My God!" cried Frank Reade, Jr., with horrible conviction, "this is awful. There is no doubt but that the Comanches have ambushed them and have taken them away captives to the hills."

CHAPTER XVI.
THE MOUNTAIN TUNNEL.

NOTHING was there to dispute this conviction and declaration of Frank Reade, Jr.'s.

Aghast with the force of the thing all stood for some moments in silence.

It was certainly an appalling reflection that Arnold and Alice Wentworth were in the power of the Comanches.

Yet such was a fact.

What was to be done?

There seemed but one possible move and this was to take the trail and follow it to the end.

It was not impossible to effect a rescue if the move was made in time.

First the body of Bill Bunch was removed from the wagon and hastily buried near the creek.

Nothing was to be seen of the outlaws, and It was evident that the Steam Man had distanced them.

It was an easy matter to follow the trail of the savages.

The ground was soft and the feet of their ponies made deep impressions.

The mesas and the table land were left far below.

The Steam Man now began to climb a steady up-grade.

Huge boulders frequently arose before them, clumps of trees, and the steep face of cliffs.

But the trail invariably led around these and was not at all difficult to follow.

Soon they reached a point from which it was easy to see the whole of the plain below.

A body of horsemen were plainly to be seen galloping in the direction of Lonely Ranch.

That they were the outlaws there was no manner of doubt; indeed, Barney declared that he could recognize Haynes.

"By me sowl, we did euchre that villyan easy enough," he chuckled. "He had the whole av us under his thumb an' now he's got divil a wan."

"That's so," agreed Frank. "It was pretty hard on him. But that is the just deserts of villainy."

"Ye're roight!"

"I jes' fink we habn't seen de whole ob dat man Haynes yit," affirmed Pomp, solemnly. "He ain' gwine to be beat so easy ef my judgment counts for sumfin'."

"You are right, Pomp!" cried Frank. "Harold Haynes is a long headed rascal, and we will do well to keep a good look out for him for some time."

"The next toime I get a chance to draw a bead on him, I'll spoil his chance for any more rascality," declared Barney, confidently.

"Hah! you cudn't hit nuffin', I'ish," chuckled Pomp, in a badgering tone."

"Bejabers, I'll show yez the misfit av' yer remarks," cried Barney, making a whack at Pomp.

But Pomp dodged the blow.

"Ki dar, you can't hit nuffin', you no good, I'ish."

"Begorra, I'll paralyze ye."

"Hold!" cried Frank, in a voice of command. "None of that. This is no place for skylarking. Look up yonder, Barney, and tell me if that is not the top-knot of a savage?"

Barney and Pomp instantly desisted in their skylarking.

Barney squinted his eyes and studied a huge boulder poised upon the mountain side above.

Then a thrilling cry escaped his lips. It was with horror that all three now witnessed a terrifying spectacle.

The boulder began to move.

It swayed slightly to one side and then they saw the bodies of half a score of savages behind it. Their purpose was apparent.

They meant to roll the boulder down upon the Steam Man and demolish it.

"My soul!" cried Frank, "they mean to smash us."

The words were not off his lips when the boulder began its downward course.

At first it took an unwieldy lunge, then it rolled over once, dropped over a slight step in the ground, rebounded, and then came down in lightning career, sweeping devastation in its path.

Down it bore like a race-horse.

Frank Reade, Jr., in desperation had swayed the Steam Man to the right.

He had acted quickly and as if by instinct. It was the saving of the lives of all.

If the boulder had struck the Steam Man fairly nothing would have been left of it but a heap of broken iron.

It would have certainly meant death to the inmates of the cage.

But it did not.

The escape, however, was narrow.

The huge stone went by the machine with scarcely the breadth of a hair to spare. Down the mountain side it went. The wind was so swift from its passage that it choked the cage for a moment with dust.

When this cleared away the inmates saw below them what looked like the path of a landslide.

A mighty sycamore tree had been cleft in twain as by an ax.

A deep furrow had been plowed in the soil and a trail of ruin followed the course of the boulder.

Mad yells of fury and chagrin came from the savages above.

Bullets began to patter against the cage.

Barney and Pomp sprang to loopholes with their repeaters and opened fire upon the red demons.

This was with telling effect.

The Indians were for a moment exposed, and those in the cage shot down several of them before they recovered sufficiently to seek cover Then a desultory battle followed.

But the savages were bound to get the worst of it, for the white men were protected by the steel cage.

Bullets flew thick as hail for a time.

Frank was unable to judge the exact number of the foe, but be determined to push the conflict closer.

Accordingly, he moved the Steam Man up the mountainside a short distance.

The result was that the savages retired before it.

Frank's conclusion now was that it was but a small party.

With this conviction, he bad decided to risk a closer attack, when a surprising thing occurred.

Suddenly the firing ceased, and the savages disappeared as if by magic.

Up the mountainside the Steam Man went, hut no sign of the Indians was to be seen anywhere.

Nor did it seem possible that they could have gone further up the mountainside.

It was bare and plain to view above, and they must necessarily have been in sight.

Yet they had certainly disappeared, and as effectually as if the earth had opened and swallowed them up.

"Bejabers, that's very funny," declared Barney, in a mystified state of mind. "What the divil can it mean, anyhow?"

The Steam Man went over the ground carefully. Then Frank directed their course up the mountain.

But, though they went almost to the summit, not a sign of the redskins was to be seen anywhere.

A more perplexing state of affairs could hardly be imagined.

Frank was at a loss what to do.

Then an idea occurred to him, and be wondered why it bad not come to him before.

"It may be that they have sought refuge in a secret cave," he cried.

"Whurroo!" cried Barney. "Shure, yez have struck it, Mister Frank. Why didn't we think av that afore?"

"Golly, dat's a fac'," agreed Pomp, with sudden inspiration. "Now dis chile finks on it, I seed jes' what I finks was de mouf ob dat cave, jes' a bit below yer."

"You didn't cried Frank. "Just tell me where that was, Pomp?"

"A'right, Li'l Boss, jes' go on down de mountain a leetle bit."

Frank did this. The Steam Man, under the brake, gently glided down the mountain side for some distance.

Then Pomp shouted:

"Ki, dar! See dat big hole yonder, Boss Jun'r? I fink dat be de Injuns' cave fo' suah."

A heavy mass of vines hung over the cliff wall. In them a small hole was seen against a background of blackness.

"As I live, I believe it is the entrance to a cave!" cried Frank. "We will see pretty quick."

The famous inventor run the Steam Man up to a point from whence a close inspection of the vines could be had.

It was an indisputable fact that there was a cave back of them.

How far it extended into the mountain, or what was its size, could not be at once determined.

But Frank was resolved to know, and at once took steps with that end in view.

He felt sure that the Indians with their captives had entered this cave.

Opening the cage door, Frank sprang boldly out.

There was not a little risk in this.

There might have been one or more savages lurking behind the leafy screen, all ready to give him a bullet.

But this did not prove, fortunately, to be the case.

There was no lurking savage in the vicinity. With perfect safety Frank approached the vines and lifted them.

The result was to him a most startling surprise.

A mighty high-arched cavern was thus revealed.

It was fully twenty feet in height and fifteen in width.

It was an opening in the solid rock as clearly cut as if with a steam drill.

The floor of the cave was smooth, and Frank saw that it was a very easy matter for the Steam Man to enter the place.

Satisfied of this, the young inventor decided to take the Steam Man into the cavern.

It required but little exertion to cut a sufficient aperture in the leafy screen.

Then Frank lit the headlight, which was in the Steam Man's fore-head, and which gave a powerful calcium glare.

Into the cavern the Steam Man went at a slow gait. All were safely in the cage, and Frank look care to mark the passage carefully, so that they would know the return.

But the cavern seemed an oddity in this respect.

It did not deviate into other passages, but held one straight uniform course.

Its height and width varied but a fraction anywhere, and suddenly Barney cried:

"By me sowl, Mister Frank, if there ain't the loight av day ahead."

Frank was astounded.

Surely Barney's eye sight bad not deceived him.

There was certainly daylight ahead.

What did it mean? Had the cave another opening? This would seem to be a fact.

But all doubt was quickly set aside when the Man suddenly approached the opening, and the next moment emerged with a puff into open air.

Frank was much surprised.

CHAPTER XVII.
THE FATE OF THE LONELY RANCH.

It seemed that the supposed cavern was then, after all, but a species of natural tunnel through the mountain.

The Steam Men had come again into open air and directly upon the other side of the mountain.

The fleeing savages had shrewdly adopted this mode of retreat.

They had gained a good lead in this manner and were nowhere in sight.

A sort of table land similar to the one on the other side of the mountain existed here.

In fact, it extended from north to south, as did the other.

Frank descended from the cage and examined the ground.

Fortunately it was soft and yielding, and he had little difficulty in discovering the trail.

To his surprise, it led out upon the plateau and to the North.

This was directly toward the Lonely Ranch, and Frank was puzzled.

"Well," he mused, with a queer smile, "if the Indians should ran across the outlaws there would be a battle surely."

Events were near at hand in the nature of a great surprise to the rescuers, and Frank's surmise had hit nearer the truth than he had imagined.

The truth was, one of the outlaws had run amuck in a bar-room at one of the settlements near, and killed a Comanche brave out of pure deviltry.

This fact had roused the ire of all the hostile Comanches on the Texas line, and a great war-dance had been called.

As a result several tribes had banded together, and had decided to make a raid upon the Lonely Ranch and if possible wipe Black Mask's gang out of existence.

From near and far the warriors had been congregating in the hills about.

Already a large party was ready to attack from the east.

Another was to move upon the ranch from the west, and in fact the place was literally surrounded.

Of course this fact was not yet known to Frank Reade, Jr.

But the revelation was near at band.

Suddenly Barney pointed out over the plateau with a sharp cry.

"See!" he cried. "What is that!"

A body of horsemen were riding northward across the plateau. That they were Indians it was easy to see.

"I wonder where they are going?" mused Frank. "Affairs are getting a bit complicated."

There was no doubt of this. But Arnold and Alice were in the hands of the Indians, and it was necessary to rescue them.

In order to do this, it was imperative to go where the savages were. So Frank started the Steam Man to the north also.

He waited first until the cavalcade had vanished from sight.

Then the Steam Man was put to his best speed.

The run across the plateau was quickly made.

Very soon the Man entered a pass, which led through the hills, still following the Comanche's trail.

To his surprise this brought him suddenly back upon the other side of the range, and Pomp cried:

"Golly sakes, Boss Frank, dar be de Lonely Ranch fo' a fac'!"

This was true. The outlaw's ranch was plainly visible high up on the mountain side.

Suddenly the distant crack of fire-arms, shouts and yells were heard.

Frank ran the Steam Man up higher on the elevation, and an astounding spectacle was presented.

About one hundred of the outlaws riding toward the ranch, probably upon their return from the futile quest for the escaped fugitives, had been attacked by the Comanches.

The natives were treble the number of the outlaws and literally surrounded them.

A fierce pitched battle followed.

From the mountain side those on board the Steam Man had an admirable chance to see the conflict.

The rapid firing of revolvers and rifles, and the yells of the combatants made a most terrific din.

Ever and anon riderless horses broke from the melee and dashed across the plain.

Frank Reade, Jr., had no desire to interfere in the struggle.

It was a case of dog eat dog, and the young inventor had little choice as to whom he would like to see win.

Certainly the outlaws seemed in a terrible trap, and were apparently getting the worst of it.

"Bejabers, it's the foist toime I was iver in sympathy with an Injun!" cried Barney; "but, on me worrud, I'd loike to see thim whip the snakes out av thim outlaws."

"Golly! I'd jes' like de same fing, I'ish," cried Pomp.

The two faithful servitors seemed likely to gain their desires.

But at this moment a great cry came from the ranch.

A perfect swarm of Comanches appeared about its walls.

The stockade was manned by only a handful of the outlaws.

The Comanches charged upon them like fiends.

Suddenly a bright streak of flame shot up, and then a puff of smoke.

A great cry burst from Frank's lips.

"My soul!" he gasped, "they have set the ranch on fire."

There was no denying this.

The flames spread from one building to another, and in what seemed like a very brief space the entire ranch was in full blast.

The Comanches, aided by the fire, could be plainly seen overpowering and massacring the white men.

Under ordinary Circumstances Frank would not have stood passively by and seen men of his own color thus slaughtered.

But he knew that it was simply a visitation of God upon them.

He could not think of interfering with this conviction upon him.

There was one thing certain.

One of the worst dens of iniquity and crime in the wild west was being disposed of in a summary fashion.

Frank watched the destruction of the Lonely Ranch until well satisfied that the Comanches would be victorious.

Then he turned to Barney and Pomp.

"We must act." he said, determinedly, "There is work for us to do. If we are to rescue Arnold and the girl, this is the proper time to do it."

"Look!" cried Frank, "they are cutting the outlaws down with ease."

"Begorra, that's true!" cried Barney.

"Jes' you say de word, Mister Frank." cried Pomp, readily.

Frank went to the dasher and started the Steam Man along the mountain side.

It was a random quest.

He had not the faintest idea as to where the prisoners had been taken.

But fortune aided him.

Suddenly a quick sharp yell burst from a thicket ahead, a rifle cracked and a bullet flattened itself against the wire cage.

The yell was answered by several whoops just beyond.

Frank was astute enough to understand this.

The Indian camp was no doubt close at hand. Also the young inventor reflected that it was quite likely lightly guarded, all the available men fighting at the ranch.

It was the time to strike.

"Barney and Pomp go to the loopholes," cried Frank. "Pick off every savage you can see."

"Aright, Boss Jun'r."

The Steam Man dashed through the thicket full tilt.

An Indian brave sprang up and hurled his tomahawk at the wagon.

But Pomp gave him a shot which laid him low. The next moment the Steam Man was upon the camp.

But a handful of warriors were on guard.

These fought desperately but Barney and Pomp picked them off easily under cover of the cage.

The Steam Man made a circuit of the camp and literally cleaned It out.

At a couple of posts in the verge of the camp, Arnold and Alice were bound.

A pile of brush was heaped at their feet and it was evident that the savages meant to have a torture feast upon returning from their victorious attack upon the ranch.

Pomp leaped out of the cage and cut the prisoners' bonds.

Their joy could not be fully expressed in words.

Arnold rushed to Alice's side and supported her.

"Thank God, once more we are free," he cried. "And what a joyful realization that Mr. Reade and his wonderful Steam Man is also safe."

"I think your troubles are all at an end," said Frank Reade, Jr., as he heartily greeted them.

"Thank Heaven for that," said Alice Wentworth fervently.

"You may come aboard the Steam Man, and this moment we will start for civilization."

Of course the offer was gladly accepted.

All clambered into the cage and Frank set the Steam Man's course down the pass.

A short while later they came out upon the plateau.

A course was set to the southward.

They were no longer interested in the Lonely Ranch or the fate of the outlaws.

"I doubt If one of them will escape alive," said Frank, with conviction. "Not even Haynes himself. It is a fitting end for the scoundrels."

"Indeed, I agree with you," declared Alice, fervently.

The Steam Man made swift progress to the southward.

At night they camped upon the banks of a small creek.

Barney and Pomp shot a couple of fine antelopes, and the juicy steak was soon broiling over hot coals.

All were in high spirts now.

After passing through so many trying vicissitudes it seemed as if happiness was sure to yet crown the lot of the lovers.

For a time they forgot that they were far out in the perilous wilds of the West where a multitude of dangers menaced them.

CHAPTER XVIII.
LOST IN THE FOG.

It was decided to start at an early hour the following morning.

Accordingly all rose early and preparations were made.

But the air was hazy, heavy clouds hung in the zenith and the Steam Man had not proceeded more than ten miles before a dense fog settled down like a pall over the plain.

This was so extremely dense that indeed it was difficult to tell which was the proper course to take.

The party were wholly at sea in the matter.

The Steam Man for a time proceeded slowly through the fog trying to feel its way.

Frank dared not maintain any great degree of speed for fear of collision with something.

This was a most provoking situation.

It was necessary to go ahead as fast as possible.

It was not a hard matter for the Indians to follow their trail even in the fog and the possibility that they might come upon them at any moment was not a pleasant one to contemplate by any means.

Yet what was to be done?

It was a literal conundrum.

A solution of it was looked for in vain.

Not one in the party could suggest an available plan. The only logical method seemed to be to go ahead slowly in the fog and trust to luck.

Frank proceeded to do this.

Barney and Pomp were kept at the dasher constantly on the watch.

The Man went ahead with long strides and clanking tread.

"Bejabers I can't see the fun av this sort av bizness." declared Barney. "I don't loike it at all, at all."

"Golly, I jes' agrees wif you I'ish, on dat point," averred Pomp.

"Keep yez eyes peeled, lad, an' tell me fer shure if there's anything ahead I'm likely to run into."

"I'll jes' do dat."

In this manner for some hours the party went on.

It was quite impossible to tell where they were going.

For aught they knew they would return to the very spot they came from.

There was no other way but to guess at the course they should pursue.

This was most unsatisfactory as the result speedily showed.

Suddenly Barney brought the Steam Man to a halt.

"What's the matter?" asked Frank, coming up.

"Shure, sar, do yez hear that?"

All listened with this.

A startling sound was heard.

It was like the distant roar of falling waters. What could it be?

All exchanged startled glances.

"Those are rapids, and they are not far away!" declared Frank. "We are near some canyon I'll warrant."

"You don't mean it?" cried Jack Arnold. "Perhaps then we will come back to the very hills we left."

"It would he just the luck," averred Frank.

"What shall we do?"

This was a problem.

To go ahead was dangerous.

At any moment they might go over the edge of some cliff and down to destruction and death.

The Steam Man was brought to a complete standstill. The fog seemed to increase in intensity every moment.

Frank sat down and gave himself up to study for a few moments. Then he hit upon an idea.

"There is but one way," he declared. "I must go out upon a tour of investigation."

But this announcement did not meet with favor from the others.

"Do not do it, Mr. Reade," cried Jack Arnold. "You must not risk it. You will get lost."

"Pshaw!" said Frank, impatiently. "I take no stock in that. I will look out for myself."

"Jes' you look here, Boss Jun'r!" cried Pomp, excitedly. "You jes' let dis chile go, an' he come back fo' suah. But if he be lost it bettah dan as if it was you."

"Bejabers, it's mesilf as will go," put in Barney. "Shure, Mister Frank, yez know that I am superior to Pomp in matters av this koind."

"Jes' you hol' on, I'ish!" cried Pomp, angrily. "You way off on dat. I reckon Boss Jun'r send me."

"Begorra, I'll bet yez tin dollars he won't."

"You g'way, I'ish."

"I'll break the jaw av ye!"

"No, you won't do nuffin' like dat."

"By my sowl, I will!"

"Hold on there!" cried Frank, with authority. "Keep cool, you rascals, I am master of this job."

Barney and Pomp promptly cooled down.

But they scowled and made angry faces at each other just the same. Neither would give in.

"Really, Mr. Reade," said Jack Arnold, in an aside, "I would not risk leaving the Steam Man just now. It will be very risky. If you get lost it will be a serious matter for the rest of us."

But Frank laughed lightly.

"Have no fears," he said, "I will not get lost. However, if Pomp desires he may accompany me."

Of course the sable servitor was delighted.

Barney subsided, and his desire to go in Pomp's place was only a spirit of a mischievous sort at any rate. He had ever an impulse to hector Pomp, and Pomp vice versa.

Jack Arnold and Alice had misgivings as to the propriety of the mission.

But all deferred to Frank, whose knowledge and experience certainly should count for something.

Accordingly, heavily armed, the two men left the wagon.

In a few moments they were lost to sight in the fog.

Frank headed directly for the sound of falling waters.

As they drew nearer Frank became satisfied that the water did not flow through a deep chasm, as he had at first fancied.

Indeed, it became plain to him very soon that the rapids were on a level with the plain, though the water apparently entered a gorge in some hills not far distant.

In a short while Frank and Pomp had come out upon the banks of the stream.

It was not too wide nor deep to ferry, but the water here ran with great swiftness.

Frank went to the water's edge and examined the shore.

It was clearly too rocky to safely wade here.

So he returned to the bank above.

"Well, Pomp," he said, brusquely, "it is evident that we cannot cross here."

"Does you want to cross dis stream?" asked Pomp.

"Yes."

"But is you suah dat it be de best fing to do?"

"Why, certainly. I believe the south lies in that direction. There is no other way but to cross this stream."

"A'right, sah. I does jes' as you say, Boss Jun'r."

"Well, Pomp, I think it would be well for you to go up the stream and I will go down. We must look for a good place to ford. Return to this spot and I will meet you here."

"A'right, sah,"

"The signal will be a long whistle."

"Yes, sah."

"Now look out for yourself."

"You kin jes' bet I will, Boss Jun'r. So long!"

Pomp vanished in the fog, and Frank went in the opposite direction. Neither had any idea of imminent danger, or that they were upon the eve of thrilling incidents.

Pomp made his way for some distance up the stream.

He could find no good fording place.

He kept on consequently for a long distance, in fact much further than he dreamed of.

Suddenly be became aware of a thrilling fact.

He had reached a point where the stream was fringed with bushes and seemed to run out of a kind of swampy tract of land.

He heard voices near him, and the guttural accents told him that they were the voices of savages.

Pomp was alarmed.

"Golly!" be muttered, "I reckon I jes' bettah get back to Li'l Boss an' tell him to look out jes' as quick as eber I can."

With this idea in mind Pomp started to retrace his steps along the banks of the stream.

But be had gone but a short distance when he became aware of the appalling fact that his path was cut off by the redskins.

They were directly in front of him, and Pomp was barred from further progress in that direction.

What was to be done?

He was wholly at a loss to know how to act.

He could hear the redskins plainly enough as they jabbered away in their unintelligible way.

"Golly!" he muttered. "Boss Jun'r ought to know 'bout dis fing right away. But how ebber is I to tell him, I'd like to know?"

Pomp considered a plan of making a detour of the spot and cutting off the foe in this manner.

But at that moment an incident occurred to prevent even this.

He became aware of the fact that the red men were advancing toward him.

The startled servant was not desirous of being discovered, so he started at once to retreat.

"Cracky!" he reflected. "If dem Injins jes' gits der paws on Pomp he be a gone chile fo' suah."

Back up the stream he retreated.

Of course, this was toward the swamp. In a few moments he was at its very verge.

Here he came to a halt.

He hardly knew just what move to make.

He could hear his foes coming nearer to him. He knew well the result if they readied him.

The miry surface of the swamp seemed the only avenue of escape left open to him.

Of course, Pomp did not know the extent of the swamp, nor whether it was safe for him to penetrate it or not.

But time was speeding, and something must be done at once.

Nearer the natives drew.

"Golly, I's in fo' it!" muttered Pomp. "I might jes' as well go ahead as stay here."

So into the swamp he boldly plunged. For a ways Pomp managed to make his way over the hassocks of grass all right.

Then he was brought to a halt.

What looked like water lay before him. He had no idea of its extent or depth, and only knew that it would be folly for him to venture into it.

Here was a predicament.

The frightened older man was wholly at his wits' ends.

"Glory fo' goodness!" he gasped. "What ebber did I leave Boss Jun'r fo', anyway? I jes' reckon dis chile be done fo' dis time fo' suah. If I ebber gits out ob dis alibe, I's lucky."

Indeed, it looked as if he was right in this premise.

Pomp was hesitating whether to go ahead or give himself up to the natives, when he heard the foe close in his rear.

Suddenly a dark, sinewy form rose from the grass seemingly at his very feet and grappled with him.

Pomp was so astonished that he hardly had time to prepare for the attack.

But instinctively he recovered and grappled with his opponent.

CHAPTER XIX.
SURROUNDED BY WOLVES.

Pomp instantly found that he had a powerful antagonist.

The red man was a giant in strength and for a moment it seemed as if he must overcome the black man.

But Pomp braced up wonderfully and got a short hold upon the Indian. He knew that his life depended on the struggle.

Somewhat singularly the savage did not make an outcry or attempt to call his fellows to his aid.

The reason for this very likely was the fact that he was desirous of being the lucky one to secure Pomp's scalp.

On the other hand, Pomp was determined that he should not.

The other savages did not come up and appeared to know nothing of the contest.

This was fortunate for Pomp.

There in the mire and the deep grass the desperate straggle went on.

Now one was beneath and then up again, and so it went on in uneven fashion for a long time.

It seemed quite impossible for Pomp to outdo his opponent.

On the other hand, the redskin did not seem able to do anything with the black man. It was an even struggle.

It might have continued until both could struggle no longer, had it not been for a fortunate incident for Pomp.

The Indian tripped once over one of the hassocks.

Pomp was quick to follow up the advantage, and the next moment his knife sank to the hit in the man's breast.

The native fell without a groan.

The straggle was ended.

Pomp was victorious.

He bad good reason to congratulate himself, but this was not the end.

Hardly had the struggle ended when a wild Indian yell broke the stillness of the night air.

Pomp saw a herd of the savages swooping down upon him in the gloom.

Pop at once fled.

He did not give such great heed as to where his footsteps led him in his great haste.

Dashing through the swamp grass, he skirted the lake of water.

Either his foes lost his track, or they dared not follow, for they quickly fell out of hearing.

Pomp, breathless and exhausted, came to a halt in the midst of the tall grass.

"Golly be," he muttered, with a thrill of joy; "I's jes' mighty glad dis chile fooled dem barbarians so easy. I reckon if I kin reach de prairie now, I's jes' able to fin' Frank Reade, Jr., an' de Steam Man."

With this conclusion, Pomp started in a direction which he believed would bring him to the open plain.

For a time be floundered on through the grass and mud.

Then he saw ahead what he believed and what really was the plain.

A few more steps and be would reach it.

Pomp plunged ahead and left the mire behind him, as he believed.

He leaped forward upon what he believed to be level, hard ground. But alas for his expectations!

As it chanced, it was a muck hole right on the verge of the plain.

The moment he struck it, Pomp went in to the waist.

In vain he tried to flounder out of it.

Every exertion only caused him to sink the deeper.

Every moment he went deeper and deeper, and in a few moments he was immovably fixed to his arm-pits in the mire.

Here was a serious dilemma.

Words cannot express the poor man's sensations. He was almost beside himself with horror and despair.

"Fo' Hebben's sake!" he cried, despairingly. "Whatebber will dis chile do? I'se done gwin to sink out ob sight altogedder in dis place!"

In fact, it seemed as if he were right.

Every moment be seemed to be sinking deeper and deeper.

It seemed but a question of time when the mire would completely engulf him.

"Golly sakes, dis be a gone ole chile," wailed Pomp. "I jes' don' know what to do. If only Li'l Boss would come."

Indeed, it was a hard position for the poor man.

He dared not shout for help for fear of attracting the attention of the Comanches to the spot.

If the Indians should discover him in his present position it would be a serious matter for him.

But at this moment Pomp felt his feet touch bed rock.

He knew that he could not sink any further.

But even with this morsel of comfort his position was a desperate one.

He might escape suffocation in the mire only to become confronted with one of the most horrible of deaths, starvation, and death by slow, lingering stages.

Pomp was utterly unable to move hand or foot.

The mire held him as in a vise.

Time passed and poor Pomp felt as uncomfortable in his horrible position as could well be imagined.

Several times be was tempted to shout for help.

But he knew that this would only result in bringing down death upon him at the bands of the Comanches.

Time passed slowly and dismally.

Pomp listened for some sounds which would satisfy him that friends were near.

But no sound of the kind came to him.

All was the stillness of the grave.

Pomp began to grow nervous.

An awful horror came upon him. His brain seemed turning.

What would be the end? How long before death would come to relieve his sufferings?

These queries flashed across him and his brain seemed likely to burst with the horror upon it.

Ages were contained in the minutes which passed.

Oh, God! Would no end come? Better death than this awful suspense.

If only the fog would give way to daylight it would be a mighty relief.

But the black pall of the fog hung down gloomy and foreboding.

When it seemed as If the dead silence would burst his brain, relief came in a manner which was most unwelcome.

Suddenly a chilling, terrible sound broke the stillness.

It was the distant, mournful howl of the prairie wolf.

In a few moments it was answered again and again, until the air seemed filled with the horrible cadence.

Pomp's blood seemed to congeal.

He had no doubt that the savage horde had scented him, and were coming to tear in pieces such of him as was above the ground.

Every moment the howls of the rapacious beasts became plainer, and they drew nearer each instant.

Soon the terrified Pomp could see their shadowy forms rustling through the gloom in near proximity.

Their glaring eyeballs were like stars of fire in the fog, and their snapping jaws were easily heard.

All around the mud hole the savage crew gathered.

At first they circled about the man, making unsuccessful lunges at him, not daring to risk being engulfed in the mud hole.

Every moment Pomp expected that they would reach him, and he was in a paroxysm of fear and suspense.

"Golly, dis means I be a gone chile," he wailed. "Oh, if only Boss Jun'r would come to help dis chile one lily bit,"

But Frank Reade, Jr., at that moment was too far from the spot to be able to render any material assistance.

In vain Pomp strove to wriggle from the clinging mire.

It was an utter impossibility, and at length he desisted in the attempt.

A sort of resignation to his fate came over him, and be awaited what he believed was his certain end.

The wolves continued to howl and snap at him, but he was just beyond their reach.

They feared to enter the treacherous mire, their acute instinct keeping them from it.

Finally, one getting too near the edge went in.

In an instant the savage brute was yelping and floundering in the deep mire. His best efforts did not succeed in extricating him.

He sank deeper and deeper, until finally the suction of the mire carried him under the surface and the struggle was quickly over.

One of the brutes had gone to its final account.

Pomp realized how narrow had been his escape from death.

Had he been one foot shorter in stature his fate would surely have been sealed.

As it was his head was above the surface.

He could, however, only breathe with difficulty, as the pressure upon his chest was so very great.

One of the wolves had succumbed to the influence of the mire.

This seemed to be a sort of warning to the others.

They kept their distance. But this did not seem to diminish the hope in their savage breasts that they might yet win their prey.

They made every effort to reach the imprisoned prey.

It was with no slight amount of relief that Pomp saw that they were unable to do this.

Hope began once more to revive in the servant's breast.

The fog must lift some time. There was no doubt but that his friends would look for him.

It was possible that they would find and rescue him from his distressing position.

At least he hoped so. He had almost infallible confidence in the ability of Frank Reade, Jr., to affect his rescue.

So he began to look forward to the lifting of the fog with great hope.

But suddenly new and strange sounds burst upon the air.

The wolves dispersed like chaff before a rattling volley of rifle balls.

Then for a moment a delirium of joy seized Pomp. He believed that rescue had come.

It was his firm conviction that his friends had come to his relief at last.

But this hope was, alas, destined to be ruthlessly dashed, as had others before it.

CHAPTER XX.
IN THE HANDS OF THE SAVAGES.

The volley of rifle balls was quickly followed by a chorus of savage yells.

Pomp's heart fell.

If it had been possible he would have turned pale at that moment.

"Glory fo' goodness!" he gasped, in dismay. "It's de Injuns an' dis is a gone boy now fo' suah."

Feeling that he would rather die in the mire than to fall into the bands of the Comanches Pomp kept perfectly quiet.

But the Indians were not to be deceived by any means.

They knew that the wolves had treed something, and they were suspicious what it was.

In a few moments they had scattered the savage beasts.

Then they drew closer with a flaming torch, which served to partially dispel the gloom.

It required but a few moments of keen searching for them to discover Pomp in the mire.

The effect upon the Indians was most ludicrous.

They were disposed to treat the matter as a joke, and laughed wildly and hilariously.

They thrust the torch in his face and uttered tantalizing cries and yells. Poor Pomp's position was a most uncomfortable and perilous one.

Yet the older man did not lose courage or give his foes the satisfaction of showing temper.

He was cool and self-possessed through all, and waited until his captors had tired of such treatment.

Then a couple of saplings were felled and placed across the mud hole.

Out upon these one of the natives crawled and inserted the loop of a lariat under the arms of the imprisoned man.

This was in turn bound to the saplings. Three Indians at each end of the saplings lifted heavily enough to raise Pomp bodily from the mire pit.

Released from his fearful position, Pomp felt a strong sense of relief, even though he knew that his fate was scarcely a better one.

Pulled from the mire, Pomp was in the midst of his captors.

The mud clung to his clothes and body, and he was a sorry looking sight.

But in spite of this, he was hustled around in lively fashion by the Comanches.

They laughed and jeered at him in a mocking way, sticking the points of their hunting knives into his flesh and pinching him unmercifully.

But Pomp stood this kind of torture well, and, on the whole, got the best of his foes.

But the savages soon tired of this.

The nest move was to bind Pomp to a mustang. Then, mounting their ponies, they dashed away across the plain, with Pomp in their midst.

For several miles they rode on in the blind fog.

How they could locate themselves or their direction was a mystery to Pomp.

But they suddenly pulled up in the edge of a line of timber.

Here they turned loose the pony to which Pomp was hound.

The animal maddened with lashing blows darted out upon the plain.

Pomp now saw their purpose at a glance.

It was evident that the redskins meant to have a rough game, common among them with a captured foe.

Each savage was provided with a long lash whip made of a lariat.

This he would nourish over his head and whenever brought within reach of the prisoner, the latter would be sure of a terrible blow.

After the captive like a pack of wolves came the savages.

Now they had headed off the pony on which Pomp was.

Down upon him they came and the blows began to fall.

Given with such cutting force they nearly crazed Pomp. He could not dodge nor avoid them. It was possible that with guidance his pony might have outfooted the others.

But unguided as it was the poor animal ran hither and thither in a confused way.

At every turn Pomp was exposed to fresh blows.

It was an agonizing experience and could not be expected to last long.

This was too much to expect of human endurance. Already Pomp began to feel weak and faint.

"Golly!" he muttered, with clenched lips. "I reckon dat dis time fo' suah dis boy be done fo'."

But even in the face of what looked like such certain death Pomp was all pluck.

He did not fail to exert every means of which he could think to make his escape.

He began at first to work on the bonds which bound his wrists.

At first he could make no impression whatever upon these. But now, probably owing to the strain of the horse's gallop, he felt them relax.

A thrill shot through his frame. Was he to gain his freedom? It was a daring hope.

He kept a cool and steady head. With great calmness but celerity, he worked upon the bonds.

The gang of savage captors were just swooping down upon him upon his right hand, and he felt that he could not survive another attack.

With a desperate effort Pomp freed one hand.

In an inner pocket of his jacket he knew that he had a small sheath knife.

It required but an instant to do this.

A quick slash and his bonds were cut.

The savages saw the move and a wild wail went up. Fearful of losing their prey, they urged their horses forward at full speed.

But Pomp picked up the rawhide reins on his pony's neck.

He gave the little animal a quick blow with his hand.

Then across the plain in the fog Pomp went at full speed. After him came the red foe.

One of them, upon a fleet pony, was suddenly alongside of him.

The savage evidently was desirous of capturing Pomp alive, for he did not attempt to shoot.

On the contrary, he reined his horse close to Pomp's and throwing out his long arms, completely encircled Pomp's.

Pomp was so astonished that for a moment he could not act.

But it was only for a moment.

Pomp hung on to his pony like a Centaur. The result was that he literally pulled the Indian from his horse.

Then Pomp's fingers closed about his red foe's windpipe.

The savage made an attempt to use his knife.

The weight of the two men for a moment caused the little pony to sag.

But the shutting off of the savage's wind had the desired effect.

The Comanche reeled, and his muscles grew lax.

With a tremendous exertion Pomp threw the savage from him.

The Comanche struck the hard floor of the prairie with a rebound, and the pony, relieved of its double weight, went on like a flash.

The Indians in pursuit yelled fiercely, but at that moment the fog lifted, and Pomp beheld a wonderful and cheering sight.

There, not one hundred yards distant, was the Steam Man.

That he was seen was quickly evident, for a loud whistle went up on the air.

Then a volley was fired in the midst of the savages.

They broke and fled in wild confusion. Then Pomp tumbled from his pony close beside the Man, and the next moment was in the cage with his friends.

"Pomp, where on earth did you go to?" cried Frank Reade, Jr., as he almost embraced dark servant.

Explanations quickly followed.

It seemed that Frank had returned to the Steam Man after losing truck of Pomp.

A close search had been made for him, and by the best of good luck be had been found at a critical moment.

The fog now quickly lifted.

Frank started the Steam Man away once more on her southward course at a lively gait.

They were much relieved to find that they had not gone far out of their course, and that they were not in any close proximity to the hills.

"Begorra, it's mighty glad I am that yez are back agin, poxy lad," cried Barney, vigorously, as he embraced his colored compatriot. "Shure, it's mesilf as wud hate to see yez lose thim beautiful raven locks av yours to the Comanche, by me sowl."

"Huh! Don' you talk about my raven locks," sniffed Pomp, as he partook of the sarcasm in Barney's remarks. "I jes' tell you fo' a suttin fac' dat if dey had dem red hairs ob your'n in dere possession dey would use dem to light fires in dere wigwams wid."

Barney was bound to admit that he had got the worst of it this time.

Everybody laughed and Frank Reade, Jr., cried:

"Well, friends, if we have luck the days will not be many before we will have reached a land where scalps will be quite safe."

This evoked a cheer and the spirits of all revived. It began to look as if more auspicious things were in store in the near future.

CHAPTER XXI.
THE END.

The Steam Man kept on to the southward for many days.

They left No Man's Land far behind them. The remembrances of the Lonely Ranch were to Alice Wentworth as a vivid nightmare. Luckily they did not fall in with the Comanches upon their return. The Indians undoubtedly for several hundred miles had congregated in the vicinity of the Lonely Ranch.

That the ranch had been destroyed and the band of outlaws broken up there was no doubt.

All felt sure of this and regrets, it may be safely said, were few.

"I jes' finks dat Mistuh Haynes hab got his pay afo' dis fo' his rapscallion tricks." affirmed Pomp, confidently.

"I shall not be sorry to know that he has expiated his crimes," said Jack Arnold, sincerely.

Alice shivered and placed her hands over her eyes, as if she would fain shut out some most unpleasant pictures.

But as a rule the spirits of all were extremely bright on the return. Barney and Pomp were exuberant now that the trip had proved a success.

They were keener than ever in playing practical jokes upon each other.

Barney had thus far come out ahead, but Pomp was determined not to be beaten, and an opportunity came for him to pay off the score upon his friend in a rich manner.

One evening they camped upon the banks of a lake.

To the right of the camping place was a small bog, through which ran a brook.

The mire in the bog was very soft and slimy and deep as well.

Pomp had gone to fetch water to the camp and had made a careful examination of the bog.

He threw a stone into the slimy ooze and saw it disappear almost instantly. Then he gave a chuckle.

"Hi yi!" he muttered, jubilantly. "Der be a glorious chaince to git squar' wif dat no 'count I'ishman. I jes' fink I does dat."

He went down and examined the edge of the bog.

There was a narrow part of it which he easily leaped.

He surveyed the ground carefully and then began to make preparations for the job.

First he stretched a line loosely from a stake driven in the ground just below the most slimy part of the bog.

To a stake above be carried this, and thence diagonally across the brook.

By pulling the line it would rise full two feet in the air and then fall back again. In the deep grass it was invisible.

With these preparations completed Pomp went back to camp.

He busied himself about the evening meal.

Barney came around after awhile.

The Celt's eyes were dancing with fun. He was all ready to play some prank upon his companion.

Pomp realized this fact and grinned.

"I'll jes' fix you, I'ish," he muttered, under his breath. "I reckon you let dis chile alone hereaftah."

"Begorra, iv it ain't the eejit," chaffed Barney, coming up quietly, "the top av the aivenin' to yez, Afriky!"

"Hullo, you no 'count I'ishman," replied Pomp. "What you want here?"

"Shure, I came around to pay me respects," replied Barney, with gravity.

"If you paid yo' bills as well you would have a big credit, I'ish."

"Bejabers, I niver knew a black man to pay fer anythin'."

"I always pays a bet, I'ish, If I loses."

"Begorra, yez have to do that."

"Does I!"

"Shure, yez do."

"Well, I'll make a bet wif yoose, I'ish, which youse will haf to pay."

"Whurroo!" scoffed Barney. "Yez niver did it yet."

"Well, I'll do it dis time."

"What is it, lad!"

"I'll bet you five dollahs even, dat you can't make de jump I did dis aftuhnoon."

Now if there was one thing in the world Barney prided himself on it was his leaping ability.

He had repeatedly defeated Pomp, so that this declaration was to him like a red rag to a mad bull.

"Put up your money, eejit."

To Barney's surprise and delight Pomp pulled out a five dollar gold piece. The Irishman could not get out of covering it.

"Jes' you comes wif me, I'ish," said Pomp, warily.

He led the way to the bog. At the spot where he had looped it he halted.

"Dar, I'ish. You kain see where I jes' jumped across dar. I bet you five dollahs you kain' leap it aftah me."

Barney snickered.

"Bejabers, that's no jump at all," he cried. "Go ahead, lad, an' thin I'll give yez an opportunity to pay over yer money."

"A'right, I'ish. I pay de money if you makes de jump."

Pomp went back a few feet and cleared the bog hole at a light bound.

Barney roared with laughter.

"Ho, ho, ho!" he laughed. "Yez have a foine idea av me jumpin' ability, I must say. Jist howld yer hosses now, an' I'll show ye how Barney O'Shea can jump."

Barney went back a few feet to get a good run.

Pomp crouched down in the grass.

The Celt started for the edge of the bog hole. But just as be reached it, a surprising thing occurred.

Pomp gave the line a twitch.

It rose just as Barney reached the edge of the bog.

The Irishman's ankles struck it and he was tripped up. Like a stone out of a catapult he shot out and down into the nasty slimy ooze of the bog.

What followed was most comical.

Pomp literally rolled upon the ground with paroxysms of laughter. His scheme had worked even better than he had dared to hope that it would.

Barney floundered about in the soft ooze. He was puffing and spitting and wheezing like a rhinoceros, when he at length pulled himself out on the bank.

"Tare an' 'ounds!" he gasped. "Whativer give me such a fall as that? Shure it must av been an optical delusion, for the distance was greater thin I had supposed."

"Ho, ho, ho!" roared Pomp. "I jes' fink yous no good at all, I'ish. You kain' jump a little bit."

Barney was silent.

Through his befogged brain an inkling of the truth was just beginning to creep.

He began to suspect that Pomp had by this time got the best of him. Barney was abundantly able to appreciate a good thing even if played upon himself.

He said not a word, but crept down to the lake and washed the mud from his person and clothing, and hung the latter up to dry.

It was an hour before he showed up in camp.

Pomp made no mention of the affair, but coolly pocketed the ten dollars in stake money.

Barney did not demur, and for a time Pomp enjoyed perfect immunity from practical joking.

The Steam Man was making very rapid progress toward Texas.

One day the Man came in sight of a small settlement.

Here a stop was made.

They were short of provisions and of fuel. A coal mine chanced to be near, and the bunkers were filled.

The first evening of this stop in the settlement, which was called Prairie City, a thrilling event occurred.

It was an incident which served to bring to a close the exciting episodes of the Steam Man's incursion into No Man's Land.

There was a small tavern in the center of the town.

Upon this evening, Frank and Arnold stood upon the steps of the hotel, when the clutter of hoofs was heard and a black horse came madly careering down the street.

Upon the animal's back was the form of a man.

But the rider seemed in distress hanging over the saddle-bow, with his head fallen upon his chest.

A great cry went up from the loungers about the hotel.

The black horse dashed up to the hotel entrance, and several men sprang out to catch the rider, who would have fallen to the ground.

His person was seen to be covered with blood from many wounds.

He was carried into the bar-room and stretched out upon a bunk or cot-bed which was procured.

Frank and Arnold saw his pallid, drawn features and gave a start of surprise.

"Heavens!" gasped Arnold. "It is Harold Haynes."

The villain, for he it was, heard the exclamation, and looked up.

"Reade!" he gasped, in a husky voice, "the game is up. Come here, I want to tell you something before I die."

"I fear that you are about to die, Harold Haynes," said Frank, sternly, as he bent down over the villain. "If you wish to die easy you had better confess your crimes."

"That is what I wish to do," said Haynes feebly. "I may as well make a clean breast of it. Take my affidavit."

Frank produced pen and paper. Witnesses were at hand, and then Haynes began:

"You may put down that I make this statement in sound mind and of my own free will."

Frank did so.

"I am guilty of the murder of Hiram Wentworth. I make free and absolute confession of that crime. I am about to die and cheat the gallows, but I shall expect to be justly dealt with hereafter. I repent the crime, and with this statement end my life."

Haynes lay back upon the cot, gasping for death.

Frank signed the confession and it was duly witnessed. Then one of the bystanders who was a bit of a surgeon advanced and placed a hand upon Haynes' pulse.

"The struggle is over!" he said; "the man is dead!"

Harold Haynes was buried in Prairie City. The mystery of Hiram Wentworth's death was solved at last.

From Prairie City the Steam Man went to a station upon the Southern Pacific Railroad.

Here the Man was shipped in sections to Readestown. The great expedition to No Man's Land was ended.

The details of the affair created a great sensation in the country. Frank Reade, Jr., and Barney and Pomp became heroes in the eyes of all.

Jack Arnold and Alice Wentworth were married upon the return to Chicago, and there they are living happily to-day.

The Steam Man returned to Readestown, but it was not long to remain inactive, for Frank was suddenly called away upon yet another excursion with his wonderful invention, the thrilling incidents of which may be found in a future number.

[THE END]

Frank Reade, Jr.

With His New Steam Man In Central America

BY LUIS SENARENS

AUTHOR OF "FRANK READE, JR. WITH HIS NEW STEAM MAN IN NO MAN'S LAND; OR, ON A MYSTERIOUS TRAIL," ETC., ETC.

CHAPTER I.

A STRANGE STORY FROM YUCATAN.

Frank Reade, Jr., the distinguished inventor of many wonderful machines, and particularly the new Steam Man, sat in his library one winter's day reading a newspaper.

His wife sat near him engaged in some light needle work. She looked up to see a peculiar expression upon her husband's handsome face.

"Well, that is strange," exclaimed Frank Reade, Jr., with a whistle of surprise. "I am positive that is my old friend, Buckden, whom I knew at college. Upon my word, this breaks me all up."

"What is it, Frank?" asked Mrs. Reade, with interest.

"Why, Tony Buckden, an old college mate of mine, it seems has turned his wits to mining engineering. This has taken him down to Central America, to Yucatan, and a cablegram has just been received in New York, stating that Tony had become separated from his party and lost in the jungle. For six weeks he was searched for in vain."

"How terrible."

"It is more than likely that he has fallen a prey to wild beasts. Yet his father, the millionaire, Thomas Buckden, of New York, comes out with an offer of $50,000 to the person who will furnish positive proof that his son is alive, and bring him safely home."

"That is a large reward," ventured Mrs. Reade. "I hope somebody will win it."

Poor Tony!" exclaimed Frank, with emotion. "I declare I almost feel it my duty to go to his rescue."

"What! leave home again so soon?"

"Yet what is my duty, dear wife? It would seem that my dear friend's life is at stake. Ought I not to sacrifice something to save him?"

"What? You don't really think of going yourself?"

"I don't know," replied Frank, agitatedly pacing the floor. "I don't see who else can go and stand the rigors of that climate, dare the dangers the jungle, the wild beasts and natives, and succeed in rescuing Tony."

"Are you sure that you can do it?"

"Ought I not to be reasonably sure? Have I not the Steam Man? Barney and Pomp I am sure would go with me."

"I hope you will not be so foolish as to go."

"I cannot say yet, my dear. I must satisfy myself completely that it is my duty. But I think I will walk down to the shop and see the Steam Man."

Frank bent down and kissed his wife and children and then left the house.

But just as he was going down the steps the mail carrier handed him a letter. Thus it was superscribed:

"To Frank Reade Jr.,
Readestown, U. S. A."

Frank glanced at the foreign postmark and then broke the seal and read:

"Dear Friend Frank—I have been thinking of you of late and so feel constrained to write you. Moreover, I have a big scheme in which I want to interest you. While at Campeche I fell in with a native trader from Valladolid. I was fortunate enough to do him a service and gain his friendship, and as a reward he accorded me a most astonishing tale and secret.

"He told me of his travels in the interior through jungle and swamp and forest. Also of the deadly animals and reptiles, the poisonous insects, and all the great dangers and pitfalls of the traveler in those latitudes.

"But more than this, he told me a wonderful story of a ruined city far up in the inaccessible table lands of Peten.

"No doubt you are familiar with the accounts of the ancient cities of Palenque and others. Well, I imagine that this ruined city, Mazendla he called it, is one of the same sort.

"But Metlo, which is the name of my informant, described a vast temple in which he said there was vast treasures of gold, silver and jewels. But ever since discovered this temple has been a perfect nest of gigantic anacondas, and none of the natives have ever ventured into the place.

"Only one man ever lived to get out of the place, and he brought forth enough gold and jewels to insure his wealth for life.

"And there to-day lies untold wealth all in the possession or the anacondas.

"Many attempts have been made by the natives to destroy the snakes. A great body of men once attempted it. Six of the snakes were killed, but there seemed to be fully half a hundred left. The place seemed alive with them, and a dozen men falling victims to the monsters the attempt was abandoned.

"From that day to this no attempt has been made to recover the wealth. Metlo told me that no white man ever visited the region.

"The journey thither is a dangerous one on account of beasts and poisonous reptiles. Yet I believe it can be made. I have thought of you and your wonderful Steam Man and I feel sure that with the aid of you and your wonderful invention the treasure can be recovered.

"Now, Frank, I humbly beg of you if possible come down here and embark in this enterprise with me.

"Of course I have plenty of money, my father being a millionaire, but I have a powerful desire to visit the ruined city of Mazendla and do battle with those anacondas.

"I can do it alone, but I can succeed better with the aid of your Steam Man. As a favor I beg of you to write me at once to Campeche. And now, my dear Frank, hoping to hear from you soon and favorably, I am as ever your friend.

TONY BUCKDEN."

Frank Reade, Jr., drew a deep breath as he finished reading this stirring epistle.

His eyes shone like stars and his whole being was stirred up.

It was certainly just the kind of a trip he would fancy. His adventurous spirit was fired and he muttered:

"That is a new field to explore. And I would like to try it. But let me see! This letter has been coming by lazy stages and has been three weeks on the way. The cablegram was received a few days ago. Since then he has become lost in the jungle. Poor Tony! He must be rescued, and who is there to do it but me?"

Frank passed down the street in deep abstraction of mind.

The wind was chill and piercing, and there was snow in the air, as well as on the ground.

Suddenly around a corner came a man on the dead run.

But as his feet struck a bit of ice, they went out from under him, and he went sliding clear across the sidewalk and into a vast snow bank.

He was literally buried, but quickly dug himself out, spluttering and jawing like mad.

"I jes' pays yuh back fo' dat, I'ish. Yuh jes' stop yo' foolin' wif dis chile, or yuh gits inter trubbel right away. Jes' yuh hear dat."

"Whurroo! Bejabers, it's a foine looking buffalo yez are now. Ha, ha, ha! Yez would pass for a Santa Claus now to be shure. It's nearer white yez are than yez iver will be again."

The victim of the snow bank, who, as the reader may have guessed, was a black man, dug the snow from his ears and eyes with supreme rage and disgust.

His companion was an Irishman, as his rich brogue would indicate. They had been having a lark at snow-balling, and the Irishman was chasing the negro around the corner when he took his fall.

It required but a glance for Frank Reade, Jr., to recognize the sky-larkers.

They were faithful servitors of his, and were named Barney and Pomp.

They were a legacy from Frank's father, and in all the famous young inventor's travels these servants had accompanied him.

Nobody could be more attached to a master than they were to Frank.

And now, as they caught sight of him approaching, they straightened up and both doffed their hats.

"I's done glad, to see yuh, Boss Frank."

"I hope yez air well, Mister Frank."

"Barney and Pomp!" cried Frank, eagerly. "You are just the fellows I want to see."

"Whurroo!" shouted Barney. "We're ready for anythin', Mister Frank, from a shindy to a ruction."

"I don't doubt it," replied Frank with a smile. "But here's a letter you may read, and tell me what you think of it."

"A letter!" gasped Barney.

He took the missive, and with Pomp at his shoulder, it was read by both. Frank watched them intently.

It was evident that the letter had made a powerful impression upon them.

"Well!" said Frank, when they had finished. "What do you think of it?"

"Bejabers I'd loike nothing better than a go at some av them forty foot snakes. Shure it's a foine trip that would be fer the Steam Man, Mister Frank."

"Ki dar, Boss Jun'r!" cried Pomp, with eyes big as moons. "Kain't say dis chile likes snakes, but yuh kin jes' bet he'd like to go dar jes' de same."

"Good!" cried Frank, "then if I conclude to go, you'll be all ready?"

"Yuh kin jes' bet we will."

"Make no doubt av that."

"All right," said Frank, buttoning his coat closer, "be in readiness for I may decide to go."

The young inventor went on down the street.

In a few moments he came to the entrance of the big yards of the Reade Machine Shop.

Here at the entrance was the sumptuously furnished office. Frank entered, and an elderly patrician-looking gentleman who was pacing the floor, excitedly rushed up to him, crying:

"Are you Mr. Frank Reade, Jr.?"

"I am," replied Frank.

"Thank God you have come at last! Here is my card."

Frank took it and read:

"Thomas Buckden, New York City."

"Indeed!" exclaimed the young inventor, affably. "I am glad to welcome you here, Mr. Buckden. I believe I know your son well, and-"

"Oh, then you remember him well," cried the old gentleman, excitedly. "Thank Heaven for that! It will perhaps influence you to accede to the request I have to make. Oh, have—have you heard about my son?"

"I have heard that your son at last accounts had become lost in the jungle," replied Frank.

"Yes, yes, but we believe that he has been captured and held a prisoner by a wild tribe of savages known in that vicinity as the Petens."

"It is quite likely."

"God grant it may be so. Oh, sir, listen to an agonized father's prayers. They tell me that you have the necessary equipments and are the only man who can go into those wilds and rescue my boy.

Now I am a wealthy man and will pay—"

"Stop!" said Frank, imperatively. "Do not speak to me of pay! I knew your son; he was my college friend. I am only too glad to be able to go to his aid. I will say this much that before three days I shall start from New Orleans with my Steam Man on board a special steamer for Campeche. You may if you choose see to the chartering of the steamer."

"A fleet if you wish it!" cried Mr. Buckden. "Oh, accept my deepest gratitude, Mr. Reade, and—bring my boy safely back."

"I will try," replied Frank.

"God bless you! But this wonderful Steam Man—I have never seen it."

"Come with me and I will be glad to show it to you," said Frank. The young inventor led the way into a high roofed chamber with large doors which opened out into the yard.

Here was a sight such as Mr. Buckden had never seen the like of. Standing in the center of the huge chamber was the Steam Man, the wonder of the century.

Since his western trip Frank had had the Man thoroughly repaired, and he was now in perfect condition to go out upon a trip.

"What do you think of him?" asked Frank.

"Simply wonderful!" replied Mr. Buchden, admiringly.

"If you will please step this way I will be glad to show you how he is made, and how he is able to go."

Frank led the way to the other side of the invention, and then with pardonable pride began explicitly to illustrate the fine points of the Steam Man.

CHAPTER II.
IN YUCATAN.

"You can see that he is constructed of plates of iron," said Frank, explanatively. "The legs are reservoirs for water, the furnace is in his chest and the smoke-pipe is his high hat. The guage and indicator and throttle as well as steam chest are upon his back. In his mouth you will see the whistle.

"Then you will observe the steel driving rods down his legs. Of course it required some clever mechanical skill, but it can be seen at a glance that the machine is a practicable and feasible one. Just as much so as a locomotive."

"But ten times more wonderful," declared Mr. Buckden.

"Perhaps so. Now you can see that this is the wagon drawn by the Steam Man. In this wagon we carry a supply of coal, provisions and weapons. It is covered with a wire screen made of toughest steel and able to withstand a rifle ball.

"Through this opening in the front come the reins by which I drive the Man. The loop-holes in the sides are to fire through. Indeed, sir, the wagon is a small fortress in itself."

"I should say so," agreed the millionaire, "and what an admirable thing for this trip to Yucatan. In that land of poisonous reptiles and insects you can travel with immunity for it would puzzle a fly to get through that screen."

"I think it is the proper vehicle to travel with there," agreed Frank. "I believe that the region where your son will be likely to be found is one of level sort, flat tablelands and plains."

"I believe so!"

"Ah, well, I will promise to do the best I can to save him."

"I thank you!"

A short while later Mr. Buckden took his departure.

Now that Frank's mind had been made up to take the trip, he lost no time in making preparations.

His father, when acquainted with the project, shook his head wistfully and said:

"I only wish I was as young and supple as I once was. How I'd like to go along!"

Barney and Pomp were over-enthusiastic over the project.

They were on hand promptly and assisted in the preparations.

The wagon was quite spacious and would carry a good deal. Provisions of a portable kind were packed, and plenty of ammunition.

Frank took care also to supply himself with drugs, for he did not forget that it was a malarial country that he was going to.

One thing was much in their favor, and that was the season of the year, it being winter.

Naturally the climate would not be so hot as in mid-summer.

When the report was spread that Frank Reade, Jr., and his Steam Man were going to Central America, the whole country was deeply interested.

The newspapers contained sketches of the young inventor and his famous machine.

People traveled hundreds of miles to Readestown for a look at the great Steam Man, the wonder of the age.

Scientists and explorers were continually besieging Frank, and the young inventor was quite worn out with the importunities of many when the day set for starting came.

At length the day came.

The Steam Man was placed aboard a special car and shipped to New Orleans direct.

Here Mr. Buckden had seen to the chartering of a steamer, aboard which the travelers went.

A tremendous crowd were at the wharf to cheer the voyagers.

It was a great day for New Orleans.

But at length the steamer's bell rung for starting.

Frank shook hands warmly with Mr. Buckden.

"I feel sure that you will rescue my son," declared the agonized father. "Heaven will aid you."

"I will do all in my power," said Frank, earnestly.

The schooner cast loose from the levee and shot down into the current. A band played, the people cheered, and Frank Reade, Jr., Barney and Pomp and the Steam Man were really off upon their trip to Central America.

A short while later they passed through the jetties at the delta of the Mississippi, and were in the waters of the Gulf.

The voyage to Campeche was not a long one and most propitious.

When at length they entered the Bay of Campeche the mild land breeze and a view of the palm-studded shore told them that they were in a tropical clime.

To the surprise of our voyagers, a warm reception was accorded them at Campeche.

The Spanish people, ever of an enthusiastic, sport-loving turn, turned out in great force to welcome the distinguished visitors.

Word had been received by cablegram of their coming.

The governor of Campeche warmly welcomed Frank, and for a few hours he was taken charge of by a committee and treated to many hospitalities.

There were many of his own people in the town also—merchants connected with houses in New York that dealt in dye stuffs, fruits and many of the products of the country.

Frank was deeply impressed with the warmth of the welcome given him.

He thanked all his benefactors kindly.

Then at the most favorable moment he returned to the ship.

The Steam Man was brought ashore and exhibited to the wondering gaze of the people.

But Frank knew the importance of quick and prompt action, and was not the one to readily accede to delay.

He knew that every moment was to the success of his enterprise of vital worth.

The people were all in sympathy with his enterprise.

Tony Buckden had been well and favorably known in Campeche.

The young engineer was very popular there, and everybody was deeply interested in his fate.

But Señor Gonzales, one of the patrician gentlemen of Campeche, came to Frank and said:

"Señor Americano, I hope you will succeed with all my heart. But do not be disappointed if you do not find the young Señor Buckden."

"Ah, then you think the chances are few?" asked Frank.

"I speak of what I know. The dangers of interior Yucatan are known to none better than I. I fear the worst for your friend."

"But I can at least try."

"Si Señor. May the mother be with you," said the Spanish gentleman, warmly.

Frank lost no time now in making the Steam Man ready for the start.

One day was consumed in making a map of his route, as nearly correct as he could gather in detail from the natives who penetrated the interior.

Frank had decided to proceed at once to the table-land of Peten.

This point gained he believed that he could there learn something more of the fate of young Buckden.

He consulted with every native guide and traveler who knew anything about the route.

But now a curious thing occurred.

Every man he encountered seemed to have a different idea of the table-lands. Some were inclined to Munchausen tales, while others pooh-poohed them.

At length in sheer disgust Frank said:

"There is just one thing about it. I have got to proceed solely upon my own judgment. If I adopted all the different plans accorded me I should lead a queer course to be sure."

So with this decision Frank left Campeche.

Beyond the city, Frank found some fairly good roads which led through a section devoted to the culture of fruits and vegetables of various kinds.

Then immense fields of the coffee plant were passed and finally the country began to change its appearance.

Immense tropical forests were encountered. These of course the Steam Man could not travel through.

But generally paths were found leading through the hills, and in this way the explorers got along.

A wild region was encountered, wilder than even Barney and Pomp had seen in the heart of Africa.

They were at the moment near the verge of a mighty forest.

"Speaking of snakes," cried Frank Reade, Jr. "Just look at that."

All gazed in the direction indicated.

Hanging from the limb of a mighty forest monarch was a gigantic python or boa-constrictor.

In the monster's folds was a small wood fawn. It had been crushed all to jelly by the powerful folds of the reptile.

It reared its head and recoiled as the Steam Man appeared on the scene.

But it did not show fear, or seem to care in the least for the machine. Indeed, it acted defiant and ready for battle.

Barney shrugged his shoulders and picked up his rifle.

"Begorra, I'd loike to spoil the appetite av the baste," he cried. "An' it's that same I'll do."

So with this the Celt up and fired at the python.

The effect was curious.

The huge snake received the bullet in its sinuous folds, and a jet of blood marked the course of the ball.

Hissing savagely with pain, the python released the wood fawn, and without an instant's warning charged directly at the man.

In an instant Frank saw that they had committed an indiscretion.

While to be sure they were protected by the steel screen of the wagon, yet it was easy to reckon the effect of the python's attack.

That monster's brown body came hurtling and hissing down the slope like an avalanche.

Swifter than a railroad train the enraged python charged upon its foe.

It would have required something more than an ordinary barrier to withstand such an attack.

Frank saw this and made quick action.

With quick hand, he seized the throttle rein and started the Steam Man ahead.

Then he turned him face on to the reptile. He had barely time to do this, when the monster struck the machine.

In a flash the folds of the reptile were wound about the Steam Man.

The foresight and wisdom of Frank's move were at once seen.

If the snake had struck the wagon, he might have crushed the screen with its leviathan folds.

As it was, the air was instantly filled with the fumes of burning snake flesh.

The huge snake's body coming in contact with the almost red hot fire box of the Steam Man, received a terrific scorching.

For an instant his snakeship did not seem to mind this and made terrific blows with his head at the screen.

He strove in vain to reach the men within.

"Whurro!" yelled Barney. "Yez did a wondherfal thing thin, Mister Frank. Shure, the big divil is burnin' up."

"Golly sakes, dat's a fac'," cried Pomp, joyfully.

But Frank knew that the battle was not over yet by any means.

It had only just begun. The monster, feeling the terrible effect of the hot iron, with an almost human-like cry unwound itself quickly from the Steam Man.

It went twisting and rolling about the plain in agony for a few moments.

In its course bushes were uprooted, the ground was torn and the air filled with dust.

Frank knew that this would last but a few moments.

The enraged monster would soon recover and renew the attack with ten-fold fury.

So the famous inventor took up his elephant rifle and thrust an explosive shell into the breach.

Going to a loophole in the screen he took careful aim.

Crack!

The rifle spoke sharply. Straight to its mark went the shell. The next moment as it exploded the air was full of shreds of snake flesh and flying dirt.

The shell had torn a hole in the python's side, but had not destroyed the monster's life.

Terribly enraged, the monster snake now seemed to forget its pain, and once more with mad fury charged down full tilt upon the Steam Man.

CHAPTER III.

THRILLING ADVENTURES.

The crisis had come.

Frank knew this, and that it would be either victory for one or the other. If the python should succeed in overturning the wagon, he might do great harm to the delicate machinery of the Steam Man.

But Frank did not intend that this should happen if he could help it.

He got one more shot at the reptile as it came on with a fearful rush.

Crack!

Once more the deadly elephant rifle spoke. This time an explosive shell tore its way through the snake's side.

Yet it did not inflict a mortal wound.

"Heavens!" gasped Frank. "That snake has more lives than a cat."

He essayed to meet the reptile as he had done before.

But the wily monster, this time evaded the Steam Man and made for the wagon.

There was no such thing as turning aside that fearful attack.

Like an avalanche the snake struck the wagon. Had not the wheels been braced against a heap of stones, it would surely have been swept over upon its side.

But, by the best of good fortune it resisted the shock.

Like a flash the snake's coils went twining about the wagon. They began to draw powerfully, and the metal work began to groan and crack.

"Quick, boys!" shouted Frank Reade, Jr. "Cut the folds in two wherever you can.

But Barney and Pomp needed no bidding. They already had their knives unsheathed, and where the snake's body was exposed at the loopholes began to slash and cut.

Frank with his rifle tried to get a shot at the reptile's head.

If he could only blow it off with one of the shells, the battle would be ended.

But the monster did not give him this opportunity.

Something desperate needed to be done. The metal work of the wagon threatened to give way.

Frank saw this and at once with his accustomed hardihood accept a desperate chance.

Throwing open the door of the wagon, he sprang out.

The reptile's head was above the wagon, and Frank instantly fired at it.

He was a dead shot and, undoubtedly, would have hit it, had it not been for the snake's gyratory motion.

The reptile's attention was instantly attracted toward Frank.

Singularly enough, its folds relaxed and it slid away from the wagon and started for the young inventor.

The snake was between Frank and the cage door.

He knew that if those deadly folds were to close about him, there would be little likelihood of ever escaping alive.

The snake had acted with the rapidity of thought.

Frank had not even time to thrust another cartridge into the breech of his gun.

He started to run. For a few paces he made good time, but what is there on earth to equal the speed of an active python.

Swift as the wind the monster was upon him.

Frank felt its hot breath, and saw for a moment its glistening jaws open over him.

Instinctively he threw up one hand, and by chance his fingers clutched the monster's throat.

Frank hung to this hold with a death-like grip. He felt the mighty coils closing about him, and then with the desperation of one facing certain death he clutched the hilt of his knife with his free hand.

With all his strength he slashed at the monster's throat.

The first blow half severed the head from the body.

A huge jet of black blood spurted into Frank's face and nigh choked him. But though half suffocated he made another blow.

The snake's folds began to loosen, and the monster writhed and tried to free itself.

Frank instantly realized that he had won the victory and fought more coolly now.

Once more he made a blow at the snake's neck.

This time it severed the head from the body completely.

The body of the snake went twisting and writhing a hundred yards across the plain, while Frank fell half fainting to the ground.

Barney and Pomp were quickly by his side and the Celtic cried:

"By me sowl, Mister Frank, I did think yez wor done for, an' it was a good foight yez made to be shure. Are yez badly hurted?"

"Not a bit, Barney," said Frank, staggering to his feet. "It was only a little faintness, that was all."

Pomp turned a hand spring.

"Glory fo' goodness!" cried the overjoyed employee. "I's jes' dat glad, Li'l Boss, dat I don' jes' know what to do dat yuh was not hurt."

The snake's body now lay writhing and twisting far out on the plain.

The adventurers did not go near it. They had had snake experience enough for one day and returned to the Steam Man.

"The next time you see a big snake, Barney," said Frank, "if he is not disturbing us I think you had better let him alone."

The Steam Man now once more went on its way.

Every day now they penetrated deeper into the jungles and wild fastnesses of this wildest country on the globe.

Many strange sights were seen and some thrilling experiences were encountered.

With difficulty the Steam Man found passage through the lowlands. At times it was necessary to cut a path through a dense forest in order to reach clear country beyond.

But one day they came out of a deep wood at the very base of a mighty, volcanic mountain.

Here higher ground was reached and a broad view enjoyed.

And from here a view could he had of a part of the broad tablelands of Peten.

It began to look as if the explorers would soon reach the end of their journey.

Now the table-lands were reached the next thing was to discover the ruined city of Mazendla.

Thus far, our adventurers had seen very few natives, and none of them hostile.

The Steam Man journeyed all that day upon the broad table land of Peten.

As night was coming on, a location was selected for a camping place.

It was a green spot close to a bubbling spring of water.

Not more than one hundred yards distant was a dense grove of trees.

Barney and Pomp were busy aboard the Steam Man preparing the evening meal.

Frank fancied that through the dense foliage of the trees he could discern the white walls of a building.

Barney and Pomp could not see it, but Frank was sure that he could. The famous inventor exclaimed:

"I am not sure but that we are in the neighborhood of the ruined city of Mazendla. It may be that yonder grove of trees conceals it."

"Begorra, Mister Frank, maybe yez are roight," declared Barney, "but by Mister Murphy's pigs, I can't see that same with me own eyes!"

"Can't you? Look sharply now to the left."

Barney strained his vision.

"Divil a bit av it."

"That is queer."

"Bejabers, I think so."

"Pomp, how is your eyesight?"

"Golly, Boss Frank, dis chile kin see in de dark."

"Well, just take a look over there and tell me what you see through those trees."

Pomp readily obeyed.

But he could see nothing but the dense green foliage.

"Bejabers, the eejit can't see it if I can't," spluttered Barney. Pomp scratched his greying head.

"I mus' say, Li'l Boss, dat I kain' see none oh dat what yuh says."

"Pshaw!" exclaimed Frank, testily. "Neither one of you have good eyesight. It is plain enough to see."

With this, the famous inventor descended from the wagon.

Barney and Pomp stood looking at each other and feeling a bit crestfallen.

"Begorra, I can see it if yez kin, buffalo," exclaimed Barney.

"G'long, yuh fool I'ishman. I hasn' seen it m'se'f yet."

"You fellows look out for things until I come back," shouted Frank, starting toward the forest.

Barney grabbed up his rifle.

"Hould on a bit, Mister Frank," he cried. "It ain't a bit safe fer yez to go off out there alone."

"Jes' yuh wait dar, I'ish, I's gwin wid Boss Jun'r m'se'f."

"No, yez won't."

"Yuh jes' bet I will."

The two zealous servitors were in imminent danger of a collision. But Frank turned and said peremptorily:

"Hold where you are. I am going alone. Look out for the Man until I get back."

This settled the question.

Reluctantly they turned back, and Pomp went about his cooking duties, while Barney gazed wistfully after Frank and declared:

"By me sowl, it ain't safe for that man to go out there alone. I'll just kape me eye out all the same."

So Barney proceeded to keep an eye out, while Pomp was busy at his work.

Reaching the woods, Frank entered them without hesitation.

He was confident that be had really seen the walls of a ruined building through the thick foliage.

To his best belief it was some part of the ruined city they were in quest of.

But upon entering the forest, Frank found that progress was not so easy as he fancied.

The vines and matted shrubbery were almost impenetrable.

The famous inventor, however, used a small hatchet, and proceeded to cut his way through.

In this manner he had very soon cleared quite a path.

But suddenly he was brought to a halt in a most startling manner. Down through a network of vines he suddenly saw a glistening pair of eyeballs.

To his startled fancy they seemed veritable balls of fire, and for a moment he could not act.

They were fixed upon him with piercing and deadly earnestness.

Frank instinctively knew that they belonged to some wild animal.

Just what kind of a creature it was he could not at the moment tell.

But he was satisfied that his position was one of deadly peril.

But he was not one given to fear or hesitation. His mind was quickly made up as to what to do.

Quick as thought he brought his rifle up and fired point blank directly between the blazing eyeballs.

The result was terrific.

Frank had presence of mind enough to sink down upon his face just as a tremendous tawny body rose out of the shrubbery and sprang directly over him.

It was as he saw at that moment a monstrous puma or panther, called by the natives lion.

Indeed, the genuine lion is not a more formidable beast to encounter than the puma of Central America.

It was a narrow escape that Frank had had.

The puma had sprung clear over him and tumbled headlong into a heap of brush, where he began to flounder and make the air hideous with his cries.

Frank was not sure whether he had given the beast a mortal wound or not.

Nor did he try to find out or follow up the contest.

He knew well enough what a hand to hand encounter with one of these monsters meant.

He at once sprang out of the forest and started at full speed for the Steam Man.

But what was his horror upon looking over his shoulder to see the lion coming after him.

CHAPTER IV.

THE TEMPLE IN THE WOODS.

The sensation experienced by Frank Reade, Jr., at that moment, was a most sickening and horrible one.

He knew that it would be easy for the puma to overtake him.

To be overtaken meant death.

But still he ran with terrific speed across the plain. The panther was close upon him, however.

But, just as it began to look bad for Frank, a cry came from the Steam Man.

Barney had been upon the watch.

He had heard the shot in the woods, and knew at once that Frank was in trouble.

He shouted to Pomp:

"Come up quick, cabbage. Bejabers, the master's in a heap av trubble. I jist heerd his rifle go aff yender in the woods."

"Golly!" gasped Pomp, as he dropped his frying pan. "What's dat yuh say, l'ish?"

Barney seized the throttle rein and started the Steam Man toward the woods.

It was just at the moment when Frank emerged with the lion after him.

The lion was gaining with tremendous bounds upon Frank.

But Barney set the Steam Man after him with all speed. A terrific race followed.

Pomp was at a loophole with his rifle.

Drawing a bead on the animal, he fired. Barney lashed the throttle rein and did the same.

Both shots took effect.

But they did not stay the panther's course, though they drew a howl of pain from him.

But every moment increased Frank's danger. He seemed certain to be overtaken.

"By me sowl!" groaned Barney, in horror, "I belave the divil will overtake Mister Frank. How many lives has the baste got, anyway?"

But at that moment Barney hit upon a happy idea.

By the best of good fortune Frank's elephant rifle lay upon one of the seats.

It contained an explosive shell and was a weapon very deadly in its effects.

It did not take Barney long to make use of it.

Seizing the rifle, he sprang to a loophole. The Steam Man had gained, and was but twenty yards from the panther.

But the beast was within ten feet of Frank Reade, Jr.

Just as he made a long leap to overtake his victim Barney fired.

If ever there was a time in his life that the Celt needed nerve and accuracy of aim it was then.

And straight to the mark sped the bullet.

The explosive shell struck the panther full behind the shoulder.

It tore its way through the beast's heart and lungs. Death was instantaneous.

But the beast's body struck Frank and hurled him upon his face.

And there the famous inventor lay with the panther's form upon him, with the hot blood surging over him in a stream.

Barney loosed the throttle, applied the brakes, and brought the Steam Man to a halt.

Then the two faithful servitors rushed out of the cage and to Frank's side.

But the young inventor was unhurt, and scrambled quickly to his feet as soon as the panther's body was pulled off from him.

"Whurroo!" yelled Barney, in delight and triumph. "We've saved yez, Mister Frank, an' if we hadn't yez would shurely av' been kilt entoirely."

"Yes, I think I should," agreed Frank. "And I owe my life to you both. I shall not forget it."

The puma was the largest of his kind that our adventurers had ever seen.

It was at the time of year that his skin was worthless, being mangy, so that it was not preserved.

Frank was quite overcome with his experience, and went on board the wagon to rest.

As darkness was at hand, it was decided to make no further exploration of the forest until morning.

Frank was more than ever convinced, however, that there were ruins in the forest.

"Tomorrow we will cut our way through," he declared, "and I will satisfy you, my friends, that I am right."

"A'righ', Boss Frank," agreed Pomp. "We'se open to conviction jus' de same."

"Bejabers, that's right!" put in Barney.

It was seldom deemed safe to sleep outside the wagon.

So beds were made comfortably enough or, the seats which ran along the sides.

Here our adventurers could sleep quite soundly. Barney and Pomp were soon in the land of dreams.

But Frank Reade, Jr., could not successfully woo the gentle goddess.

Suddenly, as he lay there in a reverie, a sudden curious manifestation caused him to start up.

A ray of something, a trifle brighter than the moonlight, glinted its radiance athwart the wire netting.

For an instant Frank was puzzled.

He rose to a sitting posture and glanced out upon the level plain.

All was plain in the moonlight out there. But no sign of life was to be seen.

Then Frank turned his gaze toward the forest, and there he caught the vivid glimmer of a light.

Certainly it was not moonlight glinting on any bright substance, but such a vivid radiance as could only be made by firelight.

Either a torch or lantern it was, and its motion and changing of base suggested that it was carried by human hands.

Frank was deeply interested.

"I knew it!" he muttered. "I'll wager my life that there is a building in that forest, but I did not dream that it was inhabited."

He watched the light intently.

It moved back and forward, and was of such size as to dispel the theory of the will-o'-the-wisp or ignis fatuus.

Once from the distance Frank fancied he heard a distant outcry.

But this he could not place reliance upon, as it might have been made by some wild beast.

But of one thing he was satisfied.

There was certainly human life and habitation in the forest. On the morrow he would learn what it meant.

He was hardly able to restrain a strong desire to go alone upon an exploring tour under cover of the night.

But sober reflection persuaded him not to do this.

It would be neither safe nor right. So Frank controlled his desire until daybreak came.

The young inventor had not slept that night.

At an early hour he aroused Barney and Pomp.

He did not tell them about the mysterious light, but bluntly informed them that he meant to invade the forest that morning.

"A'righ', Boss Jun'r," agreed Pomp. "Yo' wo'd is law."

"Bejabers, that's so," cried Barney.

Accordingly Frank laid out his map of procedure.

First the Man skirted the edge of the grove looking for an entrance. Failing to find this the adventurers would cut their way through the dense undergrowth.

But luckily a passage was found.

To Frank's gratification and the surprise of Barney and Pomp, a broad paved roadway was discovered.

Flat slabs of stone composed the roadway. This was much overgrown with weeds and brush, but did not materially impede the progress of the Steam Man.

Beneath mighty overhanging trees the roadway extended for half a mile.

Then it suddenly brought the explorers out upon a wonderful scene.

Cries of surprise and admiration escaped the lips of Barney and Pomp.

"Golly, Li'l Boss, yuh was right aftah all."

"Bejabers, that's so."

Frank was intently engaged in studying the scene spread before him.

He saw a strange looking building of whitest marble and mighty dimensions before him.

About the building were acres of paved courts and walls, with open gateways and overgrown with all manner of vines and varicolored vegetation.

The building occupied a space of over an acre, and in style of architecture was not unlike some of the better class of pueblos in Mexico.

But there were richly carved balconies and hanging gardens, piazzas and porticoes, and all done in the whitest of marble.

What was stranger yet, the building did not seem to be a ruin but newly constructed and indeed not altogether finished.

There was evidence that the workmen had not been absent many hours.

Beds of fresh mortar were in the court-yard, slabs of newly cut marble were strewn about.

As the Steam Man entered the court-yard, Frank noticed this and looked for the appearance of any number of workmen.

But to his surprise they did not appear. To all appearance the temple or pueblo in the deep forest was deserted.

For some time our adventurers continued to gaze upon the wonderful building with curiosity and interest.

"Bejabers, I don't see whativer they'd want for to build sich a foine house in this place for," exclaimed Barney. "I don't undherstand it at all, at all."

"I jes' finks dat dis be a new race ob people dat we hab discobered, Li'l Boss," suggested Pomp.

"We can tell very quickly when some of them show up," replied Frank.

"I wondah if dey's hostile to de white people, or to civilized people," asked Pomp.

"Indeed!" replied Frank, "there is every indication that these people are civilized. I wish some of them would show up."

After an hour of patient waiting, Barney suggested that they take the liberty of exploring the place.

"I reckon that's the best way out av it," recommended the Celt "An' mebbe we can foind some av the gintlemen."

"It is possible," said Frank.

"P'r'aps they're as good Americans as oursilves now," rejoined Barney.

"No," dissented Frank. "No American would build this kind of a house."

"Whativer koind of people do yez think they are, Mister Frank?"

"Well," replied the young inventor, slowly, "it is my opinion that we have made a discovery valuable to science and the world.

"Indeed it is not extravagant to assume that these people are a remnant of the original inhabitants of Yucatan who built the famous cities of Palenque and Mazendla.

"If so, then I shall have the greatest curiosity to see them."

"I's a heap 'fraid we won't see 'em today, Boss Frank," said Pomp.

Another hour passed slowly.

Still the mysterious workmen did not return.

At the expiration of this time Frank decided to take a look about the premises.

The Steam Man was left carefully adjusted, and the three adventurers set out across the court-yard.

Of course they were heavily armed and did not intend to go out of sight of the Steam Man.

In crossing the court-yard they came upon a wonderful bit of work. This was a square-shaped basin cut in whitest marble, and occupied by a bubbling spring with water as pure and clear as crystal.

In this water were fish of a peculiar green and vivid blue color, of the gold fish species evidently.

It was certainly a beautiful spectacle.

Pomp tasted of the water.

It was as pure and cool as could well be desired, and far superior to the water usually found in that part of Central America.

Passing by this they entered the main hall of the pueblo, if such it could be called.

It was a massive chamber, high roofed, with polished columns.

It was a perfect wonder to the explorers, who could not conceal their amazement.

But at one end of the hall was a strange polished dais.

Towards this Barney made his way. It seemed made of some peculiar kind of beautiful stone like agate.

Barney sprang upon it.

"Bejabers!" he cried. "Iv this ain't the place where they'll set their oidol. If iver—"

He did not finish his speech. In a twinkling a thrilling thing happened. The polished stone, owing to some mysterious and inexplicable agency, turned and Barney vanished like a flash.

CHAPTER V.
BATTLE WITH THE PIGMIES.

No sooner had Barney mounted the polished dais, than with a swift movement it turned and he vanished into a black aperture beneath.

He went out of sight so suddenly that nothing could have been done to prevent or save him.

For a moment Frank Reade, Jr., and Pomp stood aghast gazing at the treacherous slab of stone.

"Great heavens!" gasped Frank. "What does it mean? Barney! Where are you? Answer if you can."

A long wail went up from Pomp's lips.

"Lor' sakes, Li'l Boss, he's gwin gone to his death. Dat big stone hab jes' crushed him to death fo' suah."

"It can't be—it must not be so!" cried Frank, with horror, and half insane, he was about to spring upon the stone himself, when Pomp pulled him hack.

"Fo' goodness, Boss, don' yuh go an' do dat same fing!" cried the affrighted servant. "Yuh'll follow Barney, an' den whatebber dis chile do?"

"But we must know Barney's fate!" cried Frank, desperately. Again and again he called the name of his faithful servitor.

But no answer came back.

All was the silence of the tomb.

Bathed in cold perspiration, Frank laid his hands upon the stone and essayed to move it.

But he could not do this.

What other resort he would have tried, it is impossible to say, but at that moment a warning cry broke from Pomp's lips.

"Fo' Hebbin's sake, Li'l Boss, jes' yuh look yender. I done fink we bettah skip fo' de Steam Man."

Frank glanced in the direction indicated. Through the arches of the temple he saw the court-yard beyond. Through this, three huge jaguars were coming at full speed.

There was not a moment to lose.

In their exposed position Frank had no hopes of overcoming three such savage brutes.

Accordingly the safest method to pursue was to fly to the Steam Man.

Without further hesitation and with one impulse, Frank and Pomp started.

They sped through the court like a flash. One of the jaguars let out a tremendous savage roar.

All of the savage beasts were in hot pursuit of the two men. Fortunately they had not far to go. Frank reached the wagon first and sprang in.

Pomp followed, and they had just time to shut the door in the cage, when the foremost of the jaguars came bounding against it.

One of the jaguars sprang on the top of the cage and crouched there, trying to claw his way through the netting. The others kept leaping against the side of the wagon ferociously. Pomp had sprung for a rifle, and would have fired at the brutes.

But a strange incident prevented.

Suddenly the notes of a strange sounding horn sounded through the arches of the temple.

Instantly the three jaguars leaped down and went skulking away across the court-yard.

Pomp and Frank were so completely amazed that they were for a moment speechless and inactive.

"Fo' massey's sake!" gasped Pomp, in utter amazement. "Whatebber abe de meanin' ob dat?"

"Why, it looks as if they were trained jaguars," replied Frank, a swift comprehension breaking over him. "And, I was right—there is their master."

Both saw, standing upon an angle of the court-yard wall, an individual, the like of which neither had ever seen before.

He was almost a pigmy in statue, but thickset and stout of frame. His complexion was the color of parchment, and his hair long, black and wiry, hung down over his shoulders.

His keen eyes looking furtively out from beneath heavy eyebrows were fixed keenly upon the Steam Man.

He was dressed in a curious-looking suit of some sort of queerly-woven cloth, a compromise between the garb of a Turk and a native Mexican.

In his hand he carried a long lance steel tipped.

For a full minute he stood gazing at the Steam Man.

"Golly, Li'l Boss," muttered Pomp. "Dat's de funniest- looking little man I eber seed."

"Well, you're right, Pomp," agreed Frank, regarding the other with interest. "If he is a specimen of the aborigines of this country they were a funny looking lot of people."

But the funny looking little man leaped down from his perch and now advanced toward the Steam Man, gesticulating and talking in some strange tongue.

Frank could not understand a word he said.

The famous inventor opened the door of the cage and stepped down into the court-yard.

At this the aborigine came to a halt not ten paces distant.

He spoke to Frank in a strange tongue.

Frank did not attempt to make it out, but replied:

"I cannot talk your language, sir."

Again the little man spoke. Frank repeated his declaration.

The pigmy gesticulated furiously and swung his lance threateningly. But Frank tried to pacify him by resorting to signs.

This had some little effect.

The pigmy understood partly the signs Frank made.

The young inventor pointed to the Steam Man and talked and gesticulated. The pigmy's confidence seemed to be gained and he approached nearer.

"Now, Pomp," said Frank, "start the Man up a little."

Pomp pulled the throttle rein.

The Steam Man gave a puff and began to move ahead.

The effect upon the pigmy was rather startling. He dropped his lance and stood for a moment trembling in abject terror.

Then wheeling, with several cat-like leaps he gained the edge of the parapet and went over it.

Frank rushed to the wall and looked over.

But the pigmy had gone.

He was nowhere to be seen.

Frank now began to fathom the mystery of the place. These strange people had methods of living vastly at variance with American ideas. None of them were visible just now.

He had read of a class of people in Africa who never showed themselves above ground in daylight.

All of their work was done at night, and during the daytime they burrowed caverns in the ground and slept.

These people of the marble pueblo might be much the same. Frank began to believe that this was the way of it.

The light which he had seen the night before was no doubt used by the workmen in laying the stone and mortar for the structure.

But where did they find hiding places during the day?

Were there chambers or caverns underneath the marble pueblo?

Certainly the pigmy could not have disappeared so easily if there was not some method of hiding in some such manner.

Frank vaulted the parapet and began to examine the stone walls.

After some moments' search to his surprise, as he touched one of the stones, it swung inward.

A long, narrow passage dark as Erebus was disclosed.

The mystery was solved at last.

This no doubt led to underground chambers where the pigmies spent their days.

And now Frank believed that he had solved the mystery of Barney's fate.

The Celt had no doubt fallen through one of the mysterious entrances into the underground abode of the pigmies.

The marble dais in the temple was then, after all, but a curious sort of entrance to the underground retreat.

By leaping upon it, one was quickly carried down to the depths below.

It had required something more than ordinary ingenuity to invent this clever door of stone so nicely balanced.

Certainly these remnants of a lost and almost extinct race were certainly far from being fools.

They were beyond doubt most clever and skillful mechanics, masons and artisans.

Frank was tempted to invade the underground retreat of the pigmies, but sober second thought forbade.

Again at this moment a warning cry came from Pomp, who was aboard the Steam Man.

"Come, quick, Boss Jun'r, fo' yo' life!" shouted Pomp.

Frank lost no time in complying.

And, as he leaped over the wall, he saw the cause of Pomp's alarm.

The court-yard was suddenly filling with a seeming legion of the pigmies.

They were all armed as well, and were inclined to a warlike attitude. Three jaguars were now held in leash.

Frank saw the first little man in the front rank.

He seemed to be the leader of the band. Fully three hundred of the pigmies had suddenly appeared.

It was a most astonishing complication to Frank Reade, Jr.

The pigmies were all armed with long lances and bore down toward the Steam Man.

Frank pulled the whistle valve and let out an ear-splitting shriek.

For a moment the pigmies appeared to be literally paralyzed.

They were thrown into the wildest confusion. Terror seemed to be predominant, until the little old man ran in front of them and exhorted them.

His words seemed to act like magic upon them.

They re-formed and once more the outlook became serious.

With bristling lances they once more advanced toward the Steam Man.-

—

There was no evading the issue now.

Frank saw this at a glance.

He was averse to killing any of the strange people unless compelled to.

Discretion seemed the better part of valor, and it appeared in order to retreat in as graceful a manner as possible.

Accordingly he started the Steam Man across the court-yard. With clanking tread the Man crossed the space.

This brought him out upon the roadway. The pigmies pursued hurling their lances at the cage.

But the steel netting was proof against them, and they fell off harmlessly.

However, Frank saw that they were planning to annihilate the Steam Man with a huge log thrown across the roadway by a party who had headed the Man off.

The tree would prevent the Man's progress in that direction, and Frank set his lips grimly.

"They are after our lives, Pomp. I hate to fire into them, but it is self-defense."

"Ob co'se it is, Li'l Boss," protested Pomp. "Yo' jes' a good right to shoot ebery one ob dem, fo' suah."

Frank picked up his rifle.

The foe were swarming down upon the Steam Man.

They evidently believed that they had their mysterious visitor cornered. Loud cries of triumph pealed from their lips.

But Frank opened fire with his Winchester repeater.

Crack—ack—ack!

The shots flew swift and true. One, two, three of the foe fell. Then Pomp joined in the battle.

Crack!

Another of the pigmies fell. This had the effect of partially checking them.

Frank started the Steam Man forward. The huge log across the road barred their progress, but a few shots from the Winchesters scattered the foe there assembled.

Then Pomp sprang down and moved the log.

It required all his considerable strength, but he succeeded and then returned to the wagon.

"Golly, Boss Frank!" cried the excited adventurer, "I reckon we'se jes' gib dem rascals a bit ob a lesson."

"I think we have, Pomp," agreed Frank, "but I fear we've not seen the last of this battle yet."

The young inventor's fears were not without foundation.

The pigmies had been for a few moments repulsed by the deadly fire of the repeating rifles.

But they had by no means given up the idea of capturing the Steam Man.

A large party of them had struck out into the forest, and now, as Frank started the Steam Man for the table-land beyond, he was again quickly brought to a halt by a new development.

Turning a bend in the road unexpectedly, he saw just ahead a large gang of the pigmies congregated there.

They had felled several tall palms, and they lay across the roadway effectually blocking the passage of the Steam Man.

Affairs had certainly reached a crisis.

CHAPTER VI.
BARNEY MEETS A FRIEND.

But what of Barney, whom we have seen disappear in such a mysterious manner beneath the stone dais?

The astounded Celt felt the stone give way beneath him, but before he had time to recover himself it had turned completely over, and he felt himself descending through space and darkness.

He struck upon his back upon some soft substance.

How far he had dropped he had no means of knowing.

All was darkness about him. He was quickly upon his feet, and began to feel about him.

The substance he had fallen upon he discovered by touch was a pile of some sort of soft cloth-covered cushions. The Celt was more than surprised.

"Begorra, whereiver am I at all, at all?" he spluttered. "What sort av a place is this, I'd loike to know?"

This was a question not easily answered owing to the dense gloom which enshrouded it.

As soon as he could collect his scattered senses Barney got upon his feet and strove to pierce the gloom about him.

Fortunately he bad a small taper in his pocket.

This he lit and its light displaced the gloom about him.

Then he saw that he was in a square chamber of stone.

He was standing upon a pile of soft cushions. Above him he could see nothing but stone, just the same as the walls about.

But leading out of this curious chamber was a narrow passageway.

Barney started towards it, but at this moment his taper went out.

The Celt muttered something not very polite and was about to light it again, when he heard a creaking sound above, and two dark forms came hurtling down through the gloom and struck the cushions near him.

Barney's eyes had become partly accustomed to the dim light, and a momentary flash of daylight as the stone above turned showed him the personnel of the intruders.

At first he had instinctively fancied them his companions Frank and Pomp.

But second thought taught him better judgment. Instinctively he shrunk back against the wall.

The two new-comers with exclamations in a peculiar tongue quickly picked themselves up.

Before Barney could fully recover from his amazement they had gone.

"Bejabers, I see it all now," muttered the enlightened Irishman, "this is only a quare sort av a dure by which the omadhowns enter their undherground abode. Weil, now, that's quite clever, but howiver am I to git back agin with Mister Frank an' the eejit?"

This was, indeed, a problem.

Barney again lit his taper and looked in vain for some method by which he might climb out of the place.

This was impossible.

There seemed but one way, and this was to follow the passage which the new-comers had just taken.

Barney made no doubt that they were of the strange people who had built the temple, but he was not by any means assured that they would be especially friendly to invaders like himself.

"Bejabers, it's well to first git acquainted with the nature av the baste," he muttered, "an' thin iv it's all right go ahead."

This was certainly sound logic, and it was well for Barney that he adopted it.

The strange people would not have received him cordially, and indeed his precaution may be said to have been the saving of his life.

But there seemed no other safe method of procedure but to attempt the passage.

Accordingly Barney entered it.

He kept on in the darkness cautiously for a short distance.

Then he saw a ray of light ahead.

Also from the distance there came the murmur of many voices.

Barney kept on with increased caution now.

Very soon he saw that the passage would bring him into a mighty illumined chamber under the temple.

Oil lamps of various grotesque shapes furnished the means of light, and a dense throng of the most curious looking people he had ever seen were present.

Barney gazed upon the scene with great interest.

"By me sowl, but ain't they bits av men," he muttered. "No wan av thim is bigger nor a good sized Irish lad."

The pigmy women dressed much the same as the men, and seemed to busy themselves in various quarters at the culinary art.

Some time Barney spent in watching the curious people.

The next moment he received the greatest surprise of his life.

"For Heaven's sake!" said a voice at his elbow. "Is it possible there is a person in this place who can speak English too?"

Barney turned like a flash.

"Tare an''ounds!" he gasped. "Who the divil are yez."

"On the other hand, let me ask the same question."

Barney was facing a young man, tall, straight and handsome.

He was dressed in the garb of a native hunter, and carried a rifle. A moment previous he had crept out of a niche in the wall just to Barney's right.

The two white men stood gaping at each other in amazement.

"Well, I niver!" gasped Barney. "Yez are not one of these haythins that own this place, are yez?"

"No. Are you?"

"Divil a bit."

"Who are you?"

"Me name is Barney O'Shea, and I'm a respictable Irish gintleman."

"Good! Give me your hand. I am an American, and the Irishman has no better friend."

"Yez talk like a man, yez do," cried Barney. "I'm delighted to meet yez. But howiver did yez come here?"

"Well," replied the young man, "I was fool enough to step upon a revolving dais in the temple above, and-"

"Bejabers. I came here that same way mesilf," cried Barney.

"So? Well, we are in for it."

"Yez are roight."

"But what may I ask has brought yon into this part of Yucatan?"

"Shure, I come here wid the Steam Man, an' Mister Frank Reade, Jr., the worruld-famous invintor."

A gurgling cry escaped the other's lips.

"Frank Reade, Jr.?" he gasped. "Do you mean to say that he is near here?"

"Well, I lift him when I fell down into this place."

"The deuce!" exclaimed the young man, excitedly. "Why, Frank Reade, Jr., is an old friend of mine. I must see him. Look here, what brought him here?"

"Shure, he's lookin' for a young man named Tony Buckden who got lost down in this haythin region."

"Well, is this not luck? Look here, man, I am Tony Buckden—"

Barney threw up his arms.

"The divil yez say?" he exploded, in a hoarse whisper. "Shure, I'd ought to have guessed that, an' Mr. Frank will be deloighted to see yez."

"And I shall be delighted to see him!" cried the millionaire's son, for such he was. "So he answered my letter in person?"

"Yis."

"And he has the Steam Man here?"

"Shure enough."

"Then the success of my plans are assured!" exclaimed Tony, jubilantly. "That is, if we succeed in escaping from here."

"Shure we must do that," declared Barney, confidently.

At this moment there arose a great commotion among the pigmy people.

Excited cries arose, and as with one accord they rushed from the place. In less than no time the place was cleared.

Tony Buckden and Barney were not a little surprised.

"I wonder what that means?" exclaimed the New Yorker.

"Bejabers, there's no tellin' but that they've heard of the Steam Man and that's what his drawn thim away."

"By Jove, I don't know but that you are right, Barney," declared Buckden. "At any rate, it looks to me like a very good opportunity to escape."

"Shure, it's a foine chance."

Not one of the pigmy people were left in the place.

Of course Barney and young Buckden did not hesitate a moment to avail themselves of the opportunity.

Buckden led the way and they crossed the broad chamber and came to a passage which seemed to lead upwards.

There were stairs cut in the stone, and up these the two imprisoned men sprung.

A moment later they came out into the main body of the temple. Now they could hear the crack of fire-arms and the yells of the pigmy people.

It was at the moment when the Steam Man was about to leave the court-yard and had been attacked by the natives, if such they could be called.

Both Buckden and Barney could see the heads of the contestants beyond a wall of stone.

It was their impulse to go to the aid of Frank and Pomp.

But this was seen at once to be clearly impossible.

They could not hope to successfully fight their way through the crowd of people. Moreover, a thrilling danger now confronted the fugitives.

The three trained jaguars from whom Frank and Pomp had so narrowly escaped were gamboling in the court-yard.

If they should chance to catch sight of young Buckden and Barney the result would not be pleasant for them.

Clearly the safest way for the two adventurers was to steal out of the place and gain the forest beyond.

Then they might trust to luck in rejoining the Steam Man. Certainly it was the best method to pursue.

This Buckden at once proceeded to do. He led the way boldly across the court-yard and to a wall at its extremity.

Fortune favored them, and they reached the wall in safety.

Vaulting it, they dashed into the forest.

Once among the thick undergrowth they were safe, at least for the time.

"Whew!" exclaimed Buckden, suddenly pausing and wiping the perspiration from his face. "We did that in fine shape, did we not, Barney?"

"To be shure, sor," replied the Celt with a chuckle.

"Now what shall we do?"

"Shure, I think we had better troi and foind the Steam Man," said Barney.

"Of course, but how shall we proceed to do that?"

"Well, bejabers, I think the bist way is to make a cut through the woods here and trust to good fortune to foind Mister Frank out on the open ground. I'm thinkin' he'll 'ave to return there after lavin' this place, for shure."

"All right," agreed Buckden. "Fortunately I know a path that will lead directly there. In fact, I came here by it."

"That's good luck!" cried Barney, joyfully. "It's dyin' I am to get back to the Steam Man once more."

"Well, we will try it hard!" declared Buckden, leading the way. "Come on, Barney."

They set out through the forest without further comment. Buckden found little difficulty in finding the path by which he had entered the place.

Along this they sped swiftly. Soon the foliage began to grow thinner and straggling rays of light ahead showed that they were approaching the verge.

A few moments later they emerged entirely from the forest and came out upon the vast table-land.

As far as the eye could reach extended the level expanse.

Barney and his companion swept the plain eagerly with their eyes for some trace of the Steam Man.

Barney felt confident that the Man would return to the open plain. Therefore it was with a glad cry that he suddenly pointed down the line of forest.

"Luk!" he cried. "Wud yez see the loikes av that! By me sowl, we're in luck, for it's the Steam Man."

Sure enough, coming along the edge of the forest at a rapid speed was the famous Steam Man.

Frank Reade, Jr., was at the throttle, and when he saw Barney waving his arms he pulled the whistle valve open and sent up a shriek of welcome.

CHAPTER VII.
THE WONDERFUL CITY.

THAT the Steam Man had escaped from the attack of the pigmies, this would make certain.

Straight for the barrier erected by the foe Frank sent the Man.

When twenty yards from it, he closed the throttle and applied the brake.

"Now, Pomp!" he cried, "it's a fight for life."

"Yuh kin jes' bet on dat, Boss Jun'r," cried the plucky old buffalo soldier.

"We must not waste a shot."

"Not a one, suh."

At the loopholes the two adventurers stationed themselves, and opened fire upon the foe.

The pigmies hurled their lances at the cage.

But they were shattered against the steel netting and did no harm at all.

On the other hand, the repeaters did deadly work.

No human power could face such a destructive fire. The pigmies were driven from the barricade.

Then Frank Reade, Jr., kept them at a distance, while Pomp dismounted and set about clearing a pathway for the Man.

This was not a very easy job, but Pomp finally succeeded and the Steam Man passed through the harrier.

A few shots were sent after the pigmies, and then the Man under Frank's skillful guidance set out for the plain.

It was not long before the Steam Man was out of the forest.

Once out upon the open plain, Frank set his course along the edge of the forest.

Suddenly Pomp sprang up with a sharp cry:

"Golly sakes, Li'l Boss, dar's dat I'ishman alibe an' well as I'm talkin'. Jes' look dar."

"Barney!" gasped Frank.

"Dat's a fac'."

"Thank Heaven."

Frank gazed in the direction indicated by Pomp, and saw Barney waving his arms frantically in the air.

At once Frank pulled the whistle valve and increased the Steam Man's speed.

A few moments later the Steam Man came to a halt upon the spot where Barney had stood.

The meeting was a joyous one. Barney and Pomp embraced, and Frank gripped Buckden's hand.

"Tony, I'm awful glad to see you," he declared. "I feared you were dead. They assured me at Campeche that you would never be found alive."

"Well, they didn't know anything about it," declared Tony, sententiously; "then you got my letter?"

"Yes."

"And you have answered it in person. Just like you."

"Look here, Tony," said Frank, seriously; "I was sent here by your father to look you up and bring you home."

"Humph!" exclaimed Tony, with a shrug of his shoulders.

"That is the truth."

"Well, I'm not ready to go home yet."

"You are not?"

"No."

"Why not?"

"Because I propose to find the ruined city and its treasure first. I thought that you had come here to help me."

"Do you believe it exists?"

"Of course I do."

"Near here?"

"Why, I believe that we are not ten miles from it."

"But if it is inhabited with people like these with whom we have just had a little experience-"

"But it is not. It is a ruined and deserted city. Come, Frank, with your Steam Man we can find it. You must agree to go."

Frank was silent a moment.

Now that he had accomplished the real object of his mission—the rescue of Tony Buckden—he was quite willing to turn about and go home.

But he knew Tony well enough to be sure that he was very much in earnest.

He would not leave his purpose unaccomplished, even though it cost him his life.

There was no doubt but that with the Steam Man the country could be safely explored.

Frank was a trifle skeptical now as to the real existence of Mazendla.

But he reasoned that it would do no great harm to give at least another week to exploration.

In that time, no doubt, Tony would be satisfied, and then of course would willingly return.

So Frank extended his hand.

"All right, Tony," he declared, "I am with you."

"Good for you, old pard!" cried Buckden, joyfully. "I knew you would do it. Now for Mazendla."

"But I must say I have no idea of the location of the city."

"But I do."

"You do?"

"Yes."

"Where is it?"

"I learned it from a native."

"Ah!"

"Go due east across this table-land. When a tall, sugar-loaf shaped mountain is directly ahead of you, bear to the right and enter a canyon. It will take you directly to Mazendla, the most wonderful of cities."

"All right," cried Frank. "We will follow your directions. All aboard, everybody!"

All scrambled into the cage, and Frank set the Steam Man in motion.

The temple in the forest and the strange race of pigmies were left behind. Nothing more was seen of them.

The Steam Man rapidly crossed the plain.

In the course of an hour the distant shadowy peak of a mountain was seen.

It was some while before its shape became sufficiently clear to decide the question as to whether it was the sugar loaf mountain they were in quest of.

But Buckden declared that it was, and that they were on the right track.

So Frank kept the Steam Man going at full speed.

Every moment now they drew nearer the mountain.

"Look!" cried Buckden, suddenly springing up, "there is the canyon. I tell you we are all right."

"Shall we go for the canyon?" asked Frank Reade, Jr.

"Yes."

A short while later the Steam Man was picking his way along through a mighty gorge-fully a thousand feet deep.

For hours the travelers toiled through this mighty gorge.

Then suddenly the Steam Man came out on a mighty plateau.

And before the explorers was now spread a most wonderful sight. Not one hundred yards distant was the mighty gateway of a city. The towers upon either side rose to a height of fully one hundred feet.

The wall was high, massive and thick. But it was time cracked and tumbling and decayed.

It required but a glance, however, to detect the evidences of former magnificence and grandeur.

"Hurrah!" shouted young Buckden, completely beside himself. "At last we have found the city of Mazendla."

All was excitement and our explorers could hardly contain themselves.

Frank steered the Steam Man straight for the gateway and passed through it.

Before them stretched the wide street of the city.

It was fully two hundred feet wide. Upon either side rose high buildings and all in a state of decay.

The wide street, which seemed to extend for miles through this mammoth city, was paved with blocks of a species of sandstone.

Between the stones grass had grown up, and in places trees had attained a great height.

Palms grew and flourished upon the roofs of many of the buildings, and everywhere clinging vines bedecked the ruins.

It was a wonderful sight, and one which our adventurers never forgot.

The sight of this wonderful city of ruins awoke many strange thoughts and sentiments in the breasts of all.

The one question occurred to each: What manner of people had built this wonderful city, how many centuries ago, and what had become of them?

How long had it been since the feet of human beings had trod these streets?

It must have been many centuries previous, as the appearance of the buildings would proclaim that they had not been erected in very recent times.

All this must remain a mystery.

One day a powerful race had here flourished, enlightened, civilized, and certainly intellectual.

Now nothing remained of them but a few crumbling palaces.

It was a wonderful thing to ponder upon. Indeed, the more one studied upon it the more befogged one became.

What had carried off this vast nation of people?

Was it a pestilence, or a war of extermination, or had their seed by some strange fate exhausted itself and they become extinct as the dodo or the megotherium, or any other antedeluvian animal?

There was nothing at hand to answer this question, and there seemed no other way but to accept it as a mystery never to be solved. The Steam Man jogged leisurely along the broad street.

The occupants of the wagon gazed with wonder upon the stupendous piles upon either side.

Suddenly Barney gave an exclamation and picked up his rifle.

From one of the buildings a spotted jaguar had leaped.

The pretty creature crouched for a moment in the Steam Man's path, snarling and defiant.

"Begorra, ain't he a beauty?" cried Barney, eulogistically. "Shure, I'm goin' to have the skin of the baste."

So without a moment's hesitation the Celt drew aim and fired.

The jaguar gave a quick, sharp yelp of pain, leaped in the air and fell dead.

The bullet had sped true to the mark. Barney was a dead shot.

"Hooray!" cried the excited Irishman. "I flunked him just off. Now iv yez plaze, Mister Frank, will yez jist howld an wan minnit?" Frank could not refuse this request, so he brought the Steam Man to a halt, saying:

"Pshaw! You don't want his skin, Barney. It is of little use."

"Don't I?" exclaimed the Celt. "Yez kin jist bate I do. I'll take it home to me friends in Ameriky, an' tell thim what a foine shot I am."

Barney opened the rear door and leaped out of the cage.

He went directly up to the jaguar, and was about to lift the creature upon his shoulders, when a thrilling thing occurred.

Suddenly, from the same building, four more of the savage animals appeared.

They saw Barney, and without further ceremony came for him like a flash.

The Irishman saw his predicament, and knew that he was in deadly peril.

It required but a moment for him to act.

"Whurroo!" he yelled. "I'm a son av a say cook if the woods ain't full av the divils. Luk out there, yez spotted imps. Be off, I say." Barney fired at the first jaguar, and the shot struck the animal's shoulder.

For a moment it wavered and then tumbled in a heap. But the next moment the three jaguars left were upon Barney.

The Celt went to the ground like a ten-pin. It began to look as if his fate was surely sealed.

With three of the animals upon him he would speedily have been clawed to death.

But fortunately for him Barney had valuable allies in the three friends aboard the Steam Man.

A startled cry came from Frank's lips as he saw the jaguars appear.

He at once snatched up his rifle.

"Heavens!" he cried. "Barney will be killed."

Pomp and Tony were no less quick in also coming to the rescue.

All three fired. As chance had it all fired at the same jaguar and every shot told.

The animal pitched forward dead across Barney's body. The other two jaguars tumbled over him, and by the time they had recovered themselves the repeaters had got into working order again.

Crack—ack—ack!

Another jaguar tumbled over. Before the marksmen could again fire the surviving animal with a snarling cry fled and was quickly out of range.

Frank descended and rushed to Barney's side.

CHAPTER VIII.
POMP'S THRILLING EXPERIENCE.

But before the famous inventor could reach him, Barney was upon his feet.

"Begorra, that's something that ivery man can't say!" he exclaimed, with twinkling eyes. "I went out to get one jaguar and was the cause av baggin' four av thim. Shure, I'll have wan av thim skins tanned and sind it to the Pope, so I will."

"You are a pretty good decoy for jaguars," laughed young Buckden. "By Jove, Barney, you're a valuable man."

"Have yez jist discovered that?" retorted the quick-witted Irishman.

It required but a short time for Barney and Pomp to take off the jaguars' skins.

There was a skin for each of them, and they were carefully stowed away in the wagon.

Once more the Steam Man went on down the broad avenue.

There were many other streets diverging from this one, but they were more narrow and had not the appearance of this one.

It was deemed best to keep to the main thoroughfare.

At intervals a halt was called before some wonderful building of curious architecture and time was spent in studying it.

"Look here, Buckden!" said Frank, finally, "how is this? What of that temple you wrote me about, which was so abundantly stocked with anacondas?"

"Oh, that is a good ways from here," replied Buckden. "This street I believe extends for a distance of twenty miles. Half way to the other end is a public square and there we will find the temple.

At least, so I was informed by the native, Metlo."

"Very good! then we shall be on the lookout for the anacondas." The words were not out of Frank's mouth when a warning cry came from Barney who was at the forward end of the wagon.

"Luk out fer yesilf, Mister Frank!" he cried; "there's a big log acrost the road an' if yez don't luk out we'll be overturned by it."

Frank quickly closed the throttle and applied the brake.

Right across the Steam Man's path was what looked like a log of palm, and it stretched from a clump of palms to a thicket which grew out of the paving stones full thirty feet away.

But quick as he had been Frank was not in time to prevent the Steam Man from stumbling against it.

The result was terrifying.

The log was instantly an animated creature. Quick as a flash it bounded in air and ran up in huge coils, while the savage head of a huge anaconda emerged from the palm clump.

Before Frank could make a move to retreat, the big snake had thrown its giant coils around the wagon and over the cage.

The huge head was thrust against the steel netting, seeking an opening.

"Tare an''ounds!" yelled Barney in terror. "Iv it ain't another wan ov the snakes! By me sowl, he's puttin' his head in at the windy!"

This was a terrifying fact.

The anaconda's head suddenly was thrust through one of the portholes.

This chanced to be one of large circumference and the snake's whole body began to slide into the cage.

Frank Reade, Jr., seized a hatchet and made a blow at the snake.

But the reptile's head struck him in the breast and knocked him over.

Its keen fangs tore his shirt and lacerated his flesh. When he picked himself up he was alone in the wagon with the snake.

The anaconda's body was sliding rapidly in through the port-hole. Barney and Pomp and Buckden had fled from the wagon through the rear door.

"Come, Frank, for God's sake!" cried Buckden, reaching in and pulling Frank toward the door. "Don't stay there, or you will be killed."

Frank saw the snake making ready to dive at him again.

He knew that it was folly to risk his life in such a manner.

So accepting discretion as the better part of valor, the young inventor dashed from the wagon.

The huge snake's body was rapidly sliding into the wagon.

The explorers dumbfounded and irresolute stood outside and watched the proceeding with curious sensations.

"Well, upon me sowl," cried Barney, "howiver will we get the omadhoun out av that? Bad cess to his ugly shape, say I."

"By Jove, that is a stickler," declared Buckden. "How will we ever get him out of the cage?"

"At present he is master of the situation," declared Frank.

"I jes' fink dat ole snake's gwin to gib us some trubble," declared Pomp.

"It looks like it."

"Begorra, why not give him a bit av cold lead?"

But the words were not off Barney's lips when an appalling thing happened.

The snake's body was now all in the cage. The huge reptile was squirming and thrashing about like mad.

Suddenly the door of the cage shut with a snap.

Then, to add to the horror and discomfort of the situation, the Steam Man started away at full speed.

The snake's movements had in some way pulled open the throttle.

A fearful groan escaped Frank's lips.

"My God! we are lost!"

Cries of dismay escaped the others.

"Catch him!"

"Shut the valve!"

But they might as well have tried to catch the wind.

The Steam Man was off like a flash. Down the avenue he went with clanking tread.

After him with despairing souls ran the explorers, vainly trying to overtake him.

In the cage, unable to extricate himself, the huge anaconda was taking an enforced ride.

What more strange or thrilling predicament could be imagined?

Down the avenue went the strange procession. The Steam Man went on and was soon out of sight through a vista of trees and overhanging vines.

The seriousness of the affair to our adventurers could not be estimated at the moment.

Left in that terrible wilderness to find their way on foot back to Campeche was not a pleasant thing to contemplate.

There did not seem to remain any doubt but that the Steam Man would keep on until it should come in disastrous collision with some object.

The result would almost surely be to smash the machinery, and in that out of the way part of the world it would be by no means easy to repair it.

All these misgivings and fears assailed the explorers.

Frank Reade, Jr., was usually possessed of iron nerves.

But if ever there was a time in his life when those nerves were sorely tried, it was now.

It did not seem to him possible that the Steam Man could escape unharmed.

"My soul!" he gasped, as he staggered on. "We are lost!"

Indeed, it seemed true.

Yet the explorers ran on, hoping at every turn to see the Steam Man all safe and sound.

But they seemed doomed to disappointment.

Suddenly a terrible cry went up from Barney.

"Howly Mither! Luk out!" he yelled. "Whativer is that ahead of us?"

Every one came to a halt.

Just ahead of them lay what looked again like a prostrate palm trunk, but the experienced gaze of our adventurers now proved its true character.

It was another huge anaconda which was stretching itself across the roadway.

The long, sinuous horrid body, in its immense proportions, was truly a terrifying thing to look at.

For a moment our adventurers stood looking at it with dismay.

It had extended itself across the street, no doubt just after the Steam Man had passed else the Man would have cut it to pieces.

" Glory fo' goodness!" cried Pomp, "Whatebber will dis yer chile do? Ugh! I nebber did like snakes!"

"Nor I, Pomp!" cried Tony Buckden, with a shiver. "What shall we do about it, Frank?"

"Discretion is valor's better part," said Frank. "We will not try to cut our way through the foe this time, but rather go around it."

"Good!" cried Tony. "But can we do it?"

The avenue was fully one hundred feet wide here.

It seemed easy enough to go the other side of the line of palms, and the explorers made a move to do so.

But they had barely reached the other side of the avenue when a thrilling thing occurred.

The space between the palms and the buildings was hardly ten feet. Suddenly, as they were passing through this narrow space, there was a rustling sound above, and a long, sinuous body shot down from a window of one of the buildings.

The next moment Pomp was encircled by the folds of a huge anaconda.

A startled yell went up from the astonished man.

The others recoiled in amazement and horror.

Then, before any of them had time to act, Pomp was drawn up like a puppet and through the window above.

He went out of sight like a flash.

But a tremendous uproar was heard in the building, and the pounding and thumping of heavy bodies was heard.

Pomp's cries for help were agonizing.

For a few moments our adventurers were so overcome with horror that they hardly knew how to act or what to say.

"My God!" cried Frank Reade, Jr., "Pomp is being killed. Why do we stand here inactive? We must save him!"

"Right!" cried Tony Buckden. "Come on, friends! Lively, now!" No second bidding was needed.

Into the building they rushed.

Some long stairs were encountered. Up these they sprung.

This brought them to a landing above, and into a large chamber.

Up through this and through the fallen roof there grew a high palm tree.

Partly wound around the trunk of this were a part of the snake's coils.

The other part of the snake's body was wound about Pomp, and the servant was seen to be unconscious, and for aught his agonized friends knew, dead.

The monster anaconda's head was erect, and its forked tongue was darting from its month as it faced the new-comers angrily.

Frank Reade, Jr., saw that if Pomp was to be saved, quick work must be made.

With a long drawn breath the young inventor sprang forward, crying:

"Aim at his head, friends. Work quickly, for I fear Pomp is dead."

But no further adjuration was needed.

The others did work quickly.

Barney raised his rifle and took aim at the monster's head.

It was an uncertain aim, as the snake's head kept gyrating and moving about in a lively manner.

But by great good luck the bullet struck the monster's lower jaw.

It was instantly broken and hung limply. The snake gave almost a shriek of agony, and its folds partly relaxed.

Instantly Frank sprang forward and made a blow at the reptile with his knife.

It was a lucky blow, and cut a deep gash in the monster's body, half severing it to the backbone.

Barney also rushed upon the snake.

The monster made a game light, however. Its mighty coils relaxed, and it dropped Pomp from them and began to thrash about in fury.

Frank and Tony Buckden were knocked down like puppets.

The snake's huge body literally filled the huge chamber, and thrashing about so furiously kept our explorers one moment upon their feet and the next upon the floor.

Hacking at the reptile with his knife, Frank had inflicted many wounds.

Blood flowed in torrents, and the reptile was evidently weakening.

Barney at an opportune moment raised his clubbed rifle and made a blow at the snake's head.

It was a lucky stroke.

The reptile was almost instantly brained, and the battle was over.

CHAPTER IX.
INTO THE DEPTHS.

The battle was won, but what of Pomp?

The old buffalo soldier lay in an inanimate heap upon the stone floor. Frank was quickly by his side, however. His first move was to feel Pomp's pulse. With a cry of joy he reached for a whisky flask which Buckden produced.

"He is alive!" he cried. "It is about certain that we shall save him."

This, however, could not yet be determined. The older man had suffered quite a severe squeezing, and there was no certainty that bones had not been broken.

Frank applied the whisky to Pomp's lips. Then the others rubbed his hands and feet vigorously.

In a few moments Pomp gasped and opened his eyes.

"Glory for goodness, Li'l Boss," he whispered, hoarsely, "Has dis chile been sabed? I done fought I was a gone ole sojer."

"You're all right, Pomp!" cried Frank, joyfully. "You're sure you can move without pain, are you? Try and roll over."

Pomp did as he was bid.

To the joy of all it was discovered that although Pomp had experienced quite a severe squeezing he was practically uninjured. In a few moments he was able to get upon his feet.

He was a trifle stiff and sore, but this bid fair to desert him in a short while.

Then it was seen that the anaconda was a monster.

Indeed its huge coils seemed to occupy the larger part of the chamber.

All had good reason to congratulate themselves upon their escape from what might have been death for Pomp at least.

But now that the affair was over there was no use in further waste of time in the vicinity.

It was necessary at once to continue their quest for the Steam Man.

Accordingly they started to descend the stairs.

But the incidents of the moment were by no means spent. A strange and startling thing occurred.

No sooner had Barney put his foot upon the topmost stairs than the whole affair crumbled and fell.

Down went the Celt through a cloud of dust and rotten stone. It was a sudden happening and took the others quite off their guard. "Heavens!" cried Frank, recoiling. "What does that mean!"

"The stairs have given way!" cried Buckden, with horror.

"Barney has gone down with them."

"He is likely killed."

"Massy sakes alibe!" cried Pomp, wildly. "Dat's awful! We must do somfin' sabe Barney."

But now as the dust cleared, a horrible realization dawned upon the explorers.

At their feet yawned a dark abyss.

How deep it was they could not guess, for the stairs and the floor beneath had succumbed and gone down with Barney.

The bottom of the abyss could not be seen.

It was safe to assume, however, that it was really a cellar underneath the building, and therefore not more than a dozen feet or more in depth.

Frank leaned over and shouted:

"Barney! If you are alive, answer me!"

"Shure an' I will that, Mister Frank," came up the Celt's voice from the abyss. "It's not kilt I am."

"Are you badly hurt?"

"Shure, an' not a bit av it, Mister Frank. Only a bit av a bruise on me head an' me arrum. Oi'm all roight."

"Thank Heaven for that."

But the question now was, how were the three men to descend from their aerial position?

There was no other stairs, and it was a little too great a height to risk a jump with safety.

But Frank Reade, Jr., was not the one to be long in a quandary. He quickly hit upon a plan.

Advancing to one of the windows, he looked down to the pavements below.

It was a height of possibly twenty feet. But a jump was out of the question.

However, some stout vines grew over the face of the building. These offered a good safe hold, and by means of these the three explorers clambered down to the ground floor.

The first thing to do now was to rescue Barney.

It was found, however, that the redoubtable Celt did not require any assistance.

He had discovered a way to clamber out of the cellar, and in a moment came rushing out of the ruin.

Congratulations were in order over the happy escape of all.

The incidents of the day had their effect upon the explorers. Already Tony Buckden had begun to sicken of the enterprise.

He had really gained the end he sought, which was to visit the city of Mazendla.

Of course he had not as yet succeeded in locating the treasure spoken of by the Indian guide Metlo.

But the treasure was only a slight inducement for Tony to remain amid the innumerable perils of the Central American wilds.

He had in fact more money at his command than he could expend, and, of course, gold had little temptation for him.

As for Frank Reade, Jr., the treasure had not constituted the object of his visit.

That he had already accomplished in finding Tony Buckden.

Not one in the party but was badly disaffected and wanted to go home.

"I jus' fink home is de bes' place aftah all," said Pomp.

"Begorra, that's true," sang Barney. "Be it iver so humble there's no place loike home, aven iv it's in a pig pen."

"Good!" cried Frank. "Well, we will soon give you a chance to see home, boys, if we can find the Steam Man intact."

"Which Heaven grant we may," said Tony, fervently.

"Then you're really ready to go home, Tony?"

"Oh, yes. I am anxious to; the way of it is, I have sickened of roaming in this accursed clime. Father says he will take me into Wall street with him, and I'm going to accept his offer."

"Good for you, Tony!" cried Frank. "It is a good time for you to settle down."

"I shall do it."

They were now once more pushing their way along the avenue. The Steam Man did not seem to be anywhere in sight.

What was the fate of the invention they could only guess.

They pushed on rapidly.

Suddenly they came out into what seemed like the plaza, or public square of the city.

Here wonderful sights were presented.

Mammoth ruins surrounded the square on all sides.

These were overgrown with vegetation of all kinds.

Clinging vines adorned the walls, and huge trees of the deciduous species grew out of the roof and piles of moldering stone. Everywhere all was desolation and decay.

But one building, massive and commanding, with huge pillars of some strange blue stone, seemed comparatively well preserved. This building at once attracted Tony Buckden's attention.

He clapped his hands excitedly.

"As I live!" he declared, "that looks like the temple described by Metlo."

"Indeed!" exclaimed Frank.

"That is the truth."

"But where are the anacondas?"

"Where?"

The two men exchanged glances.

Certainly, there was not a big snake in sight. But after all, this did not disprove Metlo's story.

"De snakes may be dar all de same, Boss Frank," declared Pomp.

"Of course," agreed Tony. "That is logical enough."

"What shall we do?"

"Enter of course."

"It is well to proceed with care."

"Very well, we can do that."

But Barney and Pomp had already sprung up the steps of the temple. The next moment they disappeared inside of the place. Frank and Tony followed.

As they entered the temple they saw that it was a high arched structure with evidences of having once been a building of great beauty.

There was not a snake to be seen.

"Upon my word," ejaculated Tony, "this has every appearance of being the building described by Metlo."

"It very likely is," said Frank. "I have no doubt of it."

"But he described it as being literally alive with anacondas."

"It may have been, and they may have lately deserted the place."

"It looks like it."

"Of course."

"Then we are in great luck."

"Yes."

"But the treasure—ah!"

Buckden paused before a ring in the stone floor.

It was an iron ring firmly joined to a slab of stone. The New Yorker bent down and began to pull upon it.

The instant he did so a thrilling thing happened.

There was a strange whirring sound as of machinery buzzing, and then a grating noise.

Quick as a flash the stone dropped and Buckden went out of sight like a meteor.

Down into a black void went the young New Yorker.

He was swallowed up as literally as if engulfed in the sea.

For an instant Frank Reade, Jr., was so overcome with horror that he did not know what to do.

Then a wailing cry broke from his lips:

"Oh, my God!" he cried. "Tony has gone to his death."

Of course Frank had no idea as to the depth of the abyss or where it went to.

Buckden, for aught he knew, had fallen to the center of the earth. The young inventor was overcome with horror and agony.

"Something must be done!" he cried, wildly. "He must be saved!"

But what was to be done?

It was an awful question.

For a moment Frank knew not what answer to make. He stood like one in a trance.

Then he made sudden and swift action. He threw himself flat upon his stomach and shouted down into the abyss of darkness.

"Tony!" he cried, at the top of his voice. "Where are you? If you can hear me, give me an answer!"

But no sound came back.

All was the stillness of the grave.

It seemed as if Tony Buckden's fate was sealed. Certainly, if alive and uninjured, he would answer.

Frank shouted again and again.

But no answer came back from the awful stillness below. It was like the silence of the grave.

A queer sensation came over Frank.

He felt as if likely to faint.

A cold perspiration broke out upon him, and he seemed dizzy and sick.

Then a strange and awful thing happened.

Suddenly and without warning, the stone beneath him began to slide. He felt himself going, and made a spasmodic effort to save himself.

In vain was this.

Just as he was about to recoil from the verge of the awful pit, there was a grinding sound as of mortar giving way, and then, wholly unable to save himself, Frank went headlong into the abyss.

Down, down he felt himself going.

He clutched at the air wildly, experienced a sense of suffocation, then he felt a sudden shock and knew that he was in water.

It seemed as if his breath must leave his body before he came up out of this water.

Coming to the surface, he drew in a deep breath, and then struck out to swim.

The water was icy cold, and he knew that its depth must be great.

Also, he believed its extent to be considerable, as the reverberations coming to his ears were far-reaching and loud.

Frank had no means of knowing into what sort of place he had fallen, or what was to be the outcome of this adventure.

CHAPTER X.
THE SEATED CHAMBER.

But he did know that he was in the embrace of some underground lake or reservoir of water.

That it was not a river he was assured as there was no current whatever.

Involuntarily he looked about for light.

There was a faint square far above his head. This he knew must be from the aperture through which he had fallen.

Certainly that must have been a fearful distance to have fallen. To have survived that fall seemed a miracle.

But that light was too far away to be of any service.

All upon the surface of the underground lake was Stygian blackness.

"I don't know where I am, nor if I shall ever get out of here alive," muttered the young inventor, "but I must try. I will swim as far as I can."

And this he proceeded to do.

Striking out he forced his way swiftly through the water.

Pausing to rest, he suddenly heard a startling sound near him.

It was a splash in the water.

At first Frank instinctively thought of the presence of some submarine monster, but recollection came to him in time.

"Tony!" he cried; "is that you?"

"Thank God!" was the reply.

Neither could see the other, but they swam side by side in the darkness.

"Thank Heaven, you are alive!" said Frank, sincerely. "I feared you were dead."

"I am alive," said Buckden, "but I fear we will never get out of this."

"Why did you not answer my call?" asked Frank.

"I did not hear it."

"Is that possible?"

"For some moments after coming to the surface the shock made me deaf."

"Oh, I see."

"What sort of a place are we in?"

"I cannot imagine."

"I pray there is an outlet somewhere. If not, we are done for."

"That is true," agreed Frank.

"Let us pray for escape."

The words had barely left his lips, when Frank's hand struck an object. In a moment his fingers closed upon it.

It was the edge of a stone coping, and quickly he drew himself out of the water upon what seemed like a platform.

It was really the shore of the underground reservoir or lake.

Frank secured a foothold and then turned to Buckden.

"Are you there, Tony?"

"Yes."

"Give me your hand and I will help you up."

"All right."

The next moment Buckden was drawn safely up out of the water. Both men now stood once more upon terra firma.

"Well, we're out of the water, anyway," cried Tony, as he proceeded to wring the water out of his coat.

"Yes."

"But where in the mischief are we?"

"Give it up."

All was Stygian darkness about them.

But Frank remembered suddenly that in an inner pocket he had a small pocket lantern.

This was in a water-proof case and consequently had not suffered by the immersion.

There were matches in the same case and Frank lit one on a dry part of the stone coping.

Then he lit the wick of the lantern and the vicinity was dimly illumined.

But the moment Frank turned the rays of the lantern to the rear both gave a wild start.

A frightful object confronted their gaze. At first sight Frank had thought it a living object.

It was a monster dragon with wide open mouth and awful jaws. But a second glance revealed the fact that it was not animate and could consequently do them no harm.

It was of some peculiar quality of dark colored greenish stone, and was a remarkably life-like representation.

"Jupiter!" exclaimed Buckden, "but that gave me a start."

"I must confess to the same," said Frank, with a smile.

"It is a clever imitation of a dragon, isn't it?"

"Indeed, it is."

Both adventurers now advanced and began to examine the monster critically.

It was a wonderful bit of workmanship in very truth.

"Indeed!" exclaimed Buckden, "I doubt if our sculptors of the present day could ever equal this."

"I do not think they could surpass it much."

"It certainly attests that the ancient inhabitants of Mazendla were a remarkably talented people."

"Right you are."

"But the question now is, how are we to get out of this place?"

"Exactly."

"There certainly must be some other way out besides that through which we came—ah!"

Frank gave a gasping cry and came to a halt.

Just at his feet was a ghastly sight.

It was a heap of bones.

In a promiscuous fashion they were heaped there. Human bones and those of the cayman, a species of crocodile, were there all piled up together.

The two explorers gazed at the spectacle with amazement.

This was the first indication of human remains that they had found thus far.

There were human skulls and the complete skeletons of the crocodiles. A quick comprehension came to Frank.

"I have it!" he cried.

"Well?"

"In my opinion this lake was once the abode of these crocodiles. The ancient rulers placed them there for a certain purpose."

"What could it have been?"

"Well, supposing a man committed some crime. It may be that he was thrown into this place as a method of punishment, for the crocodiles to tear to pieces."

"Indeed, I believe you are right, Mr. Reade," cried Buckden, "but what a number of victims they must have had."

"For aught we know the bed of this lake may be paved with human skeletons."

It was a grim, horrible thing to think of.

Both men shivered.

Then Tony reached over to pick up one of the skulls.

The mere motion caused the horrid pile to disintegrate and relapse into a heap of gray dust.

Ages had passed since these bones had been deposited there, as this very action would attest.

"Come away," said Frank with a shiver. "Let's find our way out of here."

Together they passed by the heap of moldering bones.

A deep, arched passage lay before them. It was not a long one, and suddenly came to an end in a startling manner.

A huge iron gate made of transverse bars confronted them.

It was a ponderous affair, and there were huge bolts to hold it shut.

It did not seem as if they could ever hope to pass through it.

"My soul, we are badly stuck!" cried Tony. "We'll never get out of here alive, Frank."

Frank looked aghast.

There seemed no means at command to force the mighty gate.

It certainly seemed an insurmountable barrier. It also seemed the only means of exit from the place.

The two men looked at each other in utter dismay.

What was to be done?

Could they remain here in this place and suffer tamely a death by starvation? Frank was resolute.

"There is just one thing about it," he declared. "We've got to force our way through that gate."

"Good for you!" cried Tony. "I'm with you!"

"It must be done!"

"But can it be done?"

"I see no reason why not. We will make a valiant effort. It is better than tamely submitting to death."

"Indeed, much better."

"Here goes!"

Frank advanced and placed both hands upon one of the iron bars of the gate.

It was thickly encrusted with rust; yet neither looked for the result which followed.

Frank gave the gate a quick, sharp pull. Then he gave a leap backward.

It was just in time.

He was not a moment too soon.

Down came the whole affair in a clanging heap.

If it had struck Frank he might have been seriously injured. But fortunately it did not.

The action of time had rusted hinges and locks, and the gate was just ready to fall.

A great cloud of dust was raised which nearly overwhelmed the two explorers.

They emerged from it completely covered and wheezing and puffing.

"Jupiter!" gasped Tony, "there's no question about getting out of here now, Frank."

"No, not if this dust don't kill us," replied Frank.

"Whew! it is fearful."

After a time, however, the dust cloud was dispelled and they emerged all safe.

Then the first impulse was to break through the archway.

This they did and came to a flight of stairs.

Up these they ran at full speed.

Arrived at the top, they were confronted by an astounding fact.

They stood in a small square chamber. So far as they could see there was no door or window or other mode of exit.

Only bare walls of stone were about them upon all sides.

"Well!" exclaimed Frank, in amazement. "What the deuce does this mean?"

"Where are we?"

"Sure enough."

"Can you see any way out of here?"

"I cannot."

The two men looked at each other blankly. It was some time before either ventured to speak.

"This is the toughest yet," said Buckden, finally. "What is your idea, Frank?"

A light broke across the young inventor's handsome face.

"I have an idea!" he cried.

"What is it?"

Frank went and critically examined the walls of the chamber before he ventured to answer.

"This is a sealed chamber," he said, finally. "It is sealed that nobody may find the secrets of this underground charnel house."

"A sealed chamber!" gasped Buckden. My God! then we are lost, for that is equivalent to being buried alive. Our end has come!"

CHAPTER XI.
OUT OF IMPRISONMENT.

It was a terrible despairing cry which Tony Buckden gave.

It came from the depths of his soul, and embodied utter hopelessness.

Indeed, the situation looked to be a desperate one. If it was indeed true that they were the inmates of a sealed chamber their fate seemed sealed.

What was to be done?

Surely they could not submit to a slow lingering death by starvation in that wretched place.

Frank went forward and began to examine the masonry of the chamber walls.

The stone was a peculiar sandstone, and while it showed evidence of age and the discolorations of time it was yet firm and hard.

But the mortar would yield to the point of the knife. Frank at once began work upon it.

"My plan," he declared, "is to displace the mortar as far as possible, and perhaps we can loosen some of these stones and make an aperture large enough to get out through."

"Good!" cried Buckden, joyfully. "You've hit the mark, Frank."

"I hope so," said the young inventor, modestly; "time will tell. First we must make sure that the mortar will give way."

Together they went to work upon the mortar.

It yielded readily to the points of their knives and soon had been displaced about one of the smaller stones.

To their joy this yielded and the stone was removed.

But a second layer was discovered just beyond. How many more were beyond this they could not guess.

But Frank believed that only this layer separated them from the outer air and freedom.

Accordingly with renewed hope the two imprisoned men went to work.

With a will they hacked away at the crumbling stone and mortar.

In a very short space of time another stone had been loosened. A third was quickly displaced, making an aperture sufficiently large enough to allow a body to pass through.

Now the second layer was attacked. To the agreeable surprise of both it was a very rotten stone and yielded readily.

In a very few moments daylight streamed into the place.

"Hurrah!" cried Frank. "We are sure to escape, Tony!"

"So it seems!" cried the young New Yorker, cheerily. "This is what comes of good pluck."

"You are right."

Peering through the small hole made, Frank saw that they would come out right in the main body of the temple.

Both men now worked like beavers.

In a few moments one of the stones was displaced. Another quickly followed, and then they crawled through and into the open air.

The relief experienced was beyond description.

To drink in the pure air and the health-giving sunlight once more was a boon of no small sort.

But after a time they began to think of Barney and Pomp and the Steam Man.

It was certainly advisable to find them at once.

The fate of the Steam Man was a matter of conjecture. But Frank arose from his reclining position and said:

"Come, Tony, old man, we can't stay here any longer. There's work for us to do."

"All right, Frank."

Frank started to leave the temple, but Tony chanced to glance across an inner court-yard.

"Wait a moment, Frank!" he cried.

"What is it?"

"Just look across that court-yard. What is it?"

Frank looked and gave a start of surprise.

"Upon my soul!" He exclaimed. "What sort of a creature can it be?"

"Let us investigate."

"All right."

"Lead the way."

Through a series of arches they went and reached the court-yard. Across it they made their way.

The object of their surprise was a strange looking statue.

It was sculptured out of the same peculiar greenish stone as the dragon seen below stairs.

The statue was a compromise between a man and some strange wild animal resembling the panther.

Certainly a more life like and hideous monstrosity they had never beheld before. They gazed upon it in wonderment.

"Have you ever seen its equal?" asked Tony in amazement.

"Never!"

"What is it intended to represent?"

"Like the statues of Bacchus and the Centaurs found in ancient Greece, it is a creation of mythical sort."

"I believe you're right. Hello! What is this? Another trapdoor?"

Tony paused before a heavy iron ring set in the tiled floor.

"Don't trouble it," said Frank. "It may let us down into another underground lake."

"Do you believe it?"

"I should fear it."

But Tony could not resist the temptation to insert his fingers in the ring and give the stone a lift. It was a reckless thing to do. The result was startling.

The stone yielded, and the next moment Buckden lifted it from its bed, disclosing a cavity beneath some four feet long by two wide.

Stone steps were revealed leading downward. For a moment the two explorers looked at each other.

"What will we do?" asked Buckden.

"Investigate," said Frank, tersely.

"But it is dark down there."

"That doesn't matter," said the young inventor, coolly. "We will regulate that."

Then, from his pocket, Frank produced a small folding pocket lantern, an invention of his own.

He lit this and boldly ventured down into the place.

He went down a dozen steps, and then a wonderful sight was spread before him.

A large chamber, about fifteen feet in length by ten in breadth, hewn out of solid rock, was revealed.

The walls were adorned with shelves, and about the stone floor were chests of metal.

These chests contained coins and silver and gold cups, flagons, pots and all sorts of ware, thrown about promiscuously and in heaps.

For a moment the two explorers astounded, gazed at the scene before them.

Both were so dumfounded that they could not speak.

One thing was apparent to them, and it brought the blood in surges to their temples.

The treasure of Mazendla was found.

It would be quite impossible to enumerate its mighty value.

But it would seem that it must be up in the millions. For how many centuries it had remained here it would be quite hard to say.

"Heavens!" gasped Frank. "Here is enough to enrich us many times, Tony."

"I should say so."

"It is the wealth of a king."

"To be sure."

"But what great good can it do us? We have got enough."

"That is so."

The two explorers proceeded to make an examination of the contents of the treasure room.

Among all the gold and silver Frank looked for diamonds.

But these seemed scarce.

However, he did find a few in a small silver casket. These he secured, and, with Tony, took several bags of the coins and some of the quaint silverware.

"Well," said Tony, speculatively, "what shall we do with all this stuff, Frank? It is too bad to leave it here."

"I have an idea."

"What?"

"Let us take it to New York, convert it into greenbacks and disperse it in charities."

"Good!" cried Tony, readily, "that is a fine idea."

They now ascended to the main room of the temple.

For the first time Frank thought of Barney and Pomp.

The two servitors had wandered off in some other part of the temple and were not in sight.

Frank shouted for them, but no answer came back.

This seemed a little strange to the young inventor, and he began to fear that some harm had come to the two men.

"That is queer!" he muttered. "Why don't they answer?"

Again Frank shouted. This time an answer came back, but it seemed a mile away.

Frank was not a little vexed.

"Confound the rascals!" he muttered. "Where have they gone to?"

"We had better go in quest of them," suggested Tony. "Harm may have overtaken them."

"You are right!"

They were about to follow up this plan when a startling thing occurred.

I

Suddenly from the distance beyond the temple doors there came, a thrilling and yet familiar sound.

It was a prolonged shriek, a distant note from the ear-splitting whistle of the Steam Man.

CHAPTER XII.
WHICH IS THE END.

Frank Reade, Jr., gave a great cry of surprise and joy.

"They have found the Man, he cried. "We are in luck."

"No, said Tony, putting a hand on Frank's arm. "You are wrong. That is not so. Listen!"

The shrill whistle of the Steam Man was still going.

"I have it," said Buckden, positively. "In some manner the whistle valve has opened, and it will continue to blow until steam is all blowed off!"

"Right!" cried Frank, excitedly; why didn't I think of that. Let us go at once in quest of the machine."

The two men started at once out of the temple.

But as they reached the paved street below Tony hesitated.

"Wait," he said.

"What for?" asked Frank.

"What about Barney and Pomp?"

Here was a conundrum.

There was little time in which to decide. But Frank decided quickly.

"Enough!" he cried; "they must take care of themselves. They are abundantly able. Our life all depends upon recovering the Steam Man."

"You are right!" cried Buckden.

So away the two men sped.

It was easy enough to locate the Man now, as the whistle was an infallible guide.

Straight across the plaza they ran, and turned into a broad avenue. Here, on the verge of a clump of palms, they beheld a thrilling sight.

There was the Steam Man standing motionless on the edge of the palm clump.

The huge anaconda was yet writhing in the cage. Frank guessed the meaning of all at once.

The Steam Man had been saved by a lucky chance.

The snake, in its writhings, had not only closed the throttle by twisting the rein about its body, but had also pulled open the whistle valve in the same manner.

The two explorers came to a halt at first, and regarded the spectacle with much wonder.

Then Frank cried:

"Hurrah! We've got the best of it. We can easily end the fight how."

Straight up to the cage Frank ran. It was an easy matter to climb up and draw aim at the anaconda's head through the loophole.

Crack!

The shot pierced the snake's brain.

The head dropped lifeless, but the huge body continued to writhe in the throes of death.

Frank swung the door of the cage open.

"Come, Tony!" he cried, cheerily. "Let's pull the monster out, and we will then have the Steam Man once more in our possession." Buckden needed no urging.

Both laid hold of the snake's huge coils. It was a hard tug, but the huge monster was finally pulled out of the cage.

Then the two men sprang in and proceeded to put things to rights. The snake had done no material damage, but the odor of its presence in the cage was something frightful.

However, Frank quickly dispelled this with a chemical, and then the Man's course was set for a return to the treasure temple.

No obstacle was encountered upon the return.

Soon the Steam Man came in sight of the temple.

As it did so, Barney and Pomp were seen rushing down the steps. Their joy to discover that the Steam Man had been safely recovered knew no bounds.

"I tell yuh, Li'l Boss, dat dar's big piles ob gold an' silver in dat dar temple," cried Pomp.

"Bejabers, that's so!" cried Barney. "Ani cud hardly get the eejit to come away from it."

"Where did you rascals go?" asked Frank, sharply.

"Way up in de top ob de temple," replied Pomp.

Didn't you hear me when I called?"

"Bejabers, we did that, an' it was mesilf as answered yez," replied Barney. "But I couldn't get the cabbage to come away."

"Did you hear the whistle of the Steam Man?"

"I did that, an' that brought us down quick enough," replied Barney.

"Well," said Frank, with satisfaction, "we are in luck. Now for home."

"Ki dar, Boss Jun'r. What about dat gold an' silver?" cried Pomp.

Frank looked at Buckden.

"Is it worth while to return for it?" he asked.

"Oh, I think so," replied the New Yorker.

"All right."

Barney and Pomp eagerly started for the steps of the temple, but a startling sight caused them to draw back.

Suddenly, from what seemed like a deep archway leading into black depths beyond at the lower end of the temple wall, a large anaconda glided into view.

It was a monster of its species.

"Back into the cage," shouted Barney and Pomp. The two servitors had barely time to accomplish this move when the snake glided swift as the wind up over the temple steps.

"Look—look!" cried Buckden.

An astounding sight was next witnessed. Out from the archway there emerged more of the huge reptiles.

Some of them were monstrous in proportions.

The archway was literally choked with them.

All seemed to be making for the temple. Truly, the wonderful tale rendered by Metlo was true after all.

There seemed legions of the snakes. They swarmed over the temple wall and through all the passages.

Dumfounded, our adventurers stood and watched them.

"Great heavens!" gasped Frank' Reade, Jr., "what a sight that is!"

"I never saw its equal!"

"Golly! Ain' dem de bigges' snakes we'se seed yit?"

"Tare an''ounds! iv the divils get after the Steam Man——"

"Look out!"

Several of the huge reptiles seemed making for the Steam Man. Frank's hand was on the throttle rein, and he was about to pull it, when a terrible thing happened.

There was a dull, distant rumbling like thunder.

The air became suddenly still and oppressive. Instinctively Frank knew at that moment what was coming.

"The earthquake!" he shouted. "Steady, all! Look out for yourselves!"

Frank gave the throttle rein a yank. The Steam Man ran instantly to the center of the plaza and came to a halt.

Then a mighty, sullen roar was heard, a terrific gust of wind swept down the avenue, and the earthquake came.

For a moment it seemed as if the Steam Man would be overturned.

The ground rose and fell in billows.

The air was filled with the thunder and crash of falling buildings. The temple of treasure, which was full of the anacondas, was literally leveled to the dust.

It remained a great, moldering heap of ruins. Dozens, perhaps hundreds of the huge snakes were crushed in the ruins.

The treasure of Mazendla was beyond the reach of our adventurers now.

In three minutes the entire disturbance was over.

The city presented a vastly different aspect now.

Many of the mammoth buildings were a heap of ruins. Trees were uprooted, and a scene of havoc was upon every hand.

"Golly fo' goodness!" gasped the startled Pomp, as he pulled himself together. "I kain' say dat I'm stuck on yarthquakes, is yuh, Li'l Boss?"

"No," replied Frank, as he adjusted a sprained shoulder. "And what is more, we will start this very moment for civilization, and the land where earthquakes never happen."

"Good!" cried Tony Buckden. "I'm with you."

"Bejabers, I'm the same," cried Barney,

Not one gave thought to the deeply buried treasure of Mazendla now.

It proved in after days that their decision was a wise one.

The silverware preserved by Frank and Tony, as well as coins, turned out to be a weak alloy. The diamonds were the real treasure, and Frank had secured them all.

So the treasure of Mazendla yet remains unearthed. Certainly, it was never thought worth while by our explorers to ever return for it.

It required some time to pick their way out of the ruined city.

But they finally succeeded, and emerged upon the vast table-land of Peten once more.

The Steam Man at a rapid rate of speed kept on the return route to Campeche.

But the return trip was not devoid of incident.

When two days out from Mazendla, the Steam Man came to a vast morass between high mountains, and surrounded by tall reeds.

The Steam Man on the way out had found little difficulty in skirting this to the eastward.

But rains had since fallen and the morass was a lake.

Any attempt to go over the return route now must result in sinking the Steam Man in great depths of mire.

So a halt was called and a consultation held.

There seemed to be no other way of surmounting this obstacle but to camp and wait patiently for the water to subside.

This meant a delay of several days, but it was a virtuous necessity, as it was clearly impossible for the Steam Man to climb the rough mountain sides.

Accordingly camp was made.

A good clump of palms was found and the fires in the furnace were banked.

It was entirely out of the question for four men to remain cooped up three or four days in the cage of the Steam Man, inactive and dull.

The natural project was a hunting trip and this was at once decided upon.

What sort of game our explorers were in quest of it is not easy to say. In fact, it might as well be said that their quest was as much one of exploration as quest of game.

They started early one morning and climbed the mountain side.

This was rocky, but fortunately clear of brush or dense chaparral.

Several rabbits were bagged and some birds of beautiful plumage. Then just as they were upon the verge of the crater of an extinct volcano, the stirring events of the day began.

Suddenly Barney, who was skirting the edge of the crater, gave a sharp cry, and as his companions turned, they were horrified to see him suddenly disappear from sight.

"Great heavens!" gasped Frank. "What has become of Barney?"

All rushed to an opening in the ground through which the Celt had disappeared.

As they reached it, a terrific roar came up from below.

It required but a glance for the explorers to perceive a horrible state of affairs.

Below, at a depth of some forty feet, was a cavern.

The entrance seemed to be from the crater, and clinging vines lined the passage down which Barney had fallen.

A treacherous coating of moss had covered the hole, and the unsuspecting Irishman had stepped full upon it, with the result we have seen.

In falling, Barney had clutched wildly at the vines, and now he hung twenty feet from the bottom by a single vine, which swayed and seemed likely to snap at any moment.

Just below, upon the floor of the cavern, crouched two fierce jaguars.

They roared and snarled savagely and made upward leaps to reach the Celt.

Barney was white with fear and clung desperately to the swinging vine.

"Help!" he shouted in terror. "Mister Frank, save me."

"Have courage, Barney!" cried Frank, resolutely. "Hang on and I will do my best."

Barney did hang on with all his strength, and Frank cried, turning to the others.

"Draw a bead on the jaguars. Be sure and make your shots tell."

The three rifles cracked, and one of the jaguars turned over and lay limp and lifeless upon the bottom of the cavern.

The other was hit, but not badly wounded.

The wound, however, had the effect of exciting the animal's rage and with a roar it vanished from sight for a moment.

When it came into sight again it was seen coming up over the edge of the crater to attack its human foes.

Up over the rocks it came with mad leaps.

"Look out!" cried Frank Reade, Jr., "take good aim at the beast."

The three explorers fired. Whether the bullets struck the beast or not it was not easy to say.

But the jaguar came on with long bounds.

Before the repeaters could be worked again the jaguar was upon them. He struck Pomp first and the older man went over like a ten-pin.

Buckden rushed to his rescue with clubbed rifle.

But the jaguar knocked the rifle from his hands and tumbled him over in a heap.

That moment would have been Tony's last but for Frank, who rushed forward and thrust the muzzle of his rifle close against the hide of the beast.

The bullet penetrated the jaguar's heart and he fell dead over Buckden's prostrate form.

It was a narrow escape for all, for the jaguar might have killed one of them. Haste was made to relieve Barney from his irksome position.

The exploration was continued, but no other such serious adventure befell our friends,

A few days later they were able to leave the morass behind them.

Nothing worthy of note occurred during the remainder of the trip.

Campeche was safely reached and there the party received an ovation.

Tony's many friends were overjoyed to see him back alive.

A few days later, however, saw them aboard a return steamer. New Orleans was safely reached in due time.

Here Mr. Buckden met the party and welcomed them home.

He embraced Tony joyfully and at once made out a check to Frank Reade, Jr., for the reward offered of $50,000.

But Frank politely declined it, refusing to accept more than enough to cover the actual expenses of the trip.

Tony and his father returned to New York city. At last accounts the young explorer had given up traveling and was engaged in the banking business with his father.

Frank Reade, Jr., Barney and Pomp returned to Readestown safely with the new Steam Man.

But their travels with the new Steam Man were not yet concluded by any means, and a complete account of their thrilling experiences in their next trip may be found in

NO. 4 OF THE FRANK READE LIBRARY,

ENTITLED:

"FRANK READE, JR., WITH HIS NEW STEAM MAN IN TEXAS;"

OR

"CHASING THE TRAIN ROBBERS."

BY LUIS SENARENS

Made in the USA
Las Vegas, NV
25 March 2021